W9-CCW-234

March 11th, 2017

Happy Birthday
Maeegan !

Love, Mom
xox

(Love you bigger
than the
Universe !)

ALSO BY KAMERON HURLEY

BEL DAME APOCRYPHA
(GOD'S WAR TRILOGY)

God's War

Infidel

Rapture

WORLDBREAKER SAGA

The Mirror Empire

Empire Ascendant

The Broken Heavens

The Geek Feminist Revolution

THE
STARS
ARE
LEGION

THE
STARS
ARE
LEGION

KAMERON
HURLEY

SAGA  PRESS

LONDON SYDNEY **NEW YORK** TORONTO NEW DELHI

SAGA PRESS
AN IMPRINT OF SIMON & SCHUSTER, INC.

1230 AVENUE OF THE AMERICAS, NEW YORK, NEW YORK 10020

This book is a work of fiction. Any references to historical events, real people, or real places are used fictitiously. Other names, characters, places, and events are products of the author's imagination, and any resemblance to actual events or places or persons, living or dead, is entirely coincidental.

Text copyright © 2017 by Kameron Hurley

Jacket illustration copyright © 2017 by Stephen Youll

All rights reserved, including the right to reproduce this book or portions thereof in any form whatsoever. For information address Saga Press Subsidiary Rights Department, 1230 Avenue of the Americas, New York, NY 10020.

SAGA PRESS and colophon are trademarks of Simon & Schuster, Inc.

For information about special discounts for bulk purchases, please contact Simon & Schuster Special Sales at 1-866-506-1949 or business@simonandschuster.com.

The Simon & Schuster Speakers Bureau can bring authors to your live event. For more information or to book an event, contact the Simon & Schuster Speakers Bureau at 1-866-248-3049 or visit our website at www.simonspeakers.com.

Interior design by Brad Mead

The text for this book was set in Utopia Std.

Manufactured in the United States of America

First Edition

2 4 6 8 10 9 7 5 3 1

CIP data for this book is available from the Library of Congress.

ISBN 978-1-4814-4793-5

ISBN 978-1-4814-4795-9 (eBook)

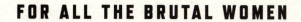

FOR ALL THE BRUTAL WOMEN

IT WAS THE EDGE THAT BROKE US.

WHEN WE WENT OVER THE EDGE,

SOMETHING CAME OVER WITH US.

THE
STARS
ARE
LEGION

PART I:

SURFACING

"THERE IS NOTHING I FEAR MORE THAN SOMEONE
WITHOUT MEMORY. A PERSON WITHOUT MEMORY
IS FREE TO DO ANYTHING SHE LIKES."
—LORD MOKSHI, ANNALS OF THE LEGION

ZAN

I remember throwing away a child.

That's the only memory I know for certain is mine. The rest is a gory blackness. All I have, then, are the things I've been told are true:

My name is Zan.

I once commanded a great army.

My mission was to destroy a world that does not exist.

I'm told my army was scattered, or eaten, or blown apart into a thousand twinkling bits of debris, and I went missing.

I don't know why I'd ever want to lead an army—especially a losing one—but I'm told I spent my life pushing hard to get to the rank and skill I attained. And when I came back, spit out by the world or wrenched free of my own will, I came back wrong. What *wrong* means I don't know yet, only that it's also resulted in my lack of memory.

The first face I see when I wake each period in my sickbed is full-lipped and luminous, like looking into the face of some life-giving sun. The woman says her name is Jayd, and it is she who has told me all I know to be true. When I ask, now, why there is a dead body on the floor behind her, she only smiles and says, "There are many bodies on the world," and I realize the words for *world* and *ship* are nearly identical. I don't know which she used.

I drift.

When I wake next, the body is gone, and Jayd is bustling around me. She helps me sit up for the first time. I marvel at the dark bruises on the insides of my arms and legs. A broad scar cuts my belly in two, low near my groin, and there is something strange about my left hand; it's clearly smaller than the right. When I try to make a fist, it closes only halfway, like a tortured claw. When I slide to the floor, I discover that the bottoms of my feet are mostly numb. Jayd does not give me time to examine them as she pulls a porous, draping robe over my shoulders. It's the same cut and heft as hers, only dark green to her blue.

"It's time for your first debriefing," Jayd says as I try to make sense of my injuries. She takes my hand and leads me from the room, down a dark, pulsing corridor. I squint. I see that our entwined hands are the same tawny color, but her skin is much softer than mine.

"You were gone for a half-dozen turns," she says, and she sits me down beside her in a room off the corridor. I stare at my palms, trying to open and close my hands. If I work at it, I can get the left to close a bit more. The room, like the corridors, is a warm, glistening space with walls that throb like a beating heart. Jayd smooths the dark hair from my brow with comforting fingers, the movement as reverent and well practiced as a prayer.

"We thought you dead," she says, "recycled."

"Recycled into what?" I say, but the wall blooms open, the door unfurling like a flower, and an older woman beckons us inside, and Jayd ignores my question.

Jayd and I go after her and sit on a damp bench on one side of the great plain of a table. The woman sits across from us. Patterns move over the surface of the table, though whether they are writing or purely decorative or something else entirely, I don't know. The more I look at them, the more my head throbs. I touch my temple, only to find that my fingers come away sticky with viscous lubricant or salve. I trace my finger along the ridge of a long scar that runs from the edge of my left brow to the curl of my left ear. I have still not seen my own face. I have encountered no reflective surfaces. There is indeed something very wrong here, but I don't think it's me.

"I'm Gavatra," the older woman says, her voice a low rumble. Her black hair is shorn short against her dark scalp, revealing four long scars like scratch marks on the side of her head. She wears a long, durable garment of shiny blue fabric, like something excreted from the walls. It's all held together with intricate knotted ties. She peers into my face and sighs. "Do you know who *you* are?"

Jayd says, "It's the same as all the other times."

"Other times?" I say, because how many times can one lose an army and get eaten by a ship and come back with injuries like these and live?

Jayd gazes deeply into my eyes, desperately searching my face for something. She has a broad, intense face with sunken eyes, and a bold beak of nose. I feel I should know or understand something from her look, but my memory is a hot, sticky void. I intuit nothing. I flex my hands again.

"Eight hundred and six of your sisters have tried to board the Mokshi," Gavatra says, tapping her fingers across the surface of the table. The patterns change, and she scrutinizes them as if scrying. "You're the only one who ever comes out, Zan. This appears to be why Lord Katazyrna keeps sending you there, despite the fact that you've never successfully led an army inside. Only yourself."

"The Mokshi," I say. "The world that doesn't exist?"

"Yes," Jayd says. "You remember?" Hopeful or doubtful?

I shake my head. The phrase means nothing to me. It has simply surfaced. "How many times has this happened to me?" I say. My left hand trembles, and I gaze at it as if it belongs to someone else. It occurs to me that maybe it once did, and that chills me. I want to know what's happened to my memory, and why there was a body on the floor in my sick room, and why I threw away a child. But I know they aren't going to be pretty answers.

"You are blessed of the War God, sister mine," Jayd says, but she is looking at Gavatra as she says it. It's like being a child again, stuck in a room with people who have a deep history between them; too deep and complicated for a child to fathom. Even more curious is that if Jayd is really my sister, then the feeling that stirs my gut when she twines her fingers in my hair is entirely wrong.

I lift my gaze to Gavatra and firm my jaw. A grim purpose fills me. "I wish to know what happened to me," I say. "You can tell me or have me wrest it from you." I can make both hands into fists now. That action feels more natural than anything I've done so far.

Gavatra barks out a laugh. She swipes at the table and pulls a nest of dancing lights from its surface and into the air. I watch them tangle above her, fascinated. She swipes them back onto another part of the table.

"You're fulfilling your duty to your mother, the Lord of Katazyrna," Gavatra says, "as are we all. But perhaps Jayd is right this time. Perhaps it's time we retire you."

"I feel you owe me a memory," I say.

"Then you must retake the Mokshi," Gavatra says. "We don't have your memory here. That ship ate it. It seems to eat it every time. You want your memory, you take the Mokshi . . . and get a squad in there with you this time."

"I will go again, then," I say.

"Mother can't afford to risk another squad," Jayd says, "not with the Bhavajas lying in wait for us in orbit around the Mokshi. The Bhavajas have taken another ship since you've been gone, Zan."

"What's a Bhavaja?" I say.

Gavatra rolls her eyes. "These cycles get tiring," she says.

"They are the greatest enemy of our family," Jayd says. "A family we have been feuding with since Mother was a child. It's only a matter of time before they take the Mokshi out from under us too. Maybe even all the Katazyrna ships." This time, I am sure she says *ship* and not *world*, because taking an entire world seems impossible.

"The Mokshi has destroyed a good many people," Gavatra says. "Your mother will just steal more from some other distressed world. If Zan is ready to assault the Mokshi again, I won't deny her."

Jayd slumps in her chair, defeated. Am I something to be fought over and won? "This is a foolish enterprise," Jayd says. "It's just as likely that Zan will die as it is she'll retrieve her memory. Some of it comes back without you going to the Mokshi, Zan. If you stay—"

"No," I say. I press my finger against the long ridge of the scar on my face again. "I would like to finish what's been started."

Gavatra waves her hand over the table, and the patterns of light fade, revealing the table surface for what it is: a smooth, stitched-together canvas of human skin.

I jerk up from the bench. The trembling in my arm becomes a spasm, and I lash out and smash the wall. The wall gives under my fist, as if I've mashed it into a lung. When I pull my hand away, it is moist. My body begins to shake; my breath comes hard and fast.

Jayd wraps her arms around me. "Hush, it will pass," she says.

I feel as if I'm watching my body from a great height, unable to contain or control it. The panic is a monstrous thing. My body is trying to fight or flee, and I can't allow it to do either until I understand what's happening here. The attack is so sudden, so consuming, that it terrifies me.

Gavatra snorts and stands. "She's going to pop again," Gavatra says, and she scratches at the scars on her head.

My heart hammers loudly in my chest. A dark and twisted impulse seizes me; an uncoiling of everything I have held back while pushed and prodded in my sick room.

I leap across the table and take Gavatra by the throat. We collide with the wall and fall into a tangle on the floor. Gavatra writhes beneath me, gasping like a dying woman, and perhaps she is. As I straddle her and look at my hands, I fear my weaker left is not up to the task of strangling a woman to death.

I bare my teeth at Gavatra. "I do not believe a word of what you have told me," I say.

Gavatra twists my weaker arm. Pain rushes through me, blinding my panic. She head-butts me in the face, so fast and unexpected that I reel back in shock as much as pain, clutching at my face as blackness judders across my vision.

Jayd rushes between me and Gavatra. She slides across the floor to wrap me again in her arms, as if I am a prize animal gone feral.

Gavatra uses the table to lever herself up. She rubs at her throat and gives a wry grin. "Perhaps there is something of the old Zan in this one," she says.

"My memory!" I say.

"You fool," Gavatra says. "You have no idea what a gift that loss is for you." And then Gavatra smiles, her wrinkles deepening, her face cavernous in the dim light. "The truth is worse than you can possibly imagine."

"Get me out of here," I say. The panic is subsiding now, but the pulsing walls feel closer, as if the room itself is going to swallow me whole.

Jayd presses her cheek to mine. I take a fistful of her hair and squeeze gently. "Who are you, really?" I whisper.

I feel her mouth turn up at the corners. "I am your sister, Zan mine."

And I smile in turn because my face is throbbing, and a trickle of blood runs from my nose, and I remember my other injuries. I have two choices here: to fight them and risk being recycled—whatever that is—or to go along with it, to give them what they want, and figure out where my memory has really gone and why these people are going to so much trouble to pretend I am their kin.

"I'm afraid," I say, and that is partly the truth. I am afraid of what I am going to have to do to this person who claims she is my sister, but who I want to take into my arms and fuck until the world ends.

"MEMORY IS A MEATY AND DELIRIOUS THING,
AND IT MAKES US PRONE TO FALSE RECOLLECTIONS.
STORIES MAKE MEMORY; IT'S MERELY A MATTER OF REPEATING
THE STORY MOST BENEFICIAL TO ONE'S PURPOSE."
—LORD MOKSHI, ANNALS OF THE LEGION

2

ZAN

I sleep in a room three paces across and eight paces long. I curl up in a filmy blanket that's slightly spongy, like porous bread. Sleeping periods are marked by the change in light across the whole of the ship, from milky green to soft blue. I'm surprised that my body responds so quickly to the change in the light, lulling me to sleep almost instantly each period. Perhaps my body remembers many things my mind does not.

"The memory will come," Jayd reassures me each sleeping period as she tucks me in after the long, sweaty exercise sessions in the tubular room at the end of the corridor outside my room. The corridor reminds me of the throat of some monster. When I ask about the rippling line of the ceiling, Jayd tells me that one of the big arteries of the ship runs overhead.

"An artery?" I say. "Does it move . . . blood?"

"Of a sort," she says. "The lifeblood of the ship. It's different from ours, but serves the same function. It brings up all the recycled proteins from the center of the world and feeds each level."

The idea of living inside the belly of an organism unsettles me. "Is it safe?" I say. "Why doesn't the ship eat us?"

She looks away. "It devours us all in the end."

During the waking periods, I work with several others in hand-to-hand combat and grappling. When I try to speak to them, Jayd tells me they do not have tongues. I think perhaps it is a figure of speech, but when they open their mouths to bark or leer, I see they have no tongues. They communicate in a sign language that seems familiar to me. After a few of these sessions, I remember what some of the signs are: *smarter*, *good effort*, and *skull-eater*. I sign *skull-eater* back at one of them and she looks as if I'd said I was going to gut her.

"What's *skull-eater*?" I ask Jayd as we walk back to my room.

Her back stiffens. "Where did you hear that?"

"Just something that came to me," I say. I don't want her to know how much of the sign language I can understand. Not yet. "I don't know," Jayd says, and it's a relief to know with certainty that she is lying. I still don't know how much of what she has told me is a lie or an exaggeration. I yearn to trust her, but my body urges caution. Once again, my body intuits what my mind has forgotten.

"Why can't you just tell me what's happened," I ask her, "the way you've told me the other things?"

"Because you will go mad," Jayd says. She opens the door to my room. My bruises are fading.

"How do you know?"

Jayd hesitates on the threshold. She speaks softly, as if to herself, without turning. "Because if we tell you too soon, you go mad," she says, "and then you could be recycled, or thrown out there at the Mokshi without the reconditioning you're doing now. You don't want to start over like that. You will have no chance, and then you will be stuck out there for turns and turns again. Or maybe the Mokshi will kill you this time. And I . . . I don't want that."

"I want my memory back, Jayd. I want what was stolen."

"You will get it," she says, "when Mother has the Mokshi."

I have no sense of time here, and though Jayd calls it a ship, or perhaps a world, for all I know, we could be deep underground at the center of some star. I spend endless nights trying to figure out how to open the door that seals behind Jayd whenever she leaves. I run my hands over the seams of the great wedged panels that purl open when Jayd enters. But though running my hands over it brings back memories of me doing this same thing again and again, it tells me nothing else.

As my bruises disappear, I resolve that this is not how I'm going to end my life, trapped in whatever cyclical horror these mad people have engineered for me.

This is what I'm thinking about when I pop one of the women in the training ring in the face with my fist. I don't pull the punch this time as I have with all the others, and she reels back, pinwheeling her arms.

I leap at her. Her companions swarm me. I duck and dodge. My fists come up. I make four solid hits. Blood spatters my face. I'm not training now, I'm fighting, and Jayd's fearful voice is just a dull buzzing at the edges of my awareness.

When Jayd takes my shoulder, I turn, fists up. She does not recoil. But the heat bleeds out of me. I let out a breath.

Around me, the three women I've been training with are all on the floor. There's blood. Not a lot, but enough to startle me.

"Go back to your room," Jayd says.

I stare down at the women. One has a burst nose. Another is spitting blood. Another crawls away from me, hand pressed to her ribs.

"I'm sorry," I say. "I don't know what—"

"Go," Jayd says. "I'll take care of them."

"I'm sorry," I say again, and turn on my heel and scuttle out of the room. I step into the corridor and take deep breaths. Stare at my fists. What am I, really? What have they made me into?

I hurry down the hall. As my haze lifts, I resolve that the last thing I want to do is go back to my cell. I change directions, picking a corridor off the main one at random. I try a few doors, but none will unfurl for me. Trapped in a maze. No way out.

I begin to run.

My bare feet slap against the moist floor. I come to the end of one corridor and turn into another. I run and I run, and as the air rushes through my lungs, I feel truly alive for the first time since waking. I take a soft left turn, and the corridor widens into a gaping mouth. An open door. I come up short and stare. Through the opening is a cavernous space with a ceiling so high, it's lost to darkness. Green, bioluminescent flora or fauna of some kind line the walls and the floor, but it's not enough to give me a sense of the depth of the room.

I step through the mouth and the ceiling lights up in green and blue. I squint and now I am the one who gapes, as I have entered a giant vehicle hangar. Row upon row of snub-nosed vehicles go on and on.

They are strange, slumbering animals, these vehicles. They are slug-like things twisted with coiled tubing, their glistening exteriors splashed in yellow, red, blue, green. I don't know what I expect vehicles to look like, but it seems odd they have no wings or wheels or feet.

As I pass, I brush them with my fingers, and they shiver and blink at my touch. They are warm, and their surfaces feel like toughened skin. Strange creatures, these. I wonder what they eat.

I crouch beside one, and it opens a massive eye, which bears an orange iris. For a long moment we stare at one another. I see that it's leaking a viscous yellow fluid from one of the tubes crisscrossing its back end. There's a workshop bench along the far wall where other vehicles are strung up in various states of disrepair. Some of them hang on bony hooks in the wall like slabs of meat.

The vehicle looks at me with its one orange eye. I feel pity for it, huffing here alone in the hangar, leaking vital fluid. I walk over to the workbench, and just like in the training room, my hands move of their own accord with some latent memory. I know how to fix this sad vehicle, and that knowledge gives me far greater pleasure than knowing how to hit someone.

I cut and stitch and smear salve across a long length of the vehicle's tubing. It has a texture and consistency somewhere between intestine and an umbilical cord; the knowledge that I know the texture of both is sobering. There's a heap of tubing in a warm bin on the workbench. I know where everything is, and I know the names of the tools: scalpel, haystitch, speculum, forebear.

I crouch next to the vehicle, a bone scalpel between my teeth, and repair the leaking tube. The vehicle hums softly beneath me. When I'm done, I'm smeared in sticky lubricant and yellow fluid. The vehicle rolls its eye at me and purrs. I pat its big snub of a front end, like thumbing a warm slug. We are probably both too happy in this moment.

"I'd heard you were alive."

I raise my head. An unfamiliar person stands at the door. She is slender and wiry where Jayd is soft and luminous. Her black hair is cut short on one side and braided into one long plait on the other, twisted atop her head like a crown. She moves toward me. I grip the scalpel, uncertain.

"Who are you?" I ask.

"Sabita," she says. "I suppose it's still too early for you to remember that." She strokes the snub nose of the vehicle. It purrs under her fingers. "I wanted to make sure you were safe this time."

"I've only met Jayd so far," I say, "and those people without tongues."

Sabita curls her lip. "Bottom-worlders."

"What does that mean?"

"People who live in the levels below here," she says. "The world is very wild in the layers beneath us. When Lord Katazyrna takes a world, she consigns those she does not recycle to the bottom levels. Most are conscripted into the army, eventually."

"Why am I here?" I ask.

Sabita presses a finger to her lips. Hesitates. "She hasn't told you yet?"

"She says I'm supposed to take the Mokshi. She says it stole my memory."

Sabita smiles, but it's a sad smile. "Then I suppose that's the truth she wants you to believe," she says.

"I have a feeling I'm getting very little of that," I say.

"I've never lied to you," Sabita says. "Though you lied to me a great deal before confiding in me. I suppose it was the same with Jayd."

I shake my head. "I've got no reason to believe you any more than I believe Jayd."

"You don't believe Jayd?"

My skin crawls. "I care very much for Jayd," I say. "I'm still working things out."

"Are you ready to return to the Mokshi? You only ever come here when you're ready to go back there."

"I'm ready," I say. "How many times have I done this?"

"You told me not to tell you."

"When?"

"Before you lost your memory. Before . . . all these hopeless missions."

"What *can* you answer, then?"

She shrugs. "Nothing about your past. Jayd tried to tell you about your past when you first came back, I heard, but it didn't go well. You became a raging, violent fool. Lord Katazyrna nearly had you recycled again. Ask about something else. The ship, the vehicles. Though you are doing very well with the vehicles already. They always did love you."

"Why would someone throw away a child?" I ask.

Sabita sees the scalpel in my hand for the first time. She takes a half-step back, though I can see she is trying to mask her fear. "Why do you ask that?"

"Something I heard," I say, which is an easy lie for her to catch because who would I have heard that from?

But she does not seem bothered by it. "Throw them away where?" she says. "You mean recycle them?"

I search the sliver of that first memory I woke with, the one I know is mine. Shake my head. "Blackness. A black pit."

"Children get recycled when they come out wrong," she says. "Just like anything else that comes out wrong." She looks me up and down. "Or anything that *goes* wrong."

"What are you doing here?" Jayd's voice.

It startles me. I tuck the scalpel under the vehicle, because I don't want to think what Jayd will do if she sees me with a weapon. When I glance over at Jayd, I see her gaze is not on me but Sabita.

"Neither of you should be here," Jayd says.

I pat the vehicle one more time. "We'll be together soon, friend," I murmur, and Jayd frowns. Let her think I remember more than I do.

Sabita smiles at Jayd; a flinty smile. Her gaze is black. "I'll leave you to her," Sabita says. She walks past Jayd.

"Don't come back here until she goes out again," Jayd says.

"Of course," Sabita says, and she is already crossing the mouth of the door, out and away.

"What did you talk about?" Jayd asks.

"Nothing," I say. I stand. "I got tired of being locked up in that room. Went for a run. Saw some work here that needed doing."

"I'll talk to the mechanics," Jayd says. "They should do a better job maintaining these for the next assault. And keep the doors closed."

"When's the next assault?"

"When you're ready."

"I'm ready."

"No," she says.

I lean against the vehicle and fold my arms. "I'm done being treated like an invalid child," I say. "I came here for my memory. You'll give it back or I'll make of you what I made of those people in the training room."

"No, you won't," Jayd says, and her certainty surprises me. "I'll tell you when you're ready."

I move toward her. I am taller than Jayd by half a hand and out-weigh her by a good measure. But she stands firm. Only raises her head to meet my look.

"I could kill you," I say.

"You could do any number of things," she says. "But you won't."

"How about this?" I say, and I reach for her. I mean to pull her into my arms and kiss her, but it startles her, and she dances away.

"Enough of that," she says, but her voice trembles, and she will not look at me now, and I know in that moment that I'm right. She's not my sister. These people are not my kin, and she is drawn to me as much as I am to her.

"Why the game?" I say. "You must know I don't believe a word you've told me."

"The game isn't for you."

"Then who?"

She smooths her hands against the fabric of her shift. She still will not look at me. "Please come back to your room, Zan."

"And if I don't?"

"Then I call Gavatra and she drugs you, and we haul you there ourselves," she says. "Would you prefer that?"

"No," I say.

"Then come with me," Jayd says. "You must trust me, Zan. I know that's difficult, but the only reason we've gotten this far is because you've trusted me."

"Gotten this far to what?" I say.

"To the Mokshi," she says. "Do you trust me?"

"No," I say.

After another round of calisthenics on my own—Jayd won't say what happened to those women I beat up last time—I tuck the spongy blanket around me back in my cell of a room, but cannot sleep. Instead, I watch the play of lights moving under the membrane of the ceiling. It's eerie, like observing the inner workings of a beast.

At some point, I must sleep, because I dream.

I dream of a woman with a great craven face walking along the surface of a massive world. She is a titan. She snatches flying vehicles from the air and crunches them in her diamond teeth. Green lubricant and yellow puffs of exhaust escape her gaping mouth. Little blue insects flitter through the ether, and when they encounter the yellow mist, they fall down dead, like leaves.

The surface of the world is covered in wavering tentacles, and the titan grabs on to them for purchase as she strides across the world, snarling and spitting out the corpses of her enemies and poisoning everything she breathes on. She snatches at one of the flying vehicles and stabs herself in the stomach with it. She cuts long and low, and though I expect her to cry out in pain, she only roars and shows her teeth as gouts of blood pour from her body and float lazily to the surface of the world, sluggish and distorted by the low gravity.

When I wake, the pulsing lights in the ceiling have dimmed. Jayd stands over me with a blade in her hand. I snap awake and snatch her wrist.

"I need to cut your hair," she says.

My heart pounds so loudly I think she can hear it, and perhaps she can, standing so close to me with that black edged weapon.

"I don't need to cut my hair to go back to the Mokshi," I say.

"The witches recommend it."

"The . . . witches?"

"We'll consider that in time," she says.

She hacks at my hair with less care than I expect, her mouth a thin line. I am surprised to see that amid the hanks of black hair she removes, some are gray. When she is satisfied, she takes me by the chin and gazes into my face, as if trying to peer up under my skull. I cannot get used to the way she looks at me, as if I am lover, sister, and enemy all at once.

"I'm ready," I say. "We go to the Mokshi now?"

She brushes my hair back from my face. "I miss you when you go."

"Now, Jayd."

Her hand trembles. "I wanted a little longer with you."

She takes me back to the hangar.

It's been cleaned up since I was last here. The workbench is tidied. I go right to the big orange-eyed vehicle I repaired before, and it opens its great eye and purrs beneath my fingers.

"How do they get around?" I ask.

"They fly," Jayd says, "through the airless spaces between us and the Mokshi."

"And how far is our . . . ship from the rogue world?"

"We are not a ship, not really," Jayd says. "You'll understand when you get outside, and inside the Mokshi, well . . ." She trails off. "You need to get a squad in there with you. Whatever happens to you in there, however you lose your memory, maybe they can prevent it and help you get it back."

"So, you don't really know if I'll get my memory back if I go."

"If the Mokshi took it, the Mokshi can give it back."

"And if I don't get out?" I say. "Isn't that the problem? That I didn't get out last time? That I've been gone for . . . how long?"

"You'll remember," she says firmly.

I hoped to remember more by now, to uncover some truth, but my memory is still as much a cipher as Jayd. All I know is that I can hurt things, I can repair things, and I once recycled a child. So far, the person I had been didn't seem to be someone I wanted to remember; seeking these memories may be like picking at a soft scab, one that barely conceals the pus and rot beneath.

Jayd points out how the assault vehicle functions while she leads me around the hangar. We pause at a long line of depressions in the wall, and she pulls out various items from the pockets of the wall's seared flesh. One item is a spray-on suit, which she tells me to coat myself in before I go out. The bulb that contains it is soft in my hand. The other is a massive weapon that I hope gets easier to carry outside, because just holding it hurts my good arm.

"You deploy the vehicle's burst scrambler when the world's defenses go up," Jayd says, pointing to a gnarled whorl in what I take to be the vehicle's control panel. "The world is dead, and nothing lives inside of it anymore, but the defenses are still active."

"If you've never been inside the Mokshi," I say, "how do you know everyone is dead inside?"

Jayd takes my good arm and repositions my fingers on the weapon. "Don't hold it like that or you will shoot your foot," she says.

A sticky memory stirs: I remember a great round ship as big as a world, bathed in wave after wave of blue-green light. The image whispers away a moment later, but the memory of it raises the fine hairs on the back of my neck. My heart pumps a little faster; I worry I might have another panic attack, like I did with Gavatra. But my body stays in check. I breathe deeply through my nose. I'm learning to control my body the way I'm learning Jayd, and the ship, and the vehicles. If I can't remember, I'll start over. We'll begin again.

"The first assault the world makes will be an energy wave," Jayd says, and though the tour of the vehicle is over, she paces now, brow knit. I want to rub the furrow there between her eyes and tell her everything is going to be all right. But what would I know?

"The second will hit after you get into the atmosphere," Jayd continues. "The burst scrambler will work to repel both, but you have to recharge it between hits. Don't press it too much, too fast. That's important." She points to the place on the soft green control panel, another gnarled, almost root-like protrusion.

I don't understand much of this, but as with the fighting and the repair of the vehicle, I'm starting to believe that some broken shards of my memory will indeed come back, hopefully when they're most needed. I wonder why Jayd and Gavatra and whoever this mother of theirs is were mad enough to keep sending me off to this fate, and why I had been mad enough to agree to it time and time again. Did this same argument work every time, this promise that I will get back a memory? Maybe there is no memory. Maybe the memory itself is a lie, and I am just like these vehicles, bred for this purpose like a sack of sorry meat.

"Won't I fall off?" I ask, pointing at the sleek tube of the open vehicle. Neither the vehicle nor the bulb containing my supposed suit looks particularly safe. I have an idea of what an airless vacuum of space is, which is odd. I can understand things like food and furniture and heat, but not who I am, or where we are, or why I dream of cannibal women cutting themselves open.

"You straddle it," Jayd says, patting the seat. "Your suit sticks to it. To unstick yourself from it, press here." She shows me the release control. It looks like a massive white pustule.

As Jayd smiles at me, a memory bubbles up: Jayd with her big eyes and full, round face reminds me of Maibe. But I have no idea who Maibe is. I want to ask how many "sisters" there are, and where all the other people are who live on the ship, like Sabita, and who all these bottom-worlders are, but there is no guarantee I'll even survive this assault. Why bother to ask about a place I have a good chance of never seeing again, with a zero chance of Jayd giving me a straight answer, anyway?

I heft the weapon. "How do I use this?" I ask.

Jayd taps the butt of the weapon, just above a soft, hooked trigger mechanism made of the same spongy stuff as the walls. "Just point and shoot," she says.

I lower the weapon, and Jayd bats it away. "Not at me." She pulls something from her pocket, a wormy little thing that she tells me to put in my ear.

"No," I say.

"It's the only way we can speak after you spray on the suit," Jayd says.

I wince. She raises her hand to do it for me, and I snatch her wrist. "I'll do it," I say, and I do as the thing slithers into the whorl of my ear canal.

I want to turn back, then. But a part of me knows that if I refuse to go on this assault, something far more terrible will happen, and this mother of ours—hers?—will recycle the lot of us, and death in service to the War God sounded a fair bit more glorious than death in the mouth of some recycler monster.

That name, that entity, the *recycler monster*, blooms into my thoughts the same way as the words *speculum* and *haystitch* had. My memory provides an image: a great lumbering one-eyed beast snarling at me from the guts of a rotten refuse heap of decaying bodies.

And then I stop thinking, stop coming up with questions, because I am terrified of what other horrors still lay locked in my broken mind.

"Time to drop," Jayd says, and a broad door unfurls from the other side of the room, and in walks my glorious army.

"THE KATAZYRNAS THINK THEMSELVES
THE MOST POWERFUL FORCE IN THE LEGION.
I AM NOT THE FIRST TO HAVE PROVEN THEM WRONG."
—LORD MOKSHI, *ANNALS OF THE LEGION*

3

ZAN

The army the Lord of Katazyrna has rallied for me is more a squad. They are nearly two hundred strong, and when I gape and ask Jayd where they have all come from, she shrugs and says, "They had no choice," and tells me to spray on my suit.

Jayd retreats into an upper bay adjacent to the hangar. The two hundred women mount two hundred vehicles. I squeeze the bulb of the spray-on suit, and it releases a thin sheen of translucent, spidery goo that hugs my body and seals off sound. For a moment, I hyperventilate, claustrophobic, but I'm able to breathe with ease, and the suit absorbs my sweat. I marvel at my suit-covered hands for a long moment until Jayd's voice tickles my ear, relayed by the worm in the casing, "Mount up," she says. "The door will open soon. You'll be pulled adrift if you aren't on a vehicle."

I sit snugly on the great purring vehicle and give it a solid pat. Above me, flickering red lights flare across the ceiling. The skin there begins to ripple. It's not opening so much as it's stretching. It becomes translucent, then tears open.

I'm sucked up toward the hole in the sky, where outside I see blackness speckled in stars. All around me, the other vehicles whoosh up and away, hurtling toward the void. It happens so fast, I gasp. Yellow and green puffs of spent fuel whirl around me while the vehicles tumble upward. It feels like drowning.

As I spin through the tear in the ceiling, I punch at the controls of the vehicle until it jerks forward of its own volition. I'm spinning slowly, but it's enough to make me dizzy and sick. I shift my weight, and the vehicle responds, sending little jets of propulsive fuel into the black. When I find my equilibrium, I raise my eyes and find that I am far above the world from which we were ejected. It hangs below us, a great brownish-green sphere covered in fleshy tentacles. It's so massive, I cannot see the bottom of it from this far away, only the curve of its top . . . or are we at the bottom? The spinning has me unsure of what's right-side-up. It's only as I gaze out at the long lines of my army, all of them flipping and pivoting into formation, an arrow pointing away from the world called Katazyrna, that I think to look beyond the world.

What I see stuns me.

Across the flat black matt of the sky, sprinkled in stars, are massive floating orbs. They hang out here in the vacuum as if attached to strings, slowly orbiting around a misty core of soft light so obscured by that mist that I can't see what is emitting the light that's reflected and refracted. My memory tells me this is the sun, and right now, it is sleeping. The orbs all around me are varying sizes but roughly spherical, like the Katazyrna below us.

It's still another long moment before I understand that these are not orbs but other worlds, other ships, made larger or smaller by how far or near they are from where we sit. Their surfaces swarm with red, blue, and purple lights; some flickering, some blackened, some clearly terribly injured. These have faces that are curled back, and they wobble in their orbits. Some have great tentacles lining their surfaces, like the Katazyrna, and when I look back again at our world, I see that toward the poles of the Katazyrna, the tentacles are blackened with rot in places, the outer skin peeling away. What happens to the people below, when the skin is breached? I watch the breach from which we've been expelled begin to close up again, like a fast-healing wound, and gaze again at the poles. There is rot and death here.

"Welcome to the Outer Rim of the Legion," Jayd says in my ear, speaking to me now from the vibrating worm casing. "You see now why I couldn't explain. We are a Legion of worlds. Ours are the Katazyrna worlds. But the Mokshi is something else. The Mokshi has escaped the Core, there beyond the misty veil that shrouds the sun. There are worlds there, we know, but no one from the Outer Rim here has ever been able to pilot a ship from the Core. Somehow, the Mokshi was able to leave the Core. Our mother must understand its secrets, and so, we must make it ours."

I power my vehicle to the point of the arrow formation my army has made. It's facing a world that appears no bigger than my fist from this distance, and I know that world on sight the way I know my own left hand.

The world called Mokshi is not supposed to be there among the others, Jayd says, and I can see that now in how it moves among the other worlds. The other worldships have far more fixed orbits; even the spaces between them are regular, but not the Mokshi. The Mokshi wobbles in the Outer Rim like a weary, derelict traveler, altering the orbits of its nearest neighbors, shimmering with blue and green auroras that snake across its poles, promising a thin atmosphere . . . yet the surface I can see from here is barren.

I raise my arm and close my fist, and I lead my army forward across the dark spaces between the worlds. We move quickly, far more quickly than I thought these vehicles could take us. There is a massive amount of detritus spinning among the worlds, and I see long lines of people tied to the tentacles of some of the worlds we power past. They are salvaging the junk that orbits their ships, packing it away into the worlds' soft underbellies. These crews are alarmed at our passing, and though we are never close enough to see their faces, I note their hasty retreat from open space into the welcoming tentacles of their worlds, hiding among them as if they were foliage. After we pass, I gaze back at them and see the scavengers carefully resuming their work.

As we approach the Mokshi, I keep our distance as I scout along the equator. I'm looking for an entry point. Circling its equator reveals a wasted wreckage of once-great cities, a forgotten empire asphyxiated by lack of oxygen, perhaps? What strikes me about this worldship are these structures—I see nothing like them on the Katazyrna or the others we have passed. I dip closer to that surface, daring the world to wake, and see now that the structures are not cities but fields of crushed bone and rocky debris that pockmark its outer skin. I cannot help but sense the world is not so much dead, though, as . . . slumbering.

And though I do not remember anything on seeing it, I do have a sense of familiarity. Perhaps it is the feeling old enemies have on meeting again, and again, and again. How many times have we danced like this: me with an army and no memory, the Mokshi with an erratic orbit and no masters?

As we come over a bone-white expanse on the Mokshi's surface, my army breaks up into two teams and fans out around the equator, as if seeing this terrain has triggered a directive that I don't know about. The soldiers are equipped with shimmering weapons and spray-on suits that catch the light of the great slumbering sun there in the misty core, which is winking awake now, unshuttering after half a turn to bathe them and the rogue world in orange radiance. I squint. The mist hiding the core swirls with light as if on fire.

The Mokshi is still moving, though, eclipsing the great orange sun, and we must move faster to keep pace with it. I look out behind us, back toward Katazyrna, and am overwhelmed at the idea that we are a Legion of worlds hurtling through an immense darkness, a space so vast I can see nothing but twinkling lights beyond Katazyrna. Are those other suns like ours? Other Legions? If they are, the distances involved make my head hurt. I turn back to the Legion. It is breathtaking, impossible, like something conjured out of my black, sticky dreams.

But this is my reality.

This is home.

Isn't it?

"Yours is the first team to enter the Mokshi's orbit in a full rotation," Jayd says, her voice so close that I jerk in my seat. I had forgotten her.

"What's a rotation?" I say.

"A turn is one sleeping and waking period," she says. "A rotation is four hundred turns."

"Then who retrieved me," I say, "when I broke free of the Mokshi?"

"The Mokshi spits you free," she says. "You come out in a pod, ejected beyond its gravity well. And no, we don't know why, and you always say you can't remember."

"What happens on that ship?" I say.

"That's what you're here to find out," she says, but of course, I'm here for far more than that. I'm here for Jayd, and her lord mother, and whatever it is they want to do with the only ship that can leave the Legion. I gaze out at those twinkling lights beyond the Outer Rim.

The wrongness in my gut roils.

"What's that debris circling the Mokshi?" I ask, trying to get a better understanding of taboo subjects.

"Our sister Nhim's dead army," Jayd says.

The scattered remnants of Nhim's army still orbit the great disk of the Mokshi: desiccated bodies in blistered suits, escort vehicles mashed into spongy, unrecognizable shapes, and warped, melted weapons that appear to have imploded, eating themselves from the inside out.

"We sent teams to recover them back when it first happened," Jayd says. "The War God wants nothing to go to waste. But they fared no better than Nhim. The Mokshi obliterated two teams outright. Six simply . . . disappeared."

"Disappeared?"

"Eaten by the world . . . or perhaps cast out of range of the Legion's gravity. When you are lost to the Legion, you are lost."

"Why does Anat want this world if it just eats her daughters?" I say.

"She must make it hers," Jayd says. "There are too many others trying to gain control of the Legion, including the Bhavaja family. The Bhavajas are winning, though Lord Katazyrna will not admit that."

I cannot imagine conquering worlds like this, not this scattered necklace of ships spinning and spinning around the core. My memory sparks and kicks and quails like a captured beast of pure, terrified energy.

I sweat hard in my suit. From my position just above the swarm of my army, I sign at them to attack. My body knows the signal just as it knows how to breathe.

The wailing starts then.

It rises from the Mokshi itself. Hearing it should be impossible, as we are still far outside its thin atmosphere. I can't even speak with my team once they are in suits.

Yet I feel the wailing in my bones, like some mournful monster roused from sleep.

I steel myself and navigate the vehicle forward, weapon raised. I am the first to pass across the Mokshi's outer security zone, and the first to see the great crimson wave of its defense grid light up. The wailing goes on and on. It shudders through my army like a physical force.

The keening brings with it a terrible memory of Jayd going in for treatments—why, or for what, I don't know. She is hidden behind a black door that pulses in time with the heartbeat of Katazyrna. Jayd had wailed like this, on and on, while I pounded my fists against the door until my hands bled and a large, squat woman—Lord Katazyrna?—slapped me and told me soldiers must endure sacrifices, and every one of her daughters is a soldier, and what Jayd had to bear would never be allowed on her ship. These were the prices the Katazyrnas must pay to rule the Outer Rim and, eventually, the Legion, she said.

If this is real memory and not dream, it confounds me further still. What would Jayd bear that is so dangerous?

The first red wave of the Mokshi's defenses peels away from the atmosphere: a massive red flare. I turn my vehicle neatly toward the Mokshi's southern pole, deploying the thorny defense scrambler at the head of my vehicle and twisting my trajectory so the vehicle collides with the wave at its weakest point. The energy wave bursts around my vehicle like a soap bubble, flashing past me toward the squad coming behind. Another wave coalesces below. I mash my hand into the indicators on my dash, recharging the scrambler or whatever it is.

Two of the squad light out ahead of me, burning so much fuel I see the yellow spores of their spent charges rippling behind them; two young, stupid kids without a burst of sense between them.

I start to sign at them, "Stay in formation," instinctively, wondering where I've gotten that sign, but they are clearly intent on being the first to cross into the atmosphere. They aren't looking behind, only forward.

"What's happening?" Jayd asks, but I am moving now, my body acting on instinct, as Jayd had promised it would. It's like being piloted by some stranger, a bag of meat pushed along at the end of a stick.

I go into another wild roll, falling past the next wave issuing from the outer defenses, pushing for the speed I need to break below the grid. I know I need to get below the grid, have done it a hundred times before, but the defense grid is only the first hurdle. Assaulting the world is like feeling my way over a familiar path.

I catch up to the kids just as they plunge through the atmosphere, skimming above the surface of the tumbled cities of calcified bone, weathered stone, and twisted amber deposits.

I see the older one sign to the younger. I swerve my vehicle close enough to that one to catch her attention before I sign, "Fall back with the formation."

The two girls fall back behind me, where six more of the squad have broken past the grid, skipping above the surface now like world-walking mechanics out on a repair run. They are below the world's defensive security zone now, but the greatest danger is yet to come. I can feel it. My whole body is taut with expectation.

I take the lead again, speeding ahead, and then I see it: a great yawning chasm at the center of the world. This is where we were going, a colossal crater that doesn't give one the impression of something having crashed into the world so much as something impossibly large having *burst out* of it.

I am very glad then that I have no memory of what that might be.

The fighters that remain form a long, jagged line at the rim of the crater. I take a fast count; sixty of the two hundred I brought with me have made it this far. The world's defenses took out the rest, or they fled from the field or collided with debris or had some malfunction along the way. It's a massive loss; more, I feel, than I should have lost to the defenses alone.

"Heavy losses," I say out loud.

"It's the Bhavajas," Jayd says, low and grim.

"That family?" I ask, scanning the horizon, looking for some other army, some mad group of monsters, maybe, crazy enough to come out here after us.

"They don't like the Katazyrnas," Jayd says. "We conquered eight of their worlds in our grandmother's time."

"We'll get on well, then, won't we?" I say, and Jayd laughs, and I wonder what I can say, what I can do, to hear that laugh again in this black place.

I hold up a fist, calling my squad's attention. My heart thuds loudly in my ears. I wonder if the Mokshi hears it. The wailing continues; it has become a part of me now, like my heartbeat, my rapid breath, the stink of myself in the cloying suit.

Below us, something flickers at the edges of the yawning black crater. A creeping yellow fog emerges, coiling into the atmosphere like the breath of some titanic god. A secondary defense mechanism.

"We are the fist of the War God," I sign to my team. "We are the inheritors of the worlds. Show yourselves worthy." The words feel ancient, a benediction, the signs something my body has done so often, it performs them by rote.

It's not until I gaze at their confused faces that I realize I have signed to them in the wrong language. I stare at my hands. I try again, using a different sign language, and their expressions turn from bewilderment to wonder. They raise their fists.

We carry on.

The army drops toward the crater. With luck, they will burst into the heart of the world and face whatever it is that waits for them and conquer it as they will conquer its world, and I will return to Jayd a hero, and our mother will not recycle me again.

I fall after them, the rush of atmosphere against my suit. I swerve to evade the curling yellow breath of the crater.

The woman beside me moves too late, and a snarl of the breath ensnares her leg, pulling her deeper into its arms. Her suit sizzles from her body. Her flesh bubbles on her bones. My vehicle and I go into free fall, tumbling into the dark mouth of the world.

I push forward, burning fuel to gain control of the fall. The two kids catch up to me again, plucky and drunk with youth, their faces euphoric.

The crater seems to grow larger as we approach, black as the inky spaces between the worlds, black as the Legion when the core shutters up, black as death, as nothingness, as the universe before the gods shook the worlds loose from their hair and ignited the spinning heart of the Legion. I have a moment to wonder who all these gods are for half a breath before a tangled shot zips past my head. It doesn't come from the blackness below us but from behind. The shot rips a great gaping hole in the girl's vehicle beside me. The girl's mouth opens, surprise more than fear, and then I am spinning down, down, down into darkness after her. Leave no one behind. Save them all.

Her young companion swerves closer to me, and we nearly collide. Another shot disturbs the mist. A thorny protuberance blooms from the falling girl's chest. We are in the Mokshi's gravity well now, and it pulls her hard.

I grab for her just as the she releases her grip on her vehicle. The vehicle falls out from under her, rushing past us both.

I clutch the girl's arm hard. She is so close now, I can see her great dark eyes. Her face is fully visible inside the transparent suit that clings to her like a second skin. I study her young, doomed face. She is just a child, not much past menarche. I want to save her so badly. My teeth ache from gritting them.

The thing blooming from her chest is a three-tentacled cephalopod projectile whose inky poison darkens the girl's transparent suit, eating holes right through the skin of it.

"What's happening?" Jayd says. Calm. So very calm.

I start babbling, trying to explain what I see happening to the girl's body.

"That's not a Mokshi weapon," Jayd says. "It's a Bhavaja one. You need to get out of there. You can't survive the Mokshi and the Bhavajas at once. We have tried that before."

I twist my head and see a full squad of soldiers behind me, not mine, riding up on the remnants of my army in three tiered lines, great angular weapons mounted to the fronts of their vehicles.

I still cling to the arm of the girl whose suit is disintegrating around her. It peels back from her head, letting her dark hair stream free of the suit, coiling through the air like snarled fingers. She gasps on air too thin to sustain her. I think of my sister Nhim and the dead army circling the Mokshi. How many went just this way? How many more will they sacrifice to control a world that can't be conquered?

I cling a long time, longer than I probably should have, until the girl's body goes limp and a third shot clips the girl's leg and sends her vehicle spinning. I drop the girl and roll my vehicle toward a billowing yellow cloud.

I punch the dash, deploying the burst shield, and cut through the cloud neatly, breaching the other side. I kick my vehicle around and face what must be the Bhavaja family. They are finishing off the last three surviving members of my army.

I snarl at them and make an obscene gesture, knowing I am too far away for them to catch it. I burn hard toward them, firing off my weapon into their lines.

The lines peel away, outmaneuvering me.

Whoever controls the Mokshi controls the Legion, another bit of wisdom bubbling up from my broken memory. Whoever said it, the Bhavajas seem to know it too, and they will never let me take it, and I'll never get my memory back, and all these girls are dead for nothing. I will never get any closer than this gaping wound, this portal to the center of the world.

I zip past a long line of Bhavajas, then tilt back toward the billowing yellow fog, gunning hard for it like some madwoman. A few of them pursue, foolishly, and why wouldn't they? They think I have burned and conquered their worlds, and they will follow me to the very limits of the Legion for revenge, wouldn't they? *I* would.

A handsbreadth from the fog, I cut the fuel to my vehicle and drop like a stone, so hard and so fast, they don't know what's happening until they plunge into the yellow fog, bubbling and sizzling, colliding with one another like broken stars.

I come out of the drop and up, fast, so fast I nearly smash into another Bhavaja vehicle, one of the ones that hung back. I circle the crater once and see not one of my soldiers still riding the Mokshi's thin atmosphere. I'm alone. The yellow mist covers the whole mouth of the crater now, blocking entry. There is no way in; I've lost the brief window between the world's first and second defensive deployments.

Another of the Bhavajas comes at me, taking lead of the group, and she signs at me: "You won't make Katazyrna space. You won't make it home."

"What's happening?" Jayd's voice.

I answer by hitting the dash and propelling myself abruptly upward, bursting through the atmosphere so fast, I feel the heat of the friction on my suit.

I pop free and let the burst of momentum push me from the weak gravity well of the world. I see the crimson wave of the defense grid coming up behind me. I try to twist my vehicle around and counter the red wave with the burst shield. The wave glances off the edge of my shield and I spin out of control, tumbling end over end through the desolate inky spaces between the worlds.

The impact of the defense wave burns the left side of my suit, blackening my vision on that side. I squint through my one good eye, blinded by the auburn glare of the misty sun of the Core.

Ahead of me, a dozen worlds burn with the auroras of their outer defenses, casting off waves of vermillion, turquoise and misty emerald light.

I see the kid's gasping face again, the thick fingers of dark hair, while light flares again and again across my field of vision.

A vehicle zips past me—not mine but Bhavaja: one on the left, then one on the right.

I fight with my vehicle's propulsion system, thighs gripping either side of it hard, trying to keep my seat.

A cephalopod thuds into my vehicle's undercarriage.

It gives me the push I need to right myself. I reorient myself and shoot past the two vehicles that flank me. I can see Katazyrna rising ahead of me. Wispy, snarling white tentacles grow out of the Katazyrna's surface. I see bits of debris caught in those sticky tentacles. If I can reach the pull of the world's gravity, I can lunge for them and climb back down planetside.

I push hard for the world. It grows into a great amber disk as I near. Another thud judders my vehicle. I correct it before I spin out.

One of the Bhavajas comes up beside me. Her expression is hard: brows meeting over deep, hooded eyes, a twist of a mouth from which peeks a pink tongue, held tightly in clenched teeth.

The Bhavaja raises her weapon and fires.

I release my vehicle, stretch out my arms, and launch myself off it like a space swimmer, catapulting toward the shimmering white tentacles of Katazyrna.

A cephalopod clips my leg. I feel the frigid rush of vacuum and the creeping horror of the suit dissolving around my leg, sickening from the outside in, peeling away like a gory fruit rind.

My grasping fingers take hold of one of the waving tentacles streaming from the surface of Katazyrna. It curls around my arm, yanking me down and down to the surface of the world and the cold, thin atmosphere of home.

I hit the spongy surface just as my suit dissolves around my face and my oxygen runs out.

I have time to suck in a painful breath of frigid, too-thin air and make an obscene gesture at the Bhavajas as they shoot out and away in the face of the world's blue defenses. Katazyrna pitches wave after wave of radiant energy after our snarling enemy.

"Home," I say through cold, parched lips into thin, crackling air, "home," and black out.

> "WE ARE ALL SERVANTS OF THE LEGION, SOME MORE SO THAN OTHERS. OUR POWER COMES IN REALIZING THAT SERVITUDE IS NOT A NATURAL STATE BUT A LEARNED ONE. OUR POWER COMES IN KNOWING WE CAN REMAKE IT ALL."
> —LORD MOKSHI, **ANNALS OF THE LEGION**

JAYD

The first time Zan came back from the Mokshi with no memory, I thought it was a blessing from the War God. We had done too many awful things to one another by then, and I feared we would never achieve what we'd set out to do. She was always more emotional than me, which made it a miracle she had achieved so much before we began to work together.

In truth, I never expected to play this game so long. But my mother, Anat, Lord Katazyrna, is stubborn, and so are the Bhavajas. They have been fighting us so long, I don't think they know how to stop, and Anat certainly can't stop them alone. Zan and I believed we had a way to end the fighting and save Katazyrna, and perhaps the Legion, too. But some people don't want to be saved.

I am thinking of this as I head down to see Anat. I've had visual confirmation from the surface-walkers that Zan has reached the well of Katazyrna's gravity, and they are going to pull her in. It makes me nervous not to be the one to welcome Zan back, but Anat is already suspicious of me, and I don't want to inflame her any more than she already is. We have come close to swaying her so many times. I touch my stomach. Everything we planned so very long ago depends on Zan being there, flinging herself at the Mokshi, and me being here, rescuing her from it, until we can convince Anat that I can better serve her in the hands of our enemies.

After this latest failed approach on the Mokshi, I prepare to debrief our mother as if I am a soldier preparing for war. It's how our mother raised us all. We are Katazyrna soldiers, born and raised for just this purpose. But I find soldiering false, a broken way to manage people who should be bound to you in love, not fear.

Love worked far better on Zan than fear, I found. At least until she found out what I did to what she loved most. I have made many mistakes. I am the first to admit that. But forgiveness is a luxury I cannot afford to court. I'm not convinced I would deserve it, even if I got down on my knees and cut open my palms and begged Zan for it.

I press the wrinkles from my slick outer coat and ask for admittance into our mother's corridor. The big women on either side of the door press the flesh of the door, and it blooms open, but it is not my mother on the other side; it is the gaggle of witches, shuffling their way down the corridor, quickly ducking from my view, fleeing my approach. Unlike Zan, witches have long memories. They remember what Zan and I had to do to them to keep them quiet. But they didn't dare give away our secrets after that. Every time the witches are recycled, they lose a little bit of their sanity on rebirth. A secret like ours is worth keeping if it means they won't have to be reborn again for another few turns, at least. Until it's Anat who tires of them.

I have not seen the witches since the day Zan came back without her memory. Some days, I wish I understood their loyalties. Do they belong to the ship or to Mother? Like everything else that belongs to the world, they are reborn in the womb of a woman, usually the same one, but if we kill that woman, the ship simply gives another one the task of birthing the witches, and we start again. We can never get rid of the witches, no matter how many times they are killed or recycled. They always come back.

Like Zan. Like me.

I find my mother in the long translucent stretch of the world called the reflective pool, though there is no water, only a sheen of filmy skin so thin that it reveals the faces and forms of the dead and half-undone floating in the guts of ship's walls. All those bits of bodies we have recycled eventually pass through here on their way to being devoured and repurposed. Sometimes, if I stand here long enough, I can see the faces of my dead sisters. Everyone is a sister here because we are all of the world, all but those we have scavenged from other worlds. The corridor stretches on and on until it comes to a crumpled ruin, something purposely destroyed to ensure no one went any farther down that way, I expect. There have been countless insurrections and blight over the rotations. I once asked Mother why she didn't fix it, and she snarled something at me—I don't even remember what—and I let it drop. I suspect Mother has far less power than she pretends. It's why I am willing to take the risks that I do.

Anat is talking loudly to three of her secretaries, all bottom-world people she has raised up to serve her. Raising them from below instead of capturing them from other worlds makes them more loyal, she always says, but I think my mother conflates fear and loyalty far too often. I fear her, yes, but I've never been loyal. She is gesturing to them with her great metal arm. The metal covers a heated green organic core, which can be seen through the grill on the underside of her arm. She likes to wave it around like the war trophy it is, but seeing it always makes my stomach turn. It reminds me of my mistakes.

"Zan came back alive from the latest assault," I say.

Anat keeps talking to the secretaries in their patois. I can speak half a dozen bottom-world languages, and I can hear them talking about trading contracts. A group in the level below has broken out in civil strife over the matter of tariffs. Anat uses those goods in her bid to win the hearts of the people she intends to conquer. The witches on every world plead with us, often, to stop sharing materials among worlds. They say it has contributed to the rotting of the Legion. Worldships are meant to be self-sustaining, they say, and the more we swap resources among worlds, the more we upset the delicate balance of the ships. But I have seen ships that never shared resources. I have conquered them. They died out faster than those who traded on the Outer Rim. When I cracked those supposedly self-sustaining worlds open, the only people alive were barely sentient, scrabbling out a living at the very center of the world, where it was still warm. I think the witches give us advice from some dead time, a time when the longevity of the worlds was never in question. But we have moved long past that. The witches haven't.

My mother's response to the witches' proclamations is less rational but just as dismissive. She says she is the only thing keeping the Legion together, and she answers only to the Lord of War. Anat believes she can do whatever she wants as long as she holds the surface of the world. That has been true here for a long time. It's why Zan and I needed to be smarter than Anat, because no one rules with a bloodier fist than Anat.

Finally, Anat dismisses her secretaries, who scuttle off on their clacking little feet, and she rounds on me. "Did Zan gain control of the Mokshi or not?" she says.

"No, but—"

"Then don't waste my time," Anat says. She nods at the reports under my arm; little slips of light escape the hemp folders. "It's gotten worse, hasn't it? The cancer on the surface of world?" she says.

"Yes," I say. "The technicians were out running another scan at the poles when Zan came back from the assault. It's the only reason we got her back inside in time. We almost lost her, Anat."

"This scheme of yours has yet to pay off. I'm getting tired of her, and you."

"She has gotten closer to the Mokshi than any of us," I say carefully, and move on to the more pressing subject, because the less we speak of my schemes, the better. "It's clear that the rot on the skin of the world is cancerous. It's eating right through the world's skin. We are only a rotation away from a breach. They hardly had to break the skin to let Zan back in."

"I know, girl," Anat says. "You leave that to me."

"How do we save the world?" I say. "We aren't going to be able to move people to the Mokshi. Zan isn't going to succeed in time. We need another option."

I have been pressing this since Zan and I began this dance, but Anat is stubborn. No one knows that better than me. She cannot be pushed into a political option if she believes a military one will achieve the same ends.

Anat peers at me and curls her lip. "The same way we've always saved the world. We must sacrifice something to it."

"I agree that there are other options," I say. "We should discuss them."

"You speak as if I'm not the Lord of the Legion," Anat says.

"I would never presume—"

"Oh, you would. You would." Anat starts pacing, and that makes me fearful, because it signals one of her violent moods. She becomes impossible to reason with during these episodes. "How are your treatments? You're not coming to term, are you?"

"The treatments are fine." Anat has never said it, but I suspect she doesn't want me to bear what I'm capable of carrying, because in the eyes of our sisters, it would make me more powerful than her. When she found out what I'd done to myself, she was not elated, but cold. She wanted to find out why I would do such a thing, why I would want to carry something like that in my womb, if not to inspire the people she ruled to overthrow her.

"I need you to stay off the skin of the world for a time," Anat says. "I have great plans for you, and they require you to stay intact. It's time to make use of what you bear."

"And what of Zan?" I say.

"Zan is failing. I should just recycle her again. Maybe she'll stay dead this time."

"Please don't do that. You know what happened last time."

"What's the use of her coming back if she can't get my army into the Mokshi with her? We still don't know what happens to her in there once she gets under the skin. Does it eat her? Remake her? If her memory loss isn't feigned—"

"It's very real," I say. It wasn't, the first time, but it has been ever since. I don't tell her that, but it's a truth I know and Zan doesn't, and it still makes my skin itch. Why does she lose her memory now, when she gets back to the Mokshi? That was never part of our plan. She had all her memories intact after she crawled her way up and went back to the Mokshi the second time. Had something happened to her down below? I would never know now.

I gaze at the ceiling, imagining the cancerous skin of the world eating into every level, striking down and down and down into the center of Katazyrna and destroying us all, level by level, cell by cell, while my mother dances with some impenetrably broken world that has already claimed hundreds of her daughters and thousands of aliens and bottom-world misfits. It is a mad vision Anat has. There is another way.

"Is that all you had?" Anat says. "Just more bad news?"

"That's all," I say. "You shouldn't—"

She raises her iron arm. "Are you trying to tell me what I should and shouldn't do again, girl?"

I cringe. I hate that I cringe, but she has struck me too often. "No," I whisper.

"Good," she says, and sweeps past me, back toward the first level of the world. I scramble to keep up with her, because I know what happens when she and Zan are alone.

> "WORLDS CAN BE REBORN, BUT THE REST OF US
> ARE DOOMED TO THE SKIN WE'VE MADE FOR OURSELVES.
> DOOMED TO LIVE WITH THE CHOICES WE'VE MADE."
> —LORD MOKSHI, *ANNALS OF THE LEGION*

5

ZAN

Blackness, then milky green.

I am sucked from the surface of the world and deep into the verdant emerald interior of Katazyrna, reborn for perhaps the millionth time, or perhaps just the tenth. Certainly only the second I remember.

As I fall, I see the Bhavajas' needled vehicles blot out the blackness. I see their dark faces, and the glinting whites of their eyes in the blue-green halo of the world's defenses. They cannot approach through those defenses, but they fire off another round from the cephalopod guns.

As the world's skin closes over me, one of the Bhavajas signs at me, "You're already dead."

I hit the floor of the ship's interior and let out a rush of air. My suit begins to dissolve into the spongy floor. I panic, struggling to my hands and knees, and begin hacking uncontrollably. The suit melts, leaving me shivering even in the humid air.

Around me, the floor blinks with a soft blue glow, turning the milky green world aqua.

Ahead, a slick squad of retaliatory troops is heading topside. I squeeze my eyes shut. My lungs and face and throat hurt. I sucked in air out there, and it hurts. I retch and gag.

"Zan!"

I raise my head, hoping it's Jayd. But it's Sabita, the woman who found me in the vehicle hangar. She is wearing a red shift, and my memory offers up a bit of wisdom. The red shift marks Sabita as an emergency tissue technician. Sabita extends her long brown arms to me and catches me up in her arms as if I am a child.

I try to speak, but my lips and tongue are blistered. Sabita takes a shimmering purple slug from the bag at her hip and fills my mouth with unguent.

"Hush now," Sabita says. She wipes more unguent around my lips, her fingers strong and sure against my battered skin.

The unguent begins to do its work. I feel my mouth and tongue again. The dead cellular tissue inside my mouth is rapidly sloughing away, choking me with pasty mucus. I gag.

"Don't vomit," Sabita says. "Give it another moment."

But I spit it all out anyway—the unguent and the dead cells from my mouth and tongue. I wipe at my face, and the skin around my lips flakes away.

"Jayd," I say.

"Jayd is with the Lord of Katazyrna," Sabita says.

"Have to tell her about the Bhavajas."

"She knows, Zan."

The flickering blue lights fade, replaced with the soft green glow. Is the blue an emergency indicator of some kind? I stare at the walls, bewildered. "I don't understand," I say. "If she knows Bhavajas are attacking us, why isn't she doing anything?"

Sabita touches my hand, briefly, as if some of the bitter cold from between the worlds still lingers on my skin.

"Your mother won't permit any retaliation against the Bhavajas," Sabita says. "The ones attacking us now probably don't know yet."

"Know what? That squad I just saw heading out, though—"

"Your mother sent those ones out to the Mokshi, to confirm your . . . failure. They weren't sent out for the raiders."

I hear the soft, irregular squelching of an approaching party.

"But—"

"So, you live. You die. You live again," Gavatra says. She holds a shimmering purple sheath of material that ripples as if alive.

I stand and step into the sheath. It conforms easily to my body. I wipe my hands against the material. It seems to be made of mites. They tickle my skin. I realize they are eating the remnants of the melted spray-on suit.

Gavatra spares a look at Sabita. "Back to the infirmary with you," she says.

"I've brought her back every time," Sabita says, "from far worse, and that is the thanks you give me?"

"We have other tissue technicians," Gavatra says.

"Where's Jayd?" I ask.

"Oh, she is coming up after me," Gavatra says. "She and your mother." I see half a dozen women dressed as Gavatra slide in from the umbilicus farther down the corridor.

"What's all this?" I ask.

"A precaution, only," Gavatra says.

Sabita steps nimbly past me, gaze lowered, and I feel a confrontation coming. I hold my ground. Sabita slips away just as the group of women parts and I see a stout, grim-faced woman striding toward me at the center of them. She is older and squatter than the others, but what really sets her apart is her great metal arm. The underside glows slightly green, and I wonder if it's hot to the touch. What does a woman do with an arm like that? Just behind her is Jayd; Jayd's expression is hard to make out from this distance in the low light, but she's moving fast after the woman with the iron arm.

This woman must be Anat, because only a woman styling herself a Lord would walk as confidently as she does while barely reaching my shoulder. I suspect the metal arm helps her ego enormously. The arm is the most metal I've seen here, and it's clearly well taken care of—it fairly gleams in the bluish light.

It's not until she's nearly on top of me, though, that I realize she is tougher than her height would have me believe.

She grabs me by the ear, which is far more painful that I would have thought, and drags me across the floor. I'm so shocked, I yelp. When I grab her hands, she releases me. She has pulled me from the open corridor into a vestibule. The six beefy women of her security team stand between us and the corridor, effectively blocking me from Jayd and anyone else passing in the hall. The security team crosses their arms and puts their backs to me and Anat. They are a wall of flesh, and I lie in their shadow.

"How close did you get?" Anat says.

"To the lip of the crater," I say, annoyed at the whole exchange, but somehow even more put off by the fact that she doesn't introduce herself. But of course she already knows me. She's likely met me many times. "The Bhavajas took out my army. They took out more than the defenses did."

"Blood-smeared Bhavajas," she says. "You were close, though. Why do you keep failing? Why are you defective?"

"We're fighting the wrong enemy," I say. "If the Bhavajas want that world, too, you need to defeat them first."

"Only a fool fights a war on two fronts," Anat says.

"That's effectively what they have you doing," I say, "whether you want to or not. It's why you're losing."

"I never lose. *You* lost."

Everyone here is insane, I think, but that's probably best kept to myself right now. "Take the army out there yourself, then," I say instead, and that's probably not going to go over well either.

Anat swings her iron arm at me.

I catch it and hold it, surprised at my own strength. The metal is warm and comforting. The green bits of skin that glow through the metal mesh give off a surprising amount of heat. I meet Anat's gaze, and in that moment we are mortal enemies, two women locked in orbit around one another. She knows her ultimate goal, but I don't know mine yet. Right now all I want is to let her know I am not some animal that will sit here and take her fist. When she gazes back, it is with the blazing maniacal eyes of a prophet or a seer, a woman who believes with absolute certainty that she is the chosen of a god.

She wrests her iron arm from my grip. "We are done dancing," she says. She pushes past her security people.

I open my arms for Jayd, but Jayd does not come to me. She runs after Anat. So I scramble up and follow Jayd, and this time, the security women don't bother to hold me back.

"I have made a bargain," Anat says to Jayd.

But just as I catch up to them, the security women decide to pull me back after all. I yell.

Jayd looks back once. Anat says something to her, and amid the stir of women, I cannot hear it, but I see something in Jayd's face change. At first I think it's fear, but as she turns away from Anat, I realize it is triumph.

"Come away!" Sabita's voice. She has come back. She snatches at me from behind.

"Get her out of here," a security woman says. "She's disturbing the Lord of the Legion."

"Quickly," Sabita says, and though I yearn for Jayd, Jayd has already disappeared after Anat, and their path is swallowed by the security women.

Sabita and I are left behind in the dim corridor. She is trembling.

"What is it?" I ask.

"Don't trust Jayd," Sabita says. "I'm sworn to help you achieve what you need to. I will keep her safe for you as you asked, but—"

"What are you talking about?" I say.

"You didn't tell me this time," she says, "another time. The first time. Before you lost your memory."

"If you know who I am—"

"Only Jayd knows that," Sabita says. "You never even told me that. Whatever is between you and her has survived all of her betrayals. I don't pretend to understand it, but you need to listen, because she will fill your head with lies. Stay true to your purpose. I was supposed to tell you that, every time. Your purpose. Not Jayd's."

"But I didn't tell you my purpose?"

She shakes her head. "I'm sorry. It frustrated me as much then as it does you now. I think you suspected that would be enough to . . . trigger a memory of some kind?"

"When did I get here, Sabita?"

"Several rotations ago," she says.

"And I'm not a Katazyrna."

"Hush," she says. "It's not safe to speak here. Let's go back to your rooms."

She takes my hand in hers, and leads me farther from Jayd and her mad mother.

> "AT THE HEART OF EVERY SHIP IS A WITCH.
> SHE IS THE ONLY ONE OF US WHO REMEMBERS EVERYTHING.
> AND IT'S THE KNOWING THAT HAS DRIVEN THEM ALL MAD."
> —LORD MOKSHI, ANNALS OF THE LEGION

6

JAYD

A bargain?" I say. Zan is yelling from the corridor, many paces behind my mother and me, but this is far more important. I stick close to Anat as she marches back to the umbilicus to head down to the second level. "With who?" My heart flutters.

"The Bhavajas."

I skip a step, and nearly stumble. "The Bhavajas? After all this time?"

"They offered peace before that last run. I told them I'd think about it. Seems they wanted to push me again and remind me of what meddlesome insects they are."

"What are their terms?" I ask.

Anat rounds on me. "You know what they want, Jayd. The same thing every world wants. They already have the ability to make new worlds. But I've always had many daughters who could do things theirs couldn't. They've raided six worlds to get what you carry. They think adding a new sort of woman and her offspring to Bhavaja can save them."

"You wouldn't do that."

"Wouldn't I?" She puts her hands on my shoulders. Grips me hard with her iron hand. "You will be the mother of worlds," she says. "The Bhavajas have asked for you to marry their general, Jayd. You know Rasida Bhavaja. And I have given my consent. It is the best decision for the Legion."

I have to turn away then. I choke on a cry, but it is not the cry she expects. It is not the cry she has been trying to wheedle out of me all along, the cry she is hoping for.

I turn away so she cannot see that it is a cry of relief. I turn away so she cannot see me smile.

I watch Anat take the umbilicus down to the second level along with her security team. It's the security team that's made it so difficult for Zan and me to overwhelm Anat, after all these cycles. To be fair, the arm makes her deadlier too, and the arm was my fault. For all her swagger, she is indeed a clever, brutish woman, and she has confounded our plans many times But not this time.

I steady my breath and my resolve. I have been pushing Anat toward this final solution with the Bhavajas for so long that I don't know what to do with myself now that it is decided. The Bhavajas need a marriage to a woman like me. They need the potential I carry. And I need to get off the ship so I can steal what they have and we don't. Everything depends on me getting off this ship. Zan can handle Anat from here.

It has taken longer than Zan and I anticipated, to twist Anat into gifting me to Rasida, and we have sacrificed more than either of us expected, but we have convinced Anat in the only way she can be convinced—through trickery and obfuscation. Yet it's a lonely victory. Zan is the only person I can tell about this change in our fortunes, but she will remember none of its significance.

I pick my way back where I came from, but Zan is no longer in the corridor. I suspect she went back to her room. I'll have to tell her this news later, even if it means nothing to her. The only living things, then, that will understand and appreciate my victory are the witches. Even if they are mad now, they'll know I beat them. Zan and I are doing the impossible. We are going to save the Legion.

I go down two levels and stop by the alcohol distillery and speak with two bottom-world brew masters. I ask where the witches are— they often drink too much—and the brew masters tell me to try the port observatory near the hangar.

I walk back up to the first level, traveling the great umbilicus that connects the levels of the world, and—wiping the mucus from my skin—I stride into the observatory overlooking the hangar.

A tangled figure crouches beneath one of the massive, misty workstations. Blue and red lights crackle from the workstation's surface in patterns whose meanings have long since been lost to us. Only the witches seem to make some sense of them; Anat once told me, in one of her drunken reveries, that even her own grandmother thought the lights just a pretty decoration.

On first look, the mash-up of arms and legs and heads beneath the console appears to be several people, but I know better. The witches rise from beneath the console as a single torso on two thick, meaty legs. Two vestigial legs hang off the back of them. This iteration has six arms, only four of them working. The smallest set hangs off the front of the torso, boneless as a vestigial tail.

They see me and begin babbling and juddering.

"I'm not here to hurt you," I say. "I wanted to tell you it worked. Despite you. It worked."

Their body and heads shake. Then they still. The three mouths gabble at me for a moment in a language I don't understand, until the far right head hits upon the right words.

"There is an anomaly in here," it says. "You've brought an anomaly from outside the world, and it is contaminating this space. You will destroy the balance of the ship's systems. You will destroy the Legion."

"We can't continue as we are," I say. "We're dying. You know that better than we do, yet you stick to that same sorry line. The worlds that stopped importing new flesh died out long ago. We are all that's left, but we've only postponed the inevitable."

"You are the embodiment of all evil," the center head says, and the three of them chatter together, clicking and hissing in some bottom-world language that I don't know.

"New world," the right says. "The world is too old and must be regenerated, but you cannot see it, can you? Cannot understand your place."

"We all have a purpose," left says. The witches lurch toward me, and I flinch. The hands flap at me, reaching for my stomach.

"Not yours!" they shriek.

I step back. "It's not up to you anymore," I say. "You've failed to preserve the Legion. We must do what you could not. Whoever put you in charge here is long dead, and you're too mad to be of any help."

The heads cackle. "Falling apart," they say, not quite in unison, and they laugh again, the mad little things.

"We have given you all such purpose," right says. "You are breaking the balance. Treachery and spite. We are here to protect and preserve—"

"You're preserving death. We won't be slaves anymore."

"You're a villain," right says, and the witches crouch beneath the console again, their four working arms poking at the guts of it. This may be the sanest thing they have ever said.

Sometimes, they try to repair things, but it doesn't usually work. Like the Legion, the witches have outlived their usefulness. We are stuck inside a closed system that's slowly coming undone. Even they know it; they just can't bear to admit it.

"We'll be free of you," I say.

The left head turns while the others remain fixed on their work. "The passengers must pay their way."

"Pay their way!" the other two heads say, and then the right head, too, turns back under the console, and they ignore me again.

I was wrong to come to them. They hardly remember more than Zan does now. We are all just so much meat to Anat, even the witches.

I won't be meat anymore.

I walk up to the observation window, the one overlooking the hangar, and gaze at the rows and rows of vehicles hooked into the spongy floor of the ship, gurgling contentedly. There are just four rows of vehicles, though the hangar stretches back and back for over a thousand paces. Heaps of spare parts take up a few areas, but the rest of the hangar is an emptiness, a boneyard for a once-great army, or perhaps . . . something else.

I dream of a world where this hangar is used for some other purpose, when we would ride vehicles out into the blackness between the worlds to help one another, to form alliances, to repair worlds together, instead of what we've become: this broken remnant of a once-great Legion.

I look out at the blackness sometimes, when I am allowed to go topside to inspect the cancer or collect detritus pulled in by the world's tentacles, and I try to imagine the Legion as it might have been in the beginning. One can see the empty spaces where other worlds used to be, the broken lines in their ranks. Anat tells me and my sisters stories of dead and dying worlds she remembers from her own youth, or stories of worlds she has known, and the sheer scope of that, of the loss, is sometimes staggering.

The Legion is dying. We will die with it if we don't act.

Anat thinks the solution lies in the Mokshi. She believes she can control it and use it to wage war on the rest of the worlds of the Legion. It's the only world that has ever clearly been able to leave its orbit, and though Anat waged a war on the Mokshi, too, when it first arrived, she was never able to board it. Not like Zan could.

Not like I could.

Maybe Anat thinks she will put it to better use than the Bhavajas, who will no doubt use it for salvage as they do every other world. But even Anat's vision is myopic. She cannot see past the Legion. Even so, she has been willing to sacrifice her daughters to achieve her ambition.

Zan and I are willing to sacrifice much more.

"IT'S A SIMPLE EXCHANGE OF GENETIC MATERIAL:
MY DAUGHTER FOR YOURS. BUT THOSE EARLY EXCHANGES
SIGNALED THE BEGINNING OF THE END. WHEN THE
WORLDS WERE NO LONGER ABLE TO BE SELF-SUSTAINING,
IT WAS ONLY A MATTER OF TIME UNTIL OUR EXTINCTION."
—LORD MOKSHI, ANNALS OF THE LEGION

7

ZAN

Sabita takes me back to my quarters to rest. "You should know that I will do what I can to help you," she whispers, as if fearing the walls themselves can hear her.

"Unless you can give me back my memory," I say, "or tell me how to board the Mokshi, there's no useful help you can offer me. Why is it Jayd tries to keep me away from everyone else?"

"You're kept cloistered while you're in recovery," Sabita says. "Some of that is for your protection, and the protection of others. Sometimes, when you come back, you have very violent fits. Perhaps that's to do with the means through which you lose your memory. I don't know. But I have cared for you in recovery. Many times."

"This is a fool's game," I mutter.

"It's coming back, isn't it? You should have had some memories resurface by now."

"How do you know that?"

"We have done this many times," she says again. A cry comes from the corridor. "I must go," she says.

"Wait—" I say, but she runs into the hall, and the door purls shut behind her.

Outside, someone is screaming.

And screaming.

I cover my ears, and the screaming stops. My legs are shaky; hunger pinches my belly.

I lie back on the bed, thinking over all that has happened, and all that I remember so far. Every new memory brings with it a knot of horror that grows every moment. The panel of the wall lights up, and tangled blue and red geometric designs dance there. Is it a language, as I suspect? What is it telling me about the ship?

I don't know how long it is before the door opens, but it's long enough for me to consider if it's possible to eat through the door.

Jayd enters, her face looking haggard and drawn.

"The bargain," I say.

"Rasida Bhavaja, Lord Bhavaja, has always loved me," Jayd says. "Or perhaps just been obsessed with me. We have parlayed with their family many times over the years. And now I carry something else that they have been fighting many other worlds to get a hold of. That combination . . . is potent. Anat proposes that I give myself to Rasida in exchange for peace, so you can board the Mokshi unhindered."

"You agreed to this?" I say, incredulous.

"One does not disagree with Anat."

"Don't do it," I say. "I can take the Mokshi without a truce. I can go in alone. No armies. If I go in alone—"

"When you go in alone, you come back without a memory," Jayd says. "To protect you from whatever happens in there, and to take the Mokshi properly, you must get more women in there with you, and we can't do that with the Bhavajas picking off whatever the Mokshi doesn't. You can't do it alone. We've tried." She presses her lips firmly together, as if she's said too much.

"We can try again," I say.

"With another army?" Jayd says. "We've lost too many of our sisters, Zan. It's not working."

"I can protect you," I say, and I know in that moment I can. I feel it fiercely.

"Oh, Zan," Jayd says, and she opens her arms and I fall into them, resting my cheek against Jayd's head, holding her close enough that I can feel the trembling of her heart. She is afraid. I don't trust anything she says, but this fear is not a lie. "This is everything we wanted, Zan. But I'm going to have to do so many terrible things."

"Why?" I say.

She does not answer, only continues stroking my hair. This is among the many things she does not want me to know. I wonder if they are the things that would make me go mad.

"You can convince Anat to hold off," I say.

"There have been many chances," Jayd says, pulling away. She wraps her hands in mine. "This is the only way to have peace."

"Peace for who?" I say. "There's no peace when you're a slave."

"It isn't like that," Jayd says. "Rasida Bhavaja is a smart, handsome woman—"

"She's bought you like some animal!"

"It will be a fair exchange," Jayd says, and her tone is dark. "I will make sure of that. She has asked for me many times. She once told Anat she would exchange a whole world for me, but Anat knows the Bhavajas too well. She knew Rasida would do something like attack and retake that world the moment we were joined."

"But you believe she'll be peaceful this time?" I say.

"I believe there will be peace long enough for you to get to the Mokshi," Jayd says. "That's all that matters. Once you have it, Anat will follow you there, and I'll take care of the rest."

"The rest of what?"

"The world is dying," Jayd says. "This is the best option."

"You didn't answer my question."

"The answers will come in time. You have to trust this."

"Don't do this." She is all I know of the world. And she will be leaving it.

"If I say no, she'll recycle me. We must be united in this. If the Bhavajas think you harbor any ill will, it can turn out very badly. Please, Zan. This is what we wanted."

I can't see any way to fight my way out of this that doesn't involve trying to turn Anat's whole army on her. The army Anat last raised is dead back at the Mokshi, and I don't know how many more conscripts she has somewhere in the other levels of the world. Getting them to fight for me instead of Anat would require me to have far more power than I command now. Right now I'm little more than a conscripted soldier, myself.

And then something far darker occurs to me, and I ask, "What will happen to me when you're gone?"

"You'll be all right," Jayd says, but she does not look at me.

"You *want* to go," I say flatly.

"This is the way it's supposed to go, Zan," she says, lowering her voice further still. "This is all we ever hoped for, I promise you."

"You speak words without saying anything."

"I'm saving you."

"Have Anat send me. Have her marry me to Rasida."

"Oh, Zan."

"Why can't they take me?"

Jayd leans into me, so close I feel her breath on my cheek. "I have something inside of me," Jayd says. "Something they want so badly they will stop fighting if I go with Rasida. This womb I carry will save us, Zan, and the Legion." She caresses my cheek. "Let this go, Zan. Let's go forward."

Something inside of me, Jayd says.

A memory blooms.

A three-headed woman, screaming. Blood on my arms. A big obsidian machete in my hand. They know too much, too much, I think as I swing the machete, and lop off one of the heads.

I jerk away from Jayd. "What are we?" I say. "What have we done?"

"We've done what we had to do," Jayd says. She pulls away from me.

"WAR MAKES MONSTERS OF US ALL. BUT WHAT HAPPENS
TO THOSE OF US WHO NO LONGER WISH TO BE MONSTERS?"
—LORD MOKSHI, *ANNALS OF THE LEGION*

JAYD

For as long as I've been alive, Rasida Bhavaja and her family have been the only things I truly fear. I fear her more than I fear my mother, because they are the only family in the Legion strong enough to defy her. My fear, however, is mixed with respect, as Rasida has been able to do what I have not. She has been able to get Anat to fear her.

Yet if the Katazyrnas are to survive, and the Legion is to be spared, it was inevitable that one of us would have to either kill Rasida or marry her to end the war. What I never told Anat was that it had to be me. She needed to think that was her idea. When I came to Anat after doing what I did during the war with the Mokshi and told her what I had stolen, she had rejoiced. For a time, she praised me as her best daughter. Her smartest daughter. Her most ruthless daughter. But I had made the wrong choice. I knew it as we recycled all those people, and Katazyrna still rotted around us. I had chosen to please Anat over my own sense, and I feared I would never be able to make it right.

But now I have the chance to do what I should have done in the first place. Now I can atone for all those bodies, all that betrayal.

Even as Anat held the iron arm aloft, that great glimmering trophy I had brought home for her, I knew that she would never make me Lord of Katazyrna as I had hoped. I would never be given the power I needed to defeat the Bhavajas and steal the womb we all knew they had, the one that could save far more than just Katazyrna. I had to go back to the Mokshi and atone.

And this was the way Zan and I came up with to get what we needed. It was a foolish, dangerous plan, but this was indeed a foolish, dangerous place.

We prepare to receive the Bhavajas in the great reception hall. All of my best sisters are with me—little Maibe with the shaved head; tall Neith, who looks nearly as old as our mother, one eye gouged out and crossed with a scar; stocky Suld with the twisted hand; Anka and Aiju, the young twins just past menarche; and Prisha, a slip of a woman with soft hands and softer features.

I pretend not to notice when Maibe slides up beside Zan, clasps her elbow, and says, "You look like a poorer copy every time you come back. Something about your eyes. Always so blankly stupid, getting stupider every time."

"Your face is stupider," Zan says, and I probably laugh too hard at that, but I'm so full of anxiety and anticipation and fear and hope that I'm almost trembling. I hope that this will all be over very soon, because to stand here much longer with Zan's desperate, innocent stare on me will break my heart.

While we wait for the arrival of the Bhavajas, Zan stares at the coiling streamers of lights dancing along the ceiling, and I follow her gaze. I'm not sure if she understands what they are yet. I don't think so. But Zan has always kept her thoughts close. The last time we went through the stumbling memory-loss-and-recovery, she had tried to kill me twice before she fully understood what had brought us to this place, and the depth of my betrayal. This is all necessary. I know that, but it doesn't make it hurt less when she remembers why.

When Anat enters, holding her iron arm aloft, its green glowing core painting harsh shadows across her face, I straighten and move closer to Zan. Even now, I feel protective of her. It's my fault she's in the position she is.

Gavatra comes in behind Anat. "Our guests have arrived," Gavatra says. "Let us assemble for the exchange."

I take a deep breath and move away from Zan so I stand halfway between Gavatra and my sisters.

Anat comes up beside me, and it is not difficult to pretend at apprehension. So much depends on this moment.

Anat's boxy face is split wide with a little half-grin that I find repulsive. Two skinny bottom-worlders stand beside her, armed with burst weapons, which I think would provoke more than reassure, but I say nothing. These talks have been going on for some time. We have fought the Bhavajas for generations, since long before the Mokshi appeared on the Outer Rim, cut loose from the Core. Whatever the

Katazyrnas want, the Bhavajas want, and vice versa. It's been a long, weary dance.

Rasida Bhavaja strides into our assembly room with a great retinue of her family behind her; a dozen, all told. I recognize her mother, Nashatra, and two of her sisters, Aditva and Samdi, and Rasida introduces them and the others to Anat and my sisters. It seems like a terrible number of Bhavajas to have on our world, but we are armed, and they would not have been allowed weapons. I honestly expected Rasida to send one of her sisters in her stead. But no. I know her face because I know all the faces of my enemies intimately. It is in my best interest to know them. I glance over at Zan.

"You've grown, Jayd," Rasida says. She is a tall, handsome woman, with not a single visible scar. I know she has others underneath the long drape she wears, but from a distance, she is untouched. One might think her soft for all that, if not for her flinty eyes. She stares at me, unblinking, as if a predator peers out from her eyes. Her gaze at once thrills and haunts me, as it has since I was small. The last time I saw her was during a parlay on another world, now long dead, when my sister Nhim commanded the Katazyrna armies, long before Zan joined us. Nhim had been an intimidating person too, but Rasida seemed to loom over her, though she was shorter and thinner than Nhim. When Nhim left the room to send a message to Anat, Rasida leaned over and whispered in my ear, "What would we do here, alone, you and I, if we were not enemies?" and the question haunted me afterward, because the desire was so thick in her voice that it made me tremble. Why is it we always want a thing we should not have?

"Growing is a thing children do," Anat barks.

I wish there was a soft, politic bone in Anat's body, but that is like wishing I could swim through the walls of the world.

Anat holds out her left arm, the great iron one, and Rasida glances from the arm to me, then to Zan. For a moment, I think Rasida is going to say something, but she lets it lie. The arm is clearly a war trophy—no one knows how to make anything so fine anymore. Wearing it in Rasida's presence could be seen as an insult, or perhaps a reminder, that all Katazyrnas are warmongers.

"You have seen my daughter," Anat says, "now where is *my* peace offering? Do I get a kiss?"

Rasida shows her teeth. "We have been at this too long, Katazyrna."

"Let's sit and pretend at friendship," I say. "I've been waiting for this war to end all my life."

Anat glares at me. Rasida's expression is more calculating. Does she think I'm insincere? It's true I've always wanted the war to end. I never said I wanted it to end like this.

Rasida clasps Anat's iron arm, and Anat grins.

The room takes a collective breath. Rasida and Anat move to the high table. Zan leans into me, whispers, "What if they'd brought some weapon with them, or are launching an assault on the Mokshi right now? How can you or her trust people who are no better than bandits?"

I gaze at the human skin stretched over the table. Zan follows my look and quiets. "We are all villains here," I say.

"I'm not," Zan says, and I do not correct her.

We assemble at the table with great ceremony. A bevy of elevated bottom-worlders begin to spin stories, accompanied by the high, thin voices of the chorus behind them. I pay only half attention to them. My gaze returns again and again to Anat and Rasida. I am passably good at reading lips, but they are eating and speaking at the same time, and that complicates things.

Rasida sneaks looks at me often, enough that Zan grumbles about it. When Anat toddles off to go relieve herself, Rasida rises and comes to me.

Zan shifts so she is pressed hard against me.

Rasida takes my hand and says, "You will be my shining star. The mother of a new world."

"I'm just a woman," I say, "not a star."

"You will be *my* star," Rasida says fiercely, and her intensity surprises me, though of course it should not. She has been waiting for this day a long time. Maybe a part of me has been too, a part I don't allow myself to think about, because it feels like another betrayal, and I am tired of being a traitor.

Zan says, "For all the talk of stars, what do you have to give her in return?"

I shush Zan, but Rasida laughs. "And what are you calling this one, Jayd?" Rasida says. "She looks like some conscript. What world is she from?"

"This is my sister Zan," I say quickly.

"Is that so?" Rasida says. "Is that who you are?"

Zan does not reply. Only stares hard at Rasida. Her shoulders are stiff, and I fear she's going to do something unwise. I pray to the Lord of War that her clean memory holds. It's never come back entirely, but with the luck we've had these many turns, some stray thought will trickle in now, and we'll be ruined. The first few times Zan came back without her memory, I had thought Zan was playing a trick on me to get back at me for what I'd done. Then I realized how much better it was this way. Now, sometimes, I pray for her to go back to the Mokshi before she remembers too much. Remembering hurts her. And me.

I put my hand over Zan's. "That's so," I say.

"Let me introduce you to my companions," Rasida says, and she points out the other women in her retinue. Her mother, a wizened old woman called Nashatra; two of her "near-sisters," she says, called Aditva and Samdi; and various security personnel. I watch Zan weigh and measure them all. It is what she is best at, after all: assessing threats.

"A pack of animals," Zan says.

Anat returns. She raises her voice. "That's enough," Anat says. "Curb your tongue, Zan, or I'll have you recycled again."

"She will," I say to Zan, low. "We don't want that." Zan has been recycled before and survived it, but I don't want to risk a second time. My pulse quickens. I feel as if I spend all of my time trying to quell Zan's darker nature, trying to turn her self-destructive impulses into action, but she could say the same of me.

Rasida picks up two fingers of mashed plantains from Zan's plate and puts both fingers into her own mouth, sucking them clean.

My physical reaction to this is less than dignified. I have to turn away from her as heat moves up my face. She is the enemy, I remind myself, but that doesn't matter. It never matters. Maybe it makes it more of a challenge for me. Rasida is a problem to be puzzled out, and my body has already announced itself more than willing to try.

"Anything else you want to fight about?" Rasida says. "I suspect you and I have played before . . . Zan. Let's play again and see how we fare this time."

"Please," I say loudly. "Zan, let us have peace."

"Let us drink!" Anat says, and raises her fist to the ceiling. The lights change colors, back to white and blue. It's a nice little trick, but a trick nonetheless. The arm is useless to her on this world. But Rasida does not know that. The lights glimmer in Rasida's gaze, and I see her hunger again. Not for me, but for all Anat has, including me.

I gaze longingly at the ceiling, begging the world for a respite. I want this over. I want to be on Bhavaja.

The bottom-worlders bring out the beer, and my sisters fill the tremulous air with their light chatter, avoiding all the contentious topics. Rasida rises and goes back to her seat. She squeezes my shoulder as she goes.

When dinner is finished, Anat asks Rasida to her quarters. I sit up a little to see if Rasida is bringing anything with her, but no. This is where they will discuss formal terms, the terms that will save Katazyrna.

When they are gone, Zan leans into me. "Don't tell me you're falling for all that," she says.

"You should be relieved."

"She'll say anything to make sure you go with her," Zan says. "Who knows what will happen when you're away from your family? I can't protect you out there, Jayd."

"I won't need protecting."

But then she says what is really at issue, and it cuts my heart. "Who'll be here to help me remember?" Zan says. "Who will care about me now, with you gone?"

> "THE COMMON PEOPLE DON'T WANT WAR.
> BETTER TO BROKER PEACE, AND BREAK IT, SO THEY ARE
> WILLING TO FIGHT FOR WHAT THEY HAVE LOST, THAN PRETEND
> THAT SPILLING COLD BLOOD WILL WARM WEARY HEARTS."
> —LORD MOKSHI, ANNALS OF THE LEGION

ZAN

The whole of Katazyrna, more people than I have yet seen, pour out into the hangar to watch Jayd go. All of them bear faces so similar to those of Jayd and Anat and the women I met in the banquet hall that it is easy to see they are related. I know from seeing it from the outside that the world is enormous, though, so even this gathering is likely only a slim number of the world's actual inhabitants.

Anat seems to pull open the skin of the world with her iron arm without letting in the cold; this display must be for the benefit of the

Bhavajas, because Jayd whispered at dinner that the arm does nothing on Katazyrna, and is just a trophy. Out there in the black waits a whole fleet of Bhavaja vehicles mounted with cephalopod cannons. I think it's disingenuous of them to come here with weapons mounted on their vehicles, but at least they didn't try to carry any inside. I'm stuck with the horde of others I've never seen before, just a spectator. I see a few people with extra limbs, and one woman with eight fingers on one hand, and I wonder what they do here. Most are thin; I doubt they've seen a meal like the one we all just ate in their whole lives. There is something about their skin that bothers me, and I see a woman beside me scratching at a lesion. Growths bloom from the necks and arms of many; several bare-chested women only have one breast. They are cancerous. This horde of women is dying of starvation and cancer, slowly but inevitably.

The crowd parts for Jayd and Rasida and the rest of the Bhavaja clan. Gavatra and our sister Neith are to accompany Jayd as well, at least for a turn. I think that's a small kindness of Anat's, but realize she probably hopes to gain keen intelligence from Gavatra about the real state of the Bhavaja worlds. I wonder if it's as bad as Katazyrna.

Peace or no, Anat has been fighting a long time, and the instincts of a fighter die hard. I know, because I still want to rip Rasida limb from limb.

The procession passes me. The first wave comes to the air port and steps inside. The film of the room closes over them, and they are whisked outside. I see them floating free out on the surface, kicking off the skin of the world and hurling themselves onto their great vehicles.

Anat did not let them park in the hangar, which is, at least, practical. Bhavaja vehicles have weapons mounted on them, and if they had something explosive . . . I ponder that thought awhile longer, wondering at my own assumptions. Is that something I would have done? Brought weapons to a peaceful trade meeting?

Jayd steps past me with barely a glance, and my heart clenches. Is this how it all ends, then? Jayd sold off to the Bhavajas so I can get to the Mokshi unhindered? What does that get her or me? Peace? Is peace worth it? What do she and I care about peace for?

Jayd walks another four steps, then turns. She breaks from Rasida's arm and runs to me. It has the feeling of a dream, or of something I've seen happen before.

I push through the crowd to meet her, and Jayd hurls herself into my embrace. For one heady moment, I believe Jayd has changed her mind. But she only holds me and whispers, "I'll bring you the world once you're on the Mokshi. Wait for me with Anat and her arm."

Then she runs back to Rasida, and Rasida wraps her arm around Jayd's waist and pulls her close, and Jayd gazes up into Rasida's face, and Jayd's gaze is so loving, so radiant, that I almost believe she never ran into my arms at all, and she didn't just promise to bring me a world.

Jayd is escaping Anat, escaping Katazyrna, escaping this rotting world. I want to be happy for her, but the darkness in Rasida's eyes is not diminished when she smiles. I can see that as well as anything. The darkness is not eclipsed by the crinkling at the edges of her eyes, by the flash of her white teeth, by the little pink tongue she bites when she is paying especial attention to Jayd's words, rapt like a hopeless lover. No, the darkness is there, always, and I worry. I worry that back on Bhavaja, away from me, from Anat, from Katazyrna, the darkness will crawl out.

Rasida sprays on her suit, then Jayd's, and they step into the air port with the last of her little party, including Rasida's mother Nashatra and her sisters, Aditva and Samdi. Their family could be a mirror of Anat's.

I watch them through the tear in the world as they are sucked onto the surface. I watch them until Jayd is secured to Rasida's vehicle, and they shoot out after the others, toward the trailing necklace of the Bhavaja worlds. So far away.

The mood becomes somber. I half-expect everyone to cheer, but it takes Anat to inspire that. Anat gets up on the backs of three bottom-worlders and shouts into the silence, "Peace! We rule the Outer Rim in peace henceforth! And soon, the Legion!"

Then the cheers rise up, from the bottom-worlders and the rest, and even a few of Jayd's sisters, who I suppose aren't cheering so much for peace as they are at the idea they weren't the ones sacrificed to it.

I stand mute in the corridor as the people sieve away from it, and Anat closes the skin of the world once again.

As the hall clears, Anat comes up to me and sets her heavy iron hand on my shoulder. "Now we get to business," Anat says. "They agreed the Mokshi is ours. After the joining on Bhavaja tomorrow, you will take the Mokshi for Katazyrna, and I will be the only Lord of the Legion."

"And what becomes of me after that?" I say.

Anat pulls her arm away. "That will depend entirely on how well you do," she says.

Without Jayd's guidance, I find myself adrift. I go to the hangar and take comfort in cleaning the vehicles. I am here again repairing broken organic tubing and removing the hard, cracked shells of the vehicle casings, and the vehicles, at least, seem to appreciate my efforts. After that disastrous attempt at boarding the Mokshi and the loss of Jayd, this effort restores some of my confidence.

I work alone and in silence for a long time. When I look up from my work, one of the sisters from the banquet hall is standing a few paces distant. I remember her name is Maibe. She's the one who told me I was a poor copy of myself.

If we were standing side by side, Maibe would barely reach my shoulder, but I am lying on my back now, covered in the juice of the organic fuel system, hands deep in the guts of a vehicle, and from that vantage Maibe looks formidable, a mountain of a woman with a face made more severe through the lack of hair. I see wounds on her head, nicks from the knife she must have used to shave away her hair. Metal seems to be a rare and expensive commodity here, and I wonder if it was a bone knife instead.

"She sending you to the Mokshi right after the joining?" Maibe asks.

"That's what they've been telling me," I say. "Been there once already, though, and not much came of that." I think about amending that based on what I've been told, but I have never been given a hard number about how many times I've been to the Mokshi.

"You should talk to the witches first," Maibe says.

"The . . . witches?"

Maibe shrugs. "That's what Mother calls them. They can . . . talk to the world. The world sees things sometimes. Things you and I don't see. They're a good source for old Legion stuff."

"Whatever the witches said about the Mokshi, Anat would have told me already."

"Would she?" Maibe says. She picks at her ragged nails. Leans over me again. "Jayd isn't here. Sabita has been reassigned. And you're practically a half-wit now, aren't you? I could do whatever I wanted to you."

I sit up. Memory stirs again, hot and uncomfortable, but nothing comes up clearly from the blackness. I hold out both of my hands. One palm open, one squeezed into a fist. "I am a half-wit who throws a spectacular punch," I say. "You should see it. Or we can skip that and share information."

Maibe shrugs. "You do what you like. It's not me she keeps throwing out there." She ignores both hands and turns to go.

"How many times?" I ask. "How many times has she sent me out to the Mokshi?"

"Hundreds," Maibe says.

Hundreds. A gaping hole in my memory comprising hundreds of missions. Failed missions.

"Not the rest of you?"

"Some of us, too," Maibe says. "But you always got the closest. Nhim's army died out there, and Ravi's. Moira's. Maybe a dozen others. But you were always the best. Jayd found you on some salvage run. Brought you in with thousands of other prisoners from some dead place, she said. Guess that worked out."

"Jayd was a general?"

"Jayd's a lot of things," Maibe says. "Don't think she's some victim in all this. I don't know what her plan is, but I can tell you it's not meant to benefit any of us."

"Why does Jayd want me to think I'm her sister?"

"Why do any of us pretend to be sisters?" Maibe says. "We all work better if we're family." She gives a little smirk. "Anat has her own reasons for doing what she does. If you're mounting another assault, you go to the witches yourself and get their advice. Don't go through Anat."

"After the joining, on Bhavaja?"

"Sure."

"Thank you."

"Don't thank me," Maibe says. "I've only told you this a hundred times. But you never listen. You never fucking listen, Zan." She leaves me.

I sit on the floor covered in the guts of the vehicles and consider my position. If I go to the witches now, it may tip off Anat that I have doubts about Anat's command. That way leads to the recycler monster. The fact that I have some memory of it makes me think I've been down that path before. But if I wait, if I go after the joining, right before the assault, Anat will have no time to stop me, not if she wants the assault to happen in time.

I get up and stick my hands into the spongy blue surface of the far wall; it absorbs the fluid from my hands, leaving my skin clean and unblemished. Some parts of how the world works still seem very strange to me, like I expect it to work a different way, like how I'd been confused about this being a ship or a world or both. Or neither.

It's the third option, the *neither* that gives me pause. I know about things outside of this world. But what they are, I have no complete idea. If Maibe's telling the truth, and I was a prisoner brought here from some dying world, why did Jayd tell me I could lead armies? Did it make me a better leader, just as telling me I was her sister was supposed to make me more loyal? If I was her sister and not her prisoner, it would certainly make me trust Jayd more.

Don't trust Jayd, they all said, and I didn't. But I couldn't help feeling that she and I were bound together, nonetheless. Some secret united us.

"I will bring you the world," Jayd had said, and it was the first thing she said that I truly believed with all my heart.

"THE HEART IS A VITAL ORGAN. CONTROL THE HEART
AND YOU CONTROL THE FLESH IT FEEDS.
WE ALL HAVE WEAKNESSES. THE HEART IS MINE."
—LORD MOKSHI, **ANNALS OF THE LEGION**

JAYD

want to hate Rasida with all my heart. I want to hate her as I hate my mother, hate her as I hate the Bhavajas, hate her as I hate the slow apocalypse of the Legion that has brought me to this place. I have wanted to hate her all my life, but as I've learned since my early days pining after Rasida, I am drawn to and desire my enemies, and it may be my worst flaw.

Rasida, for her part, is perfectly charming.

From the moment I catch sight of the Bhavajas' primary world, I can see that it, too, is dying. It's much further gone than ours. The cancerous rot that eats the outer skin of Katazyrna at the poles, leaving it soft and vulnerable, covers half the world here. Much of the outer defenses look dead. I'm surprised Anat's forces have never breached this world, but Anat has focused most of her attention on the Mokshi for some time, and I have not led an army anywhere but the Mokshi since the Mokshi entered the Outer Rim. Even the great tentacles that pull in debris from the outer edges of the Bhavaja's home atmosphere are shriveled now. I see long lines of space walkers hauling in debris by hand from a half-dissected world that hangs desolately behind Bhavaja, its resources consumed by its neighbors.

Inside, Bhavaja is not much better, though its people seem in high spirits.

They reach for me but don't touch me. Some fall to their knees before Rasida as if she is a god. And perhaps she is; in the same way Anat has styled herself Lord of the Legion, Rasida is their lord. Maybe a lord of salvation. I can't help but fold my hands over my stomach. My last treatment was not long ago, and unless Rasida means to decide the time and place at which I'll give birth to what's growing inside of me, I will give her what she married me for in less than a rotation of the Legion.

We continue down the corridors. I expect to travel through the umbilicus between levels, the way we do on Katazyrna, but we descend on staircases instead, each carved into the fleshy guts of the world. Above us, in the narrow passages, I see the shriveled brown skin of the former umbilicus. I wonder when it stopped working for them.

On the second level, Rasida asks a member of her security team to take Neith and Gavatra to their quarters.

"They aren't staying with me?" I say.

"You'll see them again at the joining tomorrow," Rasida says.

When Gavatra protests, Rasida says, "Jayd is Bhavaja now. Only Bhavajas may enter these parts of the world. I'm sorry, but you must stay in the guest quarters."

"They are my family," I say. "Doesn't that make them your family?"

"This is not my rule," Rasida says. "It is my mother's." I look around for her mother, Nashatra, but she has been swallowed by the crowd.

"We'll be at the joining," Neith says. "All I ask is that we get real food. Do you have real food?"

"Of course," Rasida says. "Samdi, take our esteemed guests to the eating hall."

Samdi makes a gesture of obeisance and peels away from us. Gavatra is still clearly not happy, and she signs something at me, fingers held low against her thigh. "Be careful," her fingers say, and I sign back, "I am always careful."

That makes Gavatra grimace. She has known me since I was a child.

Rasida's people line the halls eight and ten deep, the smaller ones sitting on the shoulders of the larger, back and back and back, so many that I find it a wonder she can care for them all here on the first level. Where is she getting the resources to care for them up here? From that dead worldship they are scavenging? How functional is the heart of her world? I stare at the spongy floor at my feet. As I walk, my footprints do not fill with a thin film of water the way they do on Katazyrna before the fleshy floor springs back up behind me. Bhavaja is dying.

I glance at Rasida beside me as we continue on, and consider the rumors I have heard about her. If she has the ability to do what Zan and I believe she can do, why has she let her world deteriorate like this? I have to understand her, and to do that, I must get close to her.

Rasida parts a shimmering curtain, and suddenly we are alone in a broad room with sweeping high ceilings. There are no patterns of light here; instead, there are fanciful geometric shapes carved into the walls, all painted in reds and blues and golds. I caress the nearest wall, running my fingers into the rivulets, and find that the walls are not porous here but hard and calcified. I snatch my fingers away.

"Your rooms are here," Rasida says, and she rolls open a great slab to reveal a long series of rooms. "I'm farther away," she says, "but you'll have access to this whole area." She waves at the great room I'm still standing in, and I see that all seven of the round slabs that ring the room like great eyes are doors like this one.

Two young girls appear from the interior of my rooms, their eyes big and black, hair bound back from identical round faces. They are painfully thin. They wear no shoes, and their feet are callused and dirty.

"These are your attendants," Rasida says.

"What are your names?" I ask, leaning over, because they look to be several rotations from menarche as yet.

"They don't speak," Rasida says.

A chill crawls up my spine, but I straighten and smile. "I see," I say.

"I don't want them to bother you with needless chatter," Rasida says. She runs her fingers down my arm, takes my hand, and opens my fingers. Her lips press against my palm. "I don't like chatter," she says.

"I see," I say again, because for all the preparation Zan and I have done these many turns, I find that I am not at all ready to be here in this place with a woman with such power and so many unknown whims. What do I know about her, really? I have seen her at negotiations and across skirmish lines. But I know nothing of her world but what I have seen, and nothing of the woman who rules it, not really.

It's not until I see her crinkling up the edges of her mouth into a smile that does not touch her eyes that I realize I have dealt with a woman just like this my whole life.

She is like Anat. She is my mother.

I smile back at her and press my fingers to her cheek.

"When will we be joined, love?" I say. "I look forward to the binding."

"Soon," Rasida says, and I cannot help but shiver.

The nameless girls comb out my hair and clean my clothes and fetch food. I feared the food would be as miserable as the rest of the world, but it's fresh tubers and broth, not some twice-baked gelatin made from the dead. That eases my concern somewhat.

Time here is strange, as the ship does not seem to regulate it anymore. It's the girls who wake the lights, rubbing their hands over the walls of the room after they have deemed my sleeping period has gone on long enough. Whatever is in the walls brightens for the length of the waking period, and then it is time to sleep, and we do it all over again.

When I wake, Rasida comes to me bearing wine and sweet treats, and sends the girls off into the main room.

"I thought you'd forgotten about me," I say lightly. "I missed your company." When I came up with this bit of fluff, I didn't think I'd mean it, but I realize on seeing her sit down at the end of my bed that it's true. The girls make for poor company. They won't look at me, and they will not speak. I found a loom in one of the far rooms, and I've been re-teaching myself how to use it. Making textiles was always a bottom-world pastime. I prefer my numbers and reports. But there's little of that here.

I have spent so many nights locked in my rooms on Katazyrna, cursing my mother, that this treatment is not surprising, only disappointing. I will need to work harder to get close to Rasida if I'm not allowed to go to her. I have already tried the great door out of the foyer, but Rasida has two stout guards there who glare at me whenever I open the door.

"You wish to know me better?" Rasida says, passing me the bulb of wine.

"We're to be paired," I say, and drink.

To my surprise, she lies down in my lap and rests her head against my stomach. She presses her ear to my belly and sighs. I carefully smooth the hair away from her brow, uncertain as to what comes next.

"You will be the mother of a new generation," she says. "My witches foretold it."

"Your witches still live?" I ask.

"Why wouldn't they?"

"Well, so much of this world is . . . I'm sorry."

"No," she says, sighing and pressing herself closer to me. "You are right. Bhavaja is deteriorating. But all that will change soon."

"How?"

She moves her mouth into that smile-that-is-not-a-smile. "You will see."

"I have heard . . ." And I must be careful here. My breath catches. "I have heard you can birth worlds. Is that what you will do?"

She sits up. My heart races, and I lean back, instinctively, fearful I have overstepped.

Rasida gets up and opens the door. She gestures to me. "Come to my quarters," she says.

I finish the wine, and I follow her. I tell myself that my smile is more convincing than hers.

Rasida takes me through a circuitous route to another level of the world. It seems we have gone up, but I can't be certain. There are heavily armed women on this level, posted every hundred paces. Rasida invites me inside a great room with high ceilings layered in lacy bones. She urges me to sit on a lavish divan layered in hemp cloth. Golden trinkets grace the walls. It takes me a moment to understand what they are. They are trophies, of a sort—pendants and religious symbols from lost worlds. I recognize two of them from a dead world called Valante, a silver-striped pin that was worn by all the daughters of the lord of that world. Now they lie scattered across whatever worlds salvaged the wreckage of that place before it rotted away.

"More wine?" Rasida asks. She opens up a great globular wardrobe made of wood, an impossible expense. I wonder which world she salvaged that from. The wood is dark and shiny, ancient.

"Yes," I say, because I have some idea of what we are here for, and I need the courage. Rasida is a handsome woman, and though she presses me close and offers me baubles, I am fighting hard to remember that she is dangerous, too.

But so are Zan and I.

Rasida pours me a drink from a very old, very used metal decanter. The liquid is poured not into bulbs but into beautiful metal glasses inscribed with fanciful geometric designs. I have seen a few such things come out of the craftspeople in the lower levels of Katazyrna, but ones this beautiful tend to be salvage. I know the Katazyrnas have murdered and pillaged many worlds, but the things Anat keeps are the people, the organics, not these sorts of objects.

I sip the wine and make an appreciative noise. I expected wine to taste more like beer. I know, vaguely, that they are made from different types of plants. I tremble. It has been a long time since I inhabited another world. A long time since I had to learn other rules.

Rasida sits next to me. I am aware of the warmth and softness of her. The room is cool, and I am drawn to her in a way I find distracting. She radiates a calm confidence. The ropy muscles in her arms, the heavy thighs, the keen, dark stare she fixes on me, as if I am the most interesting person in the world, make me want to straddle Rasida like a pleasure seeker and press myself into her, become part of her, like we are all a part of the ships.

Don't be a fool, I think, but Rasida is gazing at me with her big dark eyes now, and I get a little thrill at this idea that a woman so powerful is so smitten with me. I could control her utterly.

"This ship is yours," Rasida says, "as it is mine. You have total freedom here. I hope you understand that."

"That is kind," I say, and try to scramble back to my purpose. I am not here to fuck Rasida. I am here to get what I need from her and save the Legion.

"You are my consort," Rasida says, "not just a petty bit of organic fodder. You understand? If that was all I wanted, I could have any number of women from other worlds. What I wanted was you. Always you. From the time we were both small." She places her fingers on my arm, runs them from wrist to elbow. When she pulls her hand away, my skin is warm where she has touched me. It has been some time since anyone touched me with desire, not since the last time Zan was herself. Oh, how I love Zan, the Zan she was before all this started, before we gave up everything to get me here, trembling under Rasida's fingers.

I finish the wine, hoping for courage or perhaps sense. I wish for a message or sign from the Lord of War that tells me how to handle myself now that this plan has worked. I never counted on Rasida being so irresistible, after all this time. I never counted on the desire that lights me up like a torch when she looks at me. I feel that my body is betraying me and my purpose. I don't know why desire has to be so complicated. I know what I need and what I want, and there is a place where those two things intersect, but it is a dangerous place.

I want it nonetheless.

Rasida sets aside her own glass and gets onto her knees in front of me. She bends her head and gently parts my knees.

I freeze, uncertain of how to react. I wear only a long tunic, with nothing beneath. I feel Rasida's hot breath against my skin. Then her tongue.

I gasp. My precious metal goblet falls to the floor. The thirsty flooring laps up the wine as Rasida presses her lips to me, as if her tongue seeks to find the heart of me. She is a flickering, insistent whisper.

I dig my hands into Rasida's long hair and cry out. Rasida pushes up my tunic, stripping me bare. Rasida pulls me against her, hungry and passionate, the way Zan had taken me in the early days, before she was rewritten and erased into some pale shadow; a woman without a past, only purpose.

Is that me? Can I be a woman without a past, in this moment? I want that, desperately. I want to start over the way that Zan has.

Rasida's desire is contagious. I wrap myself around Rasida's thigh and cry out.

"I love you," Rasida says into my hair. "You make the very Lord of War tremble. I am yours. I am your lord."

"My lord," I gasp. I hold Rasida's head against my chest, feeling the warmth and power of her. How exhilarating, to hold this woman in my arms. I am drunk on her desire of me.

"You are the love of my life, the mother of worlds," Rasida murmurs, stroking my belly.

I move Rasida's hands away. "I am more than that, love," I say, and it tastes strange on my lips, to call some other woman *love*. My enemy. My love.

"Of course," Rasida says, and she strokes my cheek and moves her hands lower.

"When will we be joined?" I say, and I don't say, "Because I want to see Zan again," because I am not a fool, but with Rasida's hands on me, I see Zan again, the way she was before all of this started, and I want Zan. I want our old life. I want to see her one more time before I do what must be done.

"Soon," Rasida says. "Let us slake our thirst first."

"My family will be there?" I ask.

"They are invited to the world of the joining," Rasida says, and her fingers find me again, and I close my eyes and think of Zan. "But first," Rasida says, "I must do one last thing."

> "ONCE YOU HAVE THE HEART, TAKE THE HEAD."
> —LORD MOKSHI, **ANNALS OF THE LEGION**

ZAN

It's Sabita who wakes me while the glowing blue lights of the wall in my room tangle before me. I spray on a simple suit, something a bottom-worlder left for me before I went to sleep. It is red and black, and clings to my skin the same way my suit did, only it does not cover my hands or face.

"Maibe says you were reassigned," I say to Sabita.

Sabita gives a small smile but says nothing. She leads me to the hangar and the stir of my sisters, where we gather to attend Jayd's binding.

"Sabita?" I say as she moves away.

She opens her mouth. Her tongue is gone. I open my own mouth to cry after her, but she closes the hangar door behind her, leaving me with Anat and the others. I'm struck dumb with both shock and horror.

Anat is pulling at the collar of a suit. The others are dressed in far too many clothes, it seems to me, vests and long jackets over their regular clothing.

"Sabita—" I begin, but Anka, one of the twins, shushes me.

"Let it lie," Anka says.

"Who did that to Sabita?" I say.

"Why aren't you wearing your exterior suit?" Anat spits.

"Who did that?" I say, louder this time.

"Who do you think?" Anat says. "Jayd, of course. Sabita talks too much. She gets you overly agitated."

I gape.

Anat snorts. "Dumb idiot," she says. "Put on your exterior suit over those clothes."

Aiju, the other twin, rolls her eyes and says to me, "It's a show of strength to wear both clothes and suits. You think every world can afford clothes like these? Most wear nothing, like some kind of bottom-feeder. We're one of the wealthiest worlds on the Outer Rim."

I stare at the peeling blank walls of the hangar. It huffs gently with the thrum of the world's heartbeat. I gaze at the grungy gunk lining the corridors, the haggard faces of these women, and wonder what the poorest places must be like. And I think all this rot hides an even more rotten center, just like Jayd's smile.

"Maibe and Prisha will look after Katazyrna," Anat says. "That leaves Suld and the twins to go with us. Neith and Gavatra are already with Jayd."

She then gives careful instructions to the security team tasked with following us, and I recognize some of them as the women I sparred with while in recovery.

I know I'm not the only one to note how the security team salutes Anat and keeps their eyes on me. Why do they treat me as more of a threat than the Bhavajas?

When we are all suited up and situated on our vehicles, Anat waves her great arm, and the hangar opens, and we speed off into the black between the worlds, shooting from the comforting embrace of Katazyrna and into the cold, airless space that threatens to devour it.

I keep to the back of the party, just ahead of the rear security team. If it is a true peace, if Anat believes in it, she wouldn't have brought so many security people.

We aren't heading to Bhavaja but to some contested world, one the Bhavajas stole from Anat just a few turns before, best I can gather from Anka's signs with her twin. I like that better than the idea of riding right into enemy territory.

Anat rides at the head of the group. Great plumes of spent yellow fuel curl behind her. We pass the Katazyrna worlds, which I find that I can name: Ashorok, Musmala, Titanil, the names unwinding in my mind like a litany. As we pass Titanil, the great engine of the sun unshutters at the center of the Legion, sending a shaft of light directly into my vision.

When my vision clears, I see Anat speeding toward a new world, a great red throbbing thing with a milky atmosphere. My memory offers no name for this world, so all I know is that we and the Bhavajas both want it, and in exchange for Jayd, we get it. After seeing the cancerous rot on the outside of Katazyrna, I can see why this world must be valuable. The crimson skin of it is entirely intact, and I suspect the atmosphere, though thin, may be breathable.

We line up behind Anat and wait for the outer defenses to go down. When they do, we speed toward a ripple in the world's skin that puckers open as we advance. I see smaller tentacles on this world's surface, and they wave out at us and guide the vehicles inside. Perhaps I should consider them comforting fingers, but I can't help but think we're being pulled into the maw of some great, dangerous creature.

Inside, this world is much different from Katazyrna. We dismount inside a narrow hangar lined in pulsing orange growths all along the ceiling. Passages snake out all around us; I can't begin to think which way we should go. When the skin of the world seals behind us, Anat dismounts from her vehicle and leads us down a passage at our left. As we walk, something happens to the air around us. It's as if the skin of the passage itself normalizes the pressure as we pass through it, though I'm not sure how this is possible without having the passages properly sealed up the way they are on Katazyrna.

The passage opens up into a broad room lined in glowing statues made of a white calcified substance. It's only on peering at the faces of them that I determine they are made of bone. Human, presumably, as I've seen nothing else here. The statues are fixed in the walls as if they are trying to crawl out of them. The faces are somewhat off, not quite human, to my eye. Some of the figures have tails. Their large eyes are wide; mouths open in horror. I consider what event this room is trying to commemorate. A great war? People escaping a dying world?

I'm so intent on the statues, I don't notice Rasida's security team come out to meet us until Anka prods me from behind. I step after Anat, still frowning at the statues.

We slide through an umbilicus to a level below, and here we find the residents of the world. The ceilings here stretch up and up—I can hardly believe the umbilicus took us so far down—and there are shops and apartments carved into the walls, all lit by the glowing orbs on the ceiling, which I see now are a type of fungus.

There are people here of all types—many look like Katazyrnas, many like Bhavajas, and still more appear to be from other worlds, unless this place simply breeds many different types of people in a way I have yet to see on Katazyrna. The worlds of the Legion cannot all be like Katazyrna. What if the rules are different in every place? That leaves me feeling vertiginous. There's an entire system of worlds, each potentially with different rules, that I cannot remember. How awful to lose your knowledge of your world, but to lose knowledge of the universe? The loss overwhelms me.

The joining of Jayd and Rasida is held in a monumental temple at the center of this level of the world. We walk up steps that go on and on, all carved into the flesh of the world. Inside the temple, Anat finally releases the catch on her suit, and it falls off and is absorbed by the world. The rest of us do the same, and now I can hear and smell the world as well as see it. Sound is muffled, no doubt absorbed by the porous walls. The smell is sharp, acidic, but the air tastes richer than it does on Katazyrna. I find myself taking shallower breaths.

The joining itself takes place some time later, after we have all assembled and eaten from long tables surrounding a great dais. I have been looking for Jayd throughout the meal, but she and Rasida are still absent. A chorus of women perform from a balcony above, their voices high and warbling. I have no idea what they are singing about because I can't understand the language.

When a fat woman with a bloom of dark hair gets up on the dais and begins speaking, I can't understand her, either. I lean over and ask Aiju, "What's this language?"

"Tiltre," she says. "High Tiltre. They speak Low Tiltre on the level below." She pats my hand. "Don't worry about it. It's just formal stuff."

"Why are we here if none of it matters?" I say.

Anat glares at me. She's sitting at the head of the table, and I hoped she wasn't paying attention. I should have known better. She leans toward me. "It all matters," she says. "We have worked to free these worlds from the Bhavajas since my mother's day. We are seen as liberators."

In looking around at the wary gazes all the people here have been giving our table, I doubt that. Anat and Rasida are not so different.

I recognize Rasida's mother and other assorted relatives at a table opposite ours on the other side of the dais. The Bhavaja security team stands between the two tables, ostensibly watching all the locals as well as us, but it's clear which of us they think are more dangerous.

Finally, after the food has been cleared and the little serving women come in carrying great jugs of red liquor, I see Jayd and Rasida enter the temple from the great stairway by which we came.

I stand with the crowd—hundreds of us here—as Jayd and Rasida advance, and my heart aches as I watch Jayd walk arm in arm with Rasida, up and up to the dais where the fat local woman embraces them both. The woman gives another speech while holding hands with both Rasida and Jayd. The woman begins to cry.

"What's she saying?" I ask Aiju, but Aiju shushes me. The whole room is still on its feet, all gazes fixed on the dais.

The fat woman gets down on her knees. She has a very kind face, and though I cannot understand what she says, she says it with passion.

Rasida and Jayd lean over the woman. Each pulls out a long knife sheathed at the woman's hips.

I'm still not sure what I'm seeing. I start to ask Aiju, but she pre-emptively shushes me.

KAMERON HURLEY

Rasida and Jayd both repeat the same phrase, something in what must still be High Tiltre. Then, acting in unison, Jayd and Rasida each plunge their blades into either side of the woman's neck.

I make a choking sound and jerk out of my seat, but Aiju grabs my sleeve, shushing me again like a child. The woman on the dais sways and falls. Jayd takes a bowl from the podium and catches some of the woman's blood in it. She offers the bowl to Rasida.

Rasida drinks from it and passes it to Jayd. Jayd meets Rasida's gaze and she, too, drinks the warm blood.

When they hold up the bowl together, there is a roar from the room. Not of fear or horror, but of approval.

Aiju claps her hands and shouts with the others. Then she says to me, "They are part of this world now."

"Both of them?" I say. "I thought this would be Anat's world."

"It's a complicated treaty," Aiju says.

I see Jayd holding Rasida's hand. They raise their bloody arms aloft. Jayd's mouth is bloody. The former—what, First? Head? Leader?—woman's body lies there between them. Jayd struck her down like so much chattel. And Jayd did not flinch or hesitate in any way. No gasp, no shaking. When Jayd finally catches my eye, she grins, and her teeth are crimson.

I look away.

When Jayd and Rasida are ushered from the dais, I sit heavily in my seat. "Will they go back to Bhavaja now?" I ask Aiju.

"Most likely," she says. She peers at me. "You really shouldn't be sad. Jayd has never had your interests at heart. She has what she wants now."

"You think she always wanted to marry Rasida?"

"Of course," Aiju says. She lowers her voice, looking meaningfully at Anat, who thankfully is engaged in conversation with someone at a neighboring table. "Jayd was never going to be Lord of Katazyrna. Anat would never permit that. She will have far more power bound to Rasida."

"You think she meant to do this all along?" I ask.

Aiju pats my shoulder. "You wouldn't be the first person she used to get ahead. She's the best of us at getting Anat to do something she wants while getting Anat to think it was her idea all along. Have some drinks. You'll feel better."

I stare into my cup and see a bleary shadow stare back at me from it. It's too dark for me to see my reflection properly, but I feel old, in this moment, and foolish. Sabita warned me about Jayd, and suffered for it. Now whatever Jayd wanted from me . . . is this it? Is it over? Was this Jayd's intent all along, to get far from me and Anat so she could be co-consul of some other world?

There is more singing, more wine, and a great group of women begins to dance in three lines at the center of the room. I don't remember this place or these people. None of these things is triggering any sort of memory at all, and I am deeply angered at that. Jayd has left me alone and broken with her mad mother and sisters. I have nothing.

Anat comes up behind me and puts her arm on my shoulder. I flinch, and she leers at me.

"We're not here for Bhavaja," Anat says. "Keep your eye on the Mokshi. None of this shit matters."

But it does matter. My vision isn't clouded like Anat's with some single-minded purpose. I'm trying to see this not from Anat's perspective, or even Jayd's, but from Rasida's. What is all this? Why have a ceremony here, set between the contested Katazyrna and Bhavaja spaces? I watch the women sway together at the center of the room, their hair all done up in elaborate hanks that have been twisted and plaited into large cross sections. I see the rime of whatever it is they've put into their hair, and it looks like rusty dried blood to me. If I was Rasida, all of this would be a show, a distraction, from my real purpose. I see Anat swigging from the cup in her other hand. I see her daughters all doing the same, and even if Jayd got herself into this mess through her own devices, I fear for her anew.

If it was me suing for a true peace, I would have invited both families to my own world and offered not just some planet but an exchange of organic matter. An exchange of sisters. But Rasida offered no such thing. She did not give Anat any of her own organic matter. Nothing of her own world. Only the cast-off leavings of this one. What did that mean? It meant Rasida gave nothing of herself in this joining, only the blood of some other people.

Rasida risked nothing.

Anat gave them a daughter. And in this place, among worlds where organic matter was the literal lifeblood of the world, and the Legion, a daughter was everything.

Compared to the people of Katazyrna, many of whom seemed disfigured and cancerous, the people here appear in good health. I do not see a single person who is thin or hungry or bent under the weight of some disease or contagion.

"What will happen to these people?" I ask Anat.

She is very drunk, eyes glazed over. She smiles at me and smacks me on the back. "I'm so glad I didn't recycle you this time!" she says. "You are so amusing." She points at the ceiling. "You see how healthy this world is? The skin of the world keeps out all the radiation that ruins people. We'll strip the skin of the world here and use it to repair Katazyrna. That's how we'll last long enough to board the Mokshi and take the whole of the Legion. Rasida is such a fool, giving me this fresh world."

"But . . . what will happen to them?" I say. "How will we fix this world?"

"Fix it? Have you been listening? We are not here to fix anything. We'll plunder this world for its goods, then let the rest rot here. We'll take what we want and use it to board the Mokshi. You've seen the skin of the Mokshi. Aside from the crater, the skin is healthy and intact. The witches can fix that rupture easy enough. But we need organic material to do it. That's what this exchange is for. We aren't here to help anyone. Keep your eye on the end goal."

I stare again at the line of happy, dancing women. There are women of every age here, even some young children, though no babies. It doesn't look like anyone has borne a baby here in at least ten rotations. They are all so fat and happy and alive.

Of course Anat would want to destroy that.

"Let's go," Anat says, patting my head as if I'm a child. "Aiju! You others, let's go."

Aiju, too, pats me, this time on the shoulder, but it feels no less condescending.

"Jayd is theirs now," Aiju says. "The sooner you come to terms, the better."

As we gather to leave the world, a few faces turn to watch us go. They don't treat Anat like she is lord of their world now. If anything, this whole display made it clear that Rasida and Jayd rule here now, not Anat. But Anat appears powerfully certain that she has won something here and that this place is hers to ravage.

Rasida's security team peels away from the room to follow us. They escort us all the way back to our hangar. We stop to spray on new suits. Anat argues drunkenly with the security women for a time before the twins both pull her back. I'm the first to spray on my suit, because I don't want to listen to Anat anymore.

We go back to our vehicles, and I stare at the ceiling one last time. Then we are seated on our vehicles, and the skin of the world puckers open and we speed off into the blackness that surrounds the Legion.

When I look back, the world appears no different from before, but my memory delivers a future to me, as if it has seen just such a future on many other worlds. Soon, what is left of the world will be a soupy ruin, and Anat will send me or one of her daughters out here with an army to salvage it and feed it into the great mouth of the recycling monsters on Katazyrna, until Katazyrna is healthy again. But only for a time. Only for a time. Because the worlds are hungry beasts, and the organic matter here to feed them is finite. Eventually it will eat us all whole.

12

ZAN

Anat leads the way back to Katazyrna like the drunkard she is. She does great spiraling rolls in her vehicle, weaving between the twins, making obscene signs with her hands. She is in fine spirits. I certainly have no memory of her ever being so happy, but maybe that's because I simply have so little of it. Inside my own chest, I feel as if I have swallowed a hard black stone. The Mokshi may be able to give me back the memory it took, but I am doubting that I want it. If my memory makes these mad people and this mad life make sense, I will cast it out altogether. I don't want these people, these decisions, to be normal.

Anat speeds up over a great ring of detritus, then tumbles back through it. The ring rotates around a pitted wreck of a world at the edges of Katazyrna territory. It's long dead and picked over. I see flashes of metal among the rotted tangles of skin, slabs too big to cut out and salvage, most likely. The eye of the sun at the heart of the Legion shines through the center of the ruined world.

I squint and raise my hand to my brow to shield the light, wondering if Anat will go zooming through this wreck too, half-hoping maybe she bashes so hard into something that it knocks her senseless.

Instead, as we come around what's left of the world, following Anat's spent fuel stream, Anat's vehicle suddenly spins out.

A great thorny mass erupts from the side of Anat's vehicle, knocking Anat free.

One of our security vehicles goes next. It's hit once. Twice. Three times.

The security vehicle tumbles toward me. It happens too fast for me to react. The vehicle smashes into me. The force is so great, I'm hurled free of the vehicle and into open space. I do not scream, but I gasp, and the sound is loud and close in my suit. We aren't wearing any communications devices. We are drifting soundless and alone.

Pushed free of the group, I see the raiders coming up from beneath the orb of the rotted world. There are not a dozen, or two dozen, but sixty or more vehicles mounted with cephalopod cannons. The great tentacle weapons bash into the Katazyrna vehicles, picking us off like insects.

The twins crash into each other, smashing one another's limbs. Aiju grabs hold of Anka, and as I spin out of reach, I see Anka's suit rotting away, her leg throbbing with the bite of a three-pronged cephalopod.

Another projectile hits Aiju in the back so hard, it spins them both farther from the group, knocking them into their forgotten vehicles. They drift off into the black.

Suld holds out with a small group of security personnel. She's leapt onto one of their forgotten vehicles and now turns it toward the advancing force. She fires off a hail of energy bursts so bright they hurt my eyes.

I smack into another body rolling behind me; one of the security women, her face twisted in death, the suit mostly rotten, clinging to her body in scraps. Hitting her body slows my momentum. I try to push off her to get back to the fray, but she is at least two hundred paces away now; the only reason she isn't moving faster is because the world's gravity will only let her get so far.

The assault force swarms Suld and the security holdouts, firing round after round of their cannons. They riddle the eight of them like fine paper, hurling their bodies in every direction.

I tangle with another body behind me, one still attached to a vehicle. I hook her arm into the organic tubing of the vehicle to keep me attached to it but remain motionless as the dead. Asphyxiated, half-suited Anka is tangled beside me. Her mouth is gaping open in death, eyes and lips and tongue slowly freezing.

I do not have to get close to know who the raiders are. I know those weapons. And the vehicles. The Bhavajas betrayed us, and Anat walked right into it. As I watch, three of them find Anat's body. One takes her great iron fist. Another holds her still. A third brings up an energy weapon and fires it into Anat's elbow, severing the iron arm from her flesh.

They shoot Anat in the head for good measure and push her body into orbit with the others. The lot of them raise their weapons

KAMERON HURLEY

and shake their arms, holding the trophy of Anat's arm aloft.

When they buzz back around the wreckage they've wrought, I fix my stare straight ahead, knowing they will fire into anything that looks even remotely alive. Weapons are precious things, and the cephalopod bursts cost them. That's what I'm counting on.

They fire at me anyway. One projectile clips my leg. I let my legs and torso jerk with the push of it but keep my arm hooked in the vehicle's tubing.

I expect them to gather us all up into a net or tie us up into a caravan and recycle us. It crosses my mind that no one will leave this much good organic material to orbit some planet unless it is impossible to retrieve it, like the armies around the Mokshi.

I wait, breathing shallowly, as the sixty-odd-strong Bhavaja squad pokes and prods at the scattered wreckage of our party. After a long while, I allow myself a blink, and I see them engaged in a heated conversation in sign language. Did they get new orders?

Finally, the leaders break away, speeding back toward the rotten world. Their squad follows after them, leaving me and the dead to orbit the ruin.

I wonder if this is some trick and they've left someone behind to watch over us. But all I see is the dead that I've been told are my family, and for one terrible moment, I believe they are indeed my blood relations, and that everything I know is dead. I shake myself out of this thrall and pull myself onto Aiju's vehicle. I try to start it.

But it's dead. Just like everything else.

I swear and lean over to poke at the guts of it while Aiju's dead face looks on. I can't help but believe that if I can just remember everything, if I was just the whole person I should be, I could have not only seen this coming but convinced Anat of it too.

I find half of one of the tentacles twisted in the undercarriage of the vehicle. I carefully pull it out. Droplets of fuel snake from a torn hose. I press it closed with one finger but can't see any deeper into the guts to find other problems. I long for one of the speculums back in the hangar. It would make this much easier.

What I'm missing is something to fix the leak in the tubing. I can't just hold my hand in it. I search around and come up with nothing. Aiju's body is still tangled with the vehicle on the other side. The rest of the bodies are strewn two hundred paces distant, slowly circling back around the world. Eventually, the inhabitants of some other world will find them and have a grand recycling event. I don't intend to wait up here that long. My air will give out first. Won't it? I don't even know how long I can breathe out here in these suits.

I stare hard at Aiju's accusing face and bared torso. There is, of course, an analog to the organic tubing of the vehicle in the human body.

I work off a piece of the outer shell of the vehicle and bash it with one hand until a sharp piece comes off. I take hold of Aiju's body and plunge the piece into her frigid torso. I use both hands to tear open her body, which is not yet frozen through, only cold. I pull out the intestines and cut off a short section, squeezing out the waste.

Then I turn off the fuel line, unhook the organic tube, and slip the intestine over it before it freezes. A perfect fit, as if the vehicle is, indeed, patterned after human organs. I hook the fuel line back up and try starting it.

The vehicle comes to life, the green glowing control console blazing. I kick the vehicle forward, circling the detritus of my family once, wondering again why the squad has not netted them all up and brought them back to a Bhavaja world.

What can be more important than salvaging flesh and vehicle components? What are they off to do?

I come up alongside Anat's body. Her suit has rotted off. A giant cephalopod rises from her side. The iron arm she has menaced us all with is no more. All that remains is a stump of an arm, cut off at the elbow.

I stare long and hard at that arm and remember Anat's fake displays with it. Why haul that arm around at all, if it is worthless? And what will Rasida do to Jayd now? Has she flushed Jayd out into space too, left her to asphyxiate?

No, the key is the arm.

Why would they take the arm? Why would *I* have taken it? Probably because, after a display like Anat put on, I thought I could control Katazyrna with it.

Understanding dawns. I turn my vehicle abruptly away from the dead and speed back to Katazyrna, and the invasion I know is already underway.

The Bhavaja forces make two broad arcs around Katazyrna. I hide just behind the nearest world, hoping they will think I'm some salvager or scout from another world. But they pay me no mind. They are wholly concentrated on Katazyrna, sending wave after wave of cephalopods and bursts and scramblers into its defenses. Katazyrna is awash in blankets of red and blue and green defenses. The energy rolls off it in thick bands. The world glows so fiercely now that this close, I could almost say it rivals the sun.

Then I see them breach the skin of the world. It tears up under their weapons, curling back like burnt bark. I let out a breath. They are going to get in.

Half the Bhavajas wheel around and dive directly into the broken skin of Katazyrna, seeking to destroy all that I know of the universe, all that I know to be true.

I kick my vehicle forward, powering hard and fast for Katazyrna. I think a whole host of things in those blazing seconds as I power toward the world. The Bhavajas are very likely to fire on me. My own world might not recognize me. It is a desperate, risky move, but so is being alive.

I hurl myself toward the breach, opening up the fuel line as wide as it will go. I look back once and see the misty yellow belch of my spent fuel spiraling out behind me.

The fuel gives out four hundred paces from the surface of the world. I hunker low, though I suppose it won't matter—there is no atmospheric resistance—and ride the wave of my momentum down and down, toward the breach in the world's skin.

I zoom between two Bhavaja lines, so fast that when I glance back, I see them still signing to one another, trying to determine if I'm friend or foe.

I have no way to slow my momentum—I'm out of fuel to shoot out the front of my vehicle—so I hit the spongy floor of the first level of Katazyrna hard. The momentum throws me from the vehicle.

I crawl across the floor, trying to get clear of the breach. The massive hole in the skin of the world is mitigated by its thin atmosphere; I might be able to breathe for a while if I take off my suit, but I'm not going to risk it until I get down a few levels. I wonder if the ship has defenses against a breach in its skin.

I run down the empty corridors, past bodies hunched in the thresholds of doorways, all dressed in the black-and-red cut of security personnel. I come to a broad, fleshy wall at the end of the corridor. It's been carved open with some weapon, and now it stares balefully at me like a weary eye.

I squeeze through the busted door, realizing I not only have no weapon but also no plan. *Find a weapon, get to my sisters, and help them hold off the Bhavajas* is about as far as I can get in my reasoning.

I round a bend and come face to face with two Bhavaja women arguing. I punch the first in the face, easy as breathing. The second raises her weapon but has no time to fully draw it, let alone fire it. I have a vague recollection about how I can best a better-armed target who has not pulled a weapon so long as I'm within ten paces, but my body knew it before I consciously considered it.

I disarm the women neatly and shoot them both with the cephalopod weapon. Their suits dissolve around them. They gasp in the thin atmosphere. I heft the weight of the weapon in my hand and continue on down the corridor, navigating by sight as opposed to sound. I miss Jayd in my ear, miss the soothing sounds of the single person in the whole world who seems to give a shit.

What has Rasida done with her? Murdered her? Tossed her out into space? Or is she really as important to Rasida as she pretends?

I step through another broken corridor. A woman stands over two bodies. I heft my weapon, but as she turns, I see that inside the spray-on suit, it's my sister Maibe.

Maibe signs at me. "The others?"

I sign back. "Dead. Anat too."

"Jayd?"

"I don't know."

"Come with me," Maibe signs. "We're holding out in the cortex. This isn't the main force."

Maibe opens a gummy hatch in the corridor; it comes away from the sticky surface like pulling off a scab. I crawl after her in the darkness, dragging the weapon awkwardly in one hand while holding my weight with the other.

The darkness goes on and on. I wonder, again, how long the air in my suit will hold out. Does the suit recycle air? Do I have a limited amount? I have no idea.

Green-and-violet light spills out ahead of us. Maibe steps out and reaches a hand back for me. I have a long moment to wonder if I'm being lured into a trap.

But I take her hand anyway, and we squeeze into another long corridor. It's like a series of umbilical cords that connects the levels of the ship. We walk for some time until we come to what Maibe signs to me is the second level and the cortex. *Cortex* sounds important, and I figure it's some kind of control room.

Maibe turns off her suit, and it dissolves around her. She signs at me to do the same. "We've got good pressure on every level but the first," she signs.

I mimic her movements, sliding two fingers up my left wrist until I find a series of raised bumps. I plug in the combination, and the suit falls off, peeling quickly away like shedding my own skin. I pick the little pieces off as I follow Maibe to a big green banded security door. Maibe knocks four times.

I hear raised voices on the other side and a heavy thunking sound.

The door opens. Prisha stands there, holding a big weapon like the one I used out on the assault on the Mokshi.

"Mother?" Prisha asks.

"All dead," I say.

She narrows her eyes, as if convinced that I had something to do with Anat's death. If only.

Finally, she nods and motions us in.

I'm not sure what I expected of the cortex, but this isn't it. It's a tight, round room with high ceilings and interfaces embedded in the walls. Organic tubing sticks out from each station, like they were meant to hook up to something that has long since been removed. The room is packed with people, all my remaining sisters and many others I don't know—more family, maybe? They seem familiar. All are armed. It occurs to me that there are no children here. The youngest person is just past menarche. The oldest isn't much more senior than Anat.

If this is the center of the world, it is unassuming and in terrible disrepair. I can't tell what anything in the room is meant to do.

The whole lot of them is fixed on the origin of the thunking sound: the great round portal on the far side of the room. I can just make out the seam of it on the wall. I don't have to be told the Bhavajas are on the other side.

"How did they know where this is?" I ask Maibe.

"How do they know anything?" Maibe says. "Spies, probably. Or their witches. Some witches remember how the worlds work better than others."

"Why hold here?" I ask. "If we keep going down, we can find places to hold out and regroup on other levels. We can—"

Maibe frowns. "Zan, if they take the cortex, they take control of the world. There's no point in going on once they have this room."

"But . . . what does it do here?"

"She can hook into the mind of the world here," Prisha says, looking back at us. "She can twist it to her purposes. Maybe better than we can. It's a mad ship, but the Bhavajas . . . you've seen what they do to other worlds."

Have I? I don't remember, but the point seems moot now.

The air in the room is tense. It stinks terribly: too many unwashed bodies pushed together in sweaty fear. I survey the room, trying to assess our tactical options. When the door goes—and it will, I am sure of that—we can retreat through the secret way Maibe and I had come in, but there doesn't appear to be any other exit. And retreating through there is going to be tight, far too tight to get very many out. This is a last stand. My sisters intend to win or to die here . . . and those are in fact the only options if what Maibe says about the cortex is true.

I check the remaining cephalopods on my weapon. I don't like the idea of losing. I especially don't like the idea of losing to people who've bought Jayd as if she were a brood animal. What happens to Jayd if I'm dead? Who will go after her when I'm gone? No one. She'll be on her own.

The thunking continues. I stay posted at the entrance to the escape route, more to ensure no one comes in than in the hopes I can be the first one out. Maibe is right—running now won't mean anything if it we're just giving the world to the Bhavajas. Idiot Anat, for trusting them. Foolish Jayd, for going along with it. And here I am, useless and pinned down.

The breach comes sooner than I expect. As the first weapon punches through the door, three women try to get past me through the exit. One loses her will completely and starts screaming and tearing at her hair. I hit her in the face with the butt of my weapon. She goes down hard on her ass. For me, the breach is a relief. I don't know how to wait. But I know how to act.

Two women at the front of the room shoot back at the breached door, foolishly, because their weapons only serve to help open up the first hole.

"Hold!" I yell. "Hold until you have a clear shot!"

Something whumps against the door so hard, the whole room

trembles. The ring of the portal moves perceptibly inward.

Those at the front arm their weapons.

I know what's going to happen, but I can't figure out how to avoid it. The door is going to come inward when they push it open. It is going to crush the first twenty people on the other side of it. But we are packed so tight, they have nowhere to go.

"When it falls, come over to the breach!" I yell, but there is so much fear and confusion, I'm not certain anyone is paying attention to me. Prisha is yelling at them too, and Maibe.

There is a second powerful burst, and the door comes free.

The door crushes the first ring of women inside the door, messy and horrifying. I duck, fearing a volley. And it comes—a blast of multiple weapons. Four or five dozen cephalopods explode into the room, taking down the next ring of women. And then the Bhavajas come in after them, storming the only entrance, cutting us down like so many beasts, their faces broad and grinning and purposeful, like this is the inevitable end to the game, like they knew this was coming all along.

I fire back, yelling for order, for tactics. Prisha is hit first; a cephalopod clips her face and she goes down. Maibe fills the void where she had stood, firing her weapon into the melee of the advancing Bhavajas, as if it makes any difference.

It is a slaughter.

I meet the first line of the Bhavajas, stepping up as the lines of my family fall. I discharge my weapon three more times. Then it malfunctions. I butt the next Bhavaja in the face with it instead. I shoot two more with the fallen woman's weapon and then wrestle with a third.

They swarm me. A punch to the kidneys. The butt of a weapon in my face. A burst of darkness, a bright light. I go down. A stray blast from a Katazyrna weapon takes out my leg, and I crumple like a folding flower. I collapse onto a pile of corpses.

I claw across the bodies, making for the escape route. I grab hold of someone's face and realize it is Maibe's. Maibe is spitting up blood, clawing at a wound in her gut. The eye of the cephalopod nestled there gazes stupidly up at me, and I almost retch.

A blazing pain erupts in my shoulder, like someone has set a hammer on fire and hit me with it. I collapse on top of Maibe.

I lose some time.

The world swims. I'm aware of Maibe's watery breaths. The cries of my kin. Shots. Merry voices, joking between the sounds of the weapons. Bodies sliding across the floor. *Click, click* of piled weapons. The Bhavajas are cleaning up.

Someone rolls me over, and I gaze up into Rasida's face. Rasida is chewing on something, grinning down at me like I am some prized animal.

"Jayd," I mutter.

Rasida kicks me and yells back at someone behind her. "Recycle them," Rasida says. "Don't let a single body go to waste."

A woman grabs me by the arms and drags me painfully across the floor. Blood makes a long trail behind me, and it takes me a moment to realize a lot of it is mine. My leg is a twisted mess, and the pain in my shoulder burns white-hot. Black spots float across my vision, like burns.

They leave me next to a pile of corpses in a low room, close to a great black maw. Two Bhavajas work wordlessly, each taking one end of a corpse and throwing it into the darkness.

The recycler. The monster. The memory roars through my fuzzy head. I'm not a corpse, I try to say, but I am choking on something; my own spit, blood.

They pitch Prisha's body into the darkness.

I try to scream. No sound comes out.

One of the women takes my arms. The other grabs my twisted legs.

Pain. Fearful pain. They swing me toward the black mouth that I know leads to the monster.

Darkness, at least, can bring me some peace. I know darkness. Know it very well.

They let me go.

I make a sound then, something like a dying animal might make: a grunt, no more. Then I am falling and falling, into the sticky darkness, falling and falling to the center of the world.

> "TRUE POWER IS THE ABILITY TO MAKE THOSE
> WHO FEAR YOU DESPERATE TO LOVE YOU."
> —LORD MOKSHI, ANNALS OF THE LEGION

13

JAYD

I wake in Rasida's rooms on Bhavaja, snug in her bed, head muzzy with a terrible hangover. I sit up and find that my hands are still covered in rusty blood. It's all over me—my suit, my hair, my arms. I swing my legs over the edge of the bed and my stomach heaves. I try to put back together the events of the evening, but it's all a haze. The joining, yes, I remember some of that. I remember Rasida leading me down the dais and giving me something to drink, and passing me off to her security team and her sister Aditva, whose breath was terrible and whose eyelid kept twitching.

I had meant to turn around, to see Zan and Anat, but Aditva said that for my safety, they needed to have me sit and wait for Rasida in an apartment just outside the temple. I sat. I waited. I drank.

And now, somehow, I am back in my room on Bhavaja. Where was the rest?

Beside me, the bed is not mussed. Rasida did not sleep here. So, where is she? Though she is not here, I am comforted by the fact that she did not send me back to my rooms, as she would a prisoner. We will get close, the way I got close to Zan. That thought gives me pause, though, because what happened with Zan was something neither of us could have anticipated, and it is not a path I want to tread again.

I stare into my bloody hands and am overcome with a desire to scrub myself clean.

I go to the shower and pour oil over my body and scrape myself clean, removing the blood and smell of sex from my skin from the day before, though as I shake the dirty oil onto the sticky floor to be absorbed, I admit I could have burrowed happily into the sheets and inhaled the smell the rest of the waking period.

Maybe I am a terrible traitor. But Zan is far from here, and it is not the real Zan anyway, is it? Some pale imitation of Zan, wiped and recovered, wiped and recovered, over and over and over again. Maybe the Zan I thought I loved, the one I have spent all my time arguing with Anat about, no longer exists. What is love anyway but a hunger than no meal can satisfy?

I stare down at my belly. I've gone in for my treatments every fourteen rotations. Now the thing I carry must already be splitting and multiplying, using my body, my strength, to bring itself to fruition. Thanks to Zan, I am capable of giving birth to the most important resource in the Legion now. Rasida's world cannot live without me.

Whether Rasida truly loves me or not, I am valuable to her. I'm annoyed that she did not let me see Anat and Zan one last time. It seems strange to attend a joining and not present the two families together at the end. Maybe it was done, and it's something I don't remember?

I pull on one of Rasida's tunics, which is a little tight and too long, and venture out into the hall. A beefy woman stands outside and gives me a dark look when I leave. As I walk, the woman follows, eight or ten paces distant.

I round on her. "I'm sorry," I say, "but are you meant to be guarding me?"

"If you leave, I'm to ensure you get back to your quarters," the woman says.

"What is your name?" I say, but she does not fall for that. She presses her lips firmly together.

"Where is Rasida?"

"She is attending matters of foreign policy," the woman says.

"Take me to her," I say.

"I am to fulfill your every request," the woman says, "except when it countermands an order from Lord Rasida. Lord Rasida requests that you be escorted to your rooms. Your girls are waiting for you."

"Can I go to the banquet area?" I ask. "Perhaps eat with the rest of the family?"

"You are not family," the woman says.

That rankles, but I recognize the line. It's something Gavatra would say. Where is Gavatra? I try to tamp down my feeling of unease. Rasida professes love. I might almost call what I hold for Rasida a kind of love. I tremble at the memory of her touch. A woman who touches me like that would not make me a prisoner.

But I cannot help but think, again, of Zan. If Rasida needs me, I will use that need to manufacture her downfall. I will retain control over this situation. I got myself here, against all odds and at great cost. I can do what must be done to see the rest of it through.

I let the woman bring me back to my rooms. The girls are already there with food waiting on the table, and a stack of glowing tablets.

"What are these?" I ask, but of course they can't answer. I turn over one of the tablets and I see it is a moving storybook. I have not seen anything like this since I was small. When I concentrate hard on the image that moves across its surface, I can immerse myself in the story. This one, however, is barely comprehensible. The language is not one I know, and the setting of the world is alien. Even the people are strange—spindly and long-limbed, with squinting little eyes and flattened faces. I set the tablet down, wondering which world Rasida dug these up from.

I expect to see Rasida before the walls go dim, but she does not come for me. I think perhaps she will summon me for dinner, but that time, too, passes, and she does not come.

I'm nauseous, and vomit in the shower.

I spend time looking at the story tablets, but most are like the first— so old that they are nearly incomprehensible. And they give me strange dreams.

It's during one of these dreams that I wake with a start in the darkness. My door is open, and I see Rasida there.

I blink and rub at the walls until they brighten. I pull off my blankets and prepare to yell at her for keeping me here alone, but when the light comes up and I see her, I am mute with shock.

She is covered head to toe in blood. Not old rusty blood like I was from the day before but new, clotting blood. Her hair is a matted tangle. Clearly, some of the blood is hers. There's sticky yellow salve on her left arm. She is holding something in her hand, a weighty object that glows green.

"What's happened?" I say, and my heart catches, because I fear that Zan has done something stupid. Did she attack the Bhavajas? She is going to ruin everything.

Rasida does not meet my gaze. Instead, she gets down on her knees in front of me. She drops what she is carrying.

It is my mother's arm.

"I have brought you a war trophy," she says, and it is all I can do not to scream, because this is exactly how I presented this arm to my mother after I stole it the first time.

"My mother—" I begin, but I know what's coming now, and I want to run, but I am rooted to the spot.

Where would I go? I have nowhere to go.

Rasida takes my hands into hers, smearing dried blood and grime onto my skin, and presses my hands to her cheek.

"You are free now," she says.

"Free?" My voice is a whisper.

"I have freed you from Katazyrna," she says. "Your mother is dead. Your world is ours."

My gut twists. I must say the right thing. I can't waver in this moment, or she will murder me too. "I don't understand," I say. "We have brokered peace."

"I have done this for you," Rasida says, and she gazes up at me now with her black eyes, and in them I see absolute certainty, complete calm. "You are Bhavaja now. Katazyrna is no more."

"What have you done to my sisters?"

"They will renew the world," she says. "They have been recycled. We will eat their bones."

"No," I say, and I back away from her. I can't help it. My mind and body are split in this. I want to claw at her face. No, I want to claw at my own face, because this is my fault. I did this. "Rasida, we brokered peace. You've broken the peace. You broke your word!"

Rasida gets to her feet, slowly. I fear her then. Not as I did before, not as my enemy, but the fear one has for a mad animal, a mutant creature who has never known the light.

"I will never break my word to you," Rasida says. "But the peace was brokered with Anat, not with you. It will be difficult to adjust. But this is your home now."

"You can't . . . ," I say, and I don't want to ask her, I don't want to know if she's killed Zan too, because of course she has, and then I wonder if she knows about Zan, and who she really is. Does she suspect? Could I have given myself away? I stare at the arm. My mother's gory flesh is still inside of it; the arm was always too small for her. It pained her to wear it.

I clasp my hands together and try to control my trembling. The tears come, unbidden, but Rasida will expect tears. If I did not cry, I would be less believable when I finally said I forgave her for murdering my world.

I fall to the floor, and Rasida settles in beside me. I let her take me into her arms, and I sob against her. "What have you done?" I say. "What have you done?"

She makes a shushing sound. She wipes my sisters' blood through my hair as she strokes me.

"Hush," she says. "It's just us now."

And then, finally, I scream.

PART II:

DOWN BELOW

"THE MONSTERS DON'T LIVE IN THE BELLY OF THE WORLD
LIKE THEY ALL SAY. THE MONSTERS LIVE INSIDE OF US.
WE MAKE THE MONSTERS."
—LORD MOKSHI, **ANNALS OF THE LEGION**

14

ZAN

Everything is monstrous in the dark.

The recycler monster moves heavily in the flickering light, squelching across the detritus of the world's waste: spent suits and table scraps, bloody piss and shit and ruined bodies, corpulent or lean, old or young, mangled, deformed, mutant, or hacked to pieces, all the castoffs, the lame, the hobbled, the imperfect, the mistakes, the merely unlucky, the dead.

I wake thinking I have dreamed this horror, but it's real. My head feels heavy, stuffed with gummy ooze. I see hazy blue light shot through with blackness, as if some great light above me is swinging back and forth on a long string. It makes me dizzy. The stench is overpowering, so caustic that I dry-heave.

I can't move. As I piece together the light and shadows as they crawl across the landscape, I see that I'm lying in a heap of corpses. Someone's hand lies heavily on my face. I taste bile. I spit and slaver instead. A deep, shuddering sob bubbles up inside of me, so powerful I think I might burst with it. Out in the darkness, among the oozing piles of waste and half-rotten body parts, I see the dim shape of something terrible moving among the piles. I have met this monster before, in some other life, some other time. I know this moment in my bones.

I try to pull myself free of the bodies around me. They have cushioned me after my long fall through the darkness. How long I fell, I don't know. Of all the things I don't want to remember, that long fall is among them, but it comes back in terrible waves: a slimy, guttering slide to death. My hands are covered in grime. My fingernails are bloody, slathered in mucus from trying to grip the walls of the garbage funnel and slow my fall.

Now I want nothing more than to be free of the bodies that saved my life. A few paces away, I see something else moving. The blue light overhead swings back, and I see Maibe on her hands and knees, spitting bile or blood onto the rotten, uncertain ground beneath her.

The great hulking thing that wanders beyond the next rise of corpses grunts, then sighs. Everything around us seems to shake and tremble as it trundles forward.

I wave to Maibe, but she must not be able to see me. And then I go still, for the monster is upon us.

Maibe raises her head as the great shape of the thing rumbles toward her. I can see only its general outline. It's an enormous beast, fifty paces or more tall, and has four great front arms, powerful haunches, and the snub of some tail. It lumbers forward. Maibe babbles something that is half-scream, half burst of ragged breath.

The light swings away. The monster grabs Maibe's body. It takes her head into its massive bony fingers and pops Maibe's head from her torso as if she's brittle as a dry stick. It tosses both pieces of her into its mouth. The crunching of the body in its powerful jaws is so loud, I feel it in my own bones.

The monster groans and shifts, causing the bodies around me to tremble again. One corpse rolls off the top of the pile.

The monster snorts and shambles closer to the pile of death that surrounds me. I hold my breath, shaking so hard, my whole body feels like one open wound.

I feel its hot breath on me. Snuffling. Reeking. The light swings back, and I see the face of the thing illuminated for the first time. I bite back a scream, gnawing on my tongue so hard, I taste blood.

It has a roughly human face, a bulbous nose, and a wide-lipped mouth full of jagged teeth, yet there is just one eye, one great yellowish eye that sits at the center of its forehead. A tangle of thick, matted hair is heaped across its massive shoulders. The first set of forearms are the largest, each wrist as big around as my whole body. The hands have just three fingers: a thumb, an index finger, something like a little finger, the smallest as long as my whole arm.

The monster snorts again in my direction, its eye rolling in its socket, searching for . . . what? Movement?

It paws at the pile of corpses with its three-pronged fingers, yanking bodies up. It pops off the heads and eats them. One of the bodies is still alive, like Maibe, and screams.

The monster snorts at it. It makes a deep, regular grunting sound, like laughter.

It plays with that one for a while, tossing her among its hands, slamming her into the piles of corpses until the screams go silent. I don't want to know who it is. I hope I never met her.

The munching goes on and on. Eventually, the monster snorts a final time at the disturbed pile of bodies around me and shambles off. I lie still and strain to hear it until I can hear nothing. Then I choke on a sob, because I don't know what else to do but sit in my misery. It would have been a kindness to kill me above. A kindness for me to die in the fall. But the world is not kind.

"Zan?"

It's Prisha's voice. "Where are you?" I say.

I try to pull myself clear of the bodies again, my leg and shoulder throbbing. "Can you see me? Where are you?" I ask.

"I can't move," Prisha says. She sounds at least a dozen paces away. An impossible distance, in the shape I'm in.

"Is anyone else alive?"

"It ate Soraya," Prisha says. "Lord of War, take mercy on the fallen. Lord of War, let us die here. Let me die, Lord."

I hear someone else take up the prayer, somewhere deep in the pile of the dead and almost-dead. I didn't know Soraya. I'm glad of it.

Maybe we'll all get lucky. Maybe we'll die of our wounds before the monster comes back. I want to believe in a Lord of War that gives all what they deserve, but I fear that—among these people—I am indeed getting my due.

I try to surrender myself to true darkness. Maybe I'll bleed out. But if I bleed out, who will rescue Jayd?

It's that thought that stirs me. I open my eyes. Darkness won't come.

But the monster returns.

It shambles among the dead, picking through them like sampling some fine banquet. Its massive eye fixes on a body near me. I hear a rambling prayer and a squeal.

It's Prisha.

I watch the monster waggling her body high above the ground. It gnaws off one of her legs while she shrieks. I expect it to eat her the way it did Maibe, but instead it lumbers up on its haunches and grabs something dangling from above them, some tentacle or tendril. It wraps Prisha up in the thing, knotting it around her torso, and leaves her there, bleeding and struggling, until she dies or passes out. I can't tell which. I hope she is dead.

The monster trundles off, leaving Prisha to hang like bait on a line for something far worse, far larger, and I don't like my imagination then. Not at all.

I don't know how long it's been when I hear Prisha again. I'm sweating and burning with what feels like a terrible fever. I hope that maybe this is all this is; some fever dream.

Prisha wails. I don't know how she has the strength for it. She should know better. She's just going to draw the thing back. Maybe that's what she wants. Like me, she just wants this all over.

Her wailing continues. Screams ripple out over the landscape, far off, which makes me wonder how many more have been pushed down here from other parts of the world, still alive.

I grit my teeth. I have two choices: to wait for death or to fight it. No one is coming for us. There is no one to save us but ourselves.

I heave at the bodies surrounding me, finally peeling myself free of the heap. It takes an age, and I am sweating and shaking, but I am free of the dead. Time is difficult to measure here. I have only the trembling light to go on, and the long shadows. Where is the light coming from? Are the tentacles trailing from the ceiling attached to something else, some greater horror?

If there is a way down here, there must be a way back up. How did these creatures get here?

I pass out on the other side of the corpses.

When I wake, I'm sweating and delirious. I know I'm delirious because I see little black animals crawling among the filth across from me, but when I squint hard they disappear and it is only me and sobbing Prisha dangling high above me.

Then the ground begins to tremble.

I hug the ground like it is a solid thing, though it is filled with bones and feces and darker things. I'm thirsty and shaking, but none of that is worse than the fear I feel as the monster approaches, wending its way through the corpses. I hear the crackling of bones as it moves closer.

It looms above me now like a terrible nightmare, a mother's horror story. It grabs Prisha from the dangling tentacle and makes that huff-huffing sound, the one that is like laughter, and pops her head from her body and eats her.

I grip the ground hard, hanging on for my life.

The monster makes great walloping noises behind me, poking at the refuse. A heavy force thumps my shoulder.

Its massive fingers wrap around my torso. It clutches me so hard, the breath leaves my body. The monster lifts me high and pushes me right up in front of its great yellow eye.

I kick with my good leg, but miss the eye. The monster roars. Its hot, rank breath roils over me. I wish the fever and infection had had time to take me. Let the darkness come. Anything but this.

The monster barks. It yanks at another of the tendrils on the ceiling. Knots it around my torso.

"Fuck you," I mutter, so softly I can barely hear it myself. "Just eat me. Just eat me."

But it chortles instead. And leaves me.

The sticky tentacle clings to me like a living thing; I feel sharp little needles along its flesh, digging into my own.

I hang at least twenty paces above the ground. Even if I manage to get free, the fall will hurt, and I'm already pretty far gone. I don't know how much more I can take.

I dangle there for a long time, drooling, nodding in and out of consciousness. I have enough strength on my third waking to try getting myself free of the tentacle. The blue light swings over me, and I see I am not far from a heap of very old corpses.

I shift my torso back and forth, gaining momentum on the great tentacle, making myself into a pendulum. With slow and painful steadiness, I shift back and forth, back and forth. I swing closer and closer to the pile of bloated bodies.

In the distance, I hear a tremulous bellow.

I swing faster, working my body in the terrible grip of the tentacle as I go, praying to the Lord of War, though I'm uncertain if I believe in it, or anything, here in this place.

The corpses tremble. I hear the monster lurching out there in the distance, coming closer. Ever closer.

I will not die here. I will not be eaten at the center of the world without knowing who I am. Without a mother. Without a memory. Without Jayd.

I slip free of the tentacle. I grab it before I fall, and let go just as I begin the yawning swing toward the pile of corpses.

I land heavily in the bloated, gassy bodies. They rupture, billowing great gouts of gas. I retch and cough. Pain hammers through my open wounds, judders up my bad leg. I've likely lost the leg by now. What do I care for it? Just cut it off.

I pass out. Lose time. Pain. Darkness. Something skitters around me. I wake, once, and find a humanlike creature, tall as my knee, huddled over my leg, its lips smeared with blood, smiling a bloody smile in a twisted face. I swing my arm at it, limply, and it hops away on hands and feet, looking back just once, giggling sharply.

I'm not going to die. But maybe I'm going to get eaten alive, one way or another.

I hear the monster roaring, and I try to move through the bloated mess of leaking flesh. Skin sloughs off bones. Faces are barely recognizable as human. Maybe they aren't.

I crawl to the edge of the heap of corpses.

Then I slide off it. Down and down. I land hard. Pain and blackness, pain and blackness. Some part of me wants to die, even if Jayd is alive. Even if I could save her.

Maybe that part is getting its wish.

ZAN

The smell of smoke; the warmth of fire. The stench brings with it the memory of a burning world. Whose world? I don't know, but the smell evokes a deep feeling of loss and betrayal, of a people wasted, a purpose foiled. My purpose? What would I have had invested in the future of a world? Was it Maibe or Sabita who said I was supposedly a conscript from another world? Maybe that was my world burning.

It's the smell that wakes me. I open my eyes. I am in a dripping cave or hovel of some kind. An emaciated woman crouches near a fire. The flames lick the air between us, casting the woman's face in long shadows. Her hair is thin and greasy, her hands skinny and slender, bent slightly, curved like claws. Half her face is a twisted mass of scars.

"Who are you?" I croak. I gaze at the fire and worry over the hungry look on the woman's face.

"Das Muni," the woman says softly.

"What are you?" I feel groggy again. "The Bhavajas," I say. "They've taken the world. I have to cast them out. I need to get back to Jayd."

"I know," Das Muni says.

"What are you?"

"Just a woman," she says. "My world is dead."

"What happens to dead worlds?"

Das Muni hugs her knees to her chest. "They are eaten. Salvaged for parts until they no longer hold together. Have you never seen the death of a world?"

I shiver. It's as if she has been crouching over me and reading my thoughts. "Why did—"

"Hush," Das Muni says. She holds her filthy hands to her own mouth, rolling her eyes to the entrance of the little stinking hovel of refuse. Bone and calcified organic structures make up the foundation of the thing, and the seams are stuffed with detritus.

The whole structure trembles. I hear the familiar roar of the great recycler monster shambling through the refuse.

After a few minutes, the sound of its lumbering fades, and Das Muni uncovers her mouth. "That's the worst one," she says. "That is Meatmoth. It loves you, I think. It finds you very delicious."

"There are more?" I say, and it comes out a strained squeak, like some kid who just got her first lecture about what a vacuum is. That thought leads to another, a memory of standing in front of a room full of people my age, reciting the five rules of worldwalking. We aren't speaking in the language the Katazyrnas use. It's something else. I grasp at the name of that language, but it's elusive.

"Many monsters," Das Muni says. "We're at the center of the world, or very near it. They recycle everything for the world. It's a big job. On my world, there were more of them—"

"How did you get down here?" I say.

"Same as you," Das Muni says, but she does not look at me as she says it. She is gazing out beyond the light of the fire again, to Meatmoth's world. I wonder what it is she's burning. "Someone recycled me."

"Why?"

"Why did they recycle you?"

I don't know how much to tell her. I'm still wondering if she's going to eat me or not. "The world's been breached," I say. "The Bhavajas have taken over Katazyrna."

"Oh," Das Muni says, as if I've told her I sprayed on a blue suit that morning instead of a green one.

"That's very bad," I say, pressing. "They slaughtered everyone."

"They won't slaughter everyone," Das Muni says, "only enough to make sure they can bring all their own people over here. I heard Bhavaja is dying. Once a world is dying, the only way to turn it around is to give birth to a new one. And that's . . . rare."

"How do you know so much?"

"How do you not?" Das Muni says. "I've lived on a few worlds. No one ever wants me. I am always recycled."

"What do you do?"

She cocks her head. "I give birth to the wrong sorts of things."

"You . . . give birth?"

"Everyone births things."

"I don't."

"Of course you do. There's no one who doesn't."

I search my memory for something about birth or pregnancy but come up empty. I reflexively put my hands against my soft stomach, pressing to see if I can find some other life in there. But I don't notice anything. I remember the scar there.

"How does that . . . happen?" I ask.

Das Muni raises her brows. "Have you lost your head down here?"

"Yes," I say, relieved to find some excuse that doesn't entail telling her more of my strange story. "Since I got dumped down here, I don't remember many things."

"You birth what the world wants," Das Muni says. She picks something out of the pot over the fire, something that looks like a stick, and chews on the softened end of it. "When it decides something is needed, you make it. The witches on every ship, they know all about it. Some are madder than others, but they can tell you."

"We . . . make it?" But then, who else would make what the ship needs? The ship, maybe? Are *we* the ship, living on its flesh like parasites? "What do *you* make, then?"

Das Muni eyes me over a long moment, chewing thoughtfully. Then she stands, hunching over in the low space, and picks up a tightly woven basket. It sits on the other side of the room behind stacks of corded fuel and what appears to be semi-rotten foodstuffs.

She shuffles toward me and shoves the basket at me.

Inside is a slithering mass of oily, fishlike organisms with human-shaped heads filled with spiny teeth.

I recoil.

Das Muni looks into the basket herself, frowns. "They are not so bad this time."

I feel nauseous.

"It's all right," Das Muni says. "They are also very tasty."

"I can't stay here," I say. "Thank you for looking out for me, but I have to get back up to the surface."

"There's no way back up," Das Muni says.

"But you've been inside other worlds, you said. Been recycled before. How did you get out?"

"When the scavengers come," Das Muni says, "they break open every level of the world, right to the core here, and they take out all the organic things. Without this, the world dies. It has nothing to use to regenerate itself."

"What did you do before?"

"I served people, that's all."

"How do you know so much, then?"

"I listen," Das Muni says. "I listen when people think I don't. That's the secret to staying alive. You must know more than you pretend."

"I don't know anything," I say.

"Then we are a good pair," Das Muni says, and begins clubbing her offspring to death for dinner.

> "VILLAINS SMILE BRIGHTEST.
> MY GRIN IS WIDEST BEFORE I DINE.
> ALL MY ENEMIES KNOW THIS."
> —LORD MOKSHI, **ANNALS OF THE LEGION**

JAYD

will not lose sight of what I'm here for. Now, more than ever, every word and gesture matters. But I didn't anticipate Rasida's betrayal. Not so soon. It was . . . it was something I would have done, broker peace and destroy the world. I close my eyes. I've done it before.

Rasida has the arm. I tell myself she has done me a favor. I am halfway to getting both of the things I want, but I'm on my own now. I can't rely on Zan to hold up her part of this plan. In truth, her role was most important in getting me here. The rest, I can do alone. It will be more difficult, but it's possible. I must assume Zan and my sisters are dead; it's just me now. So I have to go through with this plan Zan and I concocted so many rotations ago, and believe that what we came up with then can still work.

But it's several sleeping periods before I can make myself accept Rasida's dinner invitation. Even getting out of bed is painful. Keeping food down in the morning is difficult, though, and by the evening, I'm starving. The food the girls offer me is terrible. I suspect Rasida knows that what will finally get me to dinner is the hope of better food.

I am careful with my appearance. I ensure I am clean and well groomed. I practice smiling. The practicing helps when I step into Rasida's rooms and see her for the first time since she murdered my family.

My expression is sad but sincere, I hope.

I don't ask her about Neith and Gavatra, though I have considered a hundred ways I could ask her during the long, sleepless periods I've endured. They are dead. I have probably been eating them.

"Thank you for accepting, love," Rasida says. My gut goes icy at the endearment. She is mad like Anat was mad. But I'm here sitting across from her of my own will, so I'm no better.

Her sister Samdi serves us, which makes me wonder if Samdi is her sister after all. Like me, Rasida has shown herself to be a master in the art of deception. In part, I think it's because she absolutely believes that the things she's telling me are true when she says them. She is nurturing reality into being as she speaks.

"I have thought long on what's happened," I say. I pick at my food. We are eating a mix of clotted protein gel and fresh greens. At least something still grows on this dying world, somewhere. I've been offered nothing this fresh in my own quarters. Maybe there will be something sweet afterward. This thought bubbles up and I almost laugh at myself, that my submission can be bought with something as simple as food.

"I came here to you because of my mother," I say. "She was always overbearing. You knew her. My whole family wanted a life killing and dying for Katazyrna. I am . . . not like that. I never wanted that. The things I did . . . all those worlds. That was something she made me do, never something I wanted. But on Katazyrna, you did what Anat asked or she had you recycled."

Rasida says, "What do you want, Jayd?"

"Just you," I say. I meet her look. "I want to have a new life. Maybe it's true that I am free now. Maybe you've freed me."

She smiles at me, but it is the smile that does not touch her eyes, the black smile that goes with her black eyes. A fist of worry forms in my chest and does not go away. If she makes me a prisoner here, I will have a much more difficult time escaping.

Rasida rises and goes to her wardrobe. She pulls out my mother's iron arm. She drops it on the table between us and sits back down.

"Is there some trick to it?" she says. "We all know Anat used the arm to power the world. She put on lovely little light shows, and I heard rumors of far more. They say she had control over Katazyrna the way the witches did, using this arm. We can't find the Katazyrna witches, so we need the arm if we're to remake the world."

"I don't know," I lie. I stare at the arm. She has taken out my mother's wasted, fleshy arm from inside of it, and it's only a metal brace wrapped over the warm organic green skin now. I don't tell Rasida that the arm is not something from Katazyrna at all. We don't have the skill to build such a thing any more than she does. Only one world does.

"If you knew how to operate it—" Rasida says.

"Mother didn't trust any of us," I say. "I'm sorry, love. If I knew how it worked, I would tell you."

"Would you?"

"I would," I say.

She considers me, expression cool, calculating. She stands and picks up the arm and puts it back in her wardrobe. I note its placement, and also that it doesn't seem to be locked up in any way. Perhaps she trusts that her people fear her enough not to touch it. It's a good thing I am not hers.

"I suppose it was not important to know such things," Rasida says. "With what you can carry in that womb, such things are not your concern. How many have you birthed?"

"None," I say.

"None?" She narrows her eyes. "Then how do you know—"

"Anat had them removed before they came to fruition," I say. "She decides . . . decided who got to give birth, and to what, on the world."

"Quite a feat," she says.

"Surely," I say carefully, "you have control over the fecundity of your people, the same way you control your own."

"I administer corrections when I deem it fit," she says. She drinks from another beautiful metal goblet. This one has blue stones embedded along the rim. I cannot imagine she eats this way every rotation. But I know very little of this woman who is my enemy, far less than I thought I did before I came here.

"I have always thought it strange," I say, "that you continue to live in a world such as this when you have the power to make a new one. What do you care about a metal arm to patch up the seams of some world, when you could remake the world?"

Rasida raises her brows. "Oh, yes," she says. "I hear that often. But no one tells you what it does to you, to make a world." She refills my goblet. "Do they?"

I fold my hands over my belly. "Anat always said leading a world was far more dangerous and terrifying than making one."

"Anat was a fool," Rasida says. "Drink your wine."

I drink my wine.

I cannot help but glance at the wardrobe again and the iron arm within. My family dead, Zan dead, and here I sit with the arm just a few paces away, and the woman who can remake worlds pouring wine into my cup.

I have stepped into the belly of my enemy. I am within a whisper of everything I sought. But at what price?

Rasida leans toward me. "There is something you should know," she says.

I wait. She seems to expect a response, but when I give none, she continues. "I love you very much," she says, and grins.

"I love you also," I say.

Smile and smile, Zan would say. Smile all the brighter for being the villain.

"It does worry me," she says, "that you have yet to bear a pregnancy to term."

"Now that I have the opportunity—"

"Yes, of course," Rasida says. "We'll make sure you are cared for. You know that's all I want. To care for you."

"I know," I say.

As we finish our meal, Rasida talks of the salvage work on the neighboring world, petty insurgencies in the level below, and relates a story about how one of her sisters burned out an infestation of vermin on the upper level. The conversation seems trivial, but I note that she is careful about how much she tells me. I never hear more of her sisters' names, nor the name of the world they are salvaging from, nor what is being salvaged.

We are interrupted by Rasida's mother, Nashatra.

I make to stand as she enters, a show of respect, but Rasida waves me back down.

"What do you want, you old fool?" Rasida says.

Nashatra ducks her head. "Apologies, Lord, you're needed on the fourth level."

"The fourth? Fuck and fire," Rasida mutters. "You can't take care of it yourself?"

"You asked to be alerted any time the—"

"Shut your fool mouth," Rasida says.

I close my own mouth, even though she is not talking to me. I can't help being shocked at Rasida's tone. If I had spoken to Anat that way, I'd have been recycled.

Rasida gets up. Nashatra backs away, trying to give her room to go past, but as she does, she knocks the table, and Rasida's goblet falls to the floor.

Rasida raises her arm, but Nashatra is already getting to her knees—painfully, from the look on her face—and babbling apologies.

"I'm sorry, daughter," Nashatra says. She pulls the goblet off the floor and begins to wipe it clean on her tunic.

I try to get down beside her to help, but Rasida snaps her fingers at me. "You go back to your rooms," she says. "Samdi, escort my consort to her rooms."

"I'm sorry," I say to Nashatra stupidly, because what do I have to be sorry for? We're all just things here, owned by the most powerful person in the Legion.

When I finally go back to my rooms, the light on the walls feels very bright, and I'm exhausted from my long performance. The girls are still there, though, turning down my bed and pouring fresh, warm water into a bowl so I can wash my face before I go to sleep. I say nothing to them as I disrobe and bathe and slip into bed. The semidarkness is welcome, because it is the only time I can be certain no one can see my face.

Yet I still pull the blankets over my head before I let my face relax. The temperature inside Katazyrna was always more or less constant, but here on Bhavaja, it fluctuates. It's warm now, but in a few breaths, it could cool to something less comfortable. Cowering under the covers this way, I can pretend I'm back on Katazyrna, though I find that memory brings me little solace. Life on Katazyrna, before Zan, was little better than my situation here. It was Zan who gave me hope that we could be something else, after I nearly destroyed her.

When I wake, the girls are rubbing the walls alight, and I find I have another long cycle of nothing before me. I make myself get up and dress. When the girls run off to get my food, I walk out into the courtyard outside my rooms and begin walking the circumference of it. I'm too nauseous to eat but hope that exercise eases both my stomach and my anxiousness. I have never been a prisoner before. I understand now how Zan felt.

When the girls arrive with the food, there is someone with them. It's Nashatra.

"Hello, Mother," I say. I expect to see Rasida there behind her, but she is alone. She is lanky in the arms and legs but soft in the middle, with a round, fleshy face and firm mouth that put me in mind of Rasida. Her eyes are hooded; she doesn't fully open the lids, making her expression difficult to read. I expect that is a blessing here.

"Walk with me, child," she says.

I follow her into the foyer. We walk in silence past the guards in the outer corridor and down a series of twisting passages. Finally, we come to a large, bowed room. Half the ceiling has collapsed, revealing brittle layers of the world above it, all fused and twisted together like scar tissue.

"We are alone," she says.

"I can see that."

"Your family is dead, and you owe us your womb," she says.

"That's correct."

"I told Rasida we should trade only for your womb and have one of her sisters carry it. She refused. She wanted you. All of you, against my better judgment. I don't trust Katazyrnas."

"Yet you are here alone with me," I say.

"You are not so foolish that you'd do harm to me here. You don't yet know the full extent of Rasida's wrath, but you will, child. Rasida always gets what she wants."

"I have seen what she does to her own mother," I say.

"I never wanted war," Nashatra says. "Rasida's aunt was Lord before Rasida was. I never held the title. You can see why."

"You have nothing to be ashamed of."

"Don't I?" she says.

"Why have you taken me here?"

"The girls are Rasida's," she says, "like most people here. But not all of us. Not all of us, child. You understand? Just because I raised that girl doesn't mean I will stand by while our world rots around her."

"What are you going to do?" I ask.

"When you first came here, I thought you were a spider," she says. "Then I thought, perhaps, you loved her. Then I saw that we were the same."

"We're not the same."

"Oh, we are," she says. "We are both smart women who thought being smart could save us here. It cannot, with Rasida. Logic does not win against her. Nor does love. You have tried both, I know. I know how you got here. But neither will work. You must try something different."

"Why are you telling me this?" I ask.

"Because you are closest to her now," she says, "and if we are going to overthrow her, we need someone who can get close enough to kill her."

My expression does not change. Killing Rasida was never part of the plan, but I am desperate for allies here.

"You had best speak quickly," I say softly, because I fear the walls are listening. I fear they can divine my true intent. "Because I would never betray Rasida in that way." And when I say it out loud, I almost believe it. I almost believe I am the woman I pretend to be.

17

ZAN

Recovery nearly kills me.

I vomit and tremble. Das Muni feeds me something like water—a viscous substance—from her crooked hands. I wake once to hear Das Muni grunting while she squats over the basket. Splashing and gurgling. The soft cries of some mutant living thing, left to drown in its own afterbirth, send me to sleep.

The horror of the real world extends into my dreams. I dream that I give birth to a squalling, one-eyed recycler monster. It grows so rapidly, it eats off my arm just minutes after birth. It snuffles after me while I try to crawl away, eating me piece by piece until it devours my chest and swallows my head.

I wake screaming, often. The screaming reminds me of the screaming I heard while asleep in my room, back before the invasion. Did my sisters dream of the same things? Of people recycled? Is that what Jayd dreams about?

Das Muni squeezes water into my parched mouth and wipes my fevered brow. I piss myself often, and Das Muni replaces the spongy blanket beneath me. It absorbs most of my sweat and piss. I watch in fascination as Das Muni goes outside the hovel and wrings it dry, like a sponge.

I don't know how long it is before Das Muni finally makes me move.

"Your leg is healing well enough," Das Muni says. "You need to get up now and move it, or you'll lose your strength."

I grunt at her. I've lost something here, in all this squalor and horror, and I don't know how to get it back. As I look at Das Muni, all I can think is that dying is preferable to living down here the rest of my life. What hope is there to ever leave, if what Das Muni says is true? What if Jayd is already dead, like the rest of our so-called sisters? Anat is dead. The Katazyrna armies are dead. I want to have hope for some reality other than this, but I can't see it. My body rebels. I whimper.

Das Muni is much smaller than me but surprisingly strong. She hooks her arms under mine and yanks me past the fire, pulling me outside the hovel for the first time. The light here is not the swinging blue light I saw when I first descended into this mire, but soft green. The glow comes from the piles of refuse all around us: a slithering green light, like something alive. And it *is* something alive, I see now as a thread of green slides up my arm. They are bioluminescent worms.

I wipe it off. It twists and tumbles to the ground, squiggling in the muck.

"Up," Das Muni says. She tugs at me again.

"I can't," I say.

"If you don't get up, I'll leave you out here for Meatmoth," she says.

I don't quite believe her, but I move my legs anyway, leaning hard on Das Muni.

Pain radiates up my bad leg. I hiss at the pain. Just the act of standing, even pushing hard against Das Muni, has me sweating and trembling. When I am finally standing straight, I find that I'm head and shoulders taller than Das Muni. And even in this state, having lost much of my flesh here during recovery, I easily outweigh her by fifty or sixty pounds.

Das Muni leads me on an agonizing walk around the hovel, squelching across the slimy ground. I wear no shoes or trousers, only a long tunic woven with the same plant stuffs as the basket. Hemp, maybe? Where do all of these things grow? Certainly not here.

I sleep after, exhausted and sweating. When Das Muni rouses me again, we again walk around the hovel, twice this time, though I whine about it. The more I must rely on Das Muni, the more I hate her, but the longer I stay, the more she seems to stare at me. I'm not sure if the hunger in her gaze is desire or actual hunger. Perhaps it is a little of both. I find that it is her gaze that inspires me to move now. I must get well before she decides which compulsion she wants to act on.

When we are not circling the hovel, we listen for the recycler monster, for Meatmoth, and the others: Bonemesh, Blightdon, Ravisher, and Smorg. It's as if Das Muni has mushed all these names together like a child. I wonder how long she has been down here, really. How old was she when her world died? I ask her about the names, and she says they just came to her; they have no greater meaning.

When I ask about her past and her people, she has the same reaction.

"That time is dead," Das Muni says.

After many periods of sleeping and waking, I'm able to get around the hovel five or six times on my own, using the long femur of some great creature as a cane.

Some days, I still do not want to get up, but Das Muni prods me until I do. One day, I don't want to get up at all, but Das Muni leans over me, arms crossed, and I stare at the basket behind her and remember seeing her eat out of it. This is not someone I want to spend the rest of my days with.

So I get up, and I move slowly, painfully, to the stink hole outside the hovel and relieve myself like a civilized creature. When I try to get back in, Das Muni tells me the food is already set up—down a long, threading path between the heaps of refuse. I hate her and admire her at the same time. If our positions were reversed, I would have left this whining, grumbling hulk of flesh that is myself to die on some heap. I'd feed her to my friend Meatmoth and be done with it. Wouldn't I?

"What do you have to live for out here?" I ask her.

"There is always something to live for," Das Muni says. "The gods have a plan for each of us. They give us signs."

"Signs? And what sign have they given you here in this horrible place?"

"They did not see fit to kill you," Das Muni says. "Nor me. That's a very great sign in this place."

I'm able to mark the time now by the swinging lights and the blooming bioluminescent flora. Best I can tell, they work on cycles, in time with the rotation of the ship. Fifteen hours, roughly, of blue, broken light. Fifteen hours of complete darkness, during which the fauna give off their singular glow. I have long since stopped noticing the stink of the place, which unsettles me. I don't want this life to become normal.

Because I don't like the swinging, erratic light, I wait until the blooming of the flora to go out. I step over Das Muni's slumbering form. I get perhaps a dozen steps from the hovel before I notice Das Muni following me. She still makes my skin crawl with the memory of the sharp-toothed tadpole heads in the basket. What kind of purpose do creatures like that serve? Why do the people of every world fear her enough to throw her down here?

I creep into the green-glowing refuse, walking and walking, still leaning heavily on my bone cane. I gaze at the blackness above me. I can see no ceiling. But I know that above us are layers upon layers of the world. I only need to figure out how to get into them.

I call back at Das Muni, who hides behind a pile when I turn. Does she really think I don't see her?

"Have you ever mapped out this place?" I say. "Have you ever seen its edges?"

Das Muni scuttles toward me, spine bent, ducking her head left, right, like a puppet on a string. When she is close enough, she says, low, "It has no edges. It has no walls. It is a vast circle."

A circle, just like the rest of the world, but one with no gates, no doors, no corridors? A vast sphere.

"There must be a way up," I say. "How are things recycled by the world? What comes down has to go up again, in some form."

Das Muni points to the ground. "The world absorbs it. Absorbs the shit that Meatmoth and the rest put out. That's what we learned from the mothers. Did you not learn this?"

I avoid the question. "There must be a way out," I say. "The top can't be so far away. The ship is vast, yes, but it has limits. If we can get in, we can get out."

"Stay here," Das Muni says. She rests her clawed hand on my forearm.

"My sister," I say, and saying it aloud breaks something in me, some terrible fog that has stolen my will and my strength all through this long recovery. "My sister is in danger. I need to save her, and I can't do it from here," I say. "It might be too late. She might be dead. But if she's dead, then I want revenge on the people that did this. On the Bhavajas." I stare long at the darkness above us. How to tackle it? I need Das Muni's help, however much she disturbs me.

"Listen," I say. "If you help me take this world from the Bhavajas, you will have an honored place topside. You can have your own space. Food whenever you want it. You can live upworld. I can do that if we win."

"You will need an army to take the world," Das Muni says.

"I will," I say. "You'll be the first among them. Will you do it?"

"We won't survive," Das Muni says.

She is probably right about that. I lean into her, biting back my revulsion. I put my hand on Das Muni's sagging, filthy shoulder. "There is a difference between living and surviving. I want to live, Das Muni. Do you?"

Das Muni quakes at my touch. "I will live," Das Muni says.

I pull my hand away. "Then we must set out on a great journey together."

"I am yours," Das Muni says, and something in her tone makes me hesitate, as if I stand on a great precipice. Why is she so devoted to me? Is she truly so starved for human company that she will travel with me? I decide to accept her answer, for however long it lasts, and for whatever reason.

"We are bound, then," I say, "until we reach the surface."

"There is no surface," Das Muni says, and for one cold moment, I wonder if Jayd and my sisters were the fever dream and this is my true reality. I shake it off.

"We'll get there," I say.

"I will go with you," Das Muni says, "but you will be disappointed."

"I cannot be more disappointed than I already am," I say, and I pray to the War God, and whatever gods Das Muni worships, that I'm making a true statement.

"WHEN I RELEASED THE MOKSHI FROM ITS ORBIT,
I NEVER EXPECTED TO ENCOUNTER RESISTANCE ON
THE WAY OUT OF THE LEGION. I SHOULD NOT HAVE BEEN
SURPRISED HOW MANY FEARED THE FUTURE."
—LORD MOKSHI, *ANNALS OF THE LEGION*

18

ZAN

The recyclers are worse during the sleeping period.

Yet I insist on traveling during the blooming of the flora, the same ones that live now in my wounded leg. The bacteria glow from beneath my healed skin, a part of me. I fear sometimes that they will overtake me. Will they colonize me? But Das Muni has been here for a long time, and she assures me the bacteria will eventually assimilate with my body. Soon, Das Muni says, the glowing will cease as they are eaten and absorbed by my body. Yet it is disconcerting to wake each morning and see the pulsing green flora swirling up my thigh.

We walk for many cycles. I wake Das Muni when the blue worms begin to glow, and we walk. We say little. As time passes, endless walking through endless semidarkness, my strength begins to grow; at the same time, I feel my sanity begin to waver.

"Surely, you must have found an edge to this place," I say after many cycles.

Das Muni only shakes her head.

It is twenty sleeping periods before we come upon a structure I recognize.

When I see it, I fall to my knees. It's just as Das Muni says. There is no way out.

We have walked and walked, and here we are again, at the little hovel where Das Muni nursed me back to health, not far from the field of horrors where I watched my sisters die. This is the proof. There is no edge.

I make a choking sound. It's a sob. Das Muni comes up beside me and holds my hand, and I wrap my arms around her because not even when I woke up without a memory have I ever felt so lost and alone. Here, Das Muni is the whole world.

"It is not a terrible life," Das Muni says, stroking my hair. "We can live here together. We can—"

"Jayd," I say. "Let's choose a different direction. Tomorrow we go . . . we go . . ." I point ahead of us. We can divide the world into sections and explore each, like slices of a pie. I won't be ruined by this. I won't be put off. There's no alternative to finding a way up. I'm not giving in.

Time becomes meaningless. We go on for seven more periods of slogging through the world, cowering from recycler monsters. I have resolved to step in front of the next monster I see and just offer myself to it.

That is when I see the rope.

It dangles ahead of us like a living thing, a tentacle or tubular growth, and as I approach, I suspect it may be that, too, but it is being used as a rope. I see a stout figure slither down its length. I rub at my eyes, just to be sure, but the figure is still there when I open my eyes.

"Do you see that?" I whisper at Das Muni, but Das Muni is snoozing against a trembling wall of filth. Shattered bones and calcified parts poke through the rotten organic matter, visible now in the swinging blue light of this strange evening in the belly of the world.

I crouch low and keep to the heaps, tracking the figure as it goes from pile to pile. It occasionally raises its head, and when it does, I freeze, hopeful that the shadowy lights will hide me.

When I am within a dozen paces, the figure's face is lit by the swinging overhead lights, and I can verify it is human. The woman's face is clean. She wears neat, whole clothes that appear remarkably wear-free for someone scraping along down here the way Das Muni is.

But in that instant, the woman's gaze meets mine, a clandestine gaze in the wink of the light. Her eyes widen. Then she sprints away, heaving her plump body back toward the ropy tentacle.

I coast across a pile of refuse. I am nearly fully recovered, but most importantly, I know this world very well now, and I navigate the heaped mounds faster than my prey. I snatch at her tunic. Yank her back.

"How did you get in here?" I say.

The squat woman tries to twist away. I throw a punch, but the woman deflects. Scrappy, this one. I grab at her hair, but it's too short to get a proper hold. I kick with my bad leg and connect with the woman's stomach. The woman keels over, but so do I. Pain shoots up my leg, making me stumble.

The woman runs, faster than I thought she could on her muscular little legs.

I give chase; it's a slow chase because we must climb over debris. I stagger after her like a drunk woman. I hear Das Muni yelling behind me, dimly. I'm not going to give this up.

The woman leaps for the tentacle. I leap too. I grab her legs and pull her to the spongy ground.

"All right, stop!" I say. "I'm not going to hurt you."

The woman gapes at me.

"I'm Zan," I say. "This is Das Muni. We only want to get out of here. Up." I point at the rope.

"Casamir," the woman says. "I'm Casamir."

"What are you doing here?" I ask.

"Can ask the same as you," Casamir says. She rubs her leg. "I'm an engineer from Arokisa. Or that's the best translation I can think of." I note her accent and wonder what language is her native one.

"I don't know what an engineer is," I say.

"Yes, well," Casamir says, "the bottom of every world is filled with the castoffs of others. It's how the Legion has lasted so long."

"How do you know about that?"

"Engineers know things.

I lean into her. "You know who I am, then?"

Casamir cocks her head. "No. You've not got a common face."

"Are most faces common?"

"Oh, certainly." Something roars in the distance. Casamir points at the tendril. "I suggest we have this conversation on the next level."

"We can't leave," Das Muni says, coming up behind me.

"Of course you can," Casamir says. "You just have to want to."

"Who's up there?" I ask. "How many people?"

"Just me," Casamir says. "I suspect if you were going to eat me, you'd have done it by now, so I have no reason to lie about some horde of friends. I don't expect to find much alive down here but the monsters, and"—she glances at Das Muni—"the folks that want to stay."

"I need to get up there," I say.

"You hardly look fit for it."

"Then we improvise."

"We?"

"We," I say. "You know the Bhavajas are up there. They're taking over the world."

"The who?

"Bhavajas," I say. "They are usurping the Katazyrnas."

Casamir shrugs. "Sorry."

"How can you not care? They're the people who rule the world."

"Not this part of it," Casamir says. She sighs. "I've met a few people from above Arokisa, sure. Explorers, mostly. I never much cared for them."

"We need to get up there," I say. "Past all those levels. To the surface."

"Surface?" Casamir raises her brows. "Surface of what?"

"The world," I say.

She covers her mouth, as if she's going to laugh. Then sobers. "I'll take you up to Arokisa, at least, on one condition," Casamir says. "Or perhaps two. Well, one for now; maybe if I think on it, I'll find—"

I snatch her by the throat with my good hand. Casamir is a short, thick woman but lighter than she first seems. "How about no conditions," I say.

"Sure, sure, sure," Casamir gasps, kicking her legs.

I drop her. "You go first," I say. "I'll follow."

Casamir lunges for the rope. I grab her collar and pull her back. "We stick close," I say. I untangle the rope I was using as a belt and knot my wrist to Casamir's, leaving enough slack to ensure we can climb up together.

"This really isn't necessary," Casamir says.

"I'll release it when we get up," I say.

Das Muni is puttering around me, humming softly. "I can't get up," she says.

I haven't considered that part until now, and I feel some guilt about that. Of course she can't get up, not with how weak she is; not on those little legs, with her crooked back and clawed hands.

"We'll pull you up after," I say.

She ceases her puttering and gazes up at me with big glassy eyes. I have to look away. She doesn't believe I'll take her with me. She thinks I'll leave her here.

As Casamir grabs hold of the rope, I glance back once at little wretched Das Muni and think about how much easier it will be to go on without her. Casamir is stronger and clearly knows the surface. Das Muni isn't even from this world.

I crawl up after Casamir. The rope is slicker than I anticipated, and I'm not as fit as I imagined. I move painfully, slowly. Casamir has to pause and wait for me. The line between us is stretched taut.

Finally, Casamir takes hold of the lip of the seam in the sky above us and pulls herself over. I get up one more knot, and then my strength gives out. I'm an arm's length from the top. I cling hard to the knotted rope, arms shaking. I take deep breaths, willing my strength to return.

Casamir peers over the top. Her gaze goes from her wrist to mine and the long thread that binds us. If I fall, she will too. She touches the knot at her wrist. I grit my teeth. She'll untie it, and I'll be stuck here, too weak to ascend. I worried she would pull the rope up after her if we weren't bound on the way up, but of course that would mean nothing once we made it to the top. She can cut the line and run off now.

I meet her look and firm my jaw to still my trembling face. My whole body is shaking now. I have an animal fear of showing weakness. But I am weak, and she sees it.

Then she reaches down, and I brace for her to cut the rope or untie us, but she grabs my wrist instead.

"Up, now," she says, and she grins. There's a halo of flickering light above her, whiter light than that below, and I love her a little in that moment, the coy grin, the strong arm, the short, messy sweep of hair brushed back from her forehead, the easy decision to offer a hand instead of cut it off.

I let out my breath and grip her wrist with my bad hand and squeeze. She pulls while I push on the knot below me.

I slide up over the lip of the jagged rent in the floor and try to catch my breath. Casamir slumps beside me. Grins again. I can see the whites of her eyes in the dim glow. For a moment, I think the room is lined in something bioluminescent, like the recycling pit below us, but the lights are moving, flitting along the walls. They are a flying creature of some kind.

Casamir follows my look. "Moths," she says. "There's proper lights farther on. Closer to town. Come up. You'll need to help me get that friend of yours up."

I call down at Das Muni, "Tie yourself up in the end of that rope and hold on! We'll pull you up."

From this height, surrounded in the brighter light of the moths, I can't see Das Muni at all. I squint and ask Casamir, "How do you safely get down there without getting eaten?"

"You just pause along the way," she says. "Let your eyes adjust. Plus, I bring snacks."

"Snacks?"

"For the meaties."

"The meaties? Recycler monsters?"

"Recycler?" Casamir repeats the word a few times, as if trying to get a taste for it. "Yes," she says.

I yell back down at Das Muni, "Are you secure? I can't see you." I tug on the rope and feel resistance. "Das Muni?"

I hear a squeal. I jerk on the rope again. "Help me," I tell Casamir.

She takes the rope behind me, and together we pull. "Das Muni!" I yell.

More squealing. I hear "Meatmoth!"

I pull faster. She isn't heavy, but my muscles are already spent. I hear a roar: the fearful cry of those terrible recycler monsters. My skin prickles.

The pulling takes an age. Das Muni's squealing continues, high and warbling. I can see the top of her head.

I release the rope with my good hand and reach for Das Muni's arm.

She turns her head up to me, and in the light of the moths, I can see her clearly for the first time.

Das Muni's face is flat and angular, and though it is smeared in heavy grit, I can see that her eyes are enormous, twice as large as anyone's I've seen. Her cowl has fallen off her head, and I can see her hair is stringy white, but she is not old. Her skin, though paler than mine and Casamir's, is unmarked. Her ears stick out from her narrow little head like great leaves, nearly as large as her small hands. She is skinny and pallid and clearly unlike anyone else I've seen in this world, even Casamir, who is squat and round and broad in the face, freckled though it is.

I jerk my hand away. It's an unconscious movement, but it happens, and she sees it. Her expression is so sorrowful, my heart clenches. I grab her wrist. I turn my face away from her as she heaves herself up. Casamir helps, and between the two of us, we get her into the corridor.

Another roar sounds from below us. Das Muni grabs me and holds tight. She is a hot, bony mess of a thing and I find myself thinking of insects.

"You're all right," I say, but I can see in her face that she knows I don't believe that.

> "I NEVER THOUGHT I'D NEED ANYONE'S HELP
> TO COMPLETE THE CONVERSION OF THE MOKSHI
> TO A FREE WORLD. BUT INDEPENDENCE IS ONE
> OF THE GREATEST DELUSIONS OF YOUTH."
>
> —LORD MOKSHI, **ANNALS OF THE LEGION**

ZAN

Casamir picks up a lantern from the floor and shakes it. The moths inside flutter, emitting soft light. I see that the lantern is made of bone and organic green mesh.

"This way," Casamir says.

Das Muni and I follow Casamir through the low tunnel.

"It opens up here," Casamir says. "Stay close to me. Stay in the light."

"Why?" I say.

"It's dangerous outside the light," Casamir says.

I move toward her. Das Muni's fingers dig into my flesh. Her nails are long and ragged.

"Creatures?" I say. "Like the monsters down there?"

"Huh?" Casamir says. "No, it's just that the walls aren't as solid in the dark."

"What?" I say, because I think I've misheard her.

"Just stay close," Casamir says.

"Where are you going?" I say. "We need to go up to the next level. I fell a long way. There could be dozens of levels between me and the surface."

"Yes, yes," Casamir says. "Let me take you to the conclave first. They can help."

"I say I need—"

"What you need is the help of the conclave of engineers," Casamir says. "They'll know more about the . . . levels. You put your case to them. They'll listen."

"You won't?"

"Oh, I'm happy to listen," Casamir says. "I love stories."

"You don't believe a word of what I'm saying."

Casamir sighs. She turns, holding the flickering lamp aloft. She is cleaner than Das Muni and me, and now, outside of the recycling pit, I'm becoming aware of my own stink. I see that my hands are filthy, the grime worked into the seams of my skin.

"A lot of people get thrown away," she says, "for whatever reason. Whatever story you need to tell yourself about what happened—"

"There was an attack," I say, "the Bhavajas have taken over the whole world. The Katazyrnas are—"

"I haven't heard of either of those families," Casamir says.

"But the Katazyrnas rule the whole world," I say.

"Not my piece of it," Casamir says, "and not any piece of it I know. We'll get this worked out in the conclave. Are you hungry? I have apples."

"Apples?"

She pulls a spongy tuber from her pocket. It's covered in green cilia. "Delicious," she says. "Try it."

I shake my head, but Das Muni grabs it with both hands. Sniffs. She takes a big bite and chews thoughtfully.

"You know what that is?" I ask.

"No," Das Muni says as she takes a second bite. "But it tastes all right."

Casamir leads us farther down the corridor until it opens up into a vast chamber. I gasp as I look up, not caring what Casamir thinks of that, because the ceiling is webbed in what looks like porous bone carved into intricate triangles. Moisture drips from the ceiling, and the ground below us is covered in a shimmering green carpet. It takes me a moment to realize the carpet is moving. They are shiny insects. Their bodies make a soft shushing sound as they skitter around our feet.

Das Muni hisses and draws away, but Casamir waves her forward. "They're harmless," she says. "Beetles are a good sign. It means the floor is still stable here. That can change. Come on."

We hurry after her. Moths alight on my body. I try to brush them away, but after a while, I give up. There are too many of them.

"What do they eat?" I ask.

"Each other, sometimes," Casamir says. "But mostly the parasites in the walls. And the beetles eat the moths. It's all connected, just like us and the world."

As we continue, I see signs of human habitation. Bony protrusions stick up from the floor, and a long braided hair rope connects them.

Little wooden clackers are attached to the ropes. When a warm, subtle wind rises in the room, the clackers plunk together, sounding an alarm or music or signal, I don't know which.

There are discarded bits of cloth and rotten, ragged mops of woven items, toys or baskets, collecting in long fissures in the walls as we pass.

"What are these?" I ask.

"Memorials," Casamir says.

"Shouldn't it all be recycled?" I say.

"It is," she says. "The walls eat it eventually. You only throw something down the pit that you never want to see again. This way, we have some time, you know?" She glances back at me. "Maybe you don't know. Huh."

"It's just different where I'm from," I say.

"Sure," Casamir says. "We have a ways to go. Why don't you tell me all about it?"

"No," I say.

"No?"

"No."

Das Muni says, "I will tell you where I'm from. I'm not from this world."

"You're just a mutant," Casamir says matter-of-factly. "I think saying you're from another world is a stretch. There are plenty of mutants, you know, people not born right, people the world messed up."

"I *am* from another world."

Casamir shakes her head. "You two are so very interesting. The conclave will love you."

I'm liking the idea of the conclave less and less. "Why don't you just point us in the right direction?" I say. I gaze up again, but the ceiling is higher now, still lined in the same bony pattern. Getting up there on our own is going to be difficult. And then what? Hack our way through? Burn our way up?

Casamir chuckles and shakes her head. "I am offering a hand in friendship," she says. "You should take it."

"No one offers a hand without wanting it filled with something," I say.

Casamir does not reply. We arrive at a wall of debris blocking our way. It looks like the ceiling above collapsed; I'm staring at long planes of the bony ceiling, twisted and broken and gooey. The pieces have fused together like a healing wound, leaving behind great puckered scars along the surfaces where the pieces meet.

Casamir pulls a bone knife from her hip and pricks her finger. She draws three curved lines on the surface of the scar.

I wonder if it's an offering or a ritual as the face of the debris begins to bubble and slough away. A thick wedge of the skin pops open, and there's a woman with a tangle of dark, braided hair who holds it open for us. She squints at Casamir, then sizes up me and Das Muni.

"More filth," she says, and ducks away, leaving the door open.

"Lovely to see you again too, Andamis!" Casamir says, and waves us inside.

A wave of heat and sound rolls over me as I cross the threshold. I come up short, so quickly Das Muni bumps into me. I hear her sharp intake of breath.

Sweeping up and out for as far and high as I can see is a vast, bustling city. It's a riotous mass of humanity; women clustered together over trading tables and walking across a complicated network of bone and sinew bridges that crisscross the space above us. Lining the walls are living spaces and workshops, their residents clustered on the walkways outside their domiciles, hanging laundry and whistling after little clusters of creatures. There are at least a dozen types of animals here, some knee-high and hairy with one big eye at the center of their heads. Another is hairless, mostly mouth and teeth, and a school of them waddles awkwardly ahead of a woman herding them with a long reed. The ground should be smeared in filth from all these creatures inhabiting one space, but when I look down, the floor isn't slick; it's lined in little fleshy nubs, like a tongue, and its absorbing everything the city feeds it.

"Welcome to Amaris, City of Light," Casamir says.

A light drizzle is falling. I hold up my hand and rub a bit of it between my fingers. It's viscous, like mucus or saliva. "What is that?" I say.

Casamir laughs. "Rain," she says. "Have you never seen rain? Goodness, you are far gone. You must have been down there even longer than I thought. Your sanity probably isn't salvageable."

I gaze into the darkness above us. "Water?"

"Mostly," she says. "It's good for you. Good bacteria for your gut. Only way to make it here." She pushes ahead.

But it is the light that is most extraordinary. The light and the heat. The moths line the bridges, the byways, the tables. They flutter onto the intricately styled hair of the women here, all of it braided and stacked so it looks like they're wearing great hats. Above us float great balloons. They are attached to long ropes, and they ferry passengers across the upper levels of the city in baskets. Yet most of the light and heat come from great round bulbs, large as heads, mounted along the walkways and in front of every dwelling. They are filled with clear liquid, and inside swim tiny orange beasts with delicate tentacles. There are hundreds, maybe thousands, inside each sphere, and they emit both heat and a brilliant orange light.

I stare long at one as we pass, leaning in for a better look, and Das Muni tugs at my sleeve.

"Don't look too close," she whispers. "The light will steal your soul."

We get a few curious looks. Das Muni raises her cowl again, and I don't blame her. I wish I had one. The crowd babbles as we pass, speaking a language I don't recognize. I glance ahead at Casamir. She is a solid woman but nimble on her feet, and she clearly knows this place well. The crowds don't part for her so much as they resign themselves to her momentum.

Casamir takes us up a series of bone steps, then across one of the swaying bridges. Das Muni refuses to cross it unless I hold her hand, and being hungry and yearning for a bath, I sigh and take her greasy palm in mine. She is trembling. I glance over at her but cannot see her expression inside the deep hood.

"See what I've got!" Casamir says, calling into the doorway of one of the houses. I call it a doorway, but there's no actual door, just the opening. I wonder how anyone has privacy here, but as we enter, I realize the first room is just a sitting area. There's another opening on the opposite side of the room that leads deeper into the dwelling.

"Wait here," Casamir says, and she takes this door while Das Muni and I wait in the outer room.

"This is a bad idea," Das Muni whispers. "Too many people."

"Better than Meatmoth," I say.

"No," she says. "I understand Meatmoth. How she breathes. How she walks. Her hungers. Here . . . people are complicated. People don't act in normal ways."

I look for a place to sit. My leg is bothering me again. There are benches carved into the wall, made of the same spongy stuff as the rest of the world. I sit and stretch my leg out. "We'll see how it goes," I say. "We can always leave."

"Not always," Das Muni says.

I hear raised voices in the rooms behind us. Casamir's optimism about our reception may have been premature.

"All I want is a bath," I mutter.

"I can lick you clean," Das Muni says.

I stare hard at her, trying to figure out if she's serious. Talking to her is like listening to broken pieces of my own memory tangling together. If Casamir weren't here to confirm that Das Muni is real, I might think I'd made her up entirely.

Casamir hustles out of the back room, arms wide. "We can't stay here," she says quickly. "I'll take you to the holding rooms until the conclave can see you."

"If they don't want us here," I say, "I'm happy to go. Das Muni and I can find our own way up."

"No, no," Casamir says. "This is very important. I promise, just have some patience. You're hungry, aren't you? How about we get you cleaned up? We can get you some new clothes."

We walk back down to the main floor, past trading shops and clusters of women boiling and steaming and weaving and sewing various bits of the world and its castoffs. Most people share Casamir's squat build, but there are some taller, thinner people with different clothing and hairstyles, and it occurs to me this must be some kind of trading hub.

"You sell what you find below?" I say. "You're scavengers?"

"Explorers," Casamir says. "I'm among the best."

Two women stand outside what I finally recognize as a door. It's not a fleshy door, though, but metal. I peer at it, as it's the first metal I've seen here. It surprises me that I know the word for something I have yet to see, but there it is in my memory. Cold, hard stuff, inert, nonsentient.

Casamir grins at the women and rattles something off in another language, the same one I've been hearing bits and pieces of as we walk.

The women argue with her. Their expressions are grim. But Casamir continues, spreading her hands wide, grinning all the while, shifting from foot to foot. Something she says convinces them, and they grudgingly grip the large handles on the door and pull it open. There is a terrible shriek, and then it slides into the wall.

I can't decide if behind every door is a new wonder or a new horror in this place. Perhaps both. The skin of the walls inside here is scorched and peeled back to reveal more metal walls and tables and compartments. There are dozens of women in here wearing long aprons who tend tables chock-full of artifacts. The material here is more clearly nonorganic. Not all of it is metal, though. It's hard, slick material, like bone, only less porous. They are constructing strange things with all of these things, stringing bits together with tendons and grafts of human skin. Whatever they are making in here, it makes my own skin crawl.

"What is this?" I ask Casamir.

She waves to some of the women, calling greetings in that other language. "We're engineers," she says. "I told you I was an engineer. Well, training to be one, anyway."

"What language is everyone speaking?"

"Oh, it's the human language."

"But . . . we're speaking human right now. All languages are human."

Casamir laughs. "Some languages are more human than others," she says. "We trade a lot with other people, so I know, I don't know, a couple dozen languages."

"A couple . . . dozen? How many people are here?"

"Lots," Casamir says.

As we move to the back of the room, I see great bone cages full of people. I recoil. They are heavily disfigured, naked. One is completely blind, both her eyes gouged out.

Das Muni shrieks when she sees them.

"Oh, that's nothing," Casamir says. "Those are enemies of the conclave. It's all right."

One of the women in the cage snatches my sleeve. I try to jerk away, but her grip is strong. Her face is a map of wrinkles. Her thinning hair has been shorn short. She has only one arm, and one of her feet is missing.

"I remember you," she says. "You destroyed everything I love."

I get my sleeve free. "Who are you?" I say.

Casamir pulls me away. "Oh, that's nothing. They're nothing. They just speak nonsense. They're mad. Don't worry about them."

"Where did they come from?" I ask.

"Here and there," Casamir says. "Here's your holding room."

She pushes a bony protrusion, and a door blooms open. I find myself relieved to see something that reminds me of the world above.

Inside are two raised platforms, some folded woven blankets, and what's likely a waste receptacle. I step inside and turn to ask if I can have a bath, but the door is already closing.

"No!" Das Muni says, and hurls herself at the door as it huffs closed.

I think of the workshops and skin and tendons outside and my stomach sinks. It may not be a cage of bone, but it is still a cage. This is what happens when you trust people. More the fool, me. I should have learned better from the Bhavajas and their sick cunning. This is a place where you eat or you are eaten.

Das Muni slumps in a corner.

I search the room, trying to get a better handle on it. There are no openings. One of the spidery water bulbs is affixed to a pillar at the far corner of the room, giving out heat and light. I contemplate breaking it open just to drink the water. If it's really water.

Testing the various growths and protrusions from the wall turns up a water sluice, which spills water into a shallow, crescent-shaped bowl against the far wall. I drink my fill, disrobe, and wash. The water is cold, but the room is warm, and the floor eats the damp as I pour it over my neck and shoulders.

"You thirsty?" I ask Das Muni. As I turn, I see she has been watching me wash. She lowers her gaze. Nods.

I towel myself off with one of the blankets. It's made of plant fibers. I still haven't seen any plants. I rinse off my suit, which dries quickly and doesn't soak up muck. When I dress now, the only things that still stink are my hair and Das Muni, but I can deal with that.

I pull at the blanket and rip off a long length of it. I twist it in my hands and test its strength. I remember what I did to those tongueless women. I am capable of great violence if pushed. Casamir and her people will soon see it.

Das Muni drinks from the basin and washes her face. Then we both sit and wait. I lie back on the bench, contemplating the play of the light on the fleshy ceiling. I play with the length of blanket, imagining wringing Casamir's throat with it. I think this idea should make me happy, but it doesn't. I want to believe the world is better than it is.

The door opens some time later. It's not Casamir but the same two guards we saw at the door to the engineering room. "The conclave will see you now," the tallest one says.

"Where's Casamir?" I ask, stuffing my improvised garrote into my pocket.

"She's there already," her shorter, thinner companion says. She picks at her teeth.

I keep my hands out of my pockets as we're led back out into the engineering room, which is now eerily empty. They take us up a set of tall, broad steps that lead into a massive theater. All of the engineers are here, sitting in the broad half-circle of the amphitheater. Six women reside at a broad table on the stage below. Casamir stands in front of them, gazing back at us as we enter. Her face is more serious than I've yet seen it. She looks even more frightened than when I threatened her in the recycling pits, but when I catch her eye, she gives a broad grin.

Our guards hustle us down the steps of the amphitheater and tell us to halt beside Casamir. Now I put my hand in my pocket, the one with the garrote, and I wait.

"Casamir tells us you speak Handavi," a plump, wizened woman says from the center of the table. Her hair is arranged in a spiky crown. She wears a red woven tunic and blue apron. Her hands are stained in grease.

"If that's what you call what we're speaking, then yes," I say.

Das Muni grumbles something.

"And you say you come from the top of the world," the woman says.

"I do," I say. "There is a war above, on the surface of the world, between us and another world like ours. It's between the Bhavajas and the Katazyrnas. My sisters and I were recycled."

There's a murmur in the crowd behind me.

A skinny woman, closer to my age, points a bony finger at me and snorts. "This is clearly a case of delusion," she says.

"There are other levels," Casamir says. "We have seen many of them and met many different kinds of people. It may not be . . . so incredible. Perhaps this is just how her broken mind put together what happened to her."

"None like she states," the older woman says.

I finger the garrote and consider taking Casamir hostage and fighting my way out. It will get messy. I try a different tack. "You're traders," I say. "If you help me get back to my own level, I can open up a new trade route for you. We have all sorts of wonders," I say. "Clothing that you can spray on, durable, like mine." I smooth a hand over my sleeve. "We have sentient vehicles"—well, they won't be going out into the vacuum, will they—"that can help you haul things. We have different kinds of foods and materials." From the looks on their faces, they still aren't convinced. I reach. "We have many different kinds of metals," I lie, because the most metal I've ever seen on the first level was on Anat's arm. "In browns and golds and grays. You can build a great many things with what we have to offer."

That rouses the crowd. The women at the table confer with one another in their own language. The plump older woman leans forward. "And if you are mad?"

"If I'm just some mad person, then what have you lost in helping me?" I say. "Casamir is precocious. She is a thrill-seeker, trouble. What do you lose by letting her guide us if that is what you want? You'll keep her busy and out of your hair. You lose nothing."

Casamir raises her brows at me, but says nothing.

"How will we bind her to her word?" the skinny woman says. "If you are telling the truth, and you arrive back to this . . . level of yours, then what's to keep you bound to your word?"

I shrug. "You'll have to trust me."

She snorts. "Trust? No. I say we bind her blood."

More murmurs from the crowd. I look at Casamir.

"I'm not sure that's necessary," Casamir says.

"What is that?" I say.

"They cut out a piece of your flesh," Casamir says, "and . . . make stuff out of it."

"Like what?" I ask.

Casamir shakes her head. "You don't want to know."

"Well, I won't have to," I say. "I'll keep my promise. If you can get me to the surface, I'm happy to trade with your people. But we need to get there." I pause and meet the gaze of every woman on the stage. "Safely."

They confer again. The crowd, too, shifts to low conversation, and I try to gauge the mood. Casamir doesn't look at me. I tighten my grip on the garrote.

Das Muni takes my arm. "Not yet," she says. "Not yet."

We wait. I take a long look at the ceiling and glance back at our escape route up the amphitheater. Casamir may not be the best hostage to take. I'll need one of the elders, the council. The skinny one, preferably. That will feel most satisfying. I play it out. Six steps to the table. The garrote, the threat, the hustling up the stairs . . . The metal door will be a problem, but if they care enough about this little council . . .

"We agree to your terms," the skinny woman says.

I startle out of my plan, a little shocked.

Casamir grins. Raises a fist. "Oh, you will not regret this," she says. "My first mission!"

"Let's hope it's not your last," says the plump woman. "Take her to the butchers to harvest her flesh. You are permitted the standard supplies. Go."

Leaving the amphitheater is a bit of a haze. I'm still half-stuck in the other reality, the one where I have to fight my way out. Casamir takes me to an efficient, clinical little room with a woman and a large bone scalpel.

"Where do you want me to take it from?" she asks, and I honestly have no idea. I stare at the heft of my body and wonder just how much flesh I have to spare. Who wants to sacrifice the bulk that gives them strength and presence?

"My thigh?" I say, and before I have time to reconsider, she's sliced fast and deep, two cuts.

I yell, and two more women come in and restrain me while she carves out a fist-sized lump of flesh from my thigh and plops it into a clear container.

She stuffs the wound full of a sweet-smelling compress that's clearly crawling with worms or parasites, and tells me to hold still as she wraps my wounded thigh. I curse because she's cut my good leg. Why didn't she go for the other one?

The compress stifles the pain, though, enough for me to stand and yell at Casamir, "What is that for? What's the point of that?"

"Don't worry about it," Casamir says. "You're keeping your promise, right? So, it's not important."

I want to get out of here as quickly as possible now, fearful that the council will change their mind. Casamir wants to linger and chatter with friends about the trial, because really, that's what it is, but I hound her onward. We collect supplies from a woman in the engineering room. I'm starving, weak with hunger, but I don't even want to stop to eat.

I limp beside Casamir as we push back out across the big traders' hall, heading back for the main entrance while people glide above us in their balloon baskets.

"I need to say good-bye to my family," Casamir says. "Just a moment! I'll only be a moment!" Casamir bounds for the stairs.

I sigh and wait with Das Muni, trying to stay out of the way of the women passing by us. Their stares are more open now. A few try to ask me something, but it's in their language, and I just shake my head and frown.

Das Muni leans into me. "We should just go," she says. "Let's not wait for Casamir."

"Stop that," I say. "That conversation is over. Casamir knows this area better than we do."

"You have given them flesh," she says. "You shouldn't have done that."

"The alternative is killing all of them. Would that have been better?"

"Yes," Das Muni says. She leans her head against me.

Casamir returns, more somber now.

I nearly ask her how things went with her family but decide I don't care to know. We aren't going to travel long together, just to the next level. I'll need to find more help after that. Best not to get attached.

But Casamir volunteers the information, as Casamir seems to volunteer everything I don't want to know. "They think me foolish," she says, "but that's no surprise. They think I'm reaching too high, but I'm here to be an engineer, not some recycler. Engineers must go on missions."

"Then let's do that," I say, and I take her arm and hustle her to the door because both my legs are throbbing now, and I'm not sure how much longer I can take being in this crowded place that now owns a piece of my flesh.

We exit the compound and step back into the relative dim of the outer corridor. I blink as my eyes adjust. Moths descend, covering my arms and hair. I brush them away.

"Lead the way, engineer," I say, and that brings a smile from Casamir.

"I will indeed," she says, and forges ahead.

I'll need to eat soon, but not yet, not until we put a lot of distance behind us.

"What's between us and the next level?" I ask as we trudge along. Das Muni trails far behind.

"Oh, I don't know," Casamir says. She unrolls something from her bag. It's a map written on human skin.

"What do you mean, you don't know?" I say.

"Well, I know what the map says."

I grab her shoulder. We halt. "Are you telling me you've never been to another level?"

She holds up the map. "It's all fine! I have the traders' maps." She squints at it. "According to this, there are some pits, a mountain range, some monster herds, and a couple tribes of mutants. It will be fine! A fine adventure!"

"You're joking," I say.

She shows her teeth. "Fine!" she says, and continues on her way.

I stare after her, shocked, long enough for Das Muni to catch up with me. As Das Muni passes me, she sighs and says, "I told you so."

"I LEARNED DECEPTION FROM MY MOTHER,
BUT IT WAS THE WORLD THAT TAUGHT ME
THE NECESSITY OF DECEPTION FOR SURVIVAL.
WHEN THE OTHER WORLDS CAME FOR THE MOKSHI,
I WAS PREPARED FOR THE FIGHT."
—LORD MOKSHI, ANNALS OF THE LEGION

20

JAYD

always suspect a trap, because I have been plotting traps for my own family my entire life. Nashatra seems sincere, but I put her off. I plead ignorance of such terrible schemes and say that I love Rasida. She clearly doesn't believe me, but if this is some trick she's playing on me, I'm not going to walk right into it.

Instead, I go back to my rooms and consider what I know. The people here seem to love Rasida, even if her family doesn't. If they *are* her real family. And of course, I haven't considered what family means here, and how it differs from Katazyrna. Anat raised us, but she did not birth us. She chose us from the children of the women who could bear them. I was raised with Nhim and Neith and Maibe and a dozen others, now dead. Suld and Prisha were much older than me, raised with another group, then Anka and Aiju, who were half a dozen rotations younger than me. The numbers of daughters in each age group were fewer each time. Anat liked to think that raising armies was easy, but the more she did it, the deeper into the world and across the Legion she had to go to get them, and the stranger and less malleable to her whims they were. We had child-bearers on Katazyrna several rotations before Zan joined us, but most have died out. I often suspect that was Anat's whim more than the world's, because as long as she had child-bearers who were native to Katazyrna, she always had a rival for power.

When I am taken to dinners with Rasida, I spend a great deal of time analyzing the corridors, the steps, the great peeling hunks of the walls that reveal shiny metal beneath. As the world rotted around them, the Bhavajas had no choice but to mix with all the levels. Anyone could be a Bhavaja here. Rasida was not as hierarchical as Anat. Blood was blood. Perhaps that's why it was so easy for her to proclaim that I was Bhavaja now and to have some of her people, at least, accept that.

As my pregnancy proceeds, Rasida seems to grow more distant. I try affection, though it pains me to attempt it, and she turns me away. This is something Zan could never pretend at, this affection. But I am a great pretender, sometimes so good at it that I convince myself that what I pretend is what is truly real.

"You must want me," she says. "I don't desire a thing which has no love for me. It's easy to force affection. Far more difficult to entice it."

"I do love you," I say, but even to my own ears, I am unconvincing.

"You don't," she says. She pulls my hands from her throat, and I think about how easy it would be to turn my caress into a strangle. Perhaps that's what she's thinking, too.

We are having dinner in her rooms again. The wardrobe is open; the green glow of the iron arm beckons to me from the darkness. I go back to my seat. Rasida has poured wine, but I haven't had any since the night of my joining, when I became too sick or drugged to remember anything.

"You don't want me anymore?" I say. "You only want the thing in my belly?"

"I can have anyone I want," Rasida says. "I can have the whole Legion, can't I? They bow and prostrate themselves; they tear off their clothes and beg for my favors. But that is not wanting."

"We fucked here in this room," I say, "under false pretenses." I do not make my hands into fists. I eat instead, but it's painful to pretend at decorum. I try to imagine Zan doing this without severing Rasida's head, and fail. Zan has a temper. I do too, but I have become far better at moderating it than Zan. I have the patience she does not. Which is why I'm here and she isn't.

"Whose false pretenses, though?" Rasida says. "I've told you, I never lied to you. The truce was never with you. It was with Anat. I never told you I wouldn't take the Legion."

"You can't say you love someone and then murder their family," I say. I sip my drink, my expression perfectly blank. I admire my own calm. I'm not even drunk.

"Why not?" she says, and her tone is not mocking. It sounds like a genuine question. "You didn't love your family. You loved belonging, perhaps, to something greater than yourself. But you hated Anat. You've hated her since you were a child."

"Every daughter despises her mother," I say.

"I love my mother very much," Rasida says. "She knows her place here. She performs her function well."

"I don't know why," I say. "You treat your family the way Anat treated me."

Rasida jerks out of her seat.

I start and scramble back. I'm moving more slowly than I'd like; my body is changing with the pregnancy, ungainly and sluggish.

But Rasida does not hit me. She goes to the wardrobe and pulls out the iron arm again. She throws it at my feet.

"Put it on," she says.

"I . . . can't," I say.

"Why? You are Katazyrna. It will fit you, surely."

I hold out my left arm. "It won't fit," I say. "It's not mine."

"It wasn't Anat's either," Rasida says, and I wonder at this turn in the conversation. "She had cut her arm up so it would fit in there. Whose arm was this, Jayd? What world did it come from?"

"I don't know," I say, "Anat has always had it." I snap my mouth shut, but it's too late. Rasida has seen Anat many times. She knows when Anat acquired the arm, not long before Zan joined us.

Rasida meets my gaze, and we acknowledge the lie with that one look.

"I'm sorry," I say.

"The time for lying is over," she says.

"The witches," I say, and maybe I hope that saying this so quickly, so immediately after she says the lying is over, means that she won't know that this, too, is a lie. "The witches know how it works. They gifted it to Anat. It's something very old. That's all I know. If you can find the Katazyrna witches, they could tell you."

"You could have said this before," she says.

"Maybe I feared what you would do with the arm," I say. In truth, I know what she could do with the arm, and it's not what she thinks. It's far worse than that. It would undo everything I'm trying to achieve here. The longer I can keep her from putting it on, the longer I have to find out how to steal the world, too.

"There are people here on my own world who would betray me," Rasida says, "the way you betrayed Anat."

"I didn't betray—"

"I know who Zan was, Jayd. I'm not the fool you think I am."

"No one knows who Zan is," I sputter. "Not even Zan."

"I know what you did to the Mokshi. You think I don't have spies inside Katazyrna?"

"I've never thought you a fool." Even if it was true, if she did know who Zan was, when even Anat had never intuited it, what did it matter now? Let her think Zan was a construct, something I cobbled together from bits of other women, or the spirit of some general, plopped into the body of one of my own sisters. But she mentioned the Mokshi in the same breath as Zan, and that made me fearful.

"I want you to know what happens to people who betray me," Rasida says.

"I didn't betray—"

"Not you," she says. "Not yet."

Relief floods through me. "Your people love you, Rasida. I have seen their eyes when they look at you. Why do you fear?"

"Because you are new here," Rasida says, "and everyone will try to turn you against me. We can't have that. We must cut the cancer out now, before it's too late."

She leaves the arm on the ground and goes to the door. She summons Samdi and two more security personnel.

Together, the five of us walk in silence. Rasida and I are side by side, following Samdi as the security people come up behind.

I map out the route we take in my mind, counting steps and turns. In bed, with the covers pulled up over my head, I will often retrace my mental map of Bhavaja, storing it for the day when I will need to leave this place quickly. The day I have the arm and the world.

We come through a broad corridor and into a holding room. I am not surprised to see Nashatra there, standing next to one of Rasida's sisters, Aditva.

"This is not necessary," Nashatra says when Rasida comes in.

Nashatra does not look at me. I keep my gaze focused just above Aditva's head, trying to pretend I know nothing of any of this.

Rasida takes Aditva by the shoulder. I tense.

"Tell me what you planned," Rasida says to Aditva.

Aditva begins to cry.

"Please, Rasida," Nashatra says. "I know you are displeased, but—"

"You know what we do to traitors, Mother," Rasida says.

"I know," Nashatra says again.

"The Legion is my sister," Rasida says. "We are all sisters. That means nothing when survival is at stake."

It's only now that I notice the black, gaping wound on the far wall. Its edges are dry and puckered, but I recognize it for what it once must have looked like. It's a recycling chute.

She's going to recycle her own mother. "Is this necessary?" I ask, because though I have no love for Nashatra, I fear that if she is gone, there will be no one to counter Rasida. If Nashatra is planning a coup, she may help me get what I need from Rasida in exchange for my help. The long game. I have always been good at the long game. It's another reason it had to be me here and not Zan. She understands vehicles and genetics and gooey organic sludge, but not people.

"Of course it is," Rasida says.

"But—" I say.

"Let it lie," Nashatra says, and meets my look.

I stare at her feet. Bite my tongue. If I reveal myself, then we are both done. If I—

"Stand, Aditva, and tell my consort what you did," Rasida says.

Aditva?

Aditva stands. She is a short, skinny woman, all knees and elbows. Her face is long and pained, her hair stringy and unwashed. I wonder how long she has been here.

"Tell her," Rasida says softly. She begins stroking Aditva's lank hair.

"I betrayed you, Lord," Aditva says. She begins to sob. "I am sorry, Lord. I was weak. The Lord of War—"

"Do not blame your foolishness on the Lord of War," Rasida says. "You tried to foment rebellion, is that right? An uprising. But an uprising of who, and to what? There is nowhere to go, Aditva. If you had truly listened to the Lord of War, she would have told you all this and much more, the way she spoke to me. She has whispered to me of the only way to save our people, and it is to work together to unite the Legion. It's the only way. You didn't want to unite us. You wanted to overthrow me and divide us."

"Yes, Lord," Aditva says.

I am staring at Aditva's bare, callused feet now. I don't want to see Nashatra's face. I fear that I will give her and myself away. Why should I feel guilt now, when this is not my family? When I declined Nashatra's offer? It could very well be me here, barefoot and filthy. The next time, it very well might be. What will happen then? Will

Nashatra speak for me, or let me be recycled as she is letting her own daughter be recycled?

Rasida makes little shushing sounds and draws Aditva into her arms. Aditva embraces her and continues sobbing, great heaving gasps that wrack her little body. As she grips Rasida, I see two fist-sized lumps on the back of her neck, most likely cancer, and I wonder how long she has been sick.

While Rasida comforts her sister with one hand, she moves the other to her waist and the long bone knife she keeps there. I could call out. I could, like Nashatra, beg Rasida to spare this woman, her own sister.

But I don't. I put my hands over my belly instead, and I watch as Rasida plunges the knife into Aditva's armpit. Once. Twice. A third time.

Aditva crumples.

Rasida lifts her up as blood pumps from Aditva's armpit. Rasida's expression is sad, almost kind, as if she is doing Aditva some great favor. Then she dumps Aditva into the black maw of the recycling chute.

Aditva cries out once. Then silence.

Rasida stares into the blackness.

It is only now, with Rasida's back turned, that I dare to gaze into Nashatra's face.

She signs something at me. It takes me a moment to understand it, because she's using an alternate sign language, not the Katazyrna one, but the more general one we use among worlds on the Outer Rim. She signs, "Who is your master?"

I sign back, "I am my own master."

And Rasida turns. "This is what I did to Zan," she says, "your prisoner who is not a prisoner. If you cannot love me, if you lie to me, if you betray me, you will end up here, like Aditva. Like Zan."

She means this to be a warning. It's meant to break me or perhaps Nashatra. But like Nashatra, I am not bowed. Though I cannot smile for fear of giving myself away, hope blooms in my belly in a way I have not felt since hearing that Rasida had destroyed Katazyrna. Hope blooms because I know this means it's possible that Zan is still alive. Zan has crawled up from the belly of the world before. Zan has survived it once. She can do it again. Zan will come back for me. She always comes back for me.

Nashatra sighs. "Is there anything else, Lord?" she says.

"Yes," Rasida says. "Samdi, take Mother to the witches."

"The witches?" Nashatra says. "What—"

"I heard you wanted to save the world," Rasida says, "so I decided to help you do that."

"What? No, I—"

Samdi takes Nashatra by the arm. The other security women help her, and they escort Nashatra out of the room.

"What will you do to her?" I ask.

"What do you care?" Rasida says.

"You're my family now," I say. "She's my mother too."

Rasida wipes her bloody bone knife on her tunic and sheathes it. "Walk with me, love," she says, and holds out her bloody hand.

I take it.

We walk back to my quarters. I see a familiar corridor along this route. It's the same corridor I first came down, the one leading back to the hangar. I make a note of that and count the steps back to my rooms. I'd been a fool not to do this when I first came in, but I hadn't been expecting Rasida's betrayal. I thought I had this whole situation well in hand. But I had spent so much time trying to understand Anat that I never considered what would happen with Rasida.

Rasida sits on the edge of my bed and pulls me gently down next to her. She smooths my hair from my face. "Was that enough?" she says.

"Enough for what?" I say.

"Enough to dissuade you from what you're planning."

"I don't know what you're talking about. This is my home now."

"Yes," Rasida says. "We must make sure you stay here."

"What do you mean?" My voice comes out a whisper.

"Shhhhh . . . ," she says.

There is something in her hand. It's the bone knife.

I leap up from the bed. I make it three steps. I grab the edge of the doorway.

I feel a hot, burning pain across the back of my right knee. I stumble and fall heavily onto my side, screaming.

Rasida leers over me. She wipes her bloody dagger on my shoulder. Kneels beside me. "You will be better now," she says. "Clearer-headed. Pain does that. There will be no running, love, because you have nowhere to go. Do you understand?"

She's cut the tendon in my leg. I don't want to understand. I don't want it to be true.

When I have the arm and the world, I will have to leave quickly. And now she has hobbled me.

"I hate you," I say. "I've always hated you."

"I know," Rasida says, "I know. It's why we are so perfect together." She wipes the blade of her knife on her knee. "You'll feel better in the morning."

"TO ESCAPE THE LEGION, YOU MUST FIRST
UNDERSTAND WHAT IT IS. MY MISTAKE WAS IN ASSUMING
I UNDERSTOOD HOW THE WORLDS WORKED."
—LORD MOKSHI, ANNALS OF THE LEGION

21

ZAN

We scale a range of mountains built of human bones. Mostly human, anyway. I can see as we struggle over the piles, all soldered together with some calcified substance, that some of the skulls are too big, the pelvises too wide, to be fully human. I don't know whose graveyard this is, then. Everyone's, I suppose. Everything's.

Time is impossible to measure at the bottom of the world. After a few sleeping periods, the moths become less and less, and are replaced by skittering beetles with great glowing abdomens. Sometimes we exist in complete darkness, and Casamir brings out a small, portable version of the tentacle globes, which she simply calls a torch.

The way would be grim and quiet if it were just Das Muni and I, but Casamir chatters ceaselessly. When we camp, Casamir tells stories, most of which make little sense to me. As we bed down for what must be our thirteenth or fourteenth time, Casamir tells a long and involved story about a woman with a cog that defecates in her hat each morning. I only half pay attention to it as I eat the tepid stew she's mixed up for us from her pack.

Casamir ends her story with "And that's why they call her Lord Knots!" She slaps her knee and guffaws.

I shake my head. "I don't understand," I say.

"It's a joke," Casamir says. "Because of science."

"I see," I say.

"I'm very funny," Casamir says. "Everyone loves that joke. Let me tell it again. Maybe you missed the middle. This woman—"

"That's all right," I say.

Das Muni mumbles something about defecating scientists and wanders off to, I presume, defecate.

I watch Casamir hum to herself as she eats.

"Do you believe me," I say, "that I'm from the surface?"

"Oh, sure," Casamir says.

"That means no."

Casamir shrugs. "What is reality, anyway? Reality is something we make with our minds. Yours exists as certainly as mine."

"You think I'm insane," I say.

"Oh, no," Casamir says. "Just mentally delusional. It's all right. Very common. Especially among those who've been discarded by their people."

"So, you agree there are upper levels?"

"I agree there are *different* levels," Casamir says.

"How diplomatic," I say.

Casamir covers her mouth with her hand, failing to hide a smirk.

"I'm an experiment, then?" I say. "Let me tell you something, Casamir. I'm tired of being somebody's experiment."

"Sorry," Casamir says. "It isn't like that, though. I can't become an engineer without going on this journey. Every engineer has to go up a level, has to explore. I'm tired of the pits. They always get tired of me talking and send me to the pits. Can't be an engineer unless you fight for it."

"How do you prove you got to another level?"

"I have to bring something back," she says. "There's . . ." She unrolls the map from her pack and spreads it out in the light of the torch. "There's a gateway, here," she says, pointing.

"Where are we?"

"Almost there," she says. "Another hundred thousand steps, maybe. Five sleeping periods, give or take."

"You say there were mutant hordes."

"Oh, that. Yes," she says. She rolls the map up again. "We may encounter them in the next twenty or thirty thousand steps. We'll need to keep a lookout."

"Did you bring weapons?"

"I have my knife," she says. I've seen her knife: a sharpened tibia.

"Are they dangerous, the mutants?"

"Sometimes," she says. "Mostly, they keep back from the light. We just need to stick close when we're walking the next few periods. It shouldn't be too bad."

But she isn't looking at me when she says it.

I don't sleep well. I toss and turn at every sound. The spaces here are so vast that we cannot huddle against the walls, so we sleep at the foot of the bone mountains, and the bones creak and clatter as small animals and insects scurry around inside of them. I wake twice with black, palm-sized insects sitting on my chest, and I bat them away and stab them with the tibia that I'm using as a walking stick.

When Casamir shakes me to get me up, I'm already awake, exhausted and irritable.

I follow Casamir's bobbing light as we come to the end of the bone mountains. She raises it as high as she can, and I see mounds of fleshy protuberances, some two stories high, riddled with a patchwork of holes and burrows big as my head.

I don't have to ask what lives in there, because I can see the shiny glint of their six eyes reflected back at us from the burrows. Whatever they are, they do not like the light.

Casamir smiles back at me nervously. "Onward, and all that," she says.

We move cautiously across the pitted ground. It's as if something has eaten away at the floor. I'm reminded of what Casamir had told us closer to the city, about how the walls and floors were permeable outside of the light.

There's skittering along the edges of our pool of light, and Casamir freezes.

I come up behind Casamir. Das Muni bumps into me. She grabs at the back of my suit.

"Keep going," I say.

"I just . . . maybe . . . ," Casamir says.

I step ahead of her, to the edge of the circle of light. "There's no option where I go back," I say. I think of Jayd and all I haven't yet told Casamir, or Das Muni. "There's a whole world at stake up there."

"Not my world," Casamir says.

"Your world," I say. "Come on."

Casamir inches forward. She moves the torch to her other hand and drops it. She says something in her language, probably swearing, and runs after the torch as it rolls away toward a depression in the floor.

I scramble after it as well. I lunge, too late, as it rolls into the hole, plunging us into darkness.

A hooting sound comes from all around us. One voice and then others.

I reach into the hole. My fingers brush the end of the torch, but I'm too big to get any farther.

"Cas," I say.

She's next to me, burrowing her head inside. "My arms aren't long enough!" she says.

"Let me," Das Muni says softly.

The skittering sounds grow closer. I feel the hush of breath against my ankles and kick out but don't make contact with anything.

Das Muni presses herself next to me. She crawls down after the torch. I keep hold of her legs, fearful about some creature pulling her down.

"Ouch!" Casamir says. "Something bit me!"

The hooting is a storm now; it reverberates. I want to cover my ears.

"I have it!" Das Muni says. "I have it." I pull her back up. She raises the globe, and I see that her eyes are broad and bright and there is something like triumph on her face. But as she turns and looks behind me, the expression turns to fear.

Casamir is tangled in crystalline webbing swarming with bulbous, multi-segmented beasts. They each have a dozen legs that look like long, clawed fingers lined in black hair. Their faces are fanged, lined in six eyes and hundreds of little feathery antennae.

I pull up my walking stick and swing at the webbing. "Bring the light!" I tell Das Muni, but she is frozen in shock, mouth agape.

I plunge ahead, striking at the creatures. They burst when my stick makes contact, splattering yellow guts across my face. I try to pull the webbing off Casamir. The insects turn their attention to me. I feel their feathered antennae brush my ankles.

"The light! Das Muni!" I say.

I stab and swing. Yellow gore covers my face, my hands, smears the front of my suit. They're crawling up my arms now. Pinching. Biting. I tear again at the webbing binding Casamir. She is so stuck now that she has ceased to struggle. She is screaming at me, but I don't know what she's saying because my feet are tangled in the webbing and I'm starting to panic.

"Das Muni!" I try to rise and fall. The swarm descends. I bite and kick and flail. My mouth is full of insect guts.

There is a hissing shriek. The insects skitter away.

I spit, trying to clear my mouth. Das Muni leans over me. She holds the torch high.

I yank myself free of the webbing. Das Muni helps me up. I hear the insects hooting and skittering, waiting at the edges of the light.

I hack Casamir free of the webbing. It's rooted her in place, intricate strands so tough that she's locked in a standing position. Finally she falls free, and I wrap my arm around her. She sags into me. "Are you hurt?" I say.

Casamir's head lolls. "I don't know. I don't . . . No more than usual, maybe."

I search her body for bites or scratches and find four small puncture wounds on her wrist and two more on her thigh. "Are they poisonous?" I ask. "The creatures?" I'm bitten too, far more than her.

"Poison? Why would they have poison?" Casamir says.

That may answer the question, or it may not. Casamir's knowledge is based on maps and stories.

"Let's keep going," I say. "Das Muni, I need you to lead."

"You take the light," Das Muni says, thrusting the torch at me.

"I need to help Casamir," I say. "I'm right behind you."

"But—"

The hooting starts again. It raises the hairs on the back of my neck.

Das Muni's big eyes widen, impossibly large, and I wonder just how well she can see with eyes so big. "All right," she says, and takes a few hesitant steps forward. The insects stir, retreating from the light. Many swarm back toward their caves, where they continue watching us.

We walk and walk, fearful to stop as long as we can see the mounded caves. Then the floor begins to slope downward, and we move into a great forest of fungus-lined pillars that stretch so high I cannot see where they end.

The forest goes on and on, and after walking for some time without encountering hostile life, I suggest we bed down for some rest.

We spend time cleaning our wounds and untangling the webbing from our hair. I go in search of water and find brackish pools of damp among the trees. When I tell Casamir about it, she says it's fine to drink.

"Isn't there a way to clean it?" I say. "It's salty."

"You don't need to clean water," Casamir says, like I'm the stupidest person she's ever met. "It's all wet. It doesn't hurt you. Nothing in the world is meant to hurt you."

"What about those insects?"

"Well," she says, rubbing the bites on her wrist, "I think we just startled them."

I'm not convinced, but Casamir and Das Muni both drink the water, and eventually my thirst overcomes caution. We sleep, and when I wake from my doze, I find that the whole forest is filled with wispy green lights. Casamir is awake, plucking mushrooms from the trees.

I sit up and marvel at the light. "What is that?" I say. It's a misty green luminescence, as if the air itself is glowing.

"I suspect it's pollen," Casamir says. "The trees are mating."

Das Muni wakes at the sound of our voices. For a time, we sit and stare at the misty green waves moving through the trees. There are little creatures in the upper reaches of the trees. I see them hopping back and forth between them, chittering.

I lie back on the soft ground; it's covered in dead fungi and probably the leavings of the animals up there, but it's comfortable enough. The musty smell of it is still an improvement from the recycling pits.

"This is a journey every engineer must take," Casamir says, popping another mushroom into her bag. "You learn more about the world, they say, and our place in it. I always feel we are very large, but out here, well, it's clear we are a small piece of something much larger."

"The world is massive," I say. "I've seen it from the outside. I didn't think about what was inside, though."

Casamir eats a mushroom. "That's a very persistent delusion you have."

"Isn't that the best kind?" I say. "The kind you're most interested in."

"It does keep you interesting," she says. "I never liked a bore. Did I tell you a story about—"

"I'm going back to sleep," I say.

"It's a great story!"

"Later," I say, and close my eyes.

She tells me the story anyway. It's about an engineer who wanted to become a warrior but didn't understand that you have to kill people to do it. I suppose it is meant to be funny, as she tries to kill insects and then animals, working her way up to a human, but for one reason or another, she fails at each attempted kill.

"What she realized is that we're all connected," Casamir says. I'm drifting off to sleep now. For better or worse, I've gotten used to the drone of her voice. "If you kill one thing, you kill everything."

At the end of the forest is a door.

I counted the steps through the forest, and it's upward of fifty thousand. Now I'm struck not by how far the forest stretches but how strange a door looks here at the end of it.

The door is a broad, round metal thing, like a great eye sewn into the flesh of the world. We have traveled ever upward the last thirty thousand steps. This is, almost certainly, a door to the next level.

But that doesn't please me as much as it should. I'm mostly just shocked and confused, because I know this door. I have seen it before. Not a door *like* it, but *this* door. I've gone through this door. But most importantly, I remember that I've left something important here. Something for myself.

"Zan?" Casamir says.

I've been looking at the door a long time. Casamir and Das Muni are both staring at me.

I approach the door cautiously, willing myself to remember. What is so important that I left here?

I crouch in front of the door. "You're sure you've never met me before?" I ask.

"I've never seen you before," Casamir says. "What are you going on about? We're here! Aren't you excited?"

"None of your people have seen me?"

"No, why would they? You're the one who keeps saying you aren't even from here!"

I run my hands over the seams of the door, the same way I had in my cell when Jayd first put me in it. And there, stuffed into one of the upper seams, I find a rolled-up piece of human skin.

I pull it out and unroll it. Casamir and Das Muni crowd around me.

There are markings on the parchment. I don't understand them, but there's something familiar about them. "Casamir, do you have something I can mark this with?"

"Sure," she says. She pulls a charred stick from her tool belt. I marvel at the stick a moment. Where are all these plants? And then I make the same marks on the page, seeing if it prompts a memory.

I don't remember anything new, but I'm startled to find that the marks I'm making exactly match those on parchment. I have the same handwriting.

"Can you read this, Casamir?" I say.

Casamir shakes her head. "I've never seen that language before. But it looks like you have."

"I can read it," Das Muni says. She takes it from me into her long fingers. Casamir holds the light closer.

"It says, 'If you don't have the arm and the world, you must start again.'"

"That's all?" I say.

"Yes." She hands it back to me.

"How can you read this, Das Muni?" I ask.

She shrugs. "I know the language."

"That's an odd language for a mutant to know," Casamir says. She snatches the parchment back from me and scrutinizes it. "I think she's making this up."

"I'm not," Das Muni says.

"Das Muni," I say, and wonder how I've failed to ask her this until now, until it is almost too late. "What world are you from? What is its exact name?"

"I'm from the Mokshi," Das Muni says.

> "BE CAREFUL WHAT YOU PRETEND TO BE.
> IT'S FAR TOO EASY TO BECOME WHAT YOU PRETEND."
> —LORD MOKSHI, **ANNALS OF THE LEGION**

22

JAYD

You have been so melancholy," Rasida says.

I lie in bed, resting my hands on my growing belly. I still get up sometimes, to eat and scroll through the story tablets, but my hair is unwashed. I could wash my clothes or have the girls wash them. I know these things but cannot make myself act on them.

Rasida crosses the room to me. She visits at least once every cycle. She sits beside me and takes my hand in hers. Her palms are rough and callused. I remember how lovely her fingers felt on me when I thought

I had the power here, when I thought it was all going according to plan.

"I know it's difficult," she says. "It was so, for me, when I took my first world. Sometimes, the darkness comes. It obliterates our sense of the future. But you carry Bhavaja's future, Jayd. You have worth."

Worth, I think, and turn away from her. Worth only for what I carry, as if I'm just a vessel. But of course, this is what I wanted. I just didn't want all of Katazyrna destroyed to get me here. I tell myself we will all die anyway if Zan and I aren't able to make this plan work, but it's little comfort. The Katazyrna dead in a generation is far different than the Katazyrna dead in my lifetime.

"I care very much for you, Jayd," Rasida says. "I hope we can be true lovers."

My eyes fill, and I keep my face turned away. Let her see me suffer. Let her feel sorry for me. I deserve it. I want her to suffer in turn.

"I have brought you a gift," Rasida murmurs. "We have been eagerly getting Katazyrna ready for you, you understand. Now that I have the arm, our people here can move there. Some are not so happy about that, those who followed Aditva and the other sisters I had to slay, but they will fall in line. They will understand, as you do."

I say nothing.

"Did you hear me?" she says softly. "This is my way of apologizing, love. I sometimes act very rashly. I feared for you. I feared my family would corrupt you. I see now that you would never have need to run from me. Let me make it up to you with a gift. I found one of your sisters, alive. I thought she could make a fine companion for you. Loneliness can be difficult, my mother tells me."

I roll over to face her. My heart quickens. But of course it won't be Zan, will it? Rasida has seen Zan and recycled her, and would never bring her here.

But I sit up. If nothing else, Rasida has awoken my curiosity, which I thought long dead along with my heart.

"See, there," Rasida says, and she wipes the tears from my cheeks. "I am not so monstrous. I've done all of this for you, love. Come." She holds out her hand.

I take it. My purpose comes roaring back to me as we walk into the great foyer. I will give birth in one hundred and thirty cycles, if all goes as it's supposed to. Her witches have visited me several times already to confirm that the pregnancy is progressing as promised. If I had tricked them and was doomed to carry something else, they would recycle me immediately, and Rasida's lovely words would mean nothing. But I know what I'm carrying, because Zan once carried it, before she gave her womb to me.

I smooth my hair from my face. It's agonizing for me to walk unaided now, so I take Rasida's arm and lean heavily on her as she escorts me to my "gift." Walking is torturous, but we don't have far to go.

Rasida takes me into the courtyard outside my rooms. She gestures expansively to a cluster of three women standing in the foyer. Two of them are Bhavajas. The third stands between them, a slim, lovely young woman who I recognize immediately. I feel a mixture of anger and despair. I smile.

"Sabita," I say, and my heart sinks. This is the worst possible person she could have brought me, short of bringing me Anat. I had one of our security women cut out her tongue because I feared what she would reveal to Zan. I may not have done that myself, but she will have guessed whose order it was. Anat would not have cared, because Anat never knew who Zan was. Sabita, though . . . She might have intuited something. She had to be silenced before she talked to Zan and ruined everything.

"She was quite enterprising," Rasida says. "She hid in one of the great arteries running along the corridor outside the cortex. If we hadn't noticed the fluid leak, we may never have found her. What do you think of my gift?"

"Lovely," I say. I let tears fall. She need not know why I shed them. Of all the women Rasida could bring to me, it is Sabita, the woman who hated what I did to Zan more than anyone else on Katazyrna, because she had foolishly taken Zan into her arms and comforted her after she came back up from being recycled, before Zan lost her memory. What had they spoken of, in those few hours before Zan left again for the Mokshi, never again to regain her memory? I would never know, but I knew Sabita had come to care for her these many cycles, nursing her back to health after every assault.

I make a small sign to Sabita without raising my hands. The Bhavajas shouldn't know our signing language, but it's best to be discreet with a paranoid woman like Rasida in the room.

Sabita glances at my fingers but makes no response. I wonder if it will be worse with her here. Will she murder me in my bed? But she may be the last Katazyrna besides myself who still lives. There is something to be said for the power of blood. She may know something of life on Katazyrna, something that will help me.

"Thank you, Rasida," I say. "You are . . . kind."

Rasida kisses my forehead. She takes my face in her hands and searches my expression. For what, I am uncertain, but I press my mouth to hers, lightly. I try to imagine Zan doing that, after all that Rasida has done, and cannot. Zan would murder her, and forget the plan, and throw her down a recycling chute.

"Good, you see," Rasida says. "You are just lonely."

"I am," I say. "I know you are very busy. I appreciate this gift."

Rasida escorts Sabita into my rooms and putters about, pointing out where Sabita should sleep, here on the floor beside me, instructing the girls to treat her as my handmaiden. Sabita wanders through all of this with a dull-eyed stare. I wonder what it must have been like all this time, hiding in one of the arteries above the cortex, covered in the world's blood, subsisting on blood and whatever she could peel off and choke down from the fleshy walls.

When Rasida leaves us and the girls go off to retrieve our refreshments, Sabita and I stand weary before one another. Do I look as defeated as she does?

Finally, Sabita signs at me, "I know where you got that womb. It's not yours. You bought your freedom with it, though. You traitor. Zan told me that much."

I sign, "You have no idea what you're talking about. Be pleased you're alive and Anat didn't recycle you. You always tell Zan too much, and she goes mad, doesn't she?"

"Mad with grief," Sabita signs. "She would never tell me, but I suspect her grief had to do with you. Something you did. It always does. You bring us all nothing but grief. When I spoke to her of the past, she remembered that grief, and it destroyed her every time. That's not my fault. It's yours."

"You don't know what Zan and I—"

"You're monstrous," Sabita signs, and turns her back to me.

I want to tell Sabita everything, but it occurs to me that that's exactly what Rasida might have hoped. Perhaps she rescued Sabita so I'd open up to her. Betrayals within betrayals. I resisted Nashatra, and that may have saved me from a far worse fate. I have not seen Nashatra since the day Aditva was recycled. Sabita is the first face I have seen that is not Rasida's or the girls' in some time.

Yet seeing her makes me angry. It makes me angry because no matter how hard I try, I cannot forget what I've done to get here. Zan is able to forget. I'm not. How can I pity her when she gets to start over? It's me who has to feel what happened. It's me who carries the burden. It's me who carries on while she flails about like an empty-headed child driven to one purpose. I have to feel because I can shutter it away, box it up like something that happened to someone else. She can't. She never could.

When you understand what the world is, you have two choices: Become a part of that world and perpetuate that system forever and ever, unto the next generation. Or fight it, and break it, and build something new.

The former is safer, and easier. The latter is scarier, because who is to say what you build will be any better?

But living in servitude is not living. Slavery ensures one's existence, but there is no future in it.

Zan and I believed in the future.

"Help me," I say aloud, and Sabita turns and grimaces.

"I see she's hobbled you," Sabita signs, "or did you do that to yourself, to garner pity? I wouldn't put it past you."

"Don't pretend to know me," I say out loud, and I remember the girls could walk in at any moment, so I switch back to signing. "Do you know how far the hangar is from here?"

"Planning escape? If you'd wanted to escape, I'd think you'd have done it by now."

"And go where?" I sign. "Tell me of Katazyrna."

"It's at war," Sabita signs. "If she tells you she's routed it, she's lying. Half of the people she brought there sided with us when they saw how rich the world was. They're trying to push out her people. She has a civil war over there. I couldn't believe I didn't see any signs of it here. There is a whole faction over there trying to separate itself from Bhavaja."

"Her family has turned on her here," I sign. "I didn't know it was out of control over there, though."

"I was holding out with three of her own people," Sabita signs. "She killed them and took me. I thought I was dead for sure. Where are Neith and Gavatra?"

"Dead with the rest," I sign. "I think so, anyway. We were separated before the joining."

"What a fucking disaster," Sabita signs. "You sure got what you wanted, though, didn't you?"

"What do you know about what I want?"

"Zan told me once, early on, that you two wanted to get you into Bhavaja hands. I don't know why. But I hope it's working out for you."

"Rasida is smart," I sign.

"Rasida's a fucking madwoman."

I have nothing to add to that. I just nod, and the girls come back in with refreshments. I wave them off into another room, and sit down to eat with Sabita at a small table at the end of my bed.

If Rasida turned Sabita before bringing her here, she's done a very good job. Still, I hedge my bets. It's my distrust that has kept me alive so far. I can't let it go, not yet.

We say nothing as we eat. Sabita gorges on the protein gel and greens. There are sour, soft-skin fruits as well, and she eats them greedily.

When she is done, she signs, "How are we getting out of here, then?"

"We're not," I sign.

She leans toward me. "You are the smartest of the Katazyrnas," she signs. "You conquered whole worlds. You can conquer one crazy woman."

"Soon," I sign. "I need to find something."

"What's taken you so long?" Sabita signs, and it's the look on her face—exasperated, disbelieving—that shifts something inside of me.

The Jayd she remembers would not sit here in bed, unwashed, melancholy. The Jayd she remembers would fight. And fight. And fight. I can smile and pretend at servitude, but all that pretending has finally caught up with me. It's in that moment that I realize I have become what Rasida believes me to be. I have fought so hard to convince her that I am hers that I have allowed myself to be cowed. I fear her. I want to please her. I'm not just pretending anymore. I have become everything I wanted Rasida to think I was. I can't do this anymore.

"I'm glad you're here," I sign.

Sabita raises her brows. "That is something I never thought you would say."

"Best I never say it out loud, then," I sign, and push away from the table.

It's time to court Rasida again. It's time to find the world.

> "WORLDS ARE BORN, AND WORLDS DIE.
> I JUST NEVER EXPECTED THE DYING WORLD WOULD BE MINE."
> —LORD MOKSHI, ANNALS OF THE LEGION

23

ZAN

What happened to the Mokshi?" I ask Das Muni. My fingers are trembling.

"I don't know," she says. "We were attacked. Recycled, most of us. Some there, but many here."

"Who attacked the Mokshi? The Bhavajas? The Katazyrnas?"

"I don't know," Das Muni says. "It was a long time ago."

"How long?" I've raised my voice, and she cringes.

"I don't know," she says. "It was long ago. I'm sorry. Meatmoth—"

"I don't give a care for Meatmoth," I say. I throw the parchment at the wall, because it means nothing. Das Muni scrambles after it. None of this is helpful. It's just one more mystery piled on top of another mystery. I feel like I'm being used, and that everyone in this foul place knows more about me than I do.

"If you've been here before," Casamir says, "recycled by your people up there, you have any tips on how to open this door?"

"Isn't that what you were here for?" I say, too short, again.

"Just trying to make it easier," Casamir grumbles. She pulls off her pack and unrolls an intricate kit of metal files and organic potions. "It could take a while," she says.

"Your test is getting it open?" I say.

"Yes," she says. "It's a complicated lock, organic and nonorganic. Very precise. There's a cache on the other side. I'll take an artifact from it and go back. You can carry on."

"If you get it open," I say.

"A little optimism," Casamir says. She glances over her shoulder, into the dark. "Keep watch for mutants. And all that other stuff."

I lift the torch high and stare at the door. What world was I telling myself to capture? This one? The Mokshi? I shiver, though the air is warm, and turn back to the darkness. Das Muni sits against the door, the bit of parchment gripped tightly in her hands. She is shaking. I don't want to ask her any more questions, because I'm angry, and she just shuts down when I yell. I need to wait until I'm calm again. Das Muni has lived a long time with horror. Horrifying her more won't help.

Casamir continues to work at the door. I watch her fiddle with it, hoping it evokes some shard of memory. The mechanism she is working on is a round raised disk with interlocking sections. It's less grimy than the rest of the door, which is coated in viscous ooze from above and calcified knobs of some sediment or other.

Time passes slowly. I eat one of the apples from Casamir's pack, spitting out the soft hairs buried in its interior. I peer out at the darkness and listen to the hooting of the black insects.

After a time, Das Muni gets up and sits next to me.

Casamir sweats and mutters to herself in her language. It's starting to sound familiar now. I think I understand a few words, but that may be hubris.

"I've got it!" Casamir says. The great door clicks. Something heaves and rumbles inside.

I stand back, pulling Das Muni with me. She grips my arm. I hand Das Muni the light and raise my walking stick.

Casamir glances back at me and grins as the great door thunders open. "It's all right," she says, "it's only—"

A screeching howl comes from the darkness beyond. I see a flurry of movement, a sea of gaunt limbs and massive eyes, and then the mutants are upon us.

> "MUTANTS MAKE FOR GOOD EATING.
> IT WAS NEVER MY CHOICE TO PURGE THEM FROM THE WORLD.
> IT WAS THE KATAZYRNAS WHO GOT THERE FIRST."
> —LORD MOKSHI, ANNALS OF THE LEGION

24

ZAN

Das Muni had been called a mutant by Casamir's people, but she is nothing like the horde that descends on us through the great eye of the door.

If they are or once were human, it's difficult to tell. They are a snarling, hairy mass of flesh and teeth and claws. Some gallop on all fours; others stagger forward on great clubbed feet. They are a riotous, screaming mob, and I lash out at them instinctively.

Casamir has her knife out, and she's yelling at me to fall back. I stab the first mutant to reach me in the throat. It falls, and more stream past it. I bring my stick up but find that they aren't attacking me—they're running past me, arms and other appendages flailing. They aren't attacking us. They're running away from an attack.

I push past the mob, getting bitten for my trouble. It takes only a few elbow jabs to keep the others in line. As I cross the threshold of the door, I see two women standing back to back, their fallen companions around them. They are fighting three large mutants with crescent-shaped faces and bony arms that have just two and three digits at the ends where hands should be. But their teeth are sharp, and they are holding their own against the armed women, who wield clubs layered in sharpened bone and skin, making them into effective maces.

I stagger forward and bark at the mutants. "That's enough! Get off!"

The women don't turn to me. One goes down under the jaws of the largest mutant, and I leap forward and thump the mutant hard on the back of the head. It yelps and runs. Its one big eye is watery, covered in a gray film.

Another swipes at the last woman standing. She takes the hit and bashes its head in. It crumples. The other two mutants gallop away after their herd.

I walk up to the fallen women. All but one is already dead, and she's bleeding out too fast to stop the inevitable.

The last woman standing crumples. She holds her club in front of her, baring her teeth, as if daring me to act.

"I'm here to help," I say, holding up my hands. "What are you called?"

She peers at me. Spits at my feet. "Arankadash," she says.

"Is that your name, or a curse?" I ask.

Casamir and Das Muni come up behind me. Casamir is limping. "Some help you were back there," Casamir says.

"They were running," I say, "not attacking."

"From these people?"

I nod. "You know them?"

"Maybe," Casamir says. She tries a couple more languages, but from the look this giant of a woman is giving me, I have a feeling she understands me just fine.

"I'm Zan," I say, "or at least that's what I'm told." I introduce Casamir and Das Muni and tell her we're looking to go up another level. "Above," I say, pointing. "To the surface. You know the surface of the world?"

"The sea," she says.

I know the word; in my mind I picture a flat, viscous expanse of dark water in a deep, cavernous crag of the world. "You've been to the sea?" I say, wondering if there's one of them, or many.

"Above us is the sea," she says. "We all come from the sea, and we all return to it." She crouches next to her dead companions, and I have a twinge of sympathy, remembering the slaughter of my sisters.

I kneel next to her. "I'm sorry we couldn't save them," I say.

"You saved me," she says. "It has to be enough."

"Were they attacking you?" I ask.

She shakes her head. She pulls a bracelet made of bone beads strung in sinew from the wrist of one of the dead and slides it onto her own wrist, which is already heavy with a dozen of them. "We are a hunting party," she says. "We hunt them. They kill our birthers and our chattel. They eat flesh without honor. They do not understand sacrifice."

"If you point us in the direction of the sea," I say, "we'll go."

She stares at the bodies, then her open palms. Shakes her head. "I cannot leave their bodies here for the scavengers. I must bring them back."

The six dead will not be easy to carry, not for her or for us. Das Muni won't even be able to move a single thigh, let alone a body.

"I'm not sure we're the best at helping with that," I say.

When she raises her head now, her eyes are filled with tears. "Help me bring them home," she says, "and I will guide you to the sea."

I glance back at Casamir. She hugs her shard of diamond to her chest. "You going back?" I say.

"I have what I came for," she says.

I nod and point back into the dark. "You're free to go back, then," I say.

She picks up her torch and heads to the door.

I survey the bodies and try to figure out a way to transport them. "We can make ropes," I say, "maybe haul them behind us?"

"Can we make a sledge?" Arankadash says.

I pull the twisted garrote from my pocket. "Maybe if we twist together—"

Casamir sighs and trudges back to us. She sets down her pack. "You can carry them on long bone poles," she says, "from the boneyard. Tie them up and suspend them between you. There's four of us. We can manage two, carrying two bodies apiece."

"That's still heavy," I say.

"Easier than dragging them," she says. "Must I think of everything?"

Casamir and I head back to the foot of the mountains, hunting for bones long enough to suspend between two people. Luckily, we don't have to go far. Our scavenging turns up four good-sized poles.

When we return, Das Muni is keening. I drop my bones and run through the door to find her on the ground, Arankadash on top of her, hands around her throat.

I rush Arankadash and knock her clear of Das Muni. I pin her to the ground. She fights me, but I'm heavier and faster. I lock her arms at her sides. "What are you doing?

"She is a mutant!" Arankadash spits. "She must die like the others!"

"She's my friend!" I say. "You accept my help, you accept hers. You understand? She may be a mutant, but she is my mutant. I'm responsible for her."

Arankadash sneers at me but stops struggling. "Fool," she says. "They all turn. They seem normal, for a time, but they all become mad. They eat flesh and murder and hunt. That is all they do."

"You tell me you were the one hunting," I say. "They were running from you into us. So, who's the hunter, then?"

"Do not trust her!" Arankadash says.

Casamir comes up behind me, still carrying her bones. "She's all right for a mutant," Casamir says. "Just ugly."

"Fools," Arankadash says.

"Do you want the help of us fools or not?" I say. "Because I'm happy to leave you here to haul your kin back one by one and get eaten by mutants or bugs or whatever else is up here along the way."

She snarls something in another language. Then: "Fine, but we are enemies now."

"All right," I say, "as long as you're the type of enemy who keeps her promises, and you've promised to take me to the sea."

"You are undeserving," she says.

I release her. "I can say the same of you. Apologize to Das Muni."

"No."

"Then at least promise not to harm her again. Because the next time you try, I'm not going to be so nice."

"I'm not nice either."

"We make a good pair, then," I say. "Well?"

Arankadash grimaces. "I will not harm her while she is yours," she says.

I get up.

"Great," Casamir says. "Can we get to work now? I don't want to stay here any longer than we have to."

"You're coming with us?" I say.

Casamir is already busily knotting rope from her pack onto the ends of the bones. "You would be lost without me," she says. "Besides, I've never seen the sea."

"And it's a long way home in the dark," I say.

She rolls her eyes. "I'm not afraid of the dark. I'm a scavenger. I crawl into the very bowels of the world to—"

"I've got it," I say. "We'll agree to disagree."

While Casamir and Arankadash work, I go over to Das Muni. Her cowl is thrown back. Her face is dirty again. I lick my finger and wipe a bit of blood from her face. Hers?

"You all right?" I ask.

She tilts her enormous eyes up to me. This close, I see how strange her irises are, little crescents of color. It's unnerving. Her ears are so large, I wonder how she didn't hear the mutants beyond the door well before it opened.

"I told you that traveling with others is not good," she says softly.

"If I'd thought that, I wouldn't have taken you with me either," I say. "It cuts both ways."

"I want to go home," she says. She presses her hands to her eyes.

"No one knows how to get back to the Mokshi," I say. "A lot of people have tried. Including me."

"Not the Mokshi," she says. "I was nothing there. I want to go home to Sledgemaw and Meatmoth."

"That is no place for you," I say, but I look back at Casamir and Arankadash and realize this isn't any place for her either. At least to the monsters she is just another piece of meat, no different from any other. I don't understand the hatred I see for people like her. People on every level look different. Why do they hate mutants and people off-world? It all gets recycled the same. We're all made of meat.

I help Casamir and Arankadash finish tying off the bodies to the makeshift litters. Casamir hangs her torch from the one she and Arankadash carry, and Das Muni and I come from behind. The litter is too heavy for her, I know, but I want to see how far we can get before thinking of another option.

But when Das Muni shoulders her end, I'm surprised to find that she doesn't complain at all. She keeps trekking after me, slower than I'd like, but not so slow that I lose sight of Casamir and Arankadash. There's not much to see outside our pool of light. There are long lines of bioluminescent flora or fauna lining the rolling ground and the far walls. I see the occasional protuberance or fallen fold of the ceiling. After a break for water at a bubbling pool oozing up from the spongy ground, we keep on. My mouth tastes of copper after I drink, as if the water is tinged with blood.

Eventually, we come to a broad path, a well-worn depression in the ground that signals human habitation. Casamir and I are exhausted, but Arankadash and Das Muni barely seem winded. We rest again, and Arankadash suggests sleep.

"I will keep watch," Arankadash says.

Casamir shares food from her pack. "I bet this is farther than anyone I know has gone," she says.

"You are of the Bharataiv?" Arankadash says. "The tinkers?"

"Engineers," Casamir says.

"Yes, the peddlers," Arankadash says. "Sometimes our traders meet with you, near the golden veil."

"What's the golden veil?" I ask.

"Oh, nothing," Casamir says. "You want some mushrooms?"

"No," I say. Then, to Arankadash: "What's the golden veil?"

"Thirty thousand steps back," she says, "near the mountains. It's a far easier route up here than the one you came. Going through the door is only something foolish tinkers do, because you have to cross the valley of beasts, and the mutant camps."

I stare at Casamir. "You could have taken us here through there? We'd have saved all those steps! And the bugs, those crawlers, and door—"

"I had to complete my initiation," Casamir says. "You can't take the shortcut or it doesn't count."

I rub my face. "I am so tired of your shit, Casamir."

"You would have wanted to take the shortcut!" Casamir says. "Let me tell you a story about someone who took the shortcut. It starts with—"

"Don't," I say.

"—this woman who wore her womb as a hat, because—"

"Who did what?" I say.

"On her head," Casamir says, patting her crown of braided hair, "but that's not important. It just identifies her, you see. Anyway, it made her look taller and more imposing, so she took the shortcut, thinking that—"

"Is this a real story?" I ask.

Casamir sniffs. "I only share real stories."

"People can't just take out their wombs," I say.

"Of course they can," Casamir says. "People swap wombs all the time."

"What?"

She munches at a fist-sized mushroom. Every time I think we'll run out of food, I catch her foraging for more. I wouldn't have thought there was so much of it here, but that's because I can't tell the difference between food and refuse.

"We all give birth to different stuff," Casamir says. "Sometimes, what one person wants isn't what another person wants, but you can't decide what you give birth to. The Godhead decides, but like with anything, you can change your fate. You can swap out with a family member, if you have a good surgeon."

I think of the long cut on my stomach. "Can you take it out altogether?"

"That's not advisable," Casamir says. "Don't you know anything? You two really are very mad."

"We don't do anything like that," Arankadash says. "That's an affront to the sea that birthed us."

"Whatever," Casamir says. "It's different for us."

"Aren't you afraid to anger the sea?" Arankadash says.

"I don't even know what that is," Casamir says. "No." She pops the rest of the mushroom into her mouth. "You really should try one of these. I have others."

"Won't you get an infection or something?" I ask.

"From mushrooms?"

"Cutting out body parts," I say.

"Why?" Casamir says. "We're all made of the same stuff, us and the world. Stuff doesn't rot here, really; it's just recycled. The world eats it. Eats us, too. We're all one thing. Haven't you listened to me at all? Those women we have in the engineering room, they don't get infections when we experiment on them. Your leg, too, have you noticed?

We took a fist of flesh out and you're walking as well as ever. You just need to treat it with the right stuff. Your body heals the rest. Sews itself back up, almost. Most of us, anyway."

"What does *most of us* mean?"

Casamir glances at Das Muni. "Not mutants," she says.

"Because they aren't from this world?" I say.

"Well, I wouldn't go that far. I mean, I'm not saying I don't believe you, but—"

"Your explanation is just that they're mutants?"

"Yes. Born wrong. So, they don't heal right. They don't grow right."

"What *right* is seems to be a matter of opinion."

"I feel my opinion matters highly."

"You're all so full of noise," Arankadash says. "Like nattering hipjacks."

"I'm not going to ask," I say.

"You don't want to know," Casamir says.

"I sure hear that a lot."

"Sometimes it's easier to live out here if you don't know," Casamir says.

"So I've been told," I say.

Das Muni is lying with her back to us, but she is pushed up against me for warmth, and in her hands is the scrap of parchment. I can see no great advantage to not knowing the things this world is keeping from me, except, perhaps, a great sense of despair. Das Muni has that despair, and Casamir and Arankadash too, in their own ways. They believe whatever myths and truths they are told. But I have no faith in any of it. Is this what Jayd wants me to be, a faithless woman who can carry on?

I'd say it seems to be working, but that parchment tells me that I've been this way before, and if it didn't work then, why should I think it is working now? And what was I working *toward*? Surely, I cannot have been down here for the same reasons last time. How many times can the Bhavajas take over a world?

When I wake, it's Casamir's grinning face I see. How she remains so peppy, I have no idea. Maybe I'd be happier too, if I knew stories about women wearing wombs on their heads.

We pack up and drink bitter dregs of coppery water from the bulbs Casamir filled at the last puddle.

I set down the one I'm sharing with Casamir and turn to pick up my walking stick.

Casamir is babbling at Arankadash, back turned, and out of the corner of my eye I see Das Muni lean over the water bulb. She drops something in it. I stare hard at her. She sees me watching and jerks her hand away.

"What is that?" I hiss. I snatch her hand and kick over the bulb. The water dribbles out.

I pull Das Muni away from the others.

"What's wrong?" Casamir says.

"Nothing," I say, loud. "Das Muni kicked over the water. I don't think she's well."

I take Das Muni by the shoulders and give her a little shake. I lower my voice. "What were you doing?"

"Nothing."

"Don't lie to me. I saw you put something in there. Don't lie to me or I'll leave you here to get eaten by whatever thing they've got out here."

"These people are dangerous," Das Muni says.

I shake her again. "Tell me."

"I tried . . . it is . . ."

"Were you trying to poison me?"

"Not you! You already drank!"

"Casamir, then?"

She looks down.

"Shit and fire, Das Muni, this is not a game," I say.

"It wouldn't poison her," Das Muni says. "She would just feel very sick. Things here don't kill you."

"We need these people," I say. "Do you understand? If you want to go home, to go back to your monsters and your garbage heaps, I'll find a recycling chute and happily throw you back into it."

"Why do we need their help? We can do this together," Das Muni says.

"I should leave you," I say. "I wanted to leave you in the pits, but I didn't, did I? You're making me regret that decision."

"Zan?" Casamir's voice, close.

I start, turn around. "Yeah, we're coming," I say. "I just don't like her wasting water."

"There's plenty of water," Arankadash says. "We'll get there in another fifteen or sixteen thousand steps."

As I gaze at Das Muni, I remember how she cared for me in the pits. She could have left me, too, or eaten me, or fed me to her precious monsters, but she didn't. Did I owe her, the way Arankadash now thought she owed me? Maybe.

"Let's get going," I say.

Das Muni lifts her head slowly. "You won't leave me?"

"I won't leave you," I say. "Just . . ." And I'm aware Casamir and Arankadash are listening now. "Just never do that again."

We pass great crimson formations, through dripping mist that stings our skin and numbs my tongue, and finally the path we're following takes us from the broad open caverns to a narrower corridor. If I lay down, I could probably stretch out and touch both sides.

Arankadash sets her litter down and tells us to wait as she forges ahead. There is light here, emitted from pulsing pustules in the ceiling.

Little insects scurry along the walls, flashing red, gold, and green lights, but those emissions are dim.

We wait with increasing restlessness.

"Think she'll eat us after all?" Casamir says lightly, but though it's meant to be a joke, it falls into flat silence. "You two are a tough crowd," she says, but she shifts from foot to foot now and pokes at the wall of the corridor with her bone stick.

Arankadash returns. "It's clear," she says.

"Of what?" I ask.

"Mutants," she says. "They run prey through here and lie in wait at the end of the corridor. Come quickly."

We pick up the pace through the narrow pass. The bodies we carry are heavy now, their mouths filled with bugs. Their eyes are sprouting fungus. Behind me, Das Muni stumbles, and her end of our litter jams in the wall, lodging firmly. A thick green ooze wells around the wound.

"Wait!" I call ahead, but Casamir and Arankadash are still moving, oblivious.

"I'm sorry," Das Muni says.

"Don't be sorry," I say. "Help." She does, and together we yank the bone from the wall and continue on our way. There's light enough to make out the bends in the corridor, but we've lost Casamir and Arankadash.

My heart thumps loud in my chest. I'm tired, and my sharpened walking stick isn't going to be easy to pull out if we're attacked.

Das Muni is quiet, and all I can hear for some time is the beat of our feet and the huff of our breath. Occasionally, I look up at the pustules of light.

After five or six hundred steps, I hear raised voices, and slow. Listen.

I motion to Das Muni to lower the litter. I creep ahead, putting most of my weight on the outside of my foot and rolling my step inward, a trick to minimize sound that I only now realize is a skill I know.

I peer around a bend in the corridor and see Arankadash and Casamir circled by a group of women wearing bone-and-sinew armor. Finger bones rattle in their hair. They've smeared their faces in black grit, and they have pointed bone weapons strapped to their wrists. Arankadash has her hands out, palms up, and she is speaking quickly. The bodies Arankadash and Casamir were carrying lie at their feet.

I motion to Das Muni to lower our own load of bodies, to free up my hands. I pull my walking stick free and wait. Diplomacy first, always. I've found I prefer it.

But the leader of the group is having none of it. She bashes Arankadash in the face with a bone club. Arankadash crumples.

Casamir puts her hands behind her head and gets to her knees. She is showing her teeth, babbling.

I move.

I come at them quickly, weapon up. I dive at the one nearest Casamir first and drive the end of my stick into her eye. I turn as she drops and stab my weapon into the unprotected armpit of the woman behind her. The others are moving now.

Surprise lost, I'm still outnumbered four to one. I kick out the legs of the one that comes at me from the left, head-butt the woman in front of me, and duck as the woman with the club swings. Her weapon collides with someone else's forearm. I hear the crack and cry.

I go for her eye, but she's fast and ducks, landing a punch to my gut.

I lose my breath, stagger back, and collide with the fourth woman. I swing my weapon, but her armor deflects it. I'm getting sloppy.

The woman with the club swings for me again. I catch the swing with my stick and kick her in the stomach. She goes down, and I gore her throat, and turn.

There's one woman standing, and she's running.

"Get her!" Casamir says. "She'll bring more of them! Zan!"

I bring up my stick and get ready to heft it like a spear. Hesitate. Who am I, to murder a fleeing woman in the back?

"Zan!" Casamir says.

I lower my arm. "We're almost to Arankadash's people," I say. I crouch beside Arankadash and move the hair away from her bloody wound. "Bring some water," I say. "Let's see if I can rouse her."

Casamir doesn't move. She's still staring at me, mouth pursed. "What?" I say.

"You're a coward," she says.

I point the bloody end of my stick at her. "It's easy to murder people, Casamir. There's nothing brave about it."

"They've killed Arankadash! They would have killed me!"

"She's not dead," I say.

"You are softhearted," Casamir says.

"You're not?" I say. "You could have left me and Das Muni down there in that pit. You could have cut that rope. Untied that line I put on you and left me to shake until I fell off that rope. You didn't. So, what does that make us both? Cowards? Weak?"

Das Muni runs up to us. "Is Arankadash all right?" she asks.

"No," Casamir says, folding her arms. "None of this is all right."

"We can't be much farther from her people," I say. "We'll carry her and follow the path."

"Why don't we just leave them all?" Das Muni says quietly. "The world will eat them. That's as it should be."

"I made a promise," I say. "Carry what bodies you can. We will send Arankadash's people back for the rest."

I heft Arankadash over my shoulder. I can't carry her and the bodies of her kin, too, but Casamir and Das Muni are able to lift one set of them. The three of us follow the path up a long, winding stair. It's in heavy disrepair, and I stumble. Das Muni and Casamir struggle to carry the bodies up.

We walk a long time in silence until we see a woman standing on an outcrop far ahead of us.

I wave at her. She ducks. I say, "I have Arankadash!"

She disappears.

"Scout?" Casamir says.

I nod. "Let's wait. I don't want to bumble into anyone the way we did with those other women."

"How do you know she's not with those other women?"

"Her hair is different," I say. "You should know how to pay attention to that more than me."

"I can't see that far," Casamir says, squinting. "My eyes aren't as good." But she and Das Muni let the bodies they carry rest on the steps.

After a few minutes, a long procession of women comes out to meet us. Two are armed, but the rest wear long flowing robes of hemp and waxy leaves.

Casamir greets them in their language. Arankadash is heavy. I feel her stir but don't set her down. She may have trouble walking with a head injury.

The woman at the front is middle-aged. She wears a mass of bone and a hemp necklace that cover the front of her robe, hanging nearly to her waist.

"I have not spoken Handavi in some time," she says to me.

"I'm good practice, then," I say. "There are more of her sisters back there. We couldn't carry them and her, too. She asked us to bring them home."

She gestures to the people behind her. One of the women with a weapon runs back up the steps.

"They will retrieve our sisters," she says. "Come, we offer rest and water. We will have a funerary feast. You are invited. You will be our special guests."

"No offense meant," I say, "but nothing good has come of me being a special guest."

"You have suffered," she says, not unkindly. "That is unfortunate. We are a peaceful people. You are in no danger here."

"Peaceful unless I'm a mutant," I say. Das Muni has put on her cowl again, but I'm aware of her breathing hotly next to me.

"All are welcome," she says, and she peers at Casamir and Das Muni. "You have done us a great service. To lose the bodies of ours is to lose a piece of our people. We lose our future."

I follow after her and her retinue. Two women come down the hill with a stretcher and take Arankadash from me. My hands are covered in her blood. I wipe my hands on my suit.

Das Muni takes my arm, Casamir rolls her eyes, and we go up and up, into some other world.

> "CONTROL OF FECUNDITY IS SOMETHING
> EVERY WOMAN WANTS, AND EACH BELIEVES
> IS HER BIRTHRIGHT. THE WORLDS HAVE OTHER IDEAS,
> AND IT EVENTUALLY LED TO THEIR DESTRUCTION."
> —LORD MOKSHI, **ANNALS OF THE LEGION**

25

JAYD

When I aborted the thing in my first womb, I expected to see some sad, tentacled monster in a jar, a half-baked gob of potential life, now just mutilated flesh; a collection of nubby tentacles and burst tissue. Or maybe I'd see the thing itself, whole and writhing in a pool of bloody afterbirth before the witches recycled it at Anat's order.

I fought the gauzy dream of the light anesthetic huffing through the air, and struggled to sit up when they tugged away the hungry tuber that was emptying my womb. But when the witches raised the jar over-head, I saw only a knuckle's depth of dark, frothy blood. I could see nothing within its murky depths. No mangled monsters. No tattered substance. Just blood.

"Is that all?" I asked, and my words came out slurred, muddy, like the stuff in the jar.

"That's all," the witches said. They looked amused, as if they had just told some recycler girl that the cog she bore to replace the dying one inside the core atmospheric lung of the world was just what they wanted, everything they had hoped for.

It was the first time I realized that we had some power over what the ship did to us. It was the first time I dared to hope that we could escape the Legion. I realized I could build a future instead of just a fate.

When I took the new womb, the one I knew Rasida would need, and my mother learned it wasn't going to be just another bit of organic shielding or some new recycler monster, Anat put me on a regular schedule of what she called "treatments," though the witches begged and pleaded for reason every time, because it's been so long since we had a womb like this on the first level of the world that they considered it a great portent.

"We don't need it yet," Anat said, as if what I bore could happen only so many times, and maybe she was right. I didn't know. I'd never had any contact with people who gave birth to what I could now. I started to wonder what she was saving it for.

I learned to recognize my mother's look of distaste every time the witches made their case—suspicion, fear, and something else, some-thing more—a realization that I was not the daughter she had hoped for. She had wanted me to lead an army. But I had fallen in love and given myself a valuable womb and failed to give her the Mokshi. It was not the future she wanted.

"Get rid of it," Anat said, every time.

The witches would bow and scrape before her, nodding all three of their heads. "She is necessary. It's necessary. Please, we must have this one. This one is for us. Please. We must have it."

"End it. You know what happens."

"It's the will of the world. A world without issue—"

"She hasn't birthed it yet, has she? Get rid of it or I'll have you recycled after all, the way I promised when I sent Zan out. It's not as if she's giving birth to a world, just another sorry piece of it."

This is how I know that Rasida is not taking the same treatments that I am. I know the signs and symptoms. If she is going to give birth, if she is pregnant or has recently aborted, she shows no signs of it. When Rasida invites me to dinner, I accept. When she brushes my fingers, I do not flinch. When she speaks to me of the troubles of the world, I listen with my most sympathetic expression, the one I used on Anat throughout my whole childhood.

And this is how I come to realize that Rasida doesn't have the world, the same way that Zan no longer has her own womb. Rasida has given it to someone else, and I need to find out who.

And then after dinner one night, I sit on Rasida's bed, drink in hand, and she lies down in my lap, and I stroke her cheek, and she says, "It is very lonely, being the lord."

"I imagine so," I say, and I do not say, "Because you have murdered everyone who has ever cared for you or could ever care for you." No, we are past that. I know what will happen if I say that. I have shifted how I am playing this game, though it is no easier than the last.

She presses her hands to my belly. "I can feel it moving," she says.

"Yes," I say, "sometimes it does that."

She coos at my belly. "You have never taken it this far?" she says.

"No," I say. She smiles and closes her eyes, and finally, I ask, "What about your own issue? I have not seen you pregnant in all this time."

"Pregnancy is a risk," she says. "Each of them, no matter what you birth. I need to stay fit to lead the Legion."

"What do you mean?"

"I mean exactly that," she says. "There is only one that will ever come to term. You must be absolutely sure it is the right time to birth it. It could destroy you in the birthing. As with any birth. Too dangerous for me. I did what many women do. I gave it to someone else to bear."

"Does it take a long time to come to term?" I ask, because the question of where her womb is now is far too obvious.

"No," she says. "I believe in absolute control over what I have to bear. It's incubating now. It will be born when we are ready to go to Katazyrna. While we are there, it will remake Bhavaja into a new world."

"How will it do that?" I ask. Ignorance worked with Anat.

"Did they not tell you?" Rasida asks. "How cruel, not to tell you."

"Tell me what?"

Rasida rises. Her hands move to my neck, and I stiffen, but she only rubs my shoulders, as if I am some creature in need of comfort. "I can give birth to worlds," she says. "Surely you had heard of that on Katazyrna."

"There were rumors," I say. "We always thought it was a rumor you planted to make you seem very powerful."

"Patience," Rasida says. "Everything is coming together."

"It's difficult to be patient, without answers."

"I anticipate your little experiment with Zan was also aggravating for her."

"Are you comparing what's happened with Zan with what you're doing to me?"

"Not at all," Rasida says. She shifts away from me.

"That's not convincing," I say, and my tone is wrong. I've misstepped. I wish, again, that I could slough off my memory the way Zan can. She can afford to be decent. I can't.

Rasida stands. "I look forward to your birthing time. I've never had one myself."

"Never? Not even someone else's issue?"

"No," Rasida says. She chuckles. "I suppose that is something you would ask, of course. I've seen your scars, Jayd. I know you weren't born with a womb that makes what I need. No, you got it from some-one else. Who, I wonder? Most importantly, though, I wonder why, and how you convinced her to give it to you. Or did you just take it, rip it from her body the way we ripped the life from that woman on Tiltre?"

"I wanted it," I say. "Does there need to be another reason? I was tired of fighting. I wanted to make something that lasted."

She smirks. Her smiles are becoming smirks now more often, amused and disgusted. She does not try to hide her contempt. "I like that you are not a little fool," she says.

"It could kill me too," I say, trying to find a safer subject, perhaps one that will tug at her heart, if she has one. "I could die birthing this thing for you, and then you'd have killed my family, taken my world, for nothing. Is this love?"

"I didn't do it for you," Rasida says, "not at first."

"Then who?"

"I did it for Zan," Rasida says, "to free her from that awful prison you constructed for her. She's some prisoner from the Mokshi, isn't she?

Made to throw herself at her own world. You are a bunch of monsters over there."

"And what are you, then?" I say. "You murdered my whole family." We have arrived here again, though it was exactly where I didn't want to go. How does she continue to twist me even when I know better?

Rasida laughs. "What does that make me?" she says. "I am a slayer of monsters."

"Rasida—"

"You are not ready yet," she says, dismissive. "Go back to your rooms. When you are ready to be mine and be civilized, you can return. But you are not there yet. Not by half. Will you ever be? My mother didn't think so."

"I'm yours, Rasida."

"You keep saying it," Rasida says, "and for a time, I think you believed it. Your body is mine, certainly, and what you carry. But not you. Not you. And it's *you* I want, Jayd. Body and soul."

She meets my look, and I think it, though I don't say it: "You will never have me." And though she cannot hear that thought—certainly her powers cannot go that far—she nods, once, and I feel that she's heard me, and it's twisted something in her, something that wasn't already twisted, which seems impossible. How can she be any more twisted?

"Good night, love," she says, and opens the door. And for the first time, I pity her, because when she says *love*, I think she really means it. For her, this is love. This is what she does to someone she loves. And I wonder if I am any better, because this is what I did to Zan all those rotations ago. I seduced her until she loved me with all her heart, and when it came time to do what needed to be done, I was willing to sacrifice that love, but she was not. Instead, she left me and came back to me without a memory. And we began our long dance. It's the first time I consider that perhaps she lost her memory on purpose. Maybe it was not the Mokshi that took it. Maybe loving me was too much to bear.

Rasida is a slayer of monsters.

But so am I.

"I DON'T REMEMBER A TIME BEFORE I KNEW THAT
THE LEGION WOULD KILL US. THERE WAS NEVER A TIME
WHEN I DIDN'T STRIVE TO BE FREE OF WHAT IT HAS
MADE OF US. I THOUGHT THAT COULD ONLY BE ACHIEVED
BY MURDERING EVERYTHING THAT STOOD IN MY WAY."
—LORD MOKSHI, *ANNALS OF THE LEGION*

26

ZAN

The funerary feast is exactly that: a feast of the dead.

I'm not sure what I expected as I sit at the table and the bodies of the dead we hauled back from the great doorway are laid out before us. Ribs are cooked and slathered in sauce. Mushrooms are sliced and fried with fingers. I would be more repulsed if it all didn't smell so good.

I look at Casamir beside me, who simply sighs when she sees the heads of the dead lined up on the mantel of the enormous eating hall, their faces illuminated by great green bioluminescent flora. These plants are feathery ferns, and they hang from every crevice and niche and overhang in the irregular walls.

All around us, robed women carry bowls of water and tea and dishes made from the leavings of their dead.

"Eat, eat," says the woman who met us on the stairs. I have since learned her name is Vashapaldi, and she is a religious headwoman of some sort. Not the leader, no; that is the woman at the head of the table, sitting up there with Arankadash in the place of highest honor. The leader is much older, her hair shorn short in mourning, they tell me, as two of her kin were killed in the mutant attack. Or, rather, the mutant hunting party gone wrong.

I'm not sure what I think of the fare.

Casamir leans into me. "Not hungry?" she says.

"I haven't . . . eaten this before."

"What do you think you've been eating?" Casamir says. "Us and the world, we're all made of the same stuff." She raises a bowl of bitter wine.

I ask Vashapaldi where the wine comes from.

"From the orchards, of course."

"I'd like to see them. I haven't seen any plants here. Only mushrooms and some strange creatures."

Vashapaldi nibbles at a finger bone. "After supper, yes. I have something else for you as well."

I pick at my food and finally settle for eating a broth-based soup. I try not to think what it's flavored with. The broth is good. I have to admit that.

After we eat, we retire to the rooms they've given us, which are built into great bulbous mounds that remind me of the insect caves. Das Muni is so tired that she doesn't even protest when Vashapaldi returns and escorts me away to visit the orchards. As we walk along the well-worn path, I realize this is the first time since I've descended into the belly of the world that I've been free of Das Muni.

We travel up a long spiraling stair that has been carved into the flesh of the world. The flesh has been seared but still oozes in places, viscous green mucus. The pustules of light far above illuminate our way.

At the top of the stair, I smell something sweet. I crest the peak of the stairs and gaze out over a lush plateau, high above the rest of the settlement. Tangled vines are lined up on poles, stretching as far as I can see. There are a dozen tangled trees, too, not like the fungal pillar forest, but trees made of wood. I walk up to one and press my hand to the trunk, just to be sure. I know these things, these words, though I have no memory of seeing them.

"We grow hemp as well," she says, "and several kinds of tubers and green leafy vegetables."

"How?" I say. I gaze up at the pustules of light.

"Yes," she says, "the light is a factor. Only a few settlements have it. Many of them have gone out over the generations, leaving increasingly little. We bring our waste up here, and dead fungi and other detritus, to feed them. It took a long time, more generations than many remember, but eventually, we grew things here."

"Where did the seeds come from?" I ask.

"The traders. Casamir's people. They have a surprising trove of useful items, much of it salvaged from the muck at the center of the world. It's amazing what people throw away."

I breathe in the scent of the growing things. I crouch and take up a pinch of soil. It's rich and black and pungent. "The world doesn't absorb it?" I say. "And water—"

"We have everything we need," Vashapaldi says. She laughs softly. "It surprises you now, too. That amuses me."

"What do you mean?"

She pulls a fist-sized sphere from the pocket of her robe and holds it out to me.

I take it. It's soft on the outside. It gives just a little when I squeeze it, like a ripening fruit. It's green-gray and shiny. I have a flicker of familiarity, as if I should know what to do with it, but the feeling passes.

"What's this?" I say.

"I am hoping you can tell me," Vashapaldi says. "The last time you were here, you told me to hold it for you."

A cold knife of fear strikes my gut. "You've met me before?"

"About a cycle ago."

"How long is a cycle?"

"There are sixty heartbeats in a minute, sixty minutes in an hour, six hours in a period, six periods in a day, six hundred days in a cycle."

So, I finally know how long this has been going on, then. A cycle. "That's a long time," I say. "What else did I tell you?"

"You said your name was Zan. You were on a quest to save the Legion. I didn't ask more than that, and you did not offer. There is a woman you loved, though. I know that much, because you would not succumb to the charms of any other. We did try."

I squeeze the sphere.

"You said that if I ever saw you again," Vashapaldi says, "I was to give you that. You told me you likely wouldn't remember me, or even yourself, but that I would know you just the same, and that by giving you this, I could help you on your mission to save us all. And I have. So, I have kept my promise."

"What did I do for you," I ask, "that you held on to this so long?"

"You helped us with the children," she says.

"I haven't seen any children here," I say.

"They come in waves," she says. "We haven't had a child-bearer in some time. But we have several women coming into adolescence."

"There are pregnant women down there, though."

She raises her brows. "Of course. We all become pregnant. But not everyone bears a child. Those blessed of the light to bear children are highly sought after. That's how you helped us. You went out with our rangers and found a child-bearer. She perished after just a few births, but it was enough to ensure the survival of our people."

"How did I do that?"

Vashapaldi puts a finger to her lips. "Some things I don't ask."

I shiver. Was I a murderer and a kidnapper, too? The more I learn about the woman I used to be, the less I like her. Is there a way to stop becoming her? Once the memories all come back the way Jayd says they will, will I become this other Zan again? Will I lose myself?

I pocket the sphere. "Thank you," I say. "I'll need your help one more time, though."

"Anything."

"We have to go up to the next level, and the next after that, however long it takes to get back to the surface. To my home. There is . . . there's a woman I love who is in a lot of trouble. I have to get back to her."

"Ah, yes. The eternal story," Vashapaldi says. She lays a hand on my wrist. "It's all right, I'm not going to try to make you stay."

"How much longer is it to the surface?"

"I don't know. You talked of it then as now, but I have never heard of such a place. There are other levels, certainly, but the world is a great circle. You'll find that when you reach the top, you'll be back at the bottom again, back in the pits."

"I have to believe in something else."

"We all must believe something," she says, and points to the pustules on the ceiling. "I believe in the light. Come, I will find someone to accompany you."

When I get back to our quarters, all is still. Das Muni snores softly in her sleep, and Casamir fairly rumbles in hers. I stand outside for some time, watching the lights on the ceiling and the little clusters of robed women going about their daily business. I wonder who works the fields up there. Surely not these women in their pretty robes, and I think of the mutants. Is it a peaceful and perfect society if you don't see the filth? If you don't look too hard? Perhaps every society is a utopia when you fail to peel up all the layers and look at what's underneath.

It's Das Muni who wakes me after the sleeping period, and her expression is pained. "They want that woman to go with us," she says.

"Who?" I ask, and as I sit up, I see Arankadash in the doorway, leaning on her long club.

"I'm to take you to the sea," Arankadash says, "and the hole in the sky where we leave the children who have come out wrong. I am bringing rope, but none of you look fit enough to use it to go into the sky."

"If you don't want to—" I say.

She grimaces. "Councilor Vashapaldi has reminded me of my blood debt to you. You saved my life and brought my sisters home. We owe you a debt. It must be paid."

I have to admit I like this better than leaving behind a hunk of flesh.

"How far to the hole in the sky?" I say.

"Quite far. Many sleeping periods, but we have a way to get there faster. Then we must cross the sea. Sometimes there is a boat, sometimes not."

"What do we do if there's no boat?" Casamir asks.

Arankadash shrugs. "We'll consider that when the time comes."

"This seems like a vital piece of logistics," Casamir says.

"Have you actually been to this sea?" I ask Arankadash, and glance over at Casamir. "I'm having some trouble with guides who turn out to have no idea where they're going."

"I got us here, didn't I?" Casamir sniffs.

"I have been there," Arankadash says. Her tone is darker now, and I wonder if I've offended her. "There is a road," she says. "We will take a sledge to the sea. It's not as wild as the way down to the tinkers' door."

"We're *engineers*," Casamir says.

Das Muni tugs at my sleeve. "I don't feel well," she says. She has her cowl up.

"Are you sick?" I ask.

"I think there is something wrong with my guts," she says.

"Do you need to rest?" I ask.

"No, but we should go."

"You ate a lot last night," I say.

"Please, let's go from here."

"You say that about every place."

Casamir and Arankadash have resupplied us. Arankadash gives me a pack to carry too, made of hemp and slick material like that of my suit, all sewn together with sinew. I rub the shiny patches and think of the surface. How many of these suits did my sisters up there throw into the belly of the world without a second thought? Are all of these people, all of these different settlements, this whole world within the world, is all of this encompassed in what they call "bottom-worlders"? It seems a poor term for so much.

As we leave, the council of robed women comes out to see us off. Vashapaldi takes my hands and presses her forehead to mine.

"Is there anything I should tell you the next time you pass through here?" she asks.

"There won't be a next time," I say.

"Very well," she says, but I know she doesn't believe it. Is this my fate, to be recycled again and again? No. I don't believe in fate. I believe in making my own way.

We start off back down the broad steps and out again into the dim. I get ready for another long march, but then I see the sledge and its attendants below, and I come up short, remembering what Arankadash had said about a road.

The sledge is just that—a long vehicle on great slick runners. Hitched to the sledge are eight beasts with heads twice the size of ours. They have mashed-in faces and wobbly chins. Their ears hang down almost to their feet, and when they shake their heads, the ears look like enormous tassels. They have six legs, all lined with thick, horny fingers tipped in massive claws.

"What are these?" I ask.

Das Muni leans into me. Her skin is hot against my arm. I can feel it through her clothes and mine.

"Sledgesaw," she murmurs.

"They're deercats," Arankadash says. "We breed them for protection against the mutants. But they also do well hauling the sledge, when it's necessary."

"If one of those eats me," Casamir says, "I'm going to be very disappointed."

Arankadash pats one of the big animals on the head. It slobbers and works its mouth, revealing a long purple tongue. "They are quite nice," she says. "Just don't be mean to them."

We all settle into the sledge. Arankadash secures an inflated purse of light at the front. I'm not sure what's inside of it, but if I had to guess, they'd put whatever filled the pustules above into an inflated stomach or other sort of organ. Putting our gear in the middle, me and Casamir and Das Muni can sit on benches inside, knees pressed to our luggage. Arankadash takes a seat at the front on a broad seat of bone and hollers at the deercats. The sledge lurches forward. I grab hold of my pack, fearful we're all going to fall out, but after a couple of jerks, the sledge trundles off across the plain.

After the endless slogging through the levels of the world, the jerking, rattling, uneven ride over the terrain is oddly soothing. I end up sleeping for a good part of the journey. Das Muni curls up next to me, and she is so warm that I don't even crave a blanket.

It's not until I wake to the sound of retching that I realize I've been so focused on getting to the next place that I haven't stopped to care about Das Muni's increasing temperature.

When I wake, we're stopped at the side of a bone-and-flesh edifice that looks human-made. Blue lights blink on and off across the whole of a long-abandoned settlement.

Das Muni is standing a little away from the sledge, vomiting, while the deercats snort and slather.

Casamir is looking for something in her luggage and Arankadash remains seated, her expression bored.

I climb out of the sledge and go to Das Muni. "Are you all right?" I ask.

She wipes her mouth. "I'm pregnant again, I think," she says.

"Oh," I say. "How does it . . . How do you know?"

"It's the right time," she says.

"Come on now," Arankadash says, "I'm halfway through my pregnancy and you don't see me whining about it."

"I thought there weren't any child-bearers in your settlement," I say.

"Didn't say I was pregnant with a child," Arankadash says. "Most people don't give birth to children. We give birth to things the world needs." She gestured expansively to the ruins around us. "The world always needs bits and pieces of itself to be reborn. That's why we're here."

"I've seen what Das Muni gives birth to," I say. "I don't think that's necessary for any world."

"You can't pretend to understand the will of the Lord," Casamir says. She finds what she is looking for in her pack and munches on it.

I help Das Muni back into the sledge.

"So, you all just . . . get pregnant?"

"Predictable as breathing," Casamir says. "But more dangerous, of course. It can still kill you."

"What do you . . . give birth to?" It's another question I've been afraid to ask. But it's time to start reconciling myself with the answers.

"Mine is an amsharasa," Arankadash says.

"But . . . what is that?"

"A necessary piece of the greater whole," she says.

"And mine doesn't happen often," Casamir says, "which I think is pretty lucky. Maybe once every six cycles. So, it's only happened twice. The seers all say they're necessary things, yes, but we don't always keep them."

"Blasphemer," Arankadash says.

"Engineer," Casamir says. "It's not logical to keep something you have no use for. Sometimes we just put it into vats, make protein cakes out of it."

"That sounds . . . awful," I say.

Casamir shrugs. "It's life, is all."

We continue. The sledge gets stuck occasionally in the pitted road, and once, we have to unload and lift the whole thing up over a rotten hunk of the ceiling that has fallen across the path. I lift Casamir's torch and try to see the where it's fallen from, but far above us is only darkness.

"There used to be lights along here," Arankadash says. "But it's become unstable since I was a child. It gets worse and worse. We worry sometimes that the rot will reach our home. Maybe not this generation but the next."

"Can it be stopped?" I ask.

She shrugs. "We have too much invested in our settlement. It's the strongest in the region. When this rot comes up there . . . I don't know. We try to study it, but what's there to study? The world is old. Perhaps it has a limited lifespan, the way we do. Perhaps we are coming to the end of it."

"But there are . . . thousands of people here," I say. "Where will you all go?"

"Perish with the world," Arankadash says. "Me, you, everyone."

"That's a long way off," Casamir says. "There's nothing like this on my level."

"There will be," Arankadash says. "We didn't think it was real either when traders told us stories. But after a time, the traders stopped coming, and the rot spread."

I think of Anat's great war being raged all across the Outer Rim of the Legion, and I wonder how much she knows about how rotten the world is. Is that why she wants the Mokshi? Is it a younger world? But if what everyone has told me is true about how we are bound to the worlds we're born on, then moving her people to the Mokshi won't solve anything. Will it? Or is it more complicated than that?

Much of the task I've been given since I woke is sorting out the truth from the lies, the real from the rhetoric.

We camp for five sleeping periods before I finally smell the sea. The smell is brackish and rotten. A cool wind blows over us from the direction of the sea, and I wonder, again, about where the blasts of air are coming from. It's like the whole world is breathing.

Above us, great stalactites hang from the ceiling, dripping salty moisture onto us. The formations are mottled red and orange, the colors swirling. They are met from below by stalagmites, great rearing teeth twice as tall as I am, which make navigating the sledge difficult.

We stop twice more to free the sledge from an entanglement. The deercats are impatient and tug hard. Arankadash yanks at their reins and whistles for obedience, but they have caught the smell of the sea.

We come over a low rise, and there it is. The sea is a flat viscous gray soup. Great blue lights glow and shift within it, roiling like living things. After a moment, I decide they are living things—it's their heads and spines that glow. Each is long as the sledge. I climb to the top of an outcropping along the edge of the sea and gaze out. There are lights moving along the ceiling, too, a forest of green glowing fungi. I can see far enough across the sea to note a horizon, that place where the blue-shimmering sea meets the green sky. Dark shapes are flying over the sea and occasionally skim the water. They have black leathery wings wide as hands and bulbous bodies, but that's all I can make out from this distance and in this light.

"I stood exactly there when I first saw the sea," Arankadash says. "I did not believe such a thing could exist."

"It's extraordinary," I say.

Casamir points to the flying beasts. "Can we eat those?"

"We can eat anything," Arankadash says, "but I'll tell you they are difficult to catch, and when they claw up your face, you will regret your decision to pursue them. They taste awful. Not worth the effort."

Das Muni stands at the edge of the sea, silent, her cowl up.

I have not noticed a swell in her belly, but I can see it now on Arankadash as the wind blows against her body, pushing her long robe behind her and revealing her full outline. Doesn't it terrify them all, I think, to have no control over when and what they give birth to? But it's normal here, isn't it? As normal as eating one's companions and swimming across a viscous sea. I press my hands to my own belly. What am I meant to give birth to? Is this another reason my memory is stripped away, because the truth is too much for me?

"I don't see a boat," Casamir says.

I tear my gaze from the horizon and back to the shore. She is right. There is no boat, only a long beach made up of bits of calcified deposits and ground metal pieces. I hop off the crag and take up a fistful of the stuff. No doubt Casamir's people will sift all the metal from this and make a fortune with it.

"Sometimes it's farther down," Arankadash says.

"When were you here last?" I ask her.

"When I left my child here and gave it to the light," she says. "It was born wrong."

I don't know what to say to that.

Casamir heads farther down the shore.

"Das Muni and I will look the other way," I say. Arankadash waves a hand at me.

I start in the opposite direction, but Das Muni isn't following me. She is still staring at the sea.

"What is it?" I say. "Come on."

"It's so beautiful," she says.

"The Mokshi doesn't have seas?"

"It's a very different place," she says.

"You should tell me about it."

"No. It was a long time ago. It's better to forget." She walks down the beach, head lowered.

"Is there a family in charge there?" I ask. "Like the Katazyrnas? Did you live below, like here?"

But she doesn't answer, only toes the shoreline. I sigh and march out ahead of her, swinging my walking stick. My leg has been bothering me less. The compress from Casamir's people fell out back in Arankadash's settlement, leaving a scarred chunk in my leg. When I saw it, I laughed because it seemed like I had created a secret compartment within myself, some terrible living pocket for contraband. But it also had the desired effect. It reminded me of my promise to Casamir's people.

We find many things along the shore, including a jellified animal that washed up there. It's twice as long as I am, with a tangle of tentacles and transparent body. I suspect it's one of the glowing blue things in the sea. I give it a wide berth.

Das Muni picks up little items as we walk; a metal square, a polished bone disk, a carved wooden ring tangled in slimy weeds.

But no boat.

The green fungus above begins to fade, and I realize it must be on another cycle, like the creatures down in the pits.

"We should get back to the others," I say, and Das Muni nods.

Then it begins to rain.

The drops come soft at first, like the rain in Casamir's city. Then it comes harder, big dirty drops smeared red. They soon coat our faces, and when I see Das Muni's face, it's as if she is crying blood.

Something thunks into the ground between us. A heavy stone hits my arm. Stone? Is that what it is? The hard little pellets are unfurling on the ground and wriggling away like snakes with legs. They rattle down around us, so fast and furious I raise my hands up over my head.

Das Muni points away from the beach. "Up there!"

I see a crumpled shadow on higher ground. I run after Das Muni. We crouch under a long shelf. I can't tell what it is or what it's made of in the dark, but it provides cover from the rain of snake-lizards.

They scurry up toward us, trying to take over our shelter. Das Muni kicks at them, and I help her. I don't know if they're venomous, but I don't like them.

As the rain subsides, we huddle up under the overhang and wait. I feel something behind me shift as I lean back.

"What is this?" I say. There's no light, but my eyes are adjusting to the dim. The object behind me has a long nose and a low, flat bottom. It's a little spongy, like everything seems to be, but it seems to be repelling water instead of absorbing it. The surface is slick with dewy moisture. It's warm under my hands and shifts beneath my fingers.

I jerk away.

"What is it?" Das Muni says.

"Something alive," I say.

"Oh, no," she says. "That's just a boat, I think."

Her eyes are enormous in the dim, and I remember that she can see far better than I can.

We haul the boat down to the shore. It's even stranger than I thought back in the cave. Its middle is fat, and it pulses as if it's breathing. The sides are curved up and out, expanding the breadth of the boat enough that I think we can all get in. Most peculiar are the eight fins that flop at its side.

Das Muni and I wait down on the beach for Arankadash and Casamir to return. Das Muni curls up next to the animal-boat and whispers a little song to it, so low that I cannot make out the words. I scan the water. More creatures wait there, I know. Stranger things.

I hear Arankadash and Casamir before I see them. They are arguing about what it was that fell from the sky, and why.

I stand and wave. "I found a boat. Or something like a boat?"

"Yes, that's it," Arankadash says.

We work together to get the slippery thing into the water. "Will it swim away?" I ask.

"Hold tight," Arankadash says, "and jump in quickly."

When the boat reaches the edge of the water, the fins start flapping. It shivers, as if in anticipation.

"How are we going to control this thing?" I ask.

"It knows the way," Arankadash says.

I gaze out at the hazy blue light of the creatures bobbing just below the surface of the sea. "That's not very comforting," I say.

"It's not meant to comfort," she says. "It's truth."

Casamir and Das Muni get into the craft, and Arankadash and I push it into the sea. The boat begins paddling its arms immediately, and I have to scramble to get myself inside. The viscous, watery sludge that makes up the sea clings to my trousers and soaks me through. I roll into the craft as Casamir tugs at my arms.

Arankadash is already in. She's positioned herself at the head of the craft as we glug out into the sea.

I catch my breath and peer back over the edge of the thing at the bobbing lights.

Das Muni squirms up beside me. "Do you think they'll see us?"

"I don't know," I say. "Let's just . . . be quiet."

Arankadash glances back at us. "I have been this way half a dozen times," she says. "We have never had trouble crossing."

"You couldn't even find the boat this time," Casamir says.

Arankadash sniffs. "That's not my fault. Someone who came before did not put it back where it's supposed to be. That's all."

"Who last used it?" I ask.

"I did not see a sign on it," Arankadash says. "Did you?"

"Sarcasm," I say. "Soon you'll be telling jokes."

The craft moves slowly across the sea. It's like paddling through a heavy stew. I perch on the back of the craft and watch the shoreline recede. After an hour, I cannot see the rim of the shoreline anymore, and I look ahead into the darkness. Great stalactites make an upside-down forest ahead of us, clawing down toward the sea with their thorny fingers.

We stand up and push against them when we come too close; it's the only way we have to steer the craft. And still the thing paddles onward.

I can see no shore, even after several hours on the flat sea.

"How much longer?" I ask Arankadash.

She is mending one of her weapon harnesses. "We will arrive when we arrive," she says.

"It's so still out here," Casamir says. She pokes her hand into the water.

"Stop that," I say. "You'll get it bitten off."

I continue to watch the lights of the creatures bobbing just below the surface.

"They probably don't eat things as big as us," Casamir says.

"You don't know that," I say. "There could be anything living in here."

Casamir dips her hand into the water again and comes up with a handful of the sludge. Sniffs it. "Rotten-smelling, isn't it? Think you could eat it?"

"Maybe *you* could eat it," I say. I can't fault any of them for trying to eat everything that grows out of this dark place.

Casamir leans far forward, and I turn away to look for the shore again. I'm not as patient as Arankadash.

I hear Casamir's curse and a curious gulping sound.

Das Muni is standing where Casamir used to be, and Casamir is struggling in the gooey waters of the sea.

"What did you do?" I yell at Das Muni. I reach for Casamir.

The bobbing lights all around us go very still. My fingers slip right off Casamir's skin. I can't get purchase.

"Arankadash!" I say, but she is already beside me.

We each grab one of Casamir's arms.

The lights begin to move again. They speed toward us, a dozen, maybe more.

We get Casamir halfway up. I push far over to hook my other arm under her leg. The vessel rocks and the paddling arms flail.

I hear a great moaning sound that makes the craft tremble, and I realize the moaning is coming *from* the boat. I lose my grip on Casamir and slip over the side.

I plunge into the sea. It's warm as soup. I muck about in it, grasping for the edge of the craft. My leg hits something beneath me. Lights dance past my elbow. I press back my terror and think only of what I know: the boat and Arankadash's open palm.

A massive appendage surfaces next to me. I call it an appendage because it doesn't have anything resembling a face.

Casamir shrieks and her head goes under.

I dive for her, but the sea is so heavy, it's difficult to dive. I surface and yell at Arankadash for a weapon. She tosses me her spear. I catch it and stab at the creature nearest me. The sea roils. Eight large white tentacles rise from the water and grasp at the craft.

I stab again and again until pale streamers of blue fluid fill the sea around me.

One of the creatures surfaces. I see a globular belly, a multitude of eyes. I stab at the belly. There's a squelching sound. Air and offal splatter back in my face. The animal sinks, the sac deflating as its tentacles writhe around it.

I dive again, kicking with all my strength, willing my bad leg to propel me harder and faster. I push the butt end of the spear ahead of me to extend my reach. It bumps into something. I claw forward. Snatch at a bit of cloth. Pull.

I come up gasping, dragging Casamir with me. I kick to the edge of the craft and heft Casamir toward Arankadash and Das Muni, though I see that Das Muni does not put out her hands until I meet her eyes.

I throw the spear in after Casamir and clamber up, kicking against the boat as it continues on its journey, oblivious to our concerns.

I heave in a long breath. All around us, white tentacles and frilly appendages have surfaced. They move in time with the lights of the bodies of the creatures they belong to, circling and circling as the craft powers on.

I crawl to Casamir. She isn't breathing. I turn her over and whack her on the back a few times until she vomits.

When I look up, I see Das Muni staring down at us from the front of the craft, eyes narrowed.

I leap for her, and she turns in on herself, cowering. I take her by the shoulders and shake her. "What were you thinking?" I say. "What kind of animal are you?"

"She's a mutant," Arankadash says. "Any fool can see—"

"You shut up," I say. "Das Muni? What's going on in your head? We're all in this together."

Her eyes fill, but she says nothing.

I let her go, exhausted. The watery stuff in the sea is terribly sticky and tastes like rotten flesh and soiled cotton. I pick up Arankadash's spear and heave it at the nearest tentacle.

"Don't aggravate them anymore," Arankadash says. "Sit down."

"After all that?" I say. "They nearly killed us!"

"They are curious creatures," she says. "Let them be."

"Is everyone mad here?" I say. "Every one of you?"

Casamir spits gummy water from her mouth and croaks, "I'm not mad."

"That's what a mad person would say!"

"Look," Das Muni says, pointing.

There, far ahead of us, the stalactite forest ends, and beyond that, I see the curve of what appears to be a shoreline. There's a gleaming dagger of light there, too, but I can't figure out what it is from this far.

I sag back down into the craft. "I hope there's real water over there," I say.

Casamir stares over the side of the boat, watching the creatures surfacing farther out. "They're surfacing and filling their bellies with air," she says, spitting. "They have to come up for air sooner or later."

"I'd prefer later," I say.

When we reach the shore, I hurl myself out of the boat. Arankadash leaps out after me, and we haul the boat up onto the shore.

Das Muni is shaking as I pull her out. I'm soaked in brackish bile. Casamir collapses on the beach and takes fistfuls of the sand into her fingers. She's gabbling in her language, something that sounds like a prayer.

I stare out at the cone of light that pierces the darkness. It paints a great burnt-yellow circle onto the sands.

Arankadash comes up beside me.

"What happened to your child?" I ask, staring up at the hole in the sky.

"I was given a child," Arankadash says. "The child-bearer came some time ago, and there were a dozen new children in the settlement to raise. It is a gift from the light. But . . . not all children come out right. This is where we take them when they are wrong. We give them back to the sky. We . . . we never know what happens to them after that."

"Did you ever want to?" I ask.

She doesn't reply.

I take a moment to consider how much to tell her, and then I say, "I think I threw away a child. I don't have a clear memory of it, but it was a child, no bigger than my fist, and I threw it into the darkness. I know what it is to want a resolution."

Casamir whistles softly. "That's a long way up, Zan."

"It was a long way here," I say, shaking away my memory. Arankadash is still not looking at me. What did I expect? "I'm not turning around. How do we get up there?" There's no wall to climb, no rope, only a blistered hole in the sky, just as Arankadash described it.

Casamir walks over to it, and I follow. We both stand in the streaming light coming in from above. I squint, trying to see the source of the light, but it's so dazzling, I can't see what's making it.

"Ideas?" I say.

Casamir chews her lip. She counts off six paces, then six more, bringing her to the edge of the circle of light. "Huh," she mumbles, and then she starts doing what I assume are sums in her language.

I cross my arms and examine the edges of the hole. Like the blistered folds of the hole in the Mokshi, it looks like something has burst down toward us as opposed to bursting up and out. That implies plenty of stuff falls in but not much goes out. Only the babies.

"Are you sure they ascend?" I ask Arankadash. "The babies? You're sure they're not . . . eaten?"

"I have heard . . . ," Arankadash says. "I have heard that they go up in the light."

I stare up again, long enough to be a little blinded when I look away. Whatever power the light has, it doesn't work on me or Casamir.

Casamir brings her torch over. I feel the heat of it as she raises it high. "I have an idea," she says. "But it may be a bit . . . labor-intensive."

"It's not as if we've got anywhere else to go," I say, "but up."

"Hot air rises," Casamir says, tapping the torch. "We've made sacs of heated air with torches at home to scout out the upper reaches of the sky and provide transit. It's a possible thing."

"You're kidding," I say.

"I never joke about science."

"I doubt a backpack full of air is going to be enough to carry me up," I say. "Even if we can get one of these airtight."

Casamir gestures to the sea. "We've seen that those things have got sacs they use to surface," she says. "We can use those."

"They'd need to be butchered and dried and—"

"I did say labor-intensive," Casamir says.

"Well," I say, and sigh, because nothing here is ever easy. "You want us to go back in and fish that thing out, don't you?"

"Sorry?" she says.

"Better than being stuck here."

We head back into the boat.

"THE SECRET TO LEADERSHIP IS NOT TO BE
A PARTICULARLY INTELLIGENT PERSON.
IT IS TO SURROUND ONESELF WITH THOSE FAR SMARTER
THAN ONESELF. AND TRY NOT TO KILL THEM."
—LORD MOKSHI, ANNALS OF THE LEGION

27

ZAN

Hauling and drying out the creature is a massive undertaking. I'm not sure Casamir realized what an ordeal it would be. But there are four of us and one creature, and nowhere else to go but up. We make neat work of it.

When it is done, I'm still not convinced this is going to be successful. I sit down on the beach and wipe my face on my sleeve as Casamir stuffs the torch into the end of the animal's sac.

We wait. Casamir seems utterly confident. She crouches next to the thing, muttering to herself. Arankadash is already asleep a few paces away, probably the smartest one of us. Das Muni is still picking her way up the beach, putting shiny baubles into her pocket.

I'm not sure when I first notice the bag inflating. It seems like an age has gone by. But there it is, sure enough: a rippling there at the end of the organ.

Casamir claps her hands and comes over. "It'll be a while," she says. "Let's eat."

We sit down to eat and watch the organ slowly inflate. Above us, the canopy of green fungi shifts color again. I fear another rain of little snake creatures, but there's nothing this time, only a dimming of the light.

"You still up for going this far?" I ask Casamir.

She leans back on her elbows, grins. "This is the most fun I've had in ages. Wait until they hear about it back home. No one has gone this far." She gazes up at the halo of light.

"Maybe there is a reason for that," Arankadash says, sitting down next to us. She rifles through Casamir's pack for an apple and peels away the outer skin. I wonder why I haven't thought to do that yet.

"Don't be superstitious," Casamir says.

Arankadash says, "Not everything can be explained with the mind. There are larger things than our mind, things so great we cannot comprehend them."

"Believing that is what keeps the mind weak," Casamir says.

"I know only what I've seen," I say, "and I've seen other worlds just like this one, hundreds of them, hanging in the darkness."

"Well, you're mad," Casamir says, "but I'm getting used to you."

"It's no madder than this idea," Arankadash says, nodding to the half-inflated balloon.

"It's simple science," Casamir says. "Hot air rises. You've never made a paper lantern?"

"What's paper?" Arankadash says.

"It's so strange," I say, "that we all live in the same place, but everything is so different from place to place."

"Not really," Casamir says. "If everything is the same, we wouldn't be living in a free society. It would be a tyranny. Who wants to live in a hierarchy? When you have hierarchy, someone always has to be at the bottom. I can't live comfortably, knowing someone is always suffering so I can have more."

"Maybe you'd be at the top," Arankadash says. "The priests get more resources in our city. They do important work."

"I can't speak for everyone, obviously," Casamir says, rolling her eyes.

Arankadash snorts and finishes the apple. "You tinkers, always thinking you're so much better. If we didn't kill the mutants before they stormed your level, you would all die of stupidity. You cannot even pick up a club."

Casamir says, "It's not a club getting us up there to see what happened to your child, is it?"

Arankadash says nothing.

"Sorry," Casamir says.

I glance at Arankadash. "You're coming with us?" I say. Had she told Casamir this when I was asleep? When did she decide this?

She gazes up at the hole in the sky. "I want to know," she says. "I want to know what happens to our children. What happened . . . to my child."

"I'm not sure you'll be able to get back," I say.

"I have nothing to go back for," Arankadash says. "I want to know what's up there." She gets up. "You sleep," she says. "I'll keep watch." She does not look at Casamir as she walks away, back into the halo of light.

"I'm not trying to be mean," Casamir says.

"Intent doesn't always matter," I say.

She's still trying to talk to me as I doze off. Sometimes it's just best to let her ramble.

It's Arankadash who wakes me. I'm not sure how much time has passed, but the fungi overhead are brilliant green again, and I see the pale, billowing form of the ballooned organ behind her. It squirms like a fat maggot, still rippling as it inflates.

Casamir is by its side, counting off the rope again. She holds tight to it, though it's tied off behind her on a jagged piece of metal jutting up from the beach.

"Something wrong?" I ask Arankadash.

It's Casamir who answers. "I'm not sure it's going to hold me," she says.

I walk over. "It's not full yet. Maybe—"

Casamir shakes her head. "I'm too heavy," she says. "We'll need to . . . I don't know, construct a second balloon, maybe sew it to this one?"

"Sew it with what?" I say.

She is gnawing on her lip, which I haven't seen her do before.

I glance over at Arankadash. We are both far larger than Casamir. I'm broader and taller, and though Arankadash is leaner than me, she's much taller than I am. If the balloon won't hold Casamir, it won't hold either of us.

"What about Das Muni?" I say.

"What?" Casamir says. The look she gives me tells me she didn't even consider that option.

"Das Muni's half your weight," I say. "She can get up there."

"And the rest of us?" Arankadash says.

"Casamir?" I say.

She shakes her head. "I don't . . . a pulley, maybe? But that's complicated. We can rig another line to the balloon. She gets it up there, puts it over something, and from down here, we can help pull up another person. Might save us some climbing time. Honestly, that's so far up, I'm not sure I can even do it on my own, just climbing."

"So, we'll put together more rope," I say.

"You want to leave her up there alone?" Arankadash says, low. I look for Das Muni. She is sitting far down on the beach, hugging her knees to her chest.

"She can do it," I say. "She's stronger than she looks."

"It's not her strength that concerns me," Arankadash says.

"I have more reason to trust her than you," I say. "Yet here we are."

Arankadash huffs out a breath of displeasure.

"All right," Casamir says. "We'll get more rope."

Making rope takes a lot of time, but when it's done and Casamir has explained the pulley to Das Muni, we tie her into a makeshift harness made of rope and hook her to the balloon.

As I check the knots, I say quietly, "Are you sure you can do this?"

She nods. She gazes at me with her big, glassy eyes. Her large ears twitch in the folds of her cowl. "I would do anything for you," she says softly.

"Don't do it for me," I say. "Do it for you."

"All right," she says.

I cannot bear her looking at me, so I step away. Nod at Casamir.

"Hold on," Casamir tells her. I get behind Casamir to help her guide the rope, and the balloon with it. She unties the balloon from the metal crag and Das Muni slowly begins to rise.

As Das Muni's feet leave the ground, she squeezes her eyes shut. I watch her ascent, so slow and laborious that I don't believe she will reach the hole in the sky.

Casamir does not take her gaze from Das Muni. She shifts her weight back, righting the balloon's course to ensure it doesn't hit the edges of the hole but goes up clean through it.

"Not bad for a tinker, huh?" Casamir says.

"Not for a tinker," Arankadash says.

The balloon continues drifting upward. I hope there's something for Das Muni to affix that rope to up there, because I've just started really imagining the climb up. It's at least twice the height of the climb that Casamir and I did back in the recycling pits.

Casamir hisses and steps back again. "Help me right her!" she says. "There's a wind up there!"

Das Muni is tugged hard to the left of the hole. I grab the rope and help haul the balloon back. She's only a few body lengths from the top now.

"All right, let go," Casamir says.

I do. The wind has died down and the rope is no longer pulling in the other direction.

"Think she'll get eaten by something up there?" Arankadash asks.

"Too late for that now," I say.

The balloon rises into the crack in the sky.

"All right, help me pull it flush against the side," Casamir says.

We pull against the rope so Das Muni can get her footing on the rim of the hole, but we can't see much of anything anymore. The light hurts my eyes, and by now I'm a little blinded from staring up at it for so long.

"Now what?" I say.

"Just hold it."

We wait. Sweat pours down my face. Casamir wipes her forehead on her sleeve.

I can't stare up anymore without pain, so I look down, trying to clear my vision. Arankadash is right. There could be anything up there. What's making the light? If it kills Das Muni and pops the balloon, we're stuck. What then? Turn around? Find some other way up?

"Little help!" Casamir says.

I grab the rope. The balloon is tugging more strongly now.

"That mean she's free?" I ask.

Casamir doesn't answer.

I suppose it could mean all sorts of things. It could mean something ripped her off the balloon and ate her.

I see something fall from the sky. I step forward, instinctively, ready to catch Das Muni falling.

But it's not Das Muni. It's the rope. The one we need hooked up there so we can haul each other up.

Arankadash grabs it as it snaps down. It's just barely long enough for her to reach.

"I'll go up," I say.

"No," Casamir says. "Me first."

"The heaviest person should go first," I say. "That will give us two people on the ground here to help haul me up."

"Yes," Casamir says, and sighs as if I'm an idiot, a sigh I am getting used to. "But if the heaviest person waits until last, then there will be three people to help pull them up from the other direction."

When I work it out, it makes sense, but the idea of leaving Casamir and Das Muni together, or Casamir, Arankadash, and Das Muni together without me doesn't sit right.

Casamir folds her arms. "It's science," she says.

I gaze back up at the hole in the sky. "Well," I say, "I can't argue with science, now, can I?" No more than I can argue about gods with Casamir.

We work together to pull the balloon back down and get Casamir strapped to it.

Arankadash and I pull on the rope affixed above, and with the balloon's help, we send Casamir up into the light too.

She yells something down at us when she gets up there, but I can't make it out. I only hear the second part: "Send Arankadash!"

Arankadash and I haul the balloon back down and knot her up.

"This seems to be the easiest part," she says.

"I like easy," I say. "We deserve it."

I haul from the bottom, they haul from the top, and after a few minutes, Arankadash, too, disappears into the halo of light.

I'm alone on the ground for the first time since I fell into the recycling pit. I should enjoy the silence, but I can't help but stare out at the water and the floundering boat, which has fallen over on its side.

I walk over to it and right it, then push it back into the water. It paddles off happily, hopefully back to the other side.

There's yelling from above, so I run back and haul on the balloon so they don't think I've been eaten.

I tie off the balloon on the metal crag while I knot it around me. By now, the rope is slippery and frayed. I chance one last look up into nothing, then yank the rope free and call, "Haul me up!"

The balloon lifts me just enough so my toes brush the ground, but that's it. I have to admit Casamir's reasoning about weight is sound.

I begin to rise in fits and starts as they pull me up and up, into the light.

I stare up one more time, squinting, because I want to see and understand what I'm getting into, even knowing it's far too late.

"THERE ARE TWO THINGS THAT MATTER TO THE LEGION:
TOO MANY PEOPLE. AND NOT ENOUGH."
—LORD MOKSHI, **ANNALS OF THE LEGION**

JAYD

The cycles pass, one bleeding into another, as my belly grows and the thing inside of me comes to life. It's such a strange feeling, to know that there is a potential bit of life growing inside of you, to both fear for it and hope for it all at once. Life here in the Legion seems especially precious. This thing, this life, most of all. If it dies before I bear it . . . then Rasida will surely recycle me. And then what will become of us all? When I took this womb from Zan, she admitted she had never borne anything in it to term. She did not need more life on the Mokshi. She could hardly save the lives she already had to care for.

And I certainly didn't help her in that.

When I go into labor, finally, it is Sabita who takes my hands while the girls run off to find Rasida. I had wanted to get more done before now. I had wanted to find out where Rasida was hiding her own womb. But my body has betrayed me. I've been sick and exhausted, and now I am here, writhing in pain while I birth the very thing I was brokered to the Bhavajas for.

I have never given birth before, not in all these many rotations of treatments, but I have attended so many births, I think I know what I'm in for.

I'm wrong.

My whole body seizes up as if attached to a series of wiry strings. Every muscle contracts, my body cramps up, and I can do nothing but howl.

Sabita rubs my back and legs. I yell at her only once, because I soon lose the energy for it.

Rasida and her mother arrive. I am shocked to see Nashatra here because I thought her maimed or dead or recycled.

"I expected a first birth to take longer," Nashatra says. She is clean and well kept, only slightly stooped. Her silver hair is knotted into a rope that circles her head. She puts her leathery hands on mine, and I am in so much shock and pain I don't think to sign at her and ask what's going on.

Behind her comes a two-headed woman with three legs and three arms, and as the four eyes roll at me, I suspect these are the Bhavaja witches.

"Not ours! Not ours!" the witches say, and Rasida hisses at them to be quiet and help me.

"The worlds are dying because we won't share resources," Rasida says. "The only reason we're alive now is because we are willing to merge with others to become stronger."

The witches push and prod at me while Sabita continues her shushing. I follow the heave of her breath until we are breathing together, snorting through the pain that comes in endless waves.

I don't notice what the witches are doing. I am aware only of my own pain. It is while I huff and pant and squeeze here on the bed that I wonder again why Rasida has gone through all this with me. She could have given my womb to Sabita or the girls. Someone she had more control over.

But as Rasida looms over me, I am reminded that she wants me more than what I carry. She wants to have a Katazyrna under her heel. Maybe even a Katazyrna who loves her, because she has taken away everything else I could possibly love.

Lord of War be merciful, I despise her. I despise her and she is all I have.

"Here it is," the witches say, and I squeeze Sabita's hand and wail, and it's as if my body splits in two. It's as if I can see myself and the whole room; I'm floating far away, contained only by the world's gravity.

Another heave, and the thing is out.

I come back to myself.

The witches hold my offspring aloft. I am still shuddering as they hand the gift of my womb over to Rasida. I hear a mewling cry.

Rasida takes the thing into her arms and cradles it. From here, the child appears to have the expected number of limbs, but I can't be sure. Let it be perfect.

Rasida's mother takes the child from Rasida and inspects it, as if it is some prized piece of the ship, and I suppose it is.

Finally, she nods and hands it back to Rasida. "It's a perfect child," her mother says. "Just what they promised."

I am exhausted, still trembling. Sabita pulls a blanket up over me and rubs my cramping legs. I don't have the strength to tell her to go away.

"Can I see it?" I say.

Rasida considers me a moment. She sits beside me. She does not hand me the child but holds it up near my face. It is very small, purplish and still covered in afterbirth. The child makes a little moue with its mouth, its tiny fists held tight, and I cannot help but feel a squeeze of love for this thing I carried all this time, this thing I made with Zan's help.

Zan's child. Not mine.

I caress the infant's cheek. Oh Zan, I have failed you. I don't have the arm. I don't have the world. I only have this child, this child doomed to die here, trapped in a dying world.

Rasida rests next to me with the child in her arms and coos at it. She tickles its little lips with her fingers. "It will be hungry," she says. "I have a nurse for her. You can rest."

"Yes," I say. "Rest."

Rasida leans over me. Her face is beaming, beatific. "You have achieved a lovely thing," she says. "We will celebrate when you are well. Soon, you and I will be back on Katazyrna. You'll like that, won't you? Being among the flesh where you were birthed? We will build a whole new world, love, a whole new society."

She gets up and hands the child over to her mother. Nashatra stands a moment longer over us. It's then that I see the swell of Nashatra's belly, and all the long conversations with Rasida begin to make some semblance of sense.

"You want to save the world?" Rasida said to Nashatra, and she took her mother away, and now here was her mother, long past the age at which her own womb would give issue, standing visibly pregnant beside me.

I stare hard at the ceiling as Nashatra takes the child with her and leaves the room, the witches following close beside her. Birthing a world is dangerous, but all birth is dangerous. This is Nashatra's punishment, to stay here and birth the world while the rest of Bhavaja is moved to Katazyrna to await the remaking of Bhavaja. Rasida's plan is almost as grand as mine. I admire it, even if it makes what I need to do that much more difficult.

The girls arrive with water and towels and clean me up. Sabita helps them. I have nothing for the pain, which is deep and intense, but I am so exhausted that I'm able to sleep, if only in snatches.

When I wake, it's to find Sabita trying to express the milk from my breasts. She signs at me that Rasida has requested it. I'm uncertain why, as she said she had a nurse, but no milk is forthcoming. It's not time yet.

I wonder if the milk is for Rasida, not the child, and with that thought, I sleep again.

Some time passes, and when I come to next, Sabita is lying on the floor next to me. I tap her on the arm. Her eyes open. I sign at her, "We need to move now. I know where to find what we need."

Sabita's eyes widen. I have not confided in her over all this time, but now that the child is here, my time is running short. The child will be able to breed more children, unlike many of the other child-bearers that Anat could have offered Rasida. Zan had that peculiar specialty with her womb. A specialty she had no use for. Rasida may keep me for a few more births, or not. She has me beaten.

Sabita signs, "I know you despise me, but I am not your enemy."

"We are both captive," I sign.

"I know a way out," she signs.

"I can't leave without Rasida's womb."

"What does she carry?"

I hesitate, then sign, "What she carries can save worlds. I think she's given it to her mother, Nashatra. We must get Nashatra off Bhavaja."

"You intend to save Katazyrna with it?" Sabita signs.

I'm still worried about telling her too much. So I lie and sign, "Yes."

Sabita is silent for a time. She folds her hands across her chest and gazes at the ceiling.

"Will you help me?" I sign. "She won't keep you any longer than she will keep me. This may be over now that the child's here. You understand?"

Sabita makes a quick sign. "Yes."

I let out my breath and sign, "I will need you to cover for me in my absence. Soon."

"What will you do?" Sabita signs.

"It's best you don't know," I sign. "You can tell them I forced you to it, if we're caught."

She does not answer. If she is going to betray me, she will betray me in the morning.

When I wake, it is with the knowledge that this could be my last day breathing, one way or another.

But when I see Sabita wake on the floor next to me, she signs, "Let me tell you about the tunnel I've been making," and hope blooms within me anew.

It's another ten cycles before I feel well enough to leave our quarters. Even then, it takes three attempts. The girls are always awake, always eager to please Rasida, and there are women outside the large foyer who guard our way.

But Sabita is a tissue technician, and she has been burrowing out an old doorway in one of my rooms, slowly carving away the slab of meaty flesh so that it opens now like the peel of a fruit. Sabita takes her place in my bed, pulling the covers up over her head, and I sneak out twice before eventually finding my way back to Rasida's quarters. Sneaking is painful; I cannot move very quickly. My walk is more a shuffle, but my advantage is that Rasida will not think me capable of walking even this far.

She has visited me several times during my recovery, always bringing small gifts, bits of other worlds, sheets of paper, colorful strands for the loom. I gave her a fine colorful cape I had woven for her, and she wears it now like a fine suit.

I, too, can smile like a villain.

The door to Rasida's rooms opens at my touch. Like her wardrobe, she does not bother with locks. Or perhaps there are none here. Perhaps the world doesn't know how to create them anymore. One more broken piece.

I go to her wardrobe and open it. Inside are a line of suits and some piles of embroidered bags and two obsidian machetes. Has she moved it already? I wonder where else she would have put it, and turn to look under the bed.

"What are you doing?"

Rasida is standing in the doorway.

She is wearing the iron arm.

My legs nearly give out from under me. I have to catch myself against the wardrobe. I want to scream. Seeing her wearing that arm reminds me of the last time I stole it, and what I had to sacrifice for it, but I clench my teeth and say nothing. Try to feel nothing.

Rasida smiles and holds up the arm. "Fits well, doesn't it?"

"How did you get it on?" I ask. "Anat had to . . . It didn't fit her very well."

"I have my ways," she says. She comes around the bed to me. Grabs the edge of the wardrobe door with her iron fingers. "You know what I loved about you when you were a child?" she says.

I shake my head.

"Boundless curiosity," she says. "Fearlessness. When we first came to talk peace with your mother all those rotations ago, do you remember it? You weren't even at menarche yet. My aunt still led us then, but I would supplant her soon. And when we met Anat, you stood beside her with your sisters and stared us all down. My mother, my aunt, and me. You didn't care. And when your mother and sisters left, you came right up to me, though I am ten rotations your senior, and you lit into me with a barrage of questions. Fearless." She shuts the wardrobe with her iron arm.

I flinch.

"What's your game here, Jayd?" she says. "You have given birth to my child. You say you are my family. But still you creep about, sniffing after something. What do you need this arm for, if it only works on Katazyrna? Do you think you're going back?"

"That's not what I came for," I say. "I just . . . I didn't know where you were. You haven't been to see me in some time. I thought I'd look for you."

"When I am able to see you, I come to see you. That's why I brought you Sabita, to give you comfort when I cannot. The wars I must wage to unite the Legion are many. They keep me very busy."

"I feel like a prisoner," I say, and sit on the bed.

"That is not my intention. You know that."

"If you're wearing the arm," I say, "we must be very close to going home. Did you find the Katazyrna witches?"

She flexes her fist. "You say it works on Katazyrna, but I have tried it there, with no luck. Perhaps only a Katazyrna can wield it. Your daughter will wield it."

I say nothing. She hasn't found the Katazyrna witches yet, then.

Rasida watches me. Drums her metal fingers on the wardrobe door. Finally, she sits beside me. "I am a woman who is meant to conquer worlds," she says, "not birth them."

"I would like to birth your worlds," I say.

She kisses me.

Fear and desire are tangled things in this place. She has not kissed me since that first night, and I am angry at my body's response to her touch. But Rasida simply lies beside me and holds me close. I exhale, relieved and grateful and hating myself for feeling either.

It's only as she settles her iron arm around me that I understand the importance of the gesture. She holds me close with my mother's arm.

I take the arm in mine and hold her.

"You are the mother to Bhavaja's children," she says. "Let's keep you as such."

"But who is better suited to birth worlds than you?"

"My mother," she says.

I hold the arm in my hands, but it's attached to a woman who will crush me with it as surely as Anat would. While it was unattached, I had a chance. Now . . . I don't know. Without the arm, I will never be able to get inside the Mokshi.

"Don't fret for Bhavaja," she says. "The world grows inside of my mother now. When we move enough to Katazyrna, she will stay here and birth a world. That world will begin to remake Bhavaja. When you and I return here, we will be Lords of not only Bhavaja but of the whole Outer Rim, and then the Legion."

Her mother. I have never been so disappointed to be right. With the arm, I could have carved my way to Nashatra. We could have had a chance to fight our way out of Bhavaja. Now that Rasida has put it on, I'll have to kill her in order to leave. I don't have the option of doing what I did on the Mokshi.

"It is a grand vision," I say.

"I want you by my side for it," she says.

"I will be," I say. "But, Rasida, please, I must feel less like a prisoner. I want to be happy here, but I can't feel that way as a kept thing."

Rasida kisses my neck. She rolls over on top of me, straddles me, and takes my face into her hands. Peers into my eyes. I let my expression soften. I push away the fear. I remember what it was when I first feared Zan.

"All right," Rasida say. "So long as the girls are with you."

"Thank you," I say, and I kiss her, and the gratefulness I feel in that moment is not feigned. I hold her iron arm tight and wonder how I am going to cut it off of her and leave this dismal place.

Rasida offers to lead me back to my rooms, but I challenge her. "So soon after saying I'm not a prisoner, you wish to give me escort?"

She sighs and says, "You will learn that it is more for your safety than mine. But go."

I consider that as I make my way back to the heavy foyer. The women posted there do a double take as I enter, but I ignore them.

I cross the foyer and find that the door to my rooms is open. I move over the threshold and note that the room is very still.

There's a low-hanging arch leading to my bedroom. I see a dark spill of something there and walk around it.

My bed is empty.

The girls are lying dead on the floor.

I limp into the next room, and the next, searching for Sabita, calling for her, but she is gone.

I lean against the outer door, trying to catch my breath. I've told Sabita about Nashatra. I told Sabita about the world.

What is she going to do with it?

"I CAN'T TELL YOU WHAT I THOUGHT THE FIRST TIME
THE KATAZYRNAS TRIED TO BOARD THE MOKSHI.
NO, WAIT. I CAN. I CAN TELL YOU THE WOMAN
WHO LED THEM FOUGHT LIKE A DEMON.
SHE FOUGHT LIKE THE MOTHER OF WORLDS."
—LORD MOKSHI, ANNALS OF THE LEGION

29

ZAN

come up through the hole in the sky and into a world of light. I shield my eyes. Hands grab my arms and waist and haul me over onto solid ground. Or mostly solid. My feet sink into a soggy mire.

They're untying the ropes. I can see hands if I squint. "Where's Das Muni?"

"I'm here." I see her little grayish hands and let out a breath. My eyes are starting to adjust. "Where are—"And then I look up from the hands to the room, and I stop speaking. I stop moving. I stare.

The room is a massive circular space, voluminous like the region below, but lined in row upon row of massive bodies. The bodies are suspended in glowing amber. Light beams from their eyes and mouths and wafts up to a great orb at the center of the room that hovers above them. I have a long breath where I realize the orb reminds me of the artificial sun at the center of the Legion. But the bodies?

They are giants, these bodies. Three times taller than me, with hooked noses and hairless heads and faces. They are twisted unnaturally in their amber prisons. Some are half sunk in the floor, others reach out at us from the ceiling, only their hands visible, as if they have been consumed by the ship itself.

"We think they're gods," Das Muni says.

Casamir lets the balloon go, and it wafts out across the great room. The sense of space, flooded with light, is so great that I feel almost as if I'm outside of the ship.

"Giants," I say.

Arankadash presses her hand to the amber casing of a figure, its torso bent half-backward, a rictus forever marked on its face. "Is this what they do to the babies?" she says softly.

"I'm . . . I'm sure that's not . . ." But I can't continue. "We need to go," I say.

"I want to find my child," Arankadash says. She gazes into the light-seared faces of the captured giants. Is this what becomes of these children? Trapped in amber? For what purpose?

I drop my voice low. "Whatever did this to the children will do it to us too if we don't get out of here," I say.

"Is this the place?" Arankadash says. "The place you threw away your child?"

"No," I say. "The place where I threw away my child was dark. Very, very dark. And I don't know if it is was my child, really, or someone else's."

"Can we stop talking about babies and move?" Casamir says. She's already three rows of bodies down. "I'm not staying here to find out what this is."

I head after her, and Das Muni grabs my hand and squeezes it hard. We meet up with Casamir. I turn and see Arankadash still frozen in front of the giant.

"Leave her," Casamir says. "She is locked in the past."

I let go of Das Muni's hand. "You two go ahead. Find a way out."

"Zan!" Casamir says. "Fire take you, Zan, you promised we'd see the surface."

"You will!" I say, and lower, to myself, "All of us will."

I gently take Arankadash's arm. "It's not yours," I say.

"How do we know?" she says. "What are they doing to them?"

"Do you want to go back?" I ask.

"No."

"Then we must go forward."

She sags against me. I hang onto her and gaze up at the giant's blazing eyes. "Come on," I say.

I step away, but she grabs my arm hard.

"I . . . can't," she says, and gazes down at her feet.

I look, too, and yank my own feet up from the sucking floor. The floor is running up over her boots, oozing a thick, amber sap.

"Get out of your boots," I say.

"I can't—"

"You can. You will," I say. I untie her boots, hopping from foot to foot as the ground tries to tug at me, too.

I yank her free and together we run, arm in arm, across the brilliant yellow room.

"Casamir!" I call. "Casamir! Das Muni!"

Nothing.

I pull Arankadash in the direction I last saw them in, and we sprint down another long aisle of bodies, each more grotesquely postured than the last.

I hear a terrible squealing and tug Arankadash the other way. "That sounds like Das Muni!" I say.

I'm out of breath now, but we keep on because the sticky fluid on the floor is building up on my shoes and her bare feet, and it's only a matter of time before our feet become too heavy to move.

I turn a corner and see Das Muni halfway up a broken mound. It's a shattered giant, upended. It's torn a hole through the wall, opening a portal into inky darkness.

Casamir is wallowing in amber up to her ankles at the other end of the statue, trying to paw her way after Das Muni.

I yank out my walking stick as we near and bring it down hard on Casamir's ankle.

She yelps. The amber cracks. I hit the casing around her twice, three times.

Das Muni shrieks again and slides back down the lower half of the statue. She lifts her feet up, avoiding the ground.

"Stop hitting me!" Casamir says.

"Then get up!" I say.

Casamir turns and tries to get up the statue, but like Das Muni, she slides right back down.

"Stay there!" I say.

"What—"

I don't give her time to think. I take a running jump and leap onto her back and propel myself up the side of the statue to the rift in the wall. My hands slip. Gain purchase. I struggle over the other side, feet kicking against the giant. All I can see is darkness; that doesn't mean it's dark, only that it's darker than the brilliant room.

I reach for Casamir. "Up!"

Casamir grabs my hand, and I pull her up. Arankadash heaves Das Muni over her shoulder. Das Muni squeals again, and I think of a dying animal. I grab her hand and pull her over.

Arankadash gazes up at me. I hold open my hand.

She takes it.

I pull her over, and into the darkness.

All around us is a crystal forest.

It takes us some time to realize that, because we're still half blind from the transition from light to dim. The crystals give off a faint gray-white light.

We stumble on, aimless, for at least five or six thousand steps before Casamir says, "Where are we going?"

"Away," I say.

"We should rest," Arankadash says.

I say nothing but collapse where I stand. The edges of the crystals have been smoothed by time, but they don't make comfortable seats, even so.

We drink water and eat. I try to catch my breath. The light keeps coming back to me. I'm going to dream of that light, those giants.

"I thought we had entered the den of the skull-eater," Arankadash says.

I start at the name. "What did you say?"

"The skull-eater," she says, "the Lord of War."

"Someone called me that once," I say. "Why would they call me that?"

She shrugs. "They thought you were a god?" She says it like it's amusing to her.

"Does *skull-eater* mean something else among other *people*?" I ask.

"Your people are different than mine," she says. "If they were your people who said it."

"I don't know whose people they were," I say, and that's true. I feel I know far more about the world below the Katazyrnas than I know about the Katazyrnas.

"We should keep moving while we have the strength," Casamir says. "I don't like this place."

"It's better than the last one," I say.

But we move on.

As we walk and our eyes adjust, the size of the crystals grows too. Soon they tower above us, so high they touch the ceiling, which is also covered in crystalline structures.

Das Muni picks her way ahead of us, the first time I can remember her taking the lead. I take up the rear, walking stick out. If we're going to be swarmed by creatures or giants, I want to be ready.

We walk for a long time. Arankadash is barefoot, and every time we stop, she tends to her feet. I offer a bit of my suit, which I'm able to cut off with Casamir's knife and wrap around her feet. But in the dim light I see her feet are blistered and bloody already, though she has not complained at all.

I wake sometime during a rest period to the sound of someone grunting. The light here is low but constant, so it's impossible to see how much time has passed.

Arankadash is squatting about forty paces away, leaning hard against a large crystal. She's sweating. For a moment, I think she's defecating, but the grunt turns into a long moan.

"Are you all right?" I ask. "Arankadash."

She waves me away, but I scramble over to her.

"What's wrong?" I say.

She shakes her head. Huffs out rhythmic breaths. "Birthing," she says.

I try to get closer, but the look she gives me is murderous. "Let me be," she says.

She grits her teeth and bears down. I can see nothing beneath her—her robes are too long—but I worry for whatever she's giving birth to. Will it smash itself on the crystals?

I bring her water. She drinks and pushes me away again. By now, Casamir and Das Muni are awake. Neither approaches. They simply sit and eat. Casamir is making marks on a parchment book.

Arankadash heaves one more time. I hear something fleshy slide to the ground.

She lets out a long breath that turns into another moan and leans hard on the crystal behind her. She reaches for me, and I hold out my hand. She levers herself up and reaches beneath her.

I tense, remembering the squirming, toothy creatures Das Muni gave birth to. I'm already horrified about what she might have created. What has the ship given her to carry?

Arankadash pulls up a wriggling mass of slimy flesh. For a moment, I think it's her placenta, but no—this is a round, mechanical-looking cog, like a toothy organ, something that would be affixed to a vehicle. It has a grooved, hollowed-out center. It has no eyes or face.

I expect her to toss it into her pack or throw it among the crystals like the waste it seems to be, to me. But she does not. She slumps to the ground and pulls it close to her. She coos at it like it's a child, this great mucus-slick thing.

I have to look away, but I can still hear her. She begins to hum softly to it.

I sit beside her, swallowing back my bile. This is something about the world that I can't stomach. Something I can't understand. There is a wrongness to it, women giving birth to what the world says it needs instead of what they yearn for.

Arankadash folds her offspring into her arm. It settles in, pulsing softly. It's red brown and laced in thick, ropy veins.

"What is it?" I ask, voice low.

"It's a gift from the light," she says.

"How do you get it . . . to the light?" I say.

She turns her sweaty face to me, and her expression contorts, as if I am mad. That gives me pause, because I don't feel like the mad one. She and her pulsing gob of flesh look mad to me. So mad that I wonder if I should leave her and it here while we carry on. But no. I'm the outsider. I need to understand this.

"When it's time, the light will come for it," Arankadash says. She gazes lovingly at the mass in her arms. "I need to rest." She holds out her arm to me.

I take her hand, averting my gaze from the thing in her arms again. I help her back to the circle. When I glance back at where she gave birth, I see a placenta and great gobs of afterbirth. We bleed, we birth, we bleed again.

Arankadash lies down with her new offspring and falls immediately to sleep.

I can't help but think of the squirming basket of creatures Das Muni showed me.

Das Muni is watching me from a few paces away, chewing thoughtfully on a bit of rancid tuber left in our pack.

"What do you do with yours?" I ask Das Muni. "Why don't you keep it like she does?"

"I'm not from this world," Das Muni says. "They will only recycle what I make. It doesn't need it. I give birth to things useful on some other world. But whatever she's made, well. The world will need it eventually. Probably. Unless that part of it is dead now."

And now I understand why they've taken Jayd. The Bhavajas needed something she had inside of her. I touch the scar on my belly. It is something I did not contain, so I cannot go in her place. But what does she give birth to? What do I have waiting in my own belly, and why have I yet to get pregnant like everyone else? Worse, then, is the idea that I will get pregnant at some point on this journey, and I am terrified of what it is I might nurture there. I resolve to cut it out long before it comes to fruition. Whatever it is, I don't want it.

We rest for a few long periods there, until Arankadash is recovered. But the resting costs us. Our water runs low after five sleeping periods in the crystal forest, and tempers begin to run high. I suggest rationing, with extra for Arankadash. She does not listen to me when I suggest this, as she is cooing at her cog or wheel or organ or whatever it is.

I'm not surprised when Casamir and Das Muni begin bickering on the walk after that.

"If you washed half as much as the rest of us, you wouldn't be crawling with vermin," Casamir says.

Das Muni is still in the lead, picking her way across the crystals. She is agile. Though she, too, has no boots, her feet are splayed, callused things. She crouches atop a large crystal, scouting ahead. "Dead end this way," she says.

"Of course!" Casamir yells, and takes off her pack. She throws it at her feet. "I've had enough!" she says. "You can't really see anything up there! She's leading us in circles! She's going to eat us all in our sleep!"

Das Muni cocks her head at Casamir and bares her teeth. "You will ruin your food."

"What do you care!" Casamir says. "You're going to eat us! That was probably the plan all along. Are you going to call your little mutant friends and—"

"Stop yelling," I say. Casamir's voice is echoing. It's made much louder as it reverberates among the crystals.

"And you!" Casamir says. "You delusional little psychotic! What was I thinking, coming all the way up here after you? The surface? Surface! Like the way a bubble has a surface? Let me tell you something. When you get through the skin of a bubble, it pops. Even if you can get us up there, then—"

"So, why don't you turn around?" I say, knowing I should just let her yell it out but tired of her whining. "We're all tired, Casamir."

"I had everything back home!" Casamir says. "I had a great job! It isn't so bad. And then I came here—"

"Stop shouting," I say.

Arankadash has strapped her offspring to her chest. She raises her hands now to cover her ears.

"—and you!" Casamir says to Arankadash. "You fell for it too! All her important talk! Don't pretend it's not because she's handsome. I see how you look at her. But she's mad, I tell you. A perfect study in madness, because she's drawn us all into her delusion, and now we'll rot here, starving—"

Das Muni leaps.

I think she is leaping onto Casamir, but she overshoots Casamir and hurls herself into me, so fast I don't have time to react. I fall hard onto the crystals behind me. Pain radiates up my ass. I twist my leg.

I hear the crack then. Not from my body, but from the crystals above us.

A huge hunk of crystal falls. It slides neatly and suddenly into Das Muni's back. The crystal pierces her flesh. I feel the hard thump of it through her body pressed tight against mine.

I garble out something unintelligible.

Das Muni sighs. She grips me tight. A dribble of blood colors her mouth. She grins at me with crimson-stained teeth.

"No, no," I say. I hold her in my arms. We are both of us pinned against the floor now. She by the crystal, me by her body. I don't know what to do.

Arankadash lunges at us, but I yell at her to stay back.

"Don't move her!" I say.

The crystal has not gone all the way through Das Muni. I'm unharmed but trembling. I work my way out from under Das Muni. She squirms as I break free.

"Don't move," I say softly, to Das Muni this time. I crouch beside her. She lets out little hissing breaths. "Why did you do that?" I say, but I don't expect an answer, and she does not give me one.

Casamir and Arankadash crowd next to me and lean over her. Casamir is wringing her hands. I reach for the crystal.

"Don't!" Casamir says. "If you pull out the crystal, she'll just bleed out."

"I can't leave it in there," I say. "Das Muni?"

She squeals again.

Arankadash slides out of her pack and kneels next to Das Muni. The shard of crystal is as long as my arm and half as wide. It's taken her low down on her right side, just below her ribs. I can't tell how deep it is, only that it hasn't gone all the way through her.

I press my ear to her back and listen to her breathe. I can hear a rattling sound.

"Why are you such a little fool?" I say, and I press my forehead to her shoulder. I don't know how we will move her. I don't know how we'll survive even if we can. She is the one thing I have had beside me from the beginning of this horror, and now she lies bleeding and rattling to death.

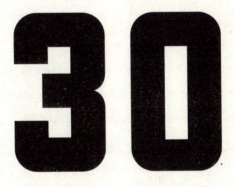

JAYD

step through the girls' blood and back through the door that Sabita made. On any other world, the blood would have been absorbed immediately, but not here on Bhavaja. Sabita did not consider this. I know because I can follow the dripping spatters of blood through the door and into the dark, narrow sub-corridors that bisect the main ones.

I am slow, terribly slow. I have no idea how far ahead of me she is, or what she means to do once she gets to where she is going. I find a dead Bhavaja security woman in the hall, her throat cut neatly. Sabita never fought in my mother's armies, but when you put people back together again, you also learn how to take them apart. She has ended this woman neatly. Much more neatly than the girls.

She stepped through the blood here and has left smeared half-footprints along the floor. I see blood along a bend in the corridor where she had paused. For breath? To catch her bearings?

I try to speed up, but with my injured leg, it's impossible. I wish I had a walking stick. I wish I'd learned to stand on my hands, the way that Zan could.

I hear raised voices, yelling.

"Sabita!" I say. "Sabita, stop!"

I hope that it gains me the time I need to reach the open doorway at the end of the hall. There is a dead end here right before the door. A great face made of rotten skin stretched over molded bone blocks the end of the hall; the corridor has partially grown around it.

I step into the lighted doorway and find Sabita dripping blood from her chin and Nashatra holding a great obsidian machete. Sabita's cunning bone knife is tiny in comparison, but the women's gazes tell me they are well matched.

"How did you find her?" I ask Sabita.

She signs, "The girls."

The girls. How had she gotten them to talk? No, of course, they could sign. I hadn't thought to sign at them, because I didn't want them to know I knew how. Sabita did not care.

"Don't kill Nashatra," I say.

Nashatra barks a laugh. "You should be telling me not to kill *her*."

"No more killing at all, then," I say. "The Bhavajas need Nashatra," I say.

"For what?" Sabita signs.

"Who will rule when Rasida is gone?"

"Rasida will just kill her anyway," Sabita signs.

"Give me the womb," I say. "I'll bear the world to term. You can't have long left."

"Are you mad?" Nashatra says.

"Yes," I say. "Sabita, you're a tissue technician. You know how to pull out my womb and give me another one. Take mine, Nashatra. You'll want children more than worlds, anyway."

"That's a serious surgery, Jayd," Sabita signs.

"I know," I say. "I've done it before, when Zan gave me her womb and we took out hers. Being able to bear children was the only leverage I would have, the only thing that could get me here. I couldn't have gotten close enough to Rasida to get the world in that womb. And it's the world we need, in the end."

Sabita signs, "When did you do that?"

I say out loud, "On the Mokshi."

"You and Zan—" Sabita signs.

"What we planned is bigger than the Legion," I say. "That's all I can tell you. We're no madder than Rasida. No madder than staying here and enduring her wrath. Where's the medical lounge?"

Nashatra considers.

"I know you don't want that world," I say. "What autonomy do you have when you cannot even decide what and when you birth? That was taken from you. We can fix it."

"This way," Nashatra says. "You'll need the witches' help or this will kill you. They will heal your—"

"All right," I say, because I want it done. I want to go on. We need to move.

Nashatra leads us to the medical lounge. We pass several women, but because we are with Nashatra, they give us only passing glances. I hope Rasida is sleeping or on another assault to Katazyrna. But part of me expects her to be in the lounge already, waiting for us, one step ahead, always.

The medical lounge is as hideous as the one on Katazyrna, maybe more so. The witches are already there, and to my horror, they are standing over a slab on which rest the bodies of the girls who once served me.

The witches raise their heads.

"These are not natural deaths," they say.

"Yours won't be either," Sabita signs, raising her bone knife. "I need healing salve, tissue repair gel, quick sutures, and liniment."

"The lord will be displeased," the witches say.

"She will not be lord much longer," I say, and get up onto the slab next to the bodies.

"ALL I'VE LEARNED OF THE WORLD HAS TOLD ME THAT IT'S NECESSARY TO GIVE UP WHO I AM TO SAVE US. CALL THAT ALTRUISTIC. I CALL IT SENSE. THERE'S NO REASON TO LIVE LIKE I AM WITHOUT A FUTURE."
—LORD MOKSHI, **ANNALS OF THE LEGION**

31

ZAN

When I wake, Das Muni is still breathing, but I cannot rouse her.

"Moving her will make her worse," Casamir says. "I think we should split up."

"We'll just get more lost," Arankadash says.

"If we each take a different direction, we might have a chance to get out," Casamir says. "Right now there's no chance. We'll die of thirst."

I had seen Casamir drinking her own urine before we slept. I don't feel that bad off yet, but it's tempting. I stare into my pack at the last half-globe of water I have. What an irony, to come this far from the belly of the world only to die for lack of water. I press my cheek to Das Muni's. We must leave her and find a way out.

Hungry, thirsty, disoriented, we wander the crystal forest. I lose track of time, and maybe that's better than whatever this is. We stumble off into opposite directions, though I can hear them all laboring not far away. Sound travels so far here. I hear Das Muni whining; it's a sound that cuts me deeply, like listening to the crying of a child.

I'm so thirsty that when I doze, I dream of water. Bathing in it. Rolling in it. Drinking until I burst. When I wake from one of these reveries, I find myself staring at my own reflection in an opaque crystal just inches from my face. The light of the bluish crystals around it illuminates me and my reflection.

I gawk at myself. It is the first time since I woke to Jayd's luminous face that I have seen my own reflection.

My skin, I know, is the same dark color as the Katazyrnas, but I am taller and broader. I have known all of this, but somehow seeing tall, lean Arankadash assured me that I was not aberrant, just different.

Now that I can see my face, I see something else entirely. I see someone who does not belong to the Katazyrnas at all. I have deep, sunken round eyes with gray irises, made to look deeper by broad, flat cheekbones unlike any I've seen here. My eyebrows are bushy and as ashen gray as my eyes, and they sweep back from my face like feathers. A long scar cuts across my brow, the same one I felt slathered in salve when I first woke. It's twisted and ugly and pulls up the left half of my face, smoothing the lines there. I'm older than I thought, probably as old as Vashapaldi.

I lean away from the crystal so my reflection distorts and blurs, becoming just another refracted bit of shadow and light.

I reach into my pocket and pull out the soft sphere that Vashapaldi gave me.

I press the face of it, trying to understand why I would have left such a trinket behind. All I can think as I stare at its spongy mass is that I was as mad in my prior lives as I am now.

I stuff the thing back into my pocket and crawl along until I lose all sense of time and myself. I know only that I'm thirsty. Perhaps I am dying.

Is there a reason I shouldn't die?

I gaze at the refracted images of my own face, fascinated.

Time skips.

Light. Reflections.

And then:

Das Muni leans over me, proffering a bit of gray flesh. I turn my face away, but she speaks in soothing tones and parts my lips with the slippery tail of the thing.

"It will make you better," she murmurs.

I know this is a dream, because Das Muni is surely dead where I left her, five hundred paces behind me. I even twist my head to look behind me where I abandoned her body, but in place of Das Muni I see a slithering mass of black, toothy fishes crawling across the crystals, flopping in a sea of afterbirth.

Since this is a dream and I am very hungry, and even thirstier, I eat what she gives me. The thing is, thankfully, dead already and does not wriggle about in my mouth as I chew and swallow. It's surprisingly salty-sweet. I feel my fog begin to lift almost immediately.

Das Muni holds me in her arms and sings to me, a song that sounds half-familiar. I lie there and stare at the crystal ceiling, trying to remember this song.

"How are you alive?" I ask. "You were dead."

"A jinni came and saved me," Das Muni says.

"What's a jinni?"

"A spirit," she says. "You must remember the spirits."

"I don't remember anything," I say.

"It's all right," Das Muni says. "Sometimes only I can see them."

"Lord of War," I sigh, "I don't know if you're speaking the truth or delirious or both."

"Both," she says."

"We are going to die here," I say.

"No," she says. "They are drawn to water."

"What is?"

"My friends," she says, and I see that in her hands are the little biting fishes that I first saw her birth back in the recycling pits.

She releases the things in her hands, and they fall to the crystals at our feet and begin to wriggle their way through the crystalline forest.

Das Muni hooks her arm under me, and we follow the snapping fishes. I stumble over Casamir. She is staring into her hands as if they, too, have become crystalline surfaces.

"Get up," I say. "Follow us."

Arankadash has made it the farthest. She stands on a great crystal, face wan and drawn. When she sees us, she squints like she can't believe we are real.

"There are living things here," she says. "I ate one."

"Where did the rest go?" I ask.

She points down a narrow, craggy precipice.

"We must follow them," I say.

I know that what I'm saying doesn't make sense, but Arankadash doesn't argue with me. She sets off ahead of us. As I walk, I begin to feel stronger, more clear-headed. Whatever is in Das Muni's offspring is a potent restorative.

When Casamir lags behind, I go back for her and help her along. Das Muni keeps on ahead, looking back at us occasionally. I hear the change long before I see it. A rushing sound fills the air, louder and louder. Cool wind blows against my face. I smell water.

Arankadash ducks under a low-hanging crystal. I slide after her with Casamir and land in deep mud up to my ankles. I gaze out at a muddy plain and there, at the far end of it, four or five hundred paces distant, is a waterfall. The water pounds down from the level above. It has carved a chasm in the ceiling. The lip of the other level has rolled downward like a knobby tongue, and the water cascades over it and into a great pool. The pool drains toward us, making a mucky river that twists and turns and disappears under the edge of the crystal forest.

I slog to the riverbed and fall to my knees. I drink, not caring what else is swimming in these dark waters. The water tastes pure, though. It is the most delicious thing I've ever tasted.

We make camp near the forest. We drink and rest and Casamir catches fist-sized creatures from the water and we eat them raw. They taste terrible, but it's better than starving.

I take the time to bathe in the water, which is warmer than I expected, warm as spit. I'm not sure how much cleaner I am after I come out of it, but I feel better, more vibrant. I feel alive.

I rinse off my suit and get dressed and stare out at the waterfall. I see that there are knobby crags along either side of the waterfall, little curls of flesh from the level above that the water has yet to wear away.

"I bet we can climb up," I say, but no one is listening to me.

Arankadash is sleeping contentedly with her offspring, and Casamir is snoring loudly. Even Das Muni has passed out, arms wrapped around herself, knees tucked to her chest. It's only then that I realize how close we all came to dying.

But I don't want to rest. I want to carry on. Every time we ascend a level, I feel that much closer to getting my revenge.

I slog toward the waterfall. I get about a hundred paces before my strength gives out. I find a damp patch of ground and lie down. I listen to the gurgle of the water. We are so close. Every step takes us closer. I sleep.

How long we rest, I don't know, but when I wake, Arankadash is already standing along the circumference of the pool where the waterfall pounds into this level.

I get up to join her. Her offspring nuzzles her chest, a great faceless blob. I try not to look at it.

"We go up?" she says.

"Always up," I say.

She pats her offspring. "Perhaps you should go first."

"I like a challenge," I say. I'm not sure if that's true, though. I've been challenged enough.

Casamir and Das Muni join us at the edge of the pool. Casamir volunteers to give it a try, but I tell her this is my lot in life.

I stretch out on the edge of the pool and head toward the right side of the waterfall, which looks like it might have more handholds. The surface is slick, but the bulbous face of the worn ceiling is varied enough that I can gain some purchase.

The way up the craggy edge of the waterfall is treacherous. I claw my way up, digging my fingernails into the soft surface to gain purchase. I tumble hard when I am just a few paces up. I flail. Hit the water with a great smack.

I swim to the shore and start again, assuring Casamir that I am fine. There is a route up. I will find it. For myself, for Das Muni, for Jayd, for us all.

I start again, more slowly this time, looking for purchase. I think of my hands as vises, too strong to let go once they have gripped an edge, and I make my way slowly up and up. I am already soaked, but the misty spray of the falls ensures I stay that way. I wipe my face on my shoulder, trying to clear my eyes of water. It's a pointless exercise.

As I near the top of the waterfall, my bad leg cramps up. I cling hard to the face of the wall. I push my toes against my foothold, trying to stretch out my tendon.

There are no calls of encouragement from below. I suspect they are all waiting for me to fall again. They're afraid to break my concentration. I realize just how strangely quiet it is to not hear Casamir complaining.

I find purchase on the lip of the wall and pull myself over while pushing with my good leg. I flop over the edge like a swollen fish and lie there gasping. Something flies above me and defecates on my face. I wipe it away and stare up. There are hundreds, maybe thousands, of flapping creatures nesting in the high, rotten walls above the water-fall. The sky here stretches up and up, and it's mostly dark. There are bioluminescent fungi here and there, glowing a faint blue, and some creature flashing white in the water. But after the disorienting maze of the crystal forest, the darkness is almost welcome.

I stagger to my feet and am pleased to see that the waterway that feeds the falls does indeed slope upward. We're continuing our climb up from the bottom of the world to its surface, however slow and agonizing.

I take a few steps, but my strength gives out. Or perhaps it's my will. I sink to my knees on the soft ground. No doubt it's covered in the excrement of whatever creatures are roosting in the walls, but I don't care. We're all the same thing. We're all shit. We're all flesh. We're all sentient.

The others have been telling me this from the very beginning, but it's not until now, saved by Das Muni's slithering offspring, revived by afterbirth and a thundering waterfall at the center of a hollowed-out world, that I really understand what they mean by it.

I pull the sphere Vashapaldi gave me from my pocket. The sequence comes easily now, like remembering the way to the home of a friend: the child, the fish, the bird, the water, the water.

The sphere warms in my hands. I drop it. It splits like an egg, revealing a gooey green core that sprays a red-green mist into the air above it. The mist coalesces into a head-and-shoulder view of a familiar face, the face I saw reflected back at me from the mirror of a crystal. This reflection of me has no scar on her face, though, and there is something different about her eyes. She is more confident, full of purpose. I see no fear in her, no indecision, only absolute faith.

"If you're seeing this," the woman who shares my face says, "it means we've been recycled again and Jayd is not with you. You have remembered enough to unlock this recording, but I expect there's still a lot that's unclear to you. That's all right. That's how it's supposed to be right now. You'll remember when you're ready. That's how it has to be. You and I both know you're too emotional to do what needs to be done when you remember . . . Well, you don't want to remember what happened. It will ruin you as it ruined me, and we must stay focused on the end goal." The woman looks away at something outside the range of the recording, then back. "If Jayd hasn't yet found her way to the Bhavajas, through marriage or prisoner exchange, then you'll need to return to the Mokshi and start again. There are more answers there. If she is with the Bhavajas this time, though, it means we are closer to success than we've ever been. Get back to the surface and find her. If she has done her part, then she will meet you at the Mokshi. Be sure the two of you have the arm and the world before you go, though, or we will have to do this again. Don't think about why this is. Trust me as one can only trust oneself. You don't want to start over. The world and the arm." She looks away again, starts to say something else, and frowns. The recording ends. The mist swirls back into the core of the sphere, and it closes.

"Who is that?" Arankadash asks. She has come up behind me. I didn't hear her over the sound of my own voice. Her offspring is pulsing softly against her chest.

"It's me," I say.

I replay the recording for the others once everyone is up the waterfall.

"This is a trick," Casamir says. "You recorded it just now."

"She doesn't have a scar in that image," Arankadash says.

Das Muni says nothing. She has pulled up her cowl again, so I cannot see her expression.

"Do you believe me now?" I ask Casamir.

"I believe this delusion is very complicated," Casamir says. "I'm going to find something to eat."

We spend some time foraging along the waterfall to restock our supplies. There are mushrooms and fish-like animals and flying things, which Casamir catches by rigging up a throwing ball she had in her pack with a rope on the end that knocks them senseless. They are about as wide as both of my hands put together, and they are mostly wings, which makes for poor eating. But Casamir enjoys catching them, and after a time, we have a whole stack of them to skin and eat.

As we sit and skin and chew, I say, "How many levels are there to the world, that you know?"

"Hundreds," Arankadash says. "That's what we've always learned." She gazes up at what will be our route very soon, following the river upward, ever upward.

Casamir says, "We have scouted and recorded eighteen. These Katazyrna people you talk about aren't recorded on any of them."

"I didn't fall far enough for there to be hundreds," I say. "Besides, I'm not the only one to fall. Das Muni has, too. She's seen another world like I have."

Casamir rolls her eyes but says nothing.

"She saved the lot of us," I say. "You can be respectful."

"Sorry," Casamir says. She glances over at Das Muni. Reluctantly hands her a skinned bat-bird. "I do appreciate it, even if you tried to fucking drown me."

Das Muni takes the offering in her long fingers and sets the bloody thing in her lap.

"We thought you dead," Arankadash says to Das Muni.

"A spirit saved me," Das Muni says.

Arankadash nods. "I understand."

Casamir grimaces but, after a quick look at me, says nothing. We all create the stories we need to survive. Let Das Muni and Arankadash have theirs.

When we are rested, we start the long walk up the waterway. When the space opens up into a broad, watery plain that runs off in many directions, I suggest we follow the main flow of the river.

"It's always going to flow downward, right?" I say. "To the center of the world. So it makes sense to follow it back up to wherever it's coming from."

The watery plain is teeming with biting bugs. We itch and scratch at them. My skin blisters, and when the blisters burst, little larvae squirm out. I should not be bothered by this after everything I've seen, but this feels like a grave imposition.

It's Casamir who stops the second cycle in and screams and screams, though. It's not a scream of fear but one of frustration.

I plant my feet in the spongy plain and I scream too. Das Muni echoes me, then Arankadash, and for several long minutes, we are a group of four women screaming at the top of our lungs in the middle of a buzzing bog. We scream until our mouths fill with bugs, and then we stop.

And we carry on.

After a time, the waves of biting insects subside, and we camp on a bit of higher ground near a long plain of water. While Arankadash and Das Muni make camp, I walk down to where Casamir is by the water.

She stands at the edge of the milky lake, throwing stones. "What's wrong?" I ask, expecting a long and convoluted story, a rant about Das Muni's table manners, or some snide remarks about Arankadash.

"I'm pregnant," she says. "I was hoping it would wait a little longer. But I guess not."

"Oh." I put my hands in my pockets. "What do you . . . Is it all right to ask what you have?"

"It's only been a couple times," she says. "Usually you get pregnant when the world has a need, I guess. It's some great organ thing, like what Arankadash has, only it grows much bigger. We kept the last one for some time, did experiments on it. They aren't living, not really. They're part of the world, I think. I think they replace parts that wear down."

"Shouldn't you always have them, then?"

"What?" Casamir says. She stops throwing stones. "Are you mad?

I'm not giving myself over to some god, some creature bigger than me. I own what I am. Nobody else."

"So, what are you going to do?"

"Maybe what Das Muni has is useful," she says grudgingly, "and maybe Arankadash is so desperate for a child that she'll try to nurse that thing, but that's not how things are for me. I'll just get rid of it."

"You can do that?"

"You can do anything you want," Casamir says. "It's your flesh, you know. If there is cancer eating out my arm, you wouldn't tell me I can't cut it off."

"These things don't seem like cancer."

"Don't they? How do we know, really, what they are or what our purpose is? We take it all on faith. But every level is the same. They all rationalize it by saying it's something they don't understand, but it's necessary. I reject that. No one's in charge of my fate but me." She jabs a finger at my belly. "You know that, or you knew it, clearly."

Casamir wanders off as we all bed down, telling us she's going to forage. I lie awake with Arankadash as she rocks her pulsing offspring in her arms. She sings it a song in her language, something soft and very soothing.

"Casamir's pregnant," I say.

"Yes," Arankadash says. "It's easy to tell."

"I can't."

"You are blind to a good many things." She raises her head from the thing in her arms. "It's odd, isn't it, that you are the only one not to become infused with a spark of life, here on this long journey?

"Is it?" I ask. "How often do people get pregnant?"

"It depends on the will of the Lord," she says. "When it needs something, it gets it from us."

"How?"

"How is there air to breathe?" Arankadash says. "It's like that."

"It sounds like we're slaves to this ship," I say.

"This world," she says. "No. It gives us shelter and food. It shields us from the black horror of the abyss that lies in wait for us after death. It keeps us warm and protected. We are as much a part of the light as it is a part of us."

I remember the great metal door that Casamir cracked open, and the Legion of worlds above, and the corridor of giant bodies whose purpose I hope I'll never know.

No, this is all very wrong. If I were a god, this is not how I would create a world, by enslaving everything that lived in it. Or would I? I gaze up at the ceiling. The world is a living thing, yes, but is it more than just a collection of organs and flesh and fluid? Is it conscious? Sentient? Is the world a literal god, some creature that's captured us the way Casamir's captured those women in the cages? I imagine us circling the misty Core of the sun for generation after generation, locked in a battle not just with ourselves but with the terrible things growing around us and inside of us, tying us so closely to themselves that we cannot exist without them.

Casamir returns a long time later. Everyone else is asleep. I peer at her from beneath my arm and watch her take off her pack and unroll her sleeping pad. She settles in. Sees me watching. Gives a little two-fingered wave.

"What is freedom, Zan?" she says.

It sounds like a saying, like something I should know. And the response comes bubbling up, the way the sign language did out in the black vacuum of space. "Freedom is the absence of outside control," I say.

"What is freedom?" Arankadash says. "It is control of the body, and its issue, and one's place in this world."

"See?" Casamir says. "We aren't all completely dead in the head."

When we wake, it's cold for the first time in my memory. A cold wind blows from above us, too high up for me to see the source. It's as if there are cracks or holes in the ceiling, and cold air is being blasted in. Fifteen thousand steps later, as we crawl out of the wetlands and onto a rocky plain, I see a bright blue light in the distance. It flickers like a flame, and as we near I see it is a flame of a sort—it's a rent in the sky oozing sulfurous blue lava.

The smell rolls over us. I cover my mouth with a hemp cloth from my pack, but it doesn't do much to filter the air.

"This is dangerous," Casamir says. "Can we go around?"

"It will take us farther from the river," I say.

Arankadash shakes her head. "I don't want to risk losing access to water again." She moves past us, taking point.

"Water's all well and good," Casamir says, "but not if you can't breathe."

But we carry on. The toxic air grows denser. I suggest going back, but Arankadash is still in the lead, and she doesn't seem to hear me over the bubbling of the burning sulfur. I wet my hemp cloth and tie it over my mouth. Das Muni has dampened her cowl and done the same.

A blast of cool air buffets us from behind, clearing the air briefly. We make our way between two dripping seas of blue blazing sulfur, up what appears to be a path.

Casamir says, "It's about time we see some people."

"Not all people are nice," Das Muni says, and passes Casamir and me as we pause to look back over the burning blue sulfur seas.

"Long way back," I say.

"Not really," Casamir says. She shoulders her pack and starts walking again. "You take me to this surface of yours, and I'll just jump right back down that recycling chute. Then I'm only a level away from home!" She laughs.

I hang back. The world is large, I know—I've seen it from the outside, but I never anticipated all of this. Maybe I thought the world was hollow, or that it was all corridors and spiraling doors like the surface. This is much more, and far more complicated. The Katazyrnas and Bhavajas were fighting for control over the Legion, but they didn't even control their own worlds. What were they actually fighting for, then? A title? An idea?

"Zan!"

Arankadash has reached the head of the path, high up on the ridge. She's waving me forward.

I start climbing again. The air is thicker with sulfur up here, but just as I think I can't stand it, there's a thread of cool air running just above me that clears the toxic cloud away.

"What is it?" I ask as I come up beside her.

Arankadash points into the valley below. "Bodies," she says.

> "I DON'T HOPE FOR THE BEST ENDING. I PLAN FOR IT."
> —LORD MOKSHI, **ANNALS OF THE LEGION**

32

JAYD

It was Zan's idea.

I would like history to believe that, but what led us to this place is not something I want recorded in any way.

"What do the Bhavajas want more than anything?" she asked me there on the Mokshi, after all my terrible betrayals, when she still took me back because she still loved me. She believed me when I said I had changed my mind, and yes, I had changed it, but I never expected her to believe that.

"They need children," I said. "It's known that they haven't had a child-bearer in at least five rotations. Like us, they've been stealing from other worlds. More than us, really. I heard they don't have as much of a hierarchy because of it."

Zan folded her hands in her lap, just below the curve of her belly. "I can give them children," she said. "Present me to them as a gift."

"What about the arm?" I said. Because I had already stolen that from her too, and given it to Anat, because I was a young fool. It was the first betrayal, but not the worst. "You said you can't restart the Mokshi without it. The Mokshi will never leave the Legion without a new world birthed on board. It's too wrecked." And I wince as I say it, but Zan doesn't notice or doesn't mind. How can she be so forgiving? Or does she not care? Does she love me at all, really, or is it all feigned, the way my love for her was feigned in the beginning?

"Can you steal the arm from Anat while I'm with the Bhavajas," she said, "the way you stole it from me?"

"And do what with it?" I said. "It only works for you, here on the Mokshi."

"What if you could bear children?" Zan says. "You convince Anat to trade you to the Bhavajas for peace. When the peace is set, I board the Mokshi, turn off the defenses, and get Anat inside. She'll walk right in. I can take the arm easily once I have her on the Mokshi. That world obeys me."

"And what," I said, "I disarm Rasida and steal the world she's got in her womb?"

Zan grinned. "You stole my arm out from under me," she said, "and my heart. I suspect you can steal far more from Rasida."

I climbed onto Zan's lap then, and she put her strong arms around me, and for a moment I let myself be held. I felt her child kick in her belly, and I said, "We'll need to do something with the child."

That idea, I admit, was mine.

* * *

It was already a complicated plan. It relied on desperation more than anything else. What we had utterly failed to consider, though, was Rasida and what she had already put into motion. I think at some point, many cycles ago, I believed I did all of this out of love for Zan, but now, drifting in a cottony haze as Sabita lifts her bloody hands from my body, I think I am doing it for the love of something far greater than Zan. I'm doing it for the love of the Legion, the love of survival. I know just how precarious life is here, and I know that I must sacrifice a lot of it in order to save any of it.

That is my burden.

When I come awake finally, it is Sabita patting my face gently. "You're still healing," she signs, "but we must be quiet. Rasida has noticed that we're gone."

I glance over at Nashatra, who was beside me when the surgery started, but she is already gone, as are the witches.

"They've gone to distract her," Sabita signs. "Can you get up? I know it's difficult, but we must get you to the hangar."

"I need the arm," I say, "I have the world, but not—"

"We'll tell Rasida you've escaped to the Katazyrna," Sabita signs. "But you need a head start."

"I don't understand," I mutter, but then I do. If I take the world to Katazyrna, Rasida will follow me. It's impossible, in my current state, to defeat her in combat. But I know Katazyrna, and I know where the witches go when Katazyrna is boarded. I will take the world to Katazyrna, and Rasida will take the arm.

"If Zan is dead . . . ," I say.

"If Zan is dead," Sabita signs, "then at least the Katazyrna will be reborn. You'll save our world. There is that. It must be enough."

"I can't fail," I say.

Sabita helps me up. Pain rolls over me. She hands me a cup of something bitter, and I drink it without question. There's a dagger of icy fire in my gut, and then the pain eases.

I don't know the way to the hangar from here, but I am not the only one who has been counting steps. Sabita takes me left, another right, and down a crumbling umbilicus. We begin to climb a long set of stairs. I hear voices on the level just below us. Sabita presses us both up against the wall at the top of the stairs, and we wait until the women pass. Stairs. Lord of War have mercy. I lean hard on the stairwell, but Sabita puts her arm under mine and half-helps, half-drags me up.

When we reach the corridor outside the hangar, Sabita carves out a new door for us and seals it behind her. Row after row of vehicles stretch out before us, all of them in far worse repair than those on Katazyrna.

Sabita yanks me forward. "Stop," I say. "Why are you helping me? You despise all I've done."

She points to a vehicle. "This is a good one," she signs, and starts it up for me. She finds several suit canisters in a bin at the back and throws me one.

"We'll go out together," she signs. "Stay close. If they spot us, I'll draw their fire."

"Sabita," I say. "I have to know whose side of this you're on."

She grimaces. "You don't know yet? I'm on Zan's side, Jayd. She came to after Anat recycled her, and she climbed up out of the pits. She came to me after you turned your back on her and told her to go out there to the Mokshi again, to do as Anat asked. She loved you, Jayd, and you broke her heart. This stopped being about your love for Zan when you let her be recycled. You never went after her. You think she dismissed that? You think she didn't care?"

"I couldn't go after her!" I say. "It would have given us away. Why would I have gone after some rogue prisoner? Anat would have known who she was."

"She told me to protect you," Sabita signs, "in case anything happened to her and your plan went wrong. It did. And I keep my promises."

There's a sound outside the hangar door.

Sabita snatches the canister from my hand and sprays my suit on me. She runs to the lights of the depressurization console and sprays her suit on as she goes. Yellow lights flash.

The hangar door leading into the corridor blinks blue.

I grip the vehicle tight and release a burst of fuel, and we are sucked up and up and pop free of Bhavaja like two vermin flicked from its skin.

We make it four hundred leaps away from Bhavaja before the first pursuers appear. It has been a long time since I fought out in open space. But it comes back to me, easy as breathing. The cephalopod guns take a moment to understand, but then I am firing back at our pursuers.

Is Rasida one of them? I don't know, but I can't risk a direct hit. I sign back at Sabita to wound them only, and her grimace tells me what she thinks of that.

I power forward, speeding through the worlds of the Legion. I have missed them and all this open space. My heart was never in leading armies—I was better at planning battles than fighting them—but the Legion from outside the worlds is a breathtaking wonder. When Zan told me she believed there were other Legions rotating around those stars in the vast distance, I told her there couldn't be anything else like the Legion in existence. *Why not?* she said, and it revealed my own sense of ego. I believed we were somehow special, blessed of the War

God. I believed She made all of this for us, and we were doomed to make of it what we will. We were stuck here in the belly of creation. There was no escaping this universe.

Zan convinced me otherwise, but I had done terrible things before I believed her.

Despite our head start, our pursuers are gaining. We come up over the contested worlds—I see Tiltre off at our left, and I have a terrible memory of the day of the joining. How long ago was it now? A full rotation ago, surely. It feels like a lifetime. I see that the skin of Tiltre has been pulled back in places; it's black and scarred. How many wars has Rasida been waging on other worlds while I lay trapped beneath the skin of Bhavaja, fighting for a future for this place?

A cephalopod clips my vehicle. I spin out. The Legion dances around me as I go whirling into the black. I recover, look back, and Sabita is powering back behind me, headed toward our pursuers.

She cannot see me, so I don't sign at her. I keep my gaze forward, ever forward, and there, as I come up over the contested worlds, I see the familiar worlds of the Katazyrnas. My worlds. I zip past salvage vehicles and roving patrols. It's impossible to give them orders to tail me, out here, unless some scout arrived ahead of me, and that hasn't happened.

They let me by unhindered, and that's good, because there is a far greater force I must face. It's my own world, the great rising face of Katazyrna there, engulfing my view as the great orb of the orange sun blooms behind me.

I think, *What if the Katazyrna doesn't recognize me? What if I've become too much like the Bhavajas? What if giving birth to Zan's child has changed me and the world no longer wants me?*

I steel myself as I dip into orbit around Katazyrna. There is a great hole blown into the side of the world now, not as terrible as the one on the Mokshi, but significant. I power toward it. My fuel is almost gone, but I can coast forward on momentum for a good long while.

I am going faster than I'd like, so I kick off the vehicle and snag one of the waving tentacles as I go past. It wraps itself around me, and I crawl down it and step onto the surface of Katazyrna, finally.

And Katazyrna welcomes me home.

"TO THE PEOPLE BELOW, THERE IS NO SURFACE,
NO OTHER WORLDS, NO LEGION. TO THE PEOPLE BELOW,
WE ARE GODS AND MONSTERS."
—LORD MOKSHI, ANNALS OF THE LEGION

33

ZAN

There are a dozen bodies piled on the shallow valley floor. They are arranged in a loose, circular group, as if they were walking up toward where we are now and fell where they stood. A few have slumped on top of each other, their long brown limbs tangled in violet robes.

The color of the robes fascinates me, because I haven't seen anyone else with clothing that color yet. Their hair is long and black and braided back into a single tail. Most of them have hair that falls nearly to their knees. They have not been dead long. If I hadn't seen so many dead already, I'd guess they were sleeping. This thought gives me pause, though. Have I really seen so many dead? I remember a field. A bright orange field of long yellow grass and tremendous white fungi, tall as I am, and bodies littered among them. Body after body, as far as I can see. I shake my head, and it's gone. I can't remember who they are, or even where, but it doesn't have the feeling of a dream.

"If there are people," I say, "there must be a settlement not much farther on."

"Settlement of dead people," Casamir says.

"Be optimistic," I say. "Sulfur probably killed them. There's a breeze now. It's clearing it out. Let's see if there are any survivors."

They are a mix of old and young women, though none younger than the age of puberty. *Still no children, even here?* I think as I pick up a staff. It has a hole carved at the top, and set into the hollow is a brilliant lavender stone. The staff itself is made of soft yellow wood. They can't be weapons—they would break in combat, or in contact with someone's head or even a strong arm.

I check the bodies, but they are already beginning to cool. I was right: they are not long dead. But they have all perished.

It's three sleeping periods more before we finally see signs of a settlement. The world here is watery and vibrant, full of twittering, buzzing life. That's great for survival but bad for comfort, as I find myself pulling the heads of little biting bugs from my flesh every morning. They nest in the seams of my suit and are easy to brush off, but my companions, with less durable clothing, are not so lucky. They carry the bugs with them every time we move.

There's a clear sleeping cycle here, as great bioluminescent trees glow more brightly during some periods and drop all of their sticky, leaf-like compounds at the end of it, only to regrow them during what passes for a sleeping cycle. The animals follow suit, with some sleeping while the trees light up, and others only coming up to chirp and bother us after the leaves have dropped.

There are human-made decorations hanging from the trees, mostly bone ornaments that click and clack in the wind. I see more signs of human habitation. Baskets left to rest under the trees. A network of paths crisscrossing the forest. Stacks of dead tree limbs and, eventually, a small lean-to made of a fallen tree and hemp covering.

Ahead of us I see something like a village proper. There's a ring of two dozen dwellings arranged around a large square made of bone and metal tree trunks. At the center of the village is a tree so large that its spidery branches make a massive canopy over the village and travel up and up into the darkness of the sky. The branches pulse with the occasional blue light speeding up and across the branches and into the ceiling above, where they ignite a series of red and orange lights in the distant ceiling. It's mesmerizing to watch and reminds me of the dancing lights I saw in my quarters when I first woke, like a secret language.

I hear only the clacking of the bone wind chimes, and the rustling of little flying creatures in the trees.

I walk to one of the huts, where someone has scraped a written passage into the face of it. I don't know the language.

"Can you read this, Casamir?" I ask.

She jogs up next to me, squints. "Huh," she says.

"Is that yes or no?" I say.

"It says there are monsters here. It says they come when the leaves fall."

"If there are monsters," Arankadash says, patting her offspring, "we should go somewhere there aren't any monsters." Her offspring has tripled in size already and pulses against her like a second stomach.

"There are monsters everywhere," I say. "Running never makes fewer of them. Let's see how we can shore up this village for an attack."

"An attack from what?" Casamir says.

"Anything," I say. I'm staring at the big tree at the center of the square and the place where its branches meet the ceiling. "I have an idea," I say.

Casamir kicks at the bones of the square. "Well, great."

"We'll need weapons," I say.

We rifle through the huts, and Casamir uncovers a number of multi-colored vials. She whistles softly. "Wizards," she says.

"Wizards?"

"There's a defensive ditch around the village," Casamir says. "These should work pretty well in it."

"Do I want to know what it is?"

"Probably not."

We open up trunks and baskets, searching for weapons. There are two obsidian machetes and some bone knives. Not enough, but something.

I watch Casamir carefully load more vials into a leather bag, and ask, "Why did you really not turn back?"

"Because you're great company," Casamir says.

"Honestly," I say.

She sighs. "There was a woman," she says.

"Not another story about wearing wombs on people's heads," I say.

"There was a woman I loved," she says. "We fought. I left her down there when we were on a run."

"Really?"

"You think I'd make up something like that?"

"It doesn't seem like you."

"When you wake up and realize you don't like yourself, you make changes," Casamir says, "or become a drunk, I guess."

"She die?" I ask.

"I don't know," Casamir says. "I thought I'd just scare her, teach her a lesson, so she wouldn't treat me like she did. There weren't any recyclers around, but . . . When I came back down a while later, she was gone. They sent a search party. I said she got lost. Never found her."

"Still doesn't answer why you don't go back."

"You're relentless."

"When you don't know anything, you get good at asking questions."

"Lots of people pop that little lock," Casamir says. She jingles the bag. "Not everybody gets this far. No, not anyone gets this far. Just me. Just us. I'm not going back until I figure out if you're mad or telling the truth."

"Thought you'd made up your mind."

"I like the suspense."

"Thanks for not dropping me," I say.

"If this is all true, all these stories about these warring families . . . How do you intend to beat them?"

"I don't know," I say. "Who knows how much things have changed since I left? The Bhavajas are bad people. I'd need an army to defeat them."

"You don't need an army. You have us."

"We've certainly got surprise on our side," I say.

I call Arankadash over, and we walk the perimeter with her while Das Muni amuses herself inside one of the huts.

"The moat is probably something they can fill with a toxic miasma,"

Casamir says. "That might work to keep most of this stuff out. We can also pull in some of those trees. The metal's rotten in a lot of them but not all. Maybe set those up as spikes."

"Are you going to tell us why we're making a stand here?" Arankadash says.

I point at the tree. "See how far it goes up?"

"I do," Casamir says. "To the sky."

"I think we can climb it and hack up into the next level," I say. "Save some time."

"If we don't get eaten first," Casamir says.

Das Muni comes out from one of the huts, humming to herself. She is digging through a basket. "What have you got over there?" I call.

"Finger bones," she says.

I get up and examine the contents of the basket for myself. Sure enough, it's full of finger bones, and possibly foot bones as well. They are small and easy to identify, though I'm curious as to why I know that.

"We need to get up that tree as fast as possible," I say. I walk around the circumference of the tree. I press my hand to it. It throbs beneath my fingers. I follow the branches up and up, and see an answering throb there in the ceiling that reminds me of the arteries that ran above the corridors on the first level of Katazyrna.

"This is an artery that runs the length of the world," I say. "I bet we can cut into it and climb all the way to the surface. Not just the next level."

Casamir, too, stares at the crown of the tree. "Only one way to find out, I suppose." She sighs. "I'm really tired of climbing things."

"How will you get into the artery, though?" Arankadash says. "There's no opening."

I heft my blade. "I'll make one," I say.

KAMERON HURLEY

"Easier said than achieved," Arankadash says. "I was going to suggest resting, but—"

"Let's not wait," I say. The tree is budding, and it makes me think of how cycles have worked across the ship, and finger bones. "I'll get some rest and then head up there."

But when I settle into one of the abandoned houses, I can't help but think of the dead we passed on the way here. Were they fleeing this place? Trying to find something better? I think all the way back the way we came, and try to imagine them finding a home somewhere there that could sustain them. They would have had to go down and down, all the way to Vashapaldi's settlement.

I gaze at the tree, which I can just see through the doorway. They were going down. I'm going up. But I'm still not certain my direction is going to have an ending that's any better.

34

ZAN

When I sleep, I dream, but I know it isn't a dream but a new memory, a harsh memory, bubbling up now, finally, just as Jayd warned me:

Wave after wave of armies break themselves against the Mokshi. I know this because I am somehow able to watch it happen from *inside* the Mokshi. Four generals die, taking their armies with them, but the fifth . . . The fifth is more tactical. She loses fewer people. She tests defenses. She flanks and folds her people and times their assaults with the flow of the Mokshi's defenses.

Yet her army, too, falls. One by one, until she is the last left. And unlike the others, she does not run away. She hurls herself at the Mokshi, one final stand.

I don't know what comes over me in that instant. But I turn off the defenses, and I welcome her. I don't know if it's the most foolish thing I've ever done or the smartest.

She is the most beautiful woman I've ever seen. Her face is full-lipped and luminous. It could be that she is the most beautiful because she is also the best fighter, the most tactical, the most brilliant. All that, yes.

She is defiant even then, and I ask her why her people fight. Why the Katazyrnas fling their young, their old, their infirm, at the Mokshi, this endless tide of flesh.

I know already that power is not in the fist or the whip or the weapon. Power lies in the flesh. Who commands the bodies. These people race to their deaths.

"What compels them?" I say.

"Fear," she says. "Fear of our mother, Lord Katazyrna."

"Is that what fuels you?"

And she hesitates, but her answer is sincere. "Yes. Surely, your people slay for you out of fear."

"No," I say. "They do it out of love."

"Love?"

"Just love. Love for those behind them. Love for those who come after them. Love."

When I wake, the light outside has changed, and my dream feels less like memory. How would I have met Jayd on the Mokshi? Why would I have spared her? And how did that start all of this?

Arankadash is sitting across from me on another mattress, speaking softly to her offspring. She seems to be struggling with it.

"You all right?" I ask.

She does not respond. The hunk of living tissue she has carried with her all this way is squirming violently in her arms. She is openly weeping.

"Arankadash?" I say, but she only shakes her head.

She slowly unties the knots of the sling she has carried it in and sets the pulsing organ-thing down on the ground. It's grown to nearly four times the size it was when she birthed it. What it's eaten, I don't know, as I haven't seen her lactating. I wonder if it's subsisting on the world itself, feeding at night on the floors, the walls, and the billions of tiny creatures that infect this place. It has taken on the shape of a large cog with a wide-open center and nubby teeth all around its circumference. It shudders once on the ground and then begins to roll away, leaving a slimy trail in its wake like a slug.

Arankadash sobs, great heaving sobs that make my chest hurt.

I crawl over to her and put my arm around her. She wraps her arms around me and cries into my shoulder so hard, I wonder that it does not break her in two.

"The light has come for it," she says. "The light has taken it."

I say nothing, because nothing I can say will bring any comfort. We are each of us alone, united only in our inability to be free of this sticky world.

After she has cried herself out, I leave Arankadash to sleep, and unpack the rope I have in my pack.

Casamir is telling Das Muni a very involved story about two women born joined at the head who were found to puzzle out logic problems four times faster than an average person. I wonder if she's told Das

Muni that the information, if true, is likely gleaned from a recycled pair that the engineers kept in cages.

"I need your rope," I tell Casamir.

She gazes up at the tree. The leaves are starting to unfurl. "I guess it's worth a try," she says.

"Our other option is to go farther up into the city," I say, "but I get the impression we'll meet more of those monsters on the way, and the positions farther along are less defensible."

"Up, then," Casamir says.

I knot Casamir's rope and mine together. I tie off the first knot when I get about twice my height up. Make the second knot a couple of paces above that. Crawl down and untie the first, make another a few paces above my second, and so on.

Casamir stares at me from below, hands on hips. "This is the first time I've seen you climb anything with a care for safety," she says.

I don't tell her that the dream makes me think we are closer to our goal now, and to die so close would be a tragedy. I keep on with my tying and untying, up and up and up as the lights flash in the tree branches beneath my palms.

I know, intellectually, that the sky is a long ways off. But I don't realize just how long until I've been climbing for some time and I dare to look down. I can already blot out Casamir's body if I hold up my palm. I gaze up, shifting the weight of my metal blade to the other shoulder, and wonder at the madness of what I have planned.

No madder than staying below, I guess.

I climb and climb. Leaves begin to break off in my hands. They are growing larger now, fully unfurled. I wonder how much time we have.

The branches become thinner, about half the size of those below, but do not become any thinner than that as I ascend, for which I'm

thankful. This high up, I see little skittering creatures with enormous eyes that remind me of Das Muni's. Their webbed feet cling to the branches. Some munch on the leaves and fling themselves off as I approach, hopping to another branch. I'm fascinated at the ecologies of all of these places, which each hold people and animals that exist nowhere else in the world. What happens when Katazyrna rots away? It will all be lost, leaves shed at the end of the season.

As I come to the top of the tree, I dare not look down. I knot the rope around me to the closest branch, in case I fall, and press my fingers to the ceiling. It's warm and slick, and I feel the pulsing heartbeat of the world beneath it.

I have the urge to look down, but close my eyes instead. Take a deep breath. I pull the blade from my back, lean back a little until the rope holding me upright is taut, and then shove the blade with all my strength into the ceiling.

The blade encounters no resistance. It cuts clean through. I work it around in the wound a bit and draw it out.

A trickle of bloody gore oozes out as I release my weapon. My blade is covered in black ichor. I'm not sure if it's really blood or just something like it. I hack again at the ceiling. Again and again, tearing out great hunks of flesh. I work until sweat streams down my face and the bloody ooze spatters my face and chest.

I hack and hack as the leaves shudder around me. The edges of them have turned orange.

I dare to look down now, and immediately regret it. The tree is in full foliage again; it's a great jeweled yellow cushion, and down and down, so far down I can nearly erase their forms with my thumb, are the people I have traveled with from the belly of the world. They are all down there now—Das Muni and Arankadash, and Casamir, staring up as I stare down.

I'm running out of time. I can feel it. Perhaps they can too. Whatever assaulted this village will come for us soon.

I get back to hacking, though I am out of breath and my arms feel heavy as lead. My muscles are burning hot. The heat from the ceiling is also increasing, which doesn't help. I'm nearing the core of the artery.

I hack out another slab of flesh and let it tumble down through the branches. It reminds me of the hunk of flesh I sacrificed to Casamir's people. What are they doing with it right now? What *will* they do with it if I die here and don't return?

I slice up into the ceiling again.

The membrane bursts.

Bloody fluid pours over me, hot and sticky. It pushes me off my feet. I fall and almost drop my blade. I swing from the branch as the warm, coppery flood gushes from the wound and pools below.

Arankadash is shouting. Casamir seems to be floating away in the flood.

I wipe the gore from my eyes as the initial tide abates. I grab for the branch and haul myself back up. I peer into the hole I've torn into the sky. The bloody stuff is still pumping from it, but only from the bottom now. It trickles over the lip of the hole with every pulse. I reach into the hole and lever myself up to get a good look inside. It's absolutely dark and stinks of copper and afterbirth.

I try to peer up, but there's nothing to see but more darkness. The artery is as wide as I am tall but has hard ridges around it. As I sit in the lip of it, I can feel it pulsing, trying to push the trickle of life that's now burst all over the world below farther up into the far reaches of the world.

"Come up!" I yell. I gaze over the edge and see that the leaves have begun to fall. It's only then, as I see them all struggling below, that I realize Das Muni is not going to be able to climb the tree by herself.

I hurriedly untie the rope from around my waist and the nearby branches and hurl it down as far as it will go.

"Casamir!" I say. "Help Das Muni up!"

There is movement below. They are all covered in red-black fluid. Casamir is coming up first, and she throws the rope down.

"Casamir!" I yell, but she does not look at me, only continues climbing.

I heft my weapon. The leaves are falling in earnest now, bursting apart as they hit Casamir's head.

Arankadash is still below, standing with Das Muni. By the time I get to the ground, it will be too late for me to get back up. I know this, but I want to go down anyway. Instead, I stare at Arankadash and Das Muni.

Will Arankadash kill her for being a mutant? Will she shrug and tell me it is for the best, after losing her own sisters and that . . . thing she birthed? Is nothing precious?

Casamir is halfway up the tree. And then I see what had caused the other women to flee. There is a gory army of women with wan skin and fungi bursting from their heads, slowly shambling toward us from out in the surrounding forest. I see that they have no fingers. I know now where the baskets of finger bones have come from. But why cut off their fingers, if . . . I gaze upward. They are coming for the tree.

"Arankadash!" I say, pointing. "They're coming."

Arankadash leans over Das Muni. I turn my head away because I can't look.

I stare up into the dark and wonder how we are going to ascend this slimy, trembling thing. Casamir says her people know of eighteen levels. We have not even traveled up half that many, and there could be twice or three times or even four times that. But there is nowhere else to go. Maybe there never was. It's just up. Always up.

I gaze back down, expecting to see Das Muni's little body there on the ground below, floating in the bloody sea.

Instead, I see Casamir's head just a few paces below, and Arankadash making her way up slowly, hand over hand, with Das Muni strapped to her back.

I help Casamir into the hole. She sits across from me. We don't say anything. She's breathing hard, and I expect some story, but no, she knows what she did.

We wait as Arankadash ascends. Below her, the diseased women swarm the tree. They batter at it with the stumps of their hands. And I see now why they cut off their hands and not their heads. The women are trying to climb the tree. They, too, want to get to the center of the world, or at least eat whatever it is up here that powers it.

Arankadash finally reaches us. I grab hold of her left hand, and Casamir takes her right. We haul her and Das Muni up into the broken artery.

For a long moment, the four of us sit up here together, exhausted, covered in grime. I gaze at each of their faces, and though Arankadash does not look at me, I see Das Muni staring at her with eyes big as globes, and Das Muni starts to cry.

Love, I think. Just love. Fear has driven too much of this world.

"We should get going," I say. "It's not a steep climb. We should be able to walk for a while. You have your torch, Casamir?"

She digs into her pack and pulls it out. Holds it high above her head. It lights up the membrane that encompasses us, like peering into the throat of some monster.

I walk around the edge of the hole and take the torch from her. "I'll lead," I say. "You take up the rear, Casamir."

She frowns but doesn't protest.

And so, we climb.

We climb so long and so far in the dark that I lose track of time completely. We all fall silent, even Casamir. We stop for water and rest, and we climb again.

When I sleep, I dream of climbing, and when I wake, I am climbing.

I squeeze the sphere in my pocket. When the climbing and sleeping all blurs together, I take out the sphere again and play the recording.

Das Muni sits next to me as I watch it, munching on a mushroom. Her eyes are big and glassy. We have all taken on a numbed, distant look. When she gazes at me, it's as if she sees through me to some other place. "I once believed that all we were is the sum of our memories," Das Muni says, "but in this place, I found that it isn't the memories that made us; it is what we decided to do with them. I tried to build a life down there, in the dark, based on the pain I've endured. But you can't do that, can you? You have to . . . remake it. Transform. We are more than the sum of what's happened to us, aren't we?"

She is pleading for an answer. "I'm afraid my memory will never come back," I say.

Das Muni rocks back on her heels. "Maybe you should be more afraid of what you'll discover if it does," she says.

We climb.

The way grows steeper. We can no longer simply walk. We must dig our fingers and toes into the ridges of the great artery and climb. We rope ourselves together, though I don't know how much good that will do. It's Casamir's idea, and I don't want to argue about it. If one of us falls, all of us will fall. But we use our weapons to steady ourselves, shoving them into the flesh to provide us with leverage and some reliable fallback holds.

It's only as the neck of the artery begins to narrow and curve off to the left that I worry we have already reached as far as this artery goes up and are coming back down again.

I climb onto the flat, curved surface of the artery and help the others up.

We sleep, exhausted from what must have been a climb over several lost sleeping periods.

When we wake, I pat the artery floor at our feet. "Here," I say.

They all look at me. "It's going down again," I say. "That means eventually it will turn back to go deep below the world again. This is as high as it goes."

Our faces look garish in the light. I think they would gnaw their way out of this thing immediately if I told them to.

But Casamir unhooks her pouch of potions and comes over to me, presses her ear to the ground. "I can get it open," she says. She pulls a vial from her bag and makes a circle of it on the fleshy floor.

There's a hissing sound and then the smell of burnt flesh.

We all come up around the edge of the hole, and we wait.

The fleshy cap half falls out, revealing a wash of blue-green light from below. I kick at the flesh. Wherever we are, I'm heading down now, not up, for the first time in this long, exhausting trek.

The flesh tears farther. I punch out another seam and squeeze through, huffing out my breath as I do it to make myself smaller. I see the ground below, and it's not too far. I let myself fall and roll onto the porous floor.

The green-blue light seems very bright after the dim of the artery, but also familiar. I raise my head—

And stare into the armed tentacles of a cephalopod gun.

PART III:

RESURRECTION

> "IF YOU CANNOT KILL WHAT YOU LOVE,
> MAKE BEST FRIENDS WITH IT."
> —LORD MOKSHI, ANNALS OF THE LEGION

35

JAYD

I stagger into the hangar on Katazyrna like a dying woman, and maybe I am. I pinch off my suit, and it dissolves around me. I take in fresh, warm air.

I fear the world inside of me will miscarry. I had to come here because I still know Katazyrna better than the Mokshi, and without the arm, the Mokshi will murder me. I can pin Rasida here. Maybe not easily, but it's far more likely than it would be on Bhavaja. We are closer to the Mokshi. Closer to Zan.

I stumble through the interior hangar door, cephalopod gun up. Rasida won't have been able to let them know that I've escaped and to look for me, but I don't look like a Bhavaja. I'll stand out for what I am.

I make for the witches, to the holdout they always use when the ship is under attack. It's how they've survived so long here when so many others have perished. If I can make it there, I know I'll have a safe haven to sit and wait for Rasida to find me. I have the world, and she has the arm. Perhaps the witches may even help me hold out there. Allegiances shift when there are fewer options.

I shoot three women along the way to the next umbilicus, and my vision tunnels. Focus. One foot. Another. Pain is a constant companion. My walk is painfully slow, like a drunk, like a mutant, like some maimed, disfigured thing. And I am all of those things now, aren't I? Some savage merging of Katazyrna, Bhavaja, and Mokshi. I've been slashed and battered and changed by all three. I'm something else now.

I find the place in the wall and drag the bodies of the women I've shot up under it so I can reach the thin scab that covers the metal hinge of the door. I lever it open and pull myself inside. I close the hatch behind me. It's dark and smells of piss and sulfur. I crawl for ten thousand steps. I know because in the heat and darkness, the counting is the only thing that can keep me calm.

The heart room where the witches are is different from the cortex. I don't know its function, but when I come up over the organic mesh above it, I can see the witches inside. They are resting on the large slab at the center of the room, gabbling to themselves in an unknown language.

They peer up at me as I punch through the organic mesh with my weapon.

The left head says, "This is a foolish final stand."

I heave the rest of my body through the opening and dangle there a moment. When I let go, I drop heavily to the spongy floor. The witches scuttle toward me, hands reaching for me, but I raise the weapon again.

"Foolish," the right head says.

"Every stand is foolish," I say.

"What will you do?" left says.

"I'm going to wait for Rasida," I say. A twinge of pain shoots through my belly. I wince. I don't want to give birth to this world on Katazyrna, but if that's what happens, so be it. At least I will have upheld my part in this long, agonizing drama. I wish only that Zan knew how close I came before the end. "I need her arm," I say. "The world and the arm. I'm going to get those two things together if it's the last thing I do with the last of my breath."

"We are all destroyed," right says.

"I'm remaking it," I say. "You never did believe that's what we were going to do, but it is. Working with other worlds is the only way to save the Legion."

Right begins to speak again, but left rides over her, says, "There has been too much death."

"If you want Lord Bhavaja here," right says, "we'll need to broadcast where we are."

"Do it," I say.

The walls light up: misty red, whorls of blue. I prepare my final stand.

> "ALL I AM, AND ALL I LOVE, IS WAR. I DON'T KNOW
> WHO I WILL BE IF I STOP. THE WORLD, IF IT IS TO SURVIVE,
> NEEDS A LEADER, NOT A WARMONGER. THE WORLD
> I WANT TO MAKE DOES NOT REQUIRE ME."
> —LORD MOKSHI, **ANNALS OF THE LEGION**

36

ZAN

When I dream in the long throat of the artery, it's often in hazy snatches, half-dream, half-memory, but what I see with the cephalopod gun in my face is not a dream but a memory, so stark and abrupt it bowls me over.

I'm in a room full of people I don't trust, but I don't trust myself, either, so none of that is very surprising.

Jayd has brought me back to Katazyrna as her prisoner. We both know this is a ruse, but it is Anat we must convince, and Anat is having none of it. I attempted my first assault on the Mokshi, pretending I was a regular conscript, and failed. Anat has one punishment for failure.

"Let Zan go again," Jayd says. "She was close. It was the Bhavajas who ruined our chance. If we had peace with the Bhavajas—"

"There will never be peace with the Bhavajas," Anat says.

I am standing along the far wall of the great banquet hall, watching the two of them talk at the table. They are standing. Jayd has reports with her, tangles of light inscribed on foamy tablets. I have been here just a few sleeping periods, and I can already see that reports will not sway Anat. Like me, she is driven with blind purpose, a fanaticism. It's what has gotten her this far. It's allowed her to survive when so many worlds out here at the edge of the Legion have fallen.

"Why didn't the Mokshi kill her like it does your sisters?" Anat says, pointing at me. "Who have you brought me?"

She is wearing the iron arm, and I want to rip it off of her, but there are security women at the doors, including Gavatra, and Gavatra especially wants nothing more than to murder me.

Jayd makes her argument for peace with the Bhavajas, again, but I have already heard it twice since I've been here, and it's not swaying Anat. I didn't expect that. Trading Jayd for peace, allowing her to get the world from Rasida and freeing me to walk into the Mokshi and take back the arm from Anat when she walks into the Mokshi behind me thinking she's a conqueror, was a fine plan back on the Mokshi. But here, in the face of Anat's myopia, I'm not seeing a clear line to that future.

I come forward. "Anat," I say, "we can take the Mokshi. You can have the only world that escaped the core of the Legion. You can use it to do whatever you like—blow up all the Bhavaja worlds, take over the core of the Legion. All of it. But sue for peace first. Let the Bhavajas think you're cowed, then turn around and destroy them at the helm of the Mokshi."

Anat turns her face slowly to me. "Are you telling me what to do, filth?"

"I'm telling you how to get what you want," I say. Jayd told me I was some great woman, some great general, but it's only now, when I remember this terrible moment, that I see it was not me who was the general; it was Jayd. I was a tactician. A very confident and high-strung tactician, full of fire. I feel like a badly copied version of her now, or maybe someone else entirely, just some woman bereft of memory who others are trying to imprint with the memories of some dead woman.

"Gavatra," Anat says, still looking at me. "Recycle this presumptuous piece of trash."

"No," Jayd says.

"What?" I say.

Gavatra and four security women advance on me.

Jayd comes forward to shield me, but Anat snatches her with her iron fingers, holding her firmly.

"What do you care," Anat says to Jayd, "when it was you who blew open the Mokshi and recycled their people? What's one more of the Mokshi's ilk sacrificed to feed Katazyrna?"

Anat does not touch me, but her words are like striking me in the chest. I stare at Jayd, incredulous. "You?" I say.

Jayd recoils from me. "Zan, don't—"

"You said it was Anat!" I yell. "You said she stole the arm and recycled my people! Did you sabotage the Mokshi, Jayd? Blow it up? You? *You?*" She had murdered everything I loved and then had the audacity to come back to me and lie about it, and beg forgiveness for not trusting my plan for the Mokshi. We started anew.

I fight, because that's what I do. I bash two women in the face. I take Gavatra by the hair and smash her skull into the wall; my fingers leave great gory scratch marks on her skull. She staggers. Grips me by the collar. Someone comes up from behind. I see a burst of light, then blackness.

So, Anat recycled me, and somehow, with the help of the people below, I crawled back up here, leaving messages for myself along the way. But why? How did I know then that I would lose my memory when I next assaulted the Mokshi? Clearly, it hadn't happened during the assaults I'd been on before learning Jayd's betrayal ran so deep. How had I trusted Jayd for so long and believed her lies? She must have known I would never have trusted her if I knew it was her who blew a hole in the Mokshi, her who recycled my people, instead of Anat. We could never have worked together if I had known.

But there are still holes in this memory. It doesn't give me everything I need. It doesn't tell me why I have no memory, or what I hoped to achieve out there on the Mokshi with the arm and the world. What happened when I returned from the bowels of Katazyrna? The version of me in this memory seems confident that she knows what the plan is, even if Jayd misled her in how they all got there.

I remember tangling my fingers in Jayd's hair when she told me she was being sold off to the Bhavajas. I remember her telling me it was all going to be all right, that she knew what she was doing and this was all part of some greater plan. But had she foreseen Rasida's betrayal and our mother's death? Now she is alone out there, captive to the Bhavajas, at the mercy of Rasida's whim, and I am here, stuck under countless megatons of rotting shit inside a dying world.

The cephalopod gun moves closer to my face.

I jerk back to the present, still reeling.

"Get up!" the woman holding the weapon barks.

I raise my hands.

My walking stick is slung across my back, and I have a bone blade at my hip, but I don't go for either of them. Arankadash is just behind me, but Casamir is at least another twenty paces down, and Das Muni is ten more after that.

"I'm here to see Rasida Bhavaja," I say.

"I'll decide who you're here to see," the woman says. I've had time to search the corridor, and I note that she's alone. I'm surprised to see a single patrol. She hasn't yet called for others.

I start to get up.

"Stop!" she says.

"You told me to get up!"

She frowns hard. She's young, not much past menarche, and I feel sorry for her. I was that young once, following orders.

"I'm going to come up slow," I say. "All right?"

She jerks her head, and I decide that's close enough to a nod. I slowly rise to my feet. I'm taller than her by a head.

"I need to see—"

"I don't give a fuck who you're here to see," she says. "Where did you come from?"

"Level below," I say. "The umbilicus isn't working."

What I'm saying is ridiculous, because we've come down from the ceiling, but it doesn't matter. She's committed a rookie error, and she hasn't spotted it yet. She's let me get too close.

I grab the stock of her weapon with my left hand and push it away from my body while punching her hard in the face with my right.

She stumbles back. I wrench the gun free and point it at her, jamming it hard in her face so the tentacles split flesh. She shrieks and goes down.

"Rasida Bhavaja!" I say.

"Outside the hangar," she says.

"The vehicle hangar?"

She nods.

I try to get my bearings, but the truth is I hardly remember my way around this place. I've spent more time underground than I have up here. At least as far as I can remember.

"Take me there," I say.

Casamir lands behind me. "What the shit?" she says.

"We'll need more of these weapons," I say. "Rasida will have people around her."

My captive looks from me to Casamir. "You don't know?" she says.

"Know what?" I ask.

"The consort has pinned herself in the heart room with the witches," the Bhavaja woman says. "There's a full civil war happening on this ship, and she's become the focus of it."

Ah, I think, resourceful Jayd and all of her plans. I remember what she told me when Rasida took her away, about this being what we wanted, what we planned for, and I wonder if this was all part of it: the blowing up of my people; this civil war; even me, here, running after her. What kind of monster was I that I kept her in my confidence, knowing what she had planned? Is that why I have no memory? Did she take it from me so I would go along with this?

"And why are you telling me this?" I say.

"Because we might be on the same side," she says.

Das Muni slips down from the ceiling too.

"How many of you *are* there?" the Bhavaja woman says.

"Weapons," I say. "Take us to a weapons cache first. Then the hangar."

The woman nods. Blood trickles from the wounds in her face. "Fine, all right."

I glance back and see Arankadash has made it as well. "We're getting weapons," I tell her, "then we're finding the woman who stole this world."

The Bhavaja woman tries to walk us right into a trap, but Casamir lobs a vial of something at the women springing the ambush and blinds them.

Arankadash and I smash the oncoming women in the face. They go down, and we take their cephalopod guns, but not before one of the women sprints away. Arankadash fires at her, but she isn't very good with a gun yet.

Casamir pulls at my sleeve as we start again, her face pained. We are a stinking, filthy bunch. The bloody arterial spray has caked our hair and skin and has been slowly flaking off. We have all lost weight, Casamir most of all, and she looks hungry and exhausted.

"We can't just walk in there," Casamir says.

"Why not?" I say.

"Because I didn't come all this way to get shot here at the end," Casamir says.

"Jayd is right up ahead!" I say.

"And what else is ahead of us?" Arankadash says. "We don't know."

"So what, we split up?" I say.

"We take the time to think it through," Casamir says.

I point my weapon at the opposite wall and fire. The cephalopod rams itself into the flesh of the wall. The wall begins to blacken and crack, making a large circle of rot around its tentacles three paces in circumference.

I point at the rotting wall. "That's what's happening to this world," I say. "All that time we traveled, what did we see? A dying world. We've got nothing to go back to, none of us. There's only up. There's only forward."

"We are not arguing with you," Arankadash says.

"We're your friends," Casamir says, "but you shouldn't have let that woman run away."

"You want me to leave behind a trail of bodies?" I say.

Casamir raises her voice. "If we're all going to die anyway, what does it matter?"

Arankadash sighs. "Stop yelling," she says. "Use your heads up here. You are heading in the opposite direction of the woman who's clearly running for reinforcements," she says. "If I was that woman, I would go straight to my commander to report you; wouldn't you?"

I stare at our captive, who looks back at me with big eyes. I hit her in the face with the butt of my gun and she goes down.

"When did you become the dumbest person here?" Casamir asks me.

I nearly butt her in the face too but check my anger. We have made it too far to screw this up.

We hear the armed party before we see them. I raise my gun and power forward. Yes, I'm the dumbest of the bunch, and I don't care.

Eight women stand outside a large round door. They're firing cephalopod guns into it, which have rotted away all the organic tissue from the outside to reveal a big metal door. The tattered, ruined bits of the surrounding wall also reveal a metal core.

The woman at the center of them is yelling up at a blinking eye above the door. I know the woman immediately for Rasida Bhavaja.

"The things I'll do to you when I get this open," she says, "are extraordinary. It's mine, Jayd. Get your—"

She sees me before her women do. I'm already firing.

Rasida drops below the first line of women and takes off. She snatches at a hand weapon at her belt as she goes but does not turn.

I press myself against the wall and fire again. The cephalopod gun is slow to reload.

Casamir and Arankadash catch up to me and exchange more fire.

We have the element of surprise. Four women are already down. One is wounded. Two more take off after Rasida.

I run up to the door and stare at the blinking eye. "Jayd?" I say. "It's me! Jayd!" No response.

I point at the door. "Can you get this open, Casamir?"

Casamir bites her lip. Nods. She hands her gun to Das Muni. "Cover us, all right?"

Das Muni stares at the gun in her hands. I pat her cheek. "We're almost home," I say.

I expect to see delight, but she only stares hollowly at me. I don't have time to understand that. I tell Arankadash to help Casamir hold the position, and pick up a second gun from the fallen women on the floor. I take off after Rasida and the other two Bhavajas.

I hear them ahead of me and pick up my pace. There's something familiar about the corridor, and when I turn and see the huge open hangar door, I recognize it immediately.

The two Bhavajas have taken up positions at it and fire on me. I hurl myself to the ground so hard, I lose my breath. I roll to one side, firing both guns. One cephalopod goes wide, hitting the top of the door. The other clips one of the women. She swears, goes down.

I fire twice more, heaving for breath, and the second woman skitters inside.

I run.

The lights in the corridor change colors. They blink blue and yellow now. I see the hangar doors closing. I shoot again. The cephalopod smacks the door, burning away the organic shell, revealing metal beneath.

I lunge through the doors just as they close, and roll to a halt inside. I bring up my other gun and fire, hitting the fleeing Bhavaja in the back. She sprawls forward.

Rasida is spraying on a suit.

I fire at her.

She ducks. Picks up a big weapon from the case of them along the far wall, and rolls behind a vehicle.

The hangar lights are on, brighter than I'm used to after so long in the dark. I squint and stay low, moving vehicle to vehicle and using them for cover.

"You don't have to go through with this, Zan!" Rasida says. "Whatever Jayd has told you is a lie!"

"How do you know I don't remember everything?" I say. I check my weapons. One of them seems to have failed to reload. I bang it on the ground next to me. It rattles. I leave it there and eye the big weapon rack that Rasida pilfered from.

"If you remembered everything, you wouldn't be trying to kill me!" Rasida says. "You'd be as keen to murder Jayd as I am."

"I thought you were in love with her," I spit. I look underneath one of the vehicles, trying to get an idea of her position. The room is so big that it distorts our voices.

"There's no such thing as love in the Legion," Rasida says. "There is birth and there is death. That's all."

I peek above one of the vehicles and fire off a test shot.

Sure enough, she fires back. I sight her position and shuffle forward. I jump over one of the vehicles and half-crouch as I hurry down the next row.

"Zan?" she says.

I stop moving. Press my back against a vehicle. I hear her footfalls and low breathing. She's close. I breathe long and slow, keeping as quiet as possible.

"You know who you are yet?" Rasida says. "I worked it out, though Jayd fought it. Refused it. She never would have told me, which is fascinating in and of itself. You aren't some grunt from the Mokshi, are you? No . . . no. You're the lord herself."

I swing around the vehicle. See her peeking over another one two rows down. I fire. The blast goes wide and buries itself in the far wall. A ring of rot appears.

"I didn't believe that for a minute," I say.

"She thought you were quite convinced," Rasida says. "You really thought you were her sister?"

I gaze over the vehicles again, but she's taken cover. I do the same. Waiting.

Rasida is silent for some time. I listen to my own heartbeat, straining to hear the sound of her movement, but there's nothing but the pulse of my blood and the purr of the vehicle behind me.

I wait for her. Rasida does not disappoint. She says, "You and I are a lot alike, Lord Mokshi."

"Don't call me that," I say. My stomach twists. The lord of the world? Wasn't I just another castoff, like Das Muni? A conscript? But a regular conscript wouldn't have been able to open up the Mokshi's defenses and let Jayd in after her army died around her.

"Lord Bhavaja and Lord Mokshi," Rasida says. "I could have offered you a great deal more than Anat. And I wouldn't have betrayed you like she did."

I close my eyes, cursing my rotten memory. How can I deny what she's saying now, after all that has bubbled up from the depths of my memory? I want to fight it. I want to fight the truth, the way I have fought everything put in front of me on the long, mad journey.

I stay quiet, and she does the same.

I breathe. Wait.

I hear the squelch of her boots.

I jump up and roll over the vehicle. I come down right on top of her.

Rasida punches me with her weapon. I reel backward, pulling the trigger on mine. The cephalopod thunks into the floor behind her. It rots beneath her. She rolls away, taking me with her.

I knock her fist against the face of a vehicle and head-butt her. It's enough to stun her. She lets go of the weapon. I overreach, trying to get it myself, but she wraps her legs around me and throws me over again. I lose my grip on the cephalopod gun.

I punch her in the face. She spits blood at me, unfazed.

She comes around and punches my kidney. Pain shoots through my body. I reel back. She smashes her fist into my nose. Blood sprays. I fall back on my seat and she's on top of me, relentless, fists flying.

I reach to my left and smack the dashboard console of the vehicle next to me. It starts up and ejects a plume of spent yellow smoke that envelopes Rasida.

She coughs and hacks. I punch her in the guts. Bowl her over. I take her by the hair and drag her away from the plume. Take a breath in the clear air. I snatch up her forgotten gun and point it at her.

"They have used you," Rasida snarls. "They took your womb and your memory and now they will take your ship, and you'll gladly give it to them, won't you?"

How does she know all this? Or is she guessing? For a moment, I think Jayd really did betray me again, and she told Rasida everything. She had looked at Rasida with such desire. Far more than she ever had for me.

"Jayd and I are on the same side," I say.

Rasida spits blood from her broken mouth. "They boarded your world, you fool. Jayd recycled all of your people to keep the heart beating on this hulking wreck of a world. Jayd betrayed you then, and she will betray you now."

"That's a lie," I say. But it's not. My memory says it's not. Das Muni was recycled, and many more like her. Who else but the Katazyrnas would recycle those on the Mokshi? Who else but Jayd? I want to weep. I admired how she fought, and opened my world to her, and told her the Legion was dying. She did not believe me. She had likely drugged me and stolen my arm and blown up my people and recycled them, and when she came back—who knows how long after?—saying she believed me now, she had changed her mind, she let me think it was her mother who had sneaked a force onto the Mokshi and killed it. How could I have been so foolish as to allow her to come back after that? Why was I so desperate? So emotional? What a fool. I hate that woman. I hate who I was. I hate the woman who endured that betrayal and welcomed Jayd back after it. I was desperate enough to save the Mokshi that I joined forces with my greatest enemy.

"I came for the arm, Rasida. You can give it to me or I can chop it off."

"You'll have to take it," she says, and spits more blood. "I never did figure out how to use it. Funny, isn't it? All this for the arm, for the world. You think you're saving the Legion, but the Legion is already dead. All you're saving is the Mokshi and yourself. You're as selfish as Jayd."

I raise my weapon. She raises her arm.

I shoot her in the chest.

She's still alive when I use the obsidian blade at my hip to cut off her arm. She shouts at me.

"You'll be sorry for this in the end." Blood flows. She goes into shock as she bleeds out.

I thought the arm was something she had to affix to the stump of her old arm, but no—it's clear that she's slipped it over her own arm, so the metal arm acted as a skin. Her arm was too large for it, though; as I wriggle the dead arm free of the casing, I see that the skin and flesh have been stripped away, not to the bone but very near it, so that her arm would fit into the metal one. The flesh of her real arm is covered in green lubricant, which must have numbed her pain and discomfort.

I pick up the metal arm with my right hand and swing around to go back to where Jayd has holed herself up. Then I stop and stare at my outstretched hands and the metal arm.

My left arm is smaller than my right. It is among the first things I noticed when I woke, after the body on the floor. I pass the arm from my right hand to my left and feel the heft of it in my palm.

I have a memory then, of waking up in a sea of pain and blood. My left arm was a red, gory wound. In the memory, I'm naked, and the first thing I do is look beside me to where I should find the woman who shares my bed. Where I should find Jayd. But she is gone. And that's when the world trembles.

Jayd stole everything from me.

The Mokshi is my world, Rasida had said. But not my world in the same way it is Das Muni's world. I built that world. I freed it from the core of the Legion, and I designed it to leave the Legion. But something went wrong. Something inside of it failed, and then the Katazyrnas attacked me. Jayd attacked me. I thought I could convince her of my purpose. But her first loyalty had been to Anat. She feared Anat far more than me.

I tremble as I slip my left arm into the metal one. The interior is slimy with the green lubricant.

But the arm fits like a glove tailored just for me.

The arm warms around me. My fingers slide into the metal sheaths at the end. I squeeze my fist, and I can feel a terrible power there at the center of it.

Why did Jayd want the arm? A trophy for her mother, no doubt, but as I stare at my fist, I see this is the key to something. It's why we needed the arm, too, and not just the world. Jayd had no idea what it contains, what it can do. To be honest, in this moment, I don't either. But it's more than a trophy.

I raise my hand; a ripple of heated air flows around me as I do. I imagine the ruined door ahead of me becoming whole. I imagine it sealing itself back up. Soldering itself together.

Green mist emanates from the center of my palm, and then the skin of the world is rippling and growing over the ruined doorway. It forms a perfect spiraling circle, then blooms open, a fresh seal without even a scab. All that's left to signal anything happened to the door at all are the blistered pieces of it lying at my feet; as I watch, they are being absorbed into the floor.

I was not a general, a leader of armies, as Jayd told me when I first woke. No, it seems my skill was in something else. My skill was never in death but in making life.

I have the arm now.

Does Jayd have the world?

Together, we'll get to the Mokshi. And I will have my real answers.

37

ZAN

I race back to the heart room and turn the corner just in time to see Arankadash and Casamir step inside.

Das Muni waits in the threshold. She gazes in, once, then back at me. She removes her cowl and stares at me with her big eyes. I see something there that makes time seem to slow down. I listen to my heartbeat and the pulse of the world beneath my feet. I see her look at me just this way in another life, another time, only that time, she is kneeling at my feet, because I am her lord.

Her lord. She must have known this whole time.

I hear a hiss. Something thuds into Das Muni's chest, and she sprawls back hard. Her little body hits the opposite wall.

I yell. What I yell, I don't know, but I run to her, still yelling whatever formless thing that's burst up from my chest.

She is lying in a pool of blood rapidly expanding from the hole in her chest. Inside her chest cavity is a pulsing black bit of charged bone or other organic material. It's neatly burst her open.

"Das Muni," I say, and I pull her into my arms. Her blood runs hot and wet into my lap. She is so light.

Her mouth moves. Blood colors her teeth and tongue. I see that she's bitten her tongue hard.

I turn, unbelieving, back toward the heart room. Jayd is there, slumped on a long console that dances with lights. Threads of red and yellow and blue tangle in the air above her. She is heavily pregnant and holding a massive weapon. I recognize it as the kind I took out on my attack on the Mokshi. Her face is drawn and haggard, and though her belly is distended, her face is hollowed: her eyes are sunken, and there are dark circles beneath her eyes. A tangled mass of arms and legs and heads is huddled up in the corner, and as they unfold themselves, I see that they are a single body. I shudder, wondering what new horror the world has for us.

Arankadash fires at Jayd and misses.

"Don't kill her!" I say. "That's Jayd."

Casamir's eyes bulge. She has her own weapon now, and she does not take her finger from the trigger. "Are you mad?" she says.

"Jayd, why did—" I begin.

"For fuck's sake!" Jayd says. "She was . . . Listen to me. She knew who you were. She was serving on this level. I can't have . . . We can't . . ." Her eyes fill. She fights it. "I can't start over. Yes, I recycled her. So what? She recognized you. We can't start over. This is the endgame, Zan. She can't . . . She can't ruin this. I just . . . I shot her without thinking. We can't start over. This is the end. This has to be the end. I can't do this again, Zan. I can't."

"Das Muni, what's she—"

Das Muni brings up her long fingers to my face and shows her teeth. "I am yours, Lord," she says.

I cradle her head in my iron arm. "I'm not just another woman from the Mokshi, am I?" I whisper, because though I know it now, have known it for too long now, I want to hear it from her.

She shakes her head.

"Why didn't you kill me down there?" I ask. "I failed the Mokshi, didn't I? Failed you and everyone who lived there. This traitor recycled you. And I took her back after. I took her back because we could not go on without her."

"You are not the same, Lord Mokshi," Das Muni says. "You are a different woman. I am too." She huffs up blood.

"You want answers?" Jayd says. She points her weapon at me now. "Get us both to the Mokshi."

I squeeze Das Muni to my chest. Her blood slicks my suit. "No," I say. "You kill her, you kill me."

"You don't care about her," Jayd says.

"Maybe some other version of me didn't," I say, "but I do. I won't leave her here to die like this."

"She is already dead," Jayd says.

Blood is bubbling on Das Muni's lips. "Save her," I say, "or kill me here with her."

Something in Jayd's face twists. Is it wonder? Surprise? She gazes back into the room and at the many-headed woman there. "Can you repair her?" Jayd asks it.

The left head says, "What will we get in return?"

"I won't shoot you," Jayd says.

"A hard bargain," the right head says. They bumble forward.

"Will you make sure she's all right?" I ask Casamir and Arankadash.

They exchange looks. Arankadash says, "Hole up here, hoping you return alive? Not a chance, after this."

"If I'm not back in an hour, come for me," I say.

Casamir knits her brows. "Come for you how?"

"I'll show you," I say.

Jayd leads us to the hangar. Or marches us there; I don't know which. Maybe both. Part of me wants to take her in my arms. The other part wants to disarm her and scream. I show Casamir the hangar and explain it. She gives a low whistle.

"You can watch from the observation window," Jayd says, motioning Casamir out.

"You sure about this?" Casamir asks me.

"No," I say, "but the Mokshi has always been where I get my answers."

"One hour," Casamir says. She shuts the hangar door behind her and goes up to the observation room.

Jayd limps toward one of the vehicles. I noticed on the way here that something had happened to her leg.

"What have you done?" I ask.

She's breathing hard and clutching at her belly. "I've done everything we promised," she says. "You clearly don't remember yet, but you will. You must. On the Mokshi. I'm sure. I'm so sure you'll remember."

"It won't let us in," I say.

"It will let you in," she says. "It always does, eventually, because you remember how to disarm it. But now you even have . . ." She trails off into a deep breath, winces. "You have the arm."

"The arm and the world," I say. "You have the world, don't you?"

She nods. "Trust me one last time, Zan. Just one last time. You remember this was our plan?"

"I remember we agreed to bring the arm and the world to the Mokshi," I say.

"Good," she says. Her tone is lighter, relieved. "Good, yes, that's something."

She gestures me toward the table where the suits and the vehicle guts are. She sprays on a suit. I do too. Then she waves me over to one of the vehicles and tells me to be still. She programs the release sequence, using a tangle of lights near the door. I look up at the observation window and see Casamir up there, hefting her weapon and peering at us. Will she be brave enough to come after me, really, once she sees the blackness of open space? She didn't believe a single word of this a rotation ago. I worry it will test her sanity.

Jayd slips onto the vehicle behind me. I feel the heat of her, and the pulsing thing inside of her. I flex my arm. The lights above us move as the skin of the world thins.

I start the vehicle, and we pop free of Katazyrna.

I have been underground so long that the sight of the Legion takes my breath away. The great orb of the artificial sun is shuttering open, and it spills across my vision like a promise of rebirth. Behind me, Jayd is tense. I am too. I wonder at both of our motives.

I pilot toward the Mokshi, and in my bones I know this route so well that it feels like the most natural thing in the world. There are dead vehicles circling Katazyrna, and abandoned bodies that no one has bothered to collect and recycle. When I gaze back at Katazyrna, I see that half the world's tentacles are now dead and withered, tucked close to the rotten black skin of the world. How long have I been gone?

I want to say something to Jayd, but we have no way to communicate in our suits except by sign language, and what I have to say is far too long and complex for that while I'm piloting a vehicle.

As we near the Mokshi, I see its defenses light up, the same blue and green auroras I saw the last time I tried to take it. This time, Jayd taps my iron arm and points to the Mokshi.

I raise the arm and make a fist.

The aurora dissipates.

I stare into my upraised hand and marvel at it. Once again, I am ushering my enemy into the Mokshi. I am inviting her and her weapons and her motives, and I understand even less of them this time than I did the last.

I fly us straight toward the hole in the world, and though Jayd points the way as we sink below the skin of the ship, I pilot my way there of my own volition, like taking a long journey home.

We part layer upon layer. I expect to see bodies, but there are none this deep into the world. Of course not. They were all recycled by Jayd. How did I forgive her? How? I don't trust who I used to be any more than I trust Jayd. There's dripping ichor from the ruined levels, much of it frozen and blistered, peeling back.

I bring the vehicle to rest in a broken hangar that contains the remnants of another sort of vehicle. These have two eyes and great bulbous bodies, not the wedged heads of the ones from the Katazyrna. We land and Jayd gestures me toward the sealed door.

I reach out my iron arm, close my fist, and the door opens. We step inside. The door closes. I look for the controls to pressurize the space, but Jayd is already ahead of me, her fingers moving over another complicated light display.

A brilliant yellow light suffuses the room. I squint. The room pressurizes. The inner door opens.

Jayd motions me forward.

I step into a long hall. Lights blink intermittently. Much of the corridor looks rotted out. I follow Jayd's lead and don't take off my suit. It's too unstable here.

We climb through a set of half-open doors, then down another corridor. The world here is much worse off than the Katazyrna. The flesh has peeled back from all the walls to reveal rusted-out metal, twisted wiring, shriveled tendons. What really makes up the core of every world? Metal skeletons? Fashioned by whom? The gods? Did a god truly come all the way out here and shit out the Legion itself and fly on across the universe, or have we been here all along?

Finally, we come to the bottom of a great stairwell. I know this stairwell. At the top of the steps is a great domed structure. It reminds me of the temple where Rasida and Jayd were joined. I don't know why I have put so much faith in coming here. Maybe because it's my only hope of finding out what's happened. But I can't think of anyone or anything I would trust to tell me the truth of the twisted story that got us to this place.

We climb. There's a spongy growth at the center of the door. I press the warm center of my iron arm to it, and the door opens. Yellow lights slowly brighten, giving my eyes time to adjust.

We are in a massive room lined in hexagonal apertures that give us a clear view of the entire Legion. It doesn't even look like the room has a floor, but Jayd walks across it, and it holds her. I stare at the worlds below us as I walk after her. There's a great round console at the center of the room. Jayd leans hard against it. She sets her weapon down and slides to the floor. She presses the bit on her suit to release it, and it falls off her. Jayd is breathing hard. She hisses and clutches at her belly again.

"Jayd—" I begin, but she shakes her head and points to the console.

There's a divot at its center, and bundles of light appear all around the circumference. On the panel in front of me are two small containers. They grow from the console, and the liquid in them seems to have bubbled up from inside. I pick one up and pour out what's inside, set it back down. It fills again.

One is full of clear liquid. The other is full of purple liquid. I have a memory of these spongy containers, of drinking them again and again.

I pull the sphere from my pocket and set it into the divot at the center of the console. Natural as breathing.

There is a feeling of static in the air; the console trembles. Light escapes the sphere and dances at the center of the console. The light shifts and weaves itself into an image of my own face and body. The image looms above me, twice as large as life. I look much younger.

"If you're here again," the image says, "and you don't have the world and the arm, you need to start again." It gestures at the console below me. "I'm sorry you don't remember much of anything, but that was necessary."

"Necessary?" she mutters. "Did you do this to *yourself*?"

"You have likely met Jayd Katazyrna," my image says. "She is your greatest love and your greatest enemy. The Mokshi, this ship, is your salvation, and the salvation of those you take with you. You've designed this ship to pilot itself out of the Legion. It was originally stationed at the very core of the Legion, where worlds are much more stable. You've programmed a destination into it that was buried in its redundant systems. Don't try to make sense of that now; it will come to you. What you need to know is that your first attempt failed. The ship failed here on the Outer Rim, and the Bhavajas and Katazyrnas attacked you for scrap."

"It was for more than that," Jayd says. She lies with her head against the console behind her, eyes glassy. "Anat wanted everything."

"You admired Jayd's fighting. You thought you had convinced her of your purpose. But she stole your arm and blew out the core of the world, ejecting your people into the vacuum and recycling them on Katazyrna."

I stare at Jayd. She looks away, says, "I thought you mad. I didn't know. . . . I didn't understand, until later, until I realized Katazyrna was dying too."

"I should have killed you," I say.

"You should have," she says. "But you didn't know, not until—"

"Until Anat had me recycled," I say, "and told me who it really was who did it."

She nods.

"You made an error," my former self says, "the error you always make. Every woman has her weaknesses. For some, it is drink. Others, abject gluttony. I once knew a woman who could not resist a bet. My weakness was always my heart. I could not sacrifice someone I loved. Things, certainly. But to lose something I loved cut me too closely. It was agony to recover. Love would destroy me as completely as any army. And I fell in love with Jayd Katazyrna."

Jayd closes her eyes. "I'm sorry," she says, and I'm not sure if she's saying it to me or the past version of me. Maybe both.

"She stole our arm, it's true," the ghost continues. "She didn't believe us. She destroyed the Mokshi, blew it all apart, and let me think it was Lord Katazyrna who did it all and captured Jayd and brought her back. It was a story only a fool in love would believe, or a fool who had never met Anat Katazyrna. Lord Katazyrna would never, ever come to retrieve any of her children. I know it now, but I didn't then. And when Jayd came back here, saying she was convinced now that the Legion was dying, I believed her. I know I'm a softhearted fool, but it got us this far. I let her in again, and we came up with a plan that would make all the betrayal worth it. I promise you."

"But we had to get the arm back," I say to Jayd, "and the world from the Bhavajas. Why was I stupid enough to take you back?"

Jayd winces and clutches at her belly again. The contractions are coming closer together. I stare up at my image, willing it to hurry, knowing I have no control over the past as it unfurls.

"Jayd took me back to Anat and said I was just another of her prisoners," my image says. "Anat didn't like me. But that wasn't the worst of it, no. No, it was learning that it was Jayd, not Anat, who stole my arm and recycled my people, that destroyed me. It made it impossible to work with her once I knew that. I was recycled, and then . . . How do you survive after that? Maybe you could. But I could not."

"I'm sorry," Jayd says, and her voice is thin. "I had to give you up to go on. No one survives being recycled."

"The plan had to proceed," my image says, "but I could not live with Jayd's betrayal." And at this, the woman with my face laughs. "You'll sit here brooding for cycles and cycles with a broken heart. A broken heart that will slay you as surely as any army. You don't want that. We have done that. It won't save the Legion. So . . . make your choice."

The image fades. I'm left in the dim with all the answers it appears I'm going to get, and a terrible choice, and Jayd wheezing beside me.

"I never knew what happened when you went here," Jayd says, and her face crumples in pain and sorrow. "I didn't know you forgot me on purpose."

"You let me be recycled," I say. "You let me come here again and again."

"We had to save the Legion."

"At the expense of my sanity?" I say. "Was the love false too, like she said? Was this really your game all along, to save the world, no matter who you would destroy? No matter how many worlds? You said I was some great general, a warmonger, but you're the cold one, Jayd. Colder than I ever was."

"It's why it had to be me," she says. "Don't you see that? I could have traded you to the Bhavajas, you and your childbearing womb. But I didn't. Because I knew you couldn't do what needed to be done. You can fight, yes, but you are too softhearted to endure the long game. You have no idea what I had to do with Rasida to get here. You wouldn't have been able to manipulate her like I did. You would have murdered her again and again, or she would have found you out and recycled you."

"I sacrificed my child," I say. My first memory. The child. The womb.

"What is a child," Jayd says, "but potential? And that's what you traded it for. The potential to free the Mokshi."

I stare hard at the fluid in the containers. Do I want to remember? Do I want to heap more heartbreak over Jayd onto my existing heartbreak? When I close my eyes and think of love, it's not Jayd in my mind now but Das Muni and Casamir and Arankadash. Jayd is fear. They are love. Do I want to exchange all of that for full knowledge of the past instead of what some old version of myself thought I should know?

As I consider my options, a second image springs up from the console.

The woman in this one is me, but not the calm, considerate one I saw before. In this one, I recognize her eyes. The haunted look. The fear.

She bows over me. She is already fairly looming, so the effect is dramatic. It's as if she's trying to see through time. She wears a tattered garment ripped through by the claws of some animal, perhaps. Her skin is red and raw in the seams of it. Half her head is scorched clean of hair.

"You don't want your memory back," she says. "I don't know how many times we've done this already, but don't get your memory back. You don't want to know what you were." She looks at something outside the frame. Shakes her head. "We are the fist of the War God. We are the inheritors of the worlds. We will show ourselves worthy."

The image bursts apart.

Jayd moans quietly in the corner.

"Jayd," I say, "what are we here to do?"

"Save the world," she says softly.

Another misty image bubbles up from the console. Myself again. My hair is shorn short. There's blood running down my head from a long gash. There seem to be great yawning distances of time between these. I didn't make a record every time I came back. Why? Did I always just choose to lose my memory? Have I always acted on blind faith? How many times had I done this before I made the second record?

"Fuck the Katazyrnas," my past self says. "Fuck the Bhavajas. We escaped the core for no fucking purpose. Neither is going to help us and we've fucked up everything. You think you want your memory back, you get it back, but you won't get all of us back, you understand? It's a fucking synthetic. The ship puts it together from the last time you left, right before this whole shit started. You're going to be all in love with Jayd again. You won't remember what she's done since." She, too, looks outside the frame. I wonder what they're all looking at.

I gaze around me at the ships of the Legion. Were they seeing someone coming for them? A ship? A vehicle? And then I see it—there's a great wall of doors behind me. Most are open and empty. I count nearly a hundred of them, all stacked up on top of one another, up and up. Here on the bottom level, there are just four left. These doors are how I escape the Mokshi each time. They propel me up and out, clear of the Mokshi's gravity. I close my eyes. I remember the feel of bursting free, but that's all. My past selves were all looking at their escape. Even knowing what they knew about what lay outside the Mokshi, they knew they could not stay here. They had to stick to the plan and remake the world, or everything we had done up until this point was for nothing.

The image bursts apart.

"Who am I, Jayd?" I say softly. "What did you do to me?"

"We did this together," Jayd says.

And maybe that is true. Maybe we became everything we hate together.

Another image pops up. Another swearing, angry version of me. Still no scar, though. This one has longer hair, and she's carrying a spear like Arankadash's. Her speech is much the same as the one before. Angry and bitter and cursing Jayd.

"What did we become?" I ask Jayd.

"I don't know," she says. She moans and lies back. The world is coming.

A misty green version of me wafts up from the sphere again. Her hair is shorn short. She looks very weary. This version of me says, "I waited four cycles this time. Got my memory back. Realized what I'd done to try to keep this ship going. We're all slaves to these worlds, these . . . beings that have overtaken our vessels. No one can escape unless they rewrite the very pattern of the world. I've done that, but I don't have the catalyst. Twelve generations, and no world-birther on Mokshi. But the Bhavajas have one. The bloody Bhavajas. I'll go back, but if you're watching this and you don't have the arm and the world, just kill yourself. Just end it. It's too much."

The recording fades.

"I fell in love with you," Jayd says. "You don't have to believe that. But you and I worked together to find a way to rebuild this ship and kill Anat and get the world without a hopeless war. You've rewritten the code for the Mokshi so it can leave the Legion. But you need . . . you need a world to rebuild this one, to reinvigorate it. Renew it. You needed Rasida. I brought you that. I did that. For you, and for the Legion."

I bend toward her. "You have a world inside of you?"

"Rasida's." She reaches her hand out to me. "We did this together, Zan. Please."

"Das Muni," I say.

She grimaces. "I'm sorry. I thought all the people from the Mokshi were dead. She was a prisoner, and she was going to betray you to Anat. She recognized you. I recycled her. I was afraid—"

"You were afraid she would tell me who I was."

"She didn't have the whole story. I did that without knowing what was at stake."

I kneel beside her and touch her belly. I feel the pulsing of the world. She grabs my hand. Above me, I can hear another recording starting. How many times have I recorded myself here? My gaze follows the long lines of doors. At least as many as there are doors, I suspect. I've used that way out many, many times. Not hundreds as Maibe would have me believe, but surely dozens.

"I threw away a child," I say. I can't let that go. I want her to say out loud what we did. What we chose.

Jayd weeps openly now. She leans hard against the console. Grips my hand. "I needed your womb," she says. "I told you, you weren't strong enough to do what needed to be done. I couldn't just give you over to the Bhavajas. Besides, they would expect a trap if we gave them some unknown woman. They would do far worse things to you because you weren't a Katazyrna. You were no one. You would have had no protection. But Rasida loved me. Lord of War, she always loved me."

"But I was already pregnant," I say.

"Yes," she says. "We had to choose. One or the other. A child with no future, or the future of the Legion."

So I threw away my child. Into the darkness of the Mokshi's recycling pit. I threw away my child to save the whole world. I think of Arankadash and her sorrow. I wonder if I felt sorrow or just relief that we had finally found a way to save the Mokshi.

I sit beside Jayd and gaze out at the worlds of the Legion. I know the worlds are dying. I know we are the only hope we have for their salvation, while also being the harbingers of their destruction.

Jayd has asked me to trust her one more time.

She grits her teeth and bears down. "You can leave me," she says. "Just leave me. When I have it . . . it will eat this whole world. Remake it. It will replicate all those patterns you programmed into it. Just . . . you need to trigger it. With the arm."

I stand up and go to the console again, searching my memory for a way to trigger this change. My gaze is drawn, again, to the clear and purple liquids.

I listen to the recording above me, a weary woman, my own voice, saying, "Who do you become when you lose your memory? I don't know. Some of it comes back, yes. But not all of it. I took the little vial, like something from a wizard, and I ate all the horror. Not just of what

I'd done but of what I planned to do. I've waited here four turns now, puttering around this dying place. And why? Because I'm afraid to start over. I'm afraid to go back. I should have used an army. I should never have saved Jayd."

"I don't understand any of this," I say.

Jayd makes a guttural laugh. "Neither do I. That's the awful part. We've done such awful things to each other, Zan. So many awful things. But it's going to end now. Just . . . leave me here. Please. I just want to end it. You have had this gift. You don't have to remember any of this. But I do. I must. And I'm tired of it."

"No," I say.

"It all worked out in the end," Jayd says. "You got back your ship, and you'll escape the Legion once it's reborn. I got revenge on the Bhavajas. We did this together, Zan."

"I don't want my bloody ship," I say. "I want an end to all this death."

Jayd chokes out a laugh and, with it, a spattering of blood. "Someone had to birth the new world, Zan. I wanted it. You didn't."

"You were my greatest enemy," I say.

"No," Jayd says. "You were always your own greatest enemy. Even here. Even now."

I place my hands on the console beside each of the growths full of liquid. Above the vials is a spongy cap. It feels familiar to me, and I open it. Inside is a bubbling mess of green gel, very much like the green skin of my arm. I dip my arm into it and watch the green liquid from my arm bleed back into the wound on the console.

When the liquid from my arm joins the rest, the whole pot of green goo turns yellow and is absorbed into the console. As I watch, spidery yellow tendrils snake out from the console and run all along the floor and up the walls of the temple room. A soft amber light fills the room, and it reminds me of the light in the hall of giants where Arankadash nearly stayed behind to find her child.

Jayd screams behind me. The world is coming. The Mokshi will be rewritten, will be reborn, will escape the Legion.

Yet here I finally sit with my memory in reach, and the means to erase everything again too. Which to choose? I have come here and chosen one or the other dozens of times. We were so single-minded in this, Jayd and this woman I once was. But do I want to become her? Lord Mokshi, the single-minded woman who was willing to sacrifice everything—her ship, her children, her womb, her memory—to power her way out of the Legion? Must I become her again, or is she, too, simply a suit, a temporary but necessary fix to get me to where I am now? I consider the pieces of my memory I have, and the pieces I've been told, and I wonder if it is all meant to bring me here, to this moment. This choice. To be someone I was, or to start over again, to fall in love again with Jayd. Am I doomed to love her and to be destroyed by that love?

One or the other.

I think of Das Muni's choices—to poison and maim, but also to heal and rebirth. I think of Arankadash and the cog she nursed until the world came for it. I think of Casamir and the love she lost to the recycler pits, and her endless stories. And I wonder if I've given myself a false choice.

There are never just two choices.

I step away from the console. Behind me, Jayd is panting. She does not need a warmonger or a general or a tactician in this moment. The tactician got us here, but someone much different needs to get us out. *I* need to get us out.

And so, I make another choice.

I choose neither. I choose the woman I've become, not the woman I was, not the woman I can be. The woman I am. Like the versions of myself before me, I stare at the long row of doors leading to my escape, but unlike those before me, I do not step into one. Not yet.

I take Jayd's hand. Together, we will remake the Mokshi, as we planned all those rotations ago.

But it must be our last act together.

> "LET IT NOT BE FORGOTTEN, NO MATTER HOW MANY
> TIMES WE GO BACK, OR HOW MANY TIMES THINGS
> ARE UNDONE, THAT I LOVED JAYD KATAZYRNA,
> HOWEVER MUCH IT HURTS MY HEART TO GIVE HER UP."
> —LORD MOKSHI, **ANNALS OF THE LEGION**

JAYD

I give birth to a world.

It does not seem so portentous. It's mostly pain and agony, as if my whole lower half is being split apart. It's worse than when I gave birth to Rasida's child . . . Zan's child. I just want it out. I want it over.

Zan takes her hand from mine and pulls the world from my body and holds it up wonderingly, as if it is a great light, though really it is only a fleshy, nubby organ of a thing. Its tentacles wriggle out from its nubs and cling to her fingers, and in the amber bloom of the room, it does not look like something that was worth all this pain and darkness.

Zan sets it on top of the console.

Above her, all of the past Zans are still playing. This last one has the long wound on her head, the one she still bore when she came to me this last time, when I thought her dead. I had seen her crash into the Mokshi that last time. She bears the same terrible wounds and scars that I would see on her when we finally retrieved her from the organic tube she used to escape the Mokshi. I thought she'd come back to us because she could not tend her own wounds. I thought she'd come back to me to be remade.

"I waited so many turns," the recording says. Zan, my Zan, the last Zan, who is not this Zan. I gaze up at her and remember how awfully things went that time, and I weep again, and I'm glad I've told Zan to leave me here, because we have been so awful to each other that there's nothing to pick up anymore.

Sometimes you can't go forward. You can't put things back together. I will die here. This will be my penance for all we've done.

Zan gets up now and wipe her hands on her suit. I lie back as the contractions still wrack my body. I begin to tremble. I lean back and wait for the world to devour me. This is how it should be. I was the stronger one. I could get us this far. I've done my part.

But Zan is holding out her arms to me. She's helping me up. I'm confused. My legs are weak. I can barely stand, but she is holding me up and helping me across the floor. I'm trailing afterbirth. My placenta slides free of my body, and the umbilicus tangles my legs.

Zan leans over and cuts me free of it. I glance back one more time at the last Zan I knew, the one before this one, the one who chose to come back to me despite all we had done.

"I don't want to go back," the other Zan says. "Who would want to go back to a dead world? But I can't leave her, can I? I can never leave her, no matter how many times I do this."

I burst into tears again because I feel like a monster, though Zan and I, the old Zan, are just the same. We were made for each other. We could have only done this being as we are. We couldn't be anything else and save the Mokshi.

"I have done terrible things," I say.

"I know," Zan says.

"Sabita," I say, because I ignored her too. I used her, and while we are here confessing all we have done wrong, she is one more thing I must atone for. "You should know she protected me. She helped me, just as you asked her. Even if you don't remember. She helped me get here. Turned around and took on the Bhavajas following us, and I . . . I just let her. I didn't look back. I didn't go back. I didn't . . ."

Zan is shushing me. I have no more breath for my guilty admissions. Zan pulls me toward the wall of doors that house the organic tubes that will jettison us from this place. She showed them to me when she first captured me, and invited me to leave any time I wished. But I wanted to stay, that first time, and sabotage this place. I was a fool then. I hadn't believed her yet that she had found a way to stop us all from dying.

"This isn't how I want it to go," I say. "I want to die. That is my story."

"Fuck that story," Zan says.

She pulls me to one of the doors and palms it open with her iron arm. It's going to be tight, and it won't have air very long for two of us. I'm afraid, more afraid to die with her than without her, because at least without her, I could pretend she had some future that outlasted us. Who will pilot the Mokshi if she dies?

She brings me into the damp tube. "You can stay if that's what you really want," she says, "But if you stay, I'll stay too. I don't leave people behind."

I am shaking hard. I gaze back at the control room. The images, all of the old Zans, have gone quiet.

"There is nothing for me here," I say.

"Good," she says. "Then let's start over."

"I HAVE SPENT MY LIFE BATTLING MONSTERS.
IT WAS ONLY IN REALIZING THAT I WAS
THE MONSTER, AND CHOOSING TO DESTROY HER,
THAT I COULD SAVE THE WORLD."
—LORD MOKSHI, ANNALS OF THE LEGION

ZAN

The massive organic tube pops free of the Mokshi and enters the long, quiet dark of the Legion. It is the silence that comforts me. I got tired of listening to my own voice. I hold Jayd against me until her trembling subsides. She drifts in and out of wakefulness.

We begin to circle the Mokshi, just another bit of detritus caught in its gravity well. This is the part I haven't thought through. When I escaped before, no doubt Jayd or Anat came for me, but now we are alone.

We are alone.

I hope that Jayd sleeps through it. I hope she does not wake to find that we're doomed out here together like two young stupid lovers. I gaze out at the Mokshi and raise my hand to it. The auroras light back up. They are beautiful to look at. A fitting final view. Maybe we can watch the Mokshi be reborn. I wonder if what I did to it means it can leave the Legion without a pilot. Maybe this reborn world will be a sentinel for the whole Legion, an ambassador to Legions that circle all those other stars. Maybe it will be ripped apart and used for scrap out there the same way it was here.

The air becomes stale. I drift in and out of consciousness as we float free. I think of all that I'm told I was, and all that I have become. All that I could be. That we could be, together, if we had the courage to start again.

Just like the Mokshi.

It's then that I see the vehicle speeding toward us from the Katazyrna. I can't make out the figure, but I can see the big cephalopod gun.

I pull Jayd closer. She murmurs something. "Sabita," she says. "Sabita held off the Bhavajas. I let her go. I let her do it."

It's only as I raise my arm that I see the rider's face.

It's Casamir.

Casamir gives me a little two-fingered salute. She clumsily attaches her vehicle to the tube's outer face. Her first walk in the blackness, her first view of the Legion. I should not be surprised that she has taken it all in stride. She has always been an intrepid explorer. I just never thought she'd take the leap and believe me.

She burns the vehicle's yellow fuel and tows us back to the open hangar of Katazyrna.

From this vantage, the world looks as if it has an open wound. I see the great blackened patches of skin surrounding the hangar and wonder how long it will hold out. How many can we move to the Mokshi? The whole world? Can we really start again? And from there, then what? The whole of Katazyrna is still swarming with Bhavajas, all of them running around without someone to lead them. It will be a mess to clean up, and doing it will require a great deal of help from the levels below.

Casamir lands. The great hangar doors close and I see the blinking tangles of light shift in the viewing port above. Casamir tugs at her suit and manages to squeeze the wrist of it to get it to melt off her. She always was a quick study. The interior hangar door opens, and Arankadash comes in and leans over our sticky translucent pod.

I figure out how to pop it open. Clean air rushes in. I breathe deeply. Jayd opens her eyes.

Casamir offers me her hand. I raise my eyebrows at her. "So," I say, "you believe me *now*?"

"Never doubted," Casamir says.

"Where's Das Muni?" I say.

"In the medical lounge," Arankadash says. "Your witches can do wonders here. We'd like some of these tricks back home."

"You'll get them," I say, "but first we need to get somewhere safe. The Bhavajas are still running around."

"The infirmary," Casamir says. "We've barricaded it up."

"Let's go, then," I say, "Jayd needs help, but . . ." I hesitate. I think of all that has been sacrificed for me. "Can you go out one more time? Can you look for a woman? Sabita. It would please Jayd."

Jayd spends time in the infirmary, or what I take to be one. There are few people left on the first level of the ship. We discover a half a dozen

Bhavajas and a whole section of Katazyrnas who have held off incursion for all this time. But I recognize none of them. Jayd is their lord now. What that makes me, I'm uncertain. But they are loyal to her; they recognize her and are willing to help secure the first level.

While Jayd is being tended by the witches, I sit down next to Das Muni. Her breathing is shallow. Her wounds are coming back together, all slathered in greenish-amber salve. Her eyelids flutter open. She squints at me. Frowns.

"Are we all dead?" she says. "Have we been freed?"

"Not dead," I say, "but free, in our own way. You'll get to go back to the Mokshi."

"I was never happy there," she says. "I didn't fit there, either."

"You will now," I say. I take her hand.

"I have always loved you, Lord," she says.

"Just Zan," I say. "I'm Zan, always."

She closes her eyes. I let her rest.

Casamir did indeed find Sabita hiding in the salvage that orbited Katazyrna. She lay snoozing now on the slab opposite Jayd. I go to Sabita's side, but she does not wake. What did I confess to her before I lost my memory? Maybe I could ask her when she wakes. Or perhaps it's best to just let it be.

Arankadash and Casamir are sitting up on a slab near Jayd now, eating prickly mushrooms. Arankadash is drawing a map of the first level on the wall, cutting into it with her knife.

"We should consider what happens when the other Bhavajas get here," I say. "The reinforcements from their world."

"No," Jayd says, and I turn to see that though her eyes are closed, she is awake. "Nashatra will want peace. There was . . . a civil war. It's a very long story. But I think she can hold them there if we can stabilize Katazyrna."

"That's our goal, then," I say. "We need to secure the first level at least. If we can hold that while the Mokshi is reborn, then we can decide who wants to go over and who wants to stay."

It's Casamir who finds the temple room on one of her excursions with a handful of Katazyrnas as they patrol the first level. When she returns, her eyes are big, and she's talking about the eyes of the War God. She takes me and Arankadash down to the room, which is one level below. I don't admonish her for taking her group a level below when our goal was to secure only the first level, because I don't think she's listening to anything I'm saying at this point. She's so excited about her find, I think her head may burst.

"The lights were simple enough to figure out," Casamir says. "They're a language, writing. They give you instructions on how to work things once you know the code."

Casamir tangles with the lights in the walls, and suddenly the whole room becomes translucent. From here I can see all the worlds around us, as if we are sitting at the very center of Katazyrna and staring out at the dark spaces that surround us. I have a perfect view of the whole of the Outer Rim.

The Mokshi is out there, a strange planet folding in on itself, wrapped in great brazen tentacles, pulsing with a bold new heart. A world that was not supposed to exist. Yet here it is, remaking itself to leave the Legion.

Arankadash says, "What will you do with that world? Will you abandon us?"

"I'll take you with me," I say, "if you'd be willing."

"I don't know," Arankadash says. "We are of the world. Leaving it . . ."

"I'm not dying with the world," Casamir says. "That's defeatist. After all you've seen, you still think we should stay?"

Arankadash gazes out at the Mokshi. I don't know what she's thinking about, but I suspect it's to do with the child she lost and all the offspring she bore for the world itself. I wonder then what Jayd did with the womb I gave her when she took Rasida's. Where is that child? Who cares for it? Because I know who should.

"I will consider it," Arankadash says. "I will put the question to my people. But they must have a choice. To stay with the world and the Legion or to risk the unknown in that new world."

"I'm not going to make anyone do what they don't want to do," I say. "I should bring Jayd here, though. This is what all the madness was for. To watch this."

When I go back to the infirmary, Jayd is sitting up and speaking to Das Muni. I stay in the doorway for a time before they notice I'm there. I enjoy that because it also gives me time to observe Sabita. Though Sabita's eyes are closed, I doubt she sleeps. I don't know how she and Jayd will ever reconcile. I don't want to know what there is between them, but I can feel it the same way I can feel what is between Jayd and Das Muni.

Das Muni is frowning, fists knotted in the sheets. She is not yet well enough to even sit up. Jayd is apologizing, though what she's done is something that no apology will fix. I appreciate the gesture, though.

"Can you walk?" I ask Jayd. "I'd like to show you something."

When she looks at me, I see a great sadness. I have two competing emotions—I want to hold her, and I want to push her away. I extend my hand instead. When you start over, you must start again with the small things. Jayd takes my hand and then my arm.

Whatever has been done to her leg is not something the witches have fixed. I wonder if they even can. Because of this, our walk to the temple room is long and slow. We have time to talk in the mostly empty corridors, but we don't. The silence is oddly soothing. Maybe we've said all we can say now.

We step inside the temple room, and Jayd gapes. Outside, the Mokshi is a heaving ball of red and orange light. There is a new band of tissue spreading out from its core, splitting the broken world in two, like a great new skin.

"It's working," she says.

"Yes," I say.

We watch the Mokshi in silence for some time.

Then she says, "I'm afraid we can't be together after what we've done to each other."

"We can't," I say.

She wipes at her face. I'm surprised she has any tears left. I don't.

"You're the Lord of Katazyrna," I say. "Your people will look to you now to figure out what to do next. I can take them on the Mokshi. We can all leave the Legion together, go out into the unknown. But that's up to you and them. You're Lord of Katazyrna now, and I'm Lord of the Mokshi. That's all we are. That's all we can be after this."

Jayd nods. "You said the Mokshi could go anywhere once it was repaired. But I'm afraid, seeing all this darkness . . . What if there's nowhere else to go? What if there's only the Legion?"

"The stars are legion," I say. "Look at them. All those other suns. There could be many other worlds like ours circling them. Maybe worlds very different from ours. We can learn from them."

"Better worlds?" Jayd says.

"Different ones," I say. "I don't know if where we'll go will be better, but we'll be free, finally. Free of what the Legion made of us."

"When we first met—"

"No," I say. "No more about the past. We're building the future now."

"I'm afraid," she says.

"I know," I say, "but it's the fear that's wounded us. We must stop being afraid."

"I don't know how," she says.

"We'll learn together," I say.

We raise our faces again to the pulsing light of the Mokshi. We are two women standing at the edge of the Legion, our armies dead, our people broken, with a history between us that I no longer want filled in any further. Instead, in my mind I construct a future. In my future, we break loose from the Legion, and Casamir helms the Mokshi, and Arankadash is at my right hand, and Jayd is at my left, and Das Muni spends her time on the shores of some sea inside the Mokshi, collecting bits of detritus and teaching herself to sing. Arankadash holds a child, and Jayd finds love with some bottom-world mechanic, and Sabita takes charge of the infirmary, and perhaps we become something more, Sabita and I, and I stand in a room like this on the Mokshi, looking forward, ever forward, into endless possibilities. It's a potential future for us, as real as the potential of the child I sacrificed to get here, as real as the dreams of the people who helped me get this far.

"I need to go back," Jayd says, tugging at my arm.

I know what she means—she wants to go lie down in the infirmary—but I still think: we can never go back, only forward. Ever forward.

I put my hand on hers. We step away from the dazzling room and the rebirth of the world, and enter the heart of Katazyrna. We walk arm in arm, two lords without a Legion, into our uncertain future.

THANK YOU FOR READING
THE STARS ARE LEGION

If you enjoyed this title, please consider reviewing it at your favorite online venue and/or recommending it to your local library for others to enjoy.

To learn more about additional titles from Kameron Hurley, and to receive special offers, sign up for the Hurley's Heroes newsletter at kameronhurley.com/newsletter.

Acknowledgments

When I first came up with the idea for this novel in 2012, I knew it was going to be a hard sell. What, you want to write an all-women space opera? Like, science fiction without *men* in it? Not even a *mention* of *men*? WHAT IS THIS, 1968?!

Props to Joe Monti at Saga Press for not only hunting us down for this book proposal, but for being even more excited to buy it when he realized the unspoken world-building bit. Thank you to everyone at Saga Press who helped shuttle the book through the publishing process. Thanks also to one of my favorite copy editors, Richard Shealy, who is not afraid to reach out to me for clarification on my wild worlds. Special thanks to Stephen Youll for the fabulous cover, and to Joe for humoring me when I said, "Dammit, Joe, it has to have a SPACESHIP ON THE COVER!" and then coming through for me.

As ever, thanks to my agent, Hannah Bowman, who helps keep me sane and on task.

Thanks also to Jayson Utz, who continues to be the bright, shining star in my own wacky universe.

Thanks to the loyal friends and fans who keep buying all these books. As a colleague said when he saw the cover for *The Stars Are Legion*: "Your name is getting bigger! That's a good sign!" Let's hope so.

My writing career continues to feel a lot like fighting through armies of mutant rats with a flashlight in one hand and a sword in the other while navigating a labyrinth designed to break my will to carry on. But so far, I have been able to tell exactly the stories I want to, in exactly the way I want to, and that gives me great pleasure. At the end of the day—however many days I get—that's the best any creator can hope for.

Thanks for coming along for the ride.

The Big Red House

Autumn, 2016